"IF I COULD EV... SOMETHING AS A ...IMPOSSIBLE,' THIS IS IT...

"Our friend Henry Cobb is going to waltz right in and snatch the head of the Strategic Rocket Forces from under the Russians' noses. What do you think of that?"

"I'd say a snatch like that is impossible," Nellie remarked blandly.

Carleton looked over at him and nodded in agreement. "Me too."

"The President says it is too. But he asked me what the next step would be if we stopped the subs up north, and if we held our own in the Med. And I told him frankly that the Russian doctrine calls for nuclear weapons, and they'll use them to show they mean business..."

First Salvo

"Taylor writes with a thorough knowledge of seapower!"
— *Seattle Times*

Books by Charles D. Taylor

CHOKE POINT
COUNTERSTRIKE
FIRST SALVO
SHOW OF FORCE
THE SUNSET PATRIOTS
SILENT HUNTER
WAR SHIP

FIRST SALVO

CHARLES D. TAYLOR

JOVE BOOKS, NEW YORK

*This book is dedicated most affectionately
to my sons, Jack and Ben*

FIRST SALVO

A Jove Book / published by arrangement with
the author

PRINTING HISTORY
Charter edition / February 1985
Jove edition / September 1988

ISBN: 0-515-10088-9

Jove Books are published by The Berkley Publishing Group,
200 Madison Avenue, New York, New York 10016.
The name "JOVE" and the "J" logo
are trademarks belonging to Jove Publications, Inc.

PRINTED IN THE UNITED STATES OF AMERICA

10 9 8 7 6 5 4

ACKNOWLEDGMENTS

It is sometimes easier to undertake the actual writing of a book than to gather the necessary support. I'm luckier than most, for I have constantly had the support of a wonderful family and valued friends. Captain William M. McDonald has, over the years, progressed from my commanding officer to good friend and a valuable source of information. Bob Donovan has the greatest patience for answering technical questions for a nontechnical writer. Dan Mundy would never let me get away with the slightest oversight and I value his criticism immensely. Bill Story enjoyed reversing positions and assuming the role of critic. Mel Parker's assistance meant a great deal to the finished manuscript. I would be lost without the other talented assistance that comes with each book I write—Candy Bergquist's typing and Laurie Meehan's mapwork. And my wife, Georgie, is the best and toughest critic.

The United States Naval Institute in Annapolis is the finest source of naval literature in this country. I often rely on the accuracy of the monthly issue of their *Proceedings,* a professional journal without peer, and I made use of the following titles from the Naval Institute Press: *Keepers of the Sea* by Fred J. Maroon and Edward L. Beach (1983),

Guide to the Soviet Navy by Norman Polmar (third ed., 1983), *The Ships and Aircraft of the U.S. Fleet* by Norman Polmar (twelfth ed., 1981), and *Combat Fleets of the World, 1980/81* edited by Jean Labayle Couhat and translated by A. D. Baker III (1980). Other books were *Soviet Military Power* by the U.S. Government Printing Office (1984), *How to Make War* by James F. Dunnigan (Morrow 1982), *The Third World War: The Untold Story* by General Sir John Hackett (Macmillan 1982), *War in Space* by James Canan (Harper and Row 1982), *The New High Ground* by Thomas Karas (Simon and Schuster 1983), and two titles by Christopher Dobson and Ronald Payne, *The Terrorists: Their Weapons, Leaders and Tactics* and *Counterattack: The West's Battle Against the Terrorists* (Facts on File 1982).

"We must decide whether we intend to remain the strongest nation in the world. The alternative is to let ourselves slip into inferiority, into a position of weakness in a harsh world where principles unsupported by power are victimized, and to become a nation with more of a past than a future. I reject that alternative."

—**U.S. Secretary of Defense Harold Brown, January, 1980**

"The battle for the first salvo is taking a special meaning in naval battle under present-day conditions. . . . Delay in the employment of weapons in a naval battle or operation inevitably will be fraught with the most serious and even fatal consequences, regardless of where the fleet is located, at sea or in port."

—**Admiral Sergei Gorshkov, Admiral of the Fleet of the Soviet Union**

WASHINGTON, D.C.

The power structure in Washington had been privy to the Soviet Union's intentions well before D minus 7. In a world made smaller by satellite reconnaissance and instant communications, no nation could conceal such tactics for long.

It had been predicted by the CIA that, about one week preliminary to a concerted ground attack against NATO forces in Central Europe, the Soviet Union would initiate a series of military-political feints in various parts of the globe. The intent would be to confuse intelligence networks as to their exact goal. It could involve an increase in terrorist activities, an instigation of localized civil wars, previously unannounced military games in critical areas, and probable overt acts against U.S. forces — all of which would be followed immediately by release of misinformation via KGB stations in major cities.

D MINUS 7

SIX MILES OFF
THE RHODE ISLAND COAST

The *Joseph and Mary* wallowed in the heavy swells, her barnacled hull heaving from one side to the other, displaying a coating of green algae. Gaspar Porcino, her captain, was exhausted. His thin, hawklike face, heavily tanned by months of summer fishing, bristled with two days' growth of beard, and the dark circles under his eyes revealed a man who lived by the sea. But his catch was poor that trip; the hold was only half full. Nothing had gone right.

An hour before departure, Porcino was forced to call his oldest son to join them when two of the crew showed up drunk. Once at sea, constant engine trouble restricted fishing time, and part of their equipment was lost in a squall the first night.

The catch had been off for weeks, and the engine was still acting up. At noon, he ordered the crew to haul in. There was no sense in challenging bad luck any further.

He headed the *Joseph and Mary*'s bow west northwest. His course would keep Block Island to port and put enough distance between them and the little pleasure boats. Then he would head west through Block Island Sound and finally due north after Fishers Island into New London and home. Captain Porcino could see Sandy Point on Block Island to port and even make out Point Judith, Rhode Island, on the horizon to starboard through the muggy, end-of-August haze. There was no need for radar, but out of habit he snapped it on just the same. The screen painted a large object off his starboard bow about four miles distant. Raising his binoculars, he could make out the familiar lines of the ferry following its standard course from Point Judith to Block Island. As usual, it would be full of families off on vacation, their station wagons parked bumper to bumper on the main deck and jammed with luggage and pets. Once the trawl was in, he would increase speed and pass her astern.

"Captain... Captain...." An anxious voice interrupted his reverie. Manuel Modica was waving his arms frantically, giving the sign to stop the engine. As he cut engine, Porcino could hear the man shouting in his Portuguese accent, "The net... she eese foul wit someting...."

Porcino jumped down the few steps from his pilothouse to the main deck and hurried aft. His men were alternately winching and peering over the side to search for whatever had become trapped in the gear.

"Very beeg," Modica reported, stretching his arms wide before the captain. "Heavy... perhaps too beeg to bring in."

"You handle the winch, Manuel," Porcino ordered. "You just watch me and I'll tell you when to haul and when to stop. We can't take a chance on losing anything more this trip." He shrugged to himself. "And so close to home." He leaned over the stern to peer into the murky water. There was nothing visible.

The captain, never looking behind him, held his right arm in the air, closing his fist to indicate that Modica should engage the winch. Whatever was fouled, Porcino could feel its bulk through the hull under his feet. The boards throbbed as the winch engine strained. The stern sank slightly with the weight.

The wail of the winch engine and the aroma of hot oil indicated their catch was unusually heavy. Porcino opened his fist, palm back toward Modica. The winch stopped. There was still nothing heaving into view. The captain arched his back, swinging his shoulders from side to side to ease the ache of almost two solid days of work. Tired, closing his eyes and squeezing them tight to ward off exhaustion, he barely heard the ceaseless chatter in Portuguese from the other hands.

Stretching again, he raised his arm and closed his fist. The whine of the winch pierced the air. Once more Porcino could feel the deck under his feet broadcasting as it had done for years, talking to him.

"There . . . down there," one of the men shouted excitedly. Porcino searched for a moment before he saw a form taking shape just off the stern. He closed his fist to halt the engine. Peering down, he could barely make out the object. He opened his fist, wagging it softly behind him for a slow speed on the haul.

Gradually, as more of his gear came into view, Porcino saw it was no fish. The hazy sun reflected brightly off the object. Hastily he closed his fist. He knew what it was even before the sun caught the metal—a torpedo!

The others recognized the object. "What we have there, Captain?" one of them inquired nonchalantly. "Another one of those practice torpedoes?"

"More than likely," he sighed half to himself, slamming his fist on the railing. His catch wasn't bad enough, now the Navy was finishing his day! He glanced back at the object again. It was too big and too shiny for one of those practice loads the subs used. It should have been dirty and covered with mud. This one looked new. "Haul it in a little closer, Manuel," he shouted behind him, arm raised, fist closed once again. "Very slowly."

Rising through the cloudy water, the object took on a new perspective as the sun outlined its form in more detail. Captain Porcino had fouled dummy torpedoes before, and once even an old German one, but none compared in size to this. Longer than any he had seen, it was wider and more lethal looking, and judging by the metal, which was shiny and untarnished, it was of recent vintage. He recognized what looked like Navy markings on its body. It had not been in the water long.

"That's it, Manuel," he shouted, opening his fist as the torpedo bobbed to the surface, tearing the netting with its weight. A cable was still tangled around the fins. It was drawn against the fishing boat, bumping the hull each time the boat rolled in the opposite direction. Porcino ordered his men to swing the outrigger to haul the torpedo away from the boat, but the outrigger jammed.

Captain Porcino was not taking any chances. He had no desire to see this evil machine punch a hole in the side of the *Joseph and Mary*. As he started his cranky engine, an especially large swell heaved the round-bottomed boat first to starboard toward the torpedo, then even more wildly to port, yanking it sharply against the hull. With a cracking sound, the weapon smashed into the boat. That was immediately followed by a growling sound from the torpedo.

"Captain, she ees running!" Manuel shouted.

The torpedo drove against the boat's hull once, then twice, as the projectile's propellers picked up speed.

"Cut the cable!" Porcino shouted.

But Manuel had already seen the problem. With a huge fire ax, he slashed again and again at the woven metal cable until the combination of his blows and the surging of the boat parted the final strands.

Porcino watched helplessly as the torpedo banged once more against the *Joseph and Mary*'s hull, then turned and ran in a line directly off the bow. At the same time, the last section of cable slid off the fins. Captain Porcino crossed himself and muttered a Hail Mary as the torpedo moved away, increasing speed rapidly as it slipped just below the surface.

Looking ahead, the captain gasped. Not more than a mile off his bow was the Block Island ferry, her rails lined with vacationers enjoying their brief ride. Mouth ajar, Porcino stared helplessly at the ferry as the telltale wake of the torpedo left no doubt of its direction.

He reached for the mike on his radio, checking to make sure he was still on the Coast Guard emergency frequency. "New London Coast Guard...New London Coast Guard

.... this is *Joseph and Mary*.... Emergency... please..." he pleaded.

A voice came back instantly. "Go ahead, *Joseph and Mary.*"

There was no answer for a moment. Then the Coast Guard operator heard a voice repeat over and over again. "Mother of God... Mother of God... Mother of God..." It was all Captain Porcino could say as the large pleasure boat erupted in a sheet of flame. He gazed in horror at the bodies blown skyward, the flaming cars tumbling lazily through the air.

The Block Island ferry disintegrated.

D MINUS 6

ISTANBUL, TURKEY

The man squinted at the sun's reflection on the face of his watch. Religious services would end soon and the Premier and his party would be leaving the mosque. It was the largest, most ornate building in that part of Istanbul. The plaza in front and the wide main street were heavily guarded by Turkish security forces. No one for the past five minutes had been allowed into an area cordoned off by the army.

It was a high holy day, one of the most significant. That's what he had been told the day before in Simferopol, a city in the Crimea northeast of Sevastopol. Not only was it a major Russian port on the Black Sea, Simferopol was also the headquarters for a major Soviet terrorist school run by the KGB. Each member of his so-called "guild" had been trained there and, like him, had departed only the day before.

Some of them would be performing the same acts near the other mosques in other major Turkish cities—Izmir, Konya, Adana, Ankara. He couldn't begin to remember all those foreign names, nor had anyone ever answered his question about why the Premier had chosen to attend services in Istanbul rather than the capital in Ankara. But he didn't care either. His one and only requirement was to follow through with his orders.

This wasn't his first assassination, and he was sure it wouldn't be his last. Most of the new guild members, the first-timers, would be caught, he knew. They would be too excited, too interested in seeing the spoils of their work. Security forces would notice them quickly. The bodies and the gore and the blood meant nothing to him. He enjoyed his job and would be satisfied simply to read about it in the papers when he returned to Russia. His superiors always had copies of the foreign papers.

He saw the Premier exiting, a retinue of guards surrounding him. The assassin never looked up, never made any motion that might attract attention. It was simple caution. He was more than a block away and it was unlikely anyone would notice him. As the Turkish leader walked briskly with his escort toward the car, the assassin thought briefly about his comrades in those other cities. In the next few hours, and certainly by the end of the day, Turkey would be in chaos. Government and military bases would be damaged. Many important officials would be dead, along with hundreds of innocent people unfortunate enough to be nearby.

The Premier was within twenty yards of his car as the man watching him shook out a cigarette, sticking it in his mouth at enough of an angle to maintain his view. He extracted a cigarette lighter from a breast pocket, snapping it into flame. When he judged the positioning of everyone was as close to perfect as possible, he depressed a small pin on the underside of the lighter.

The explosion of the fire hydrant closest to the Premier's limousine was tremendous, the blast flattening people as far as fifty yards away. But the most exacting part of his job involved attaining the correct angle of explosion, for men could survive even mightier blasts at equivalent ranges. At the moment of the detonation, secondary charges propelling tiny cylindrical pieces of metal blossomed out in an arc that took in the Premier and his guards ten yards to either side of him. Like grapeshot, the metal shards ripped through them, tearing flesh to ribbons, shattering vital organs, amputating limbs. There was no chance of survival within that arc of metal.

Even as the agonizing, terrified screams echoed back to him, the man calmly finished lighting his cigarette. Then he arose, acting as startled and horrified as anyone around him.

As confusion mounted into chaos, he chose the appropriate moment to slip away. It would be many hours before he was delivered back to the coast of the Black Sea, north of the entrance to the Bosporus. Then he could sleep. But he knew he wouldn't sleep well until he returned to Simferopol and read the papers.

At the same moment, and at selected times throughout that same day, other terrorists from his guild would also slip away unnoticed. But some of them would be captured. They would be relieved to learn that the cyanide capsules would work quickly. But they would never know they had been set up by their own people, or that they would be identified as Greeks. They were not aware that the objective was war between Turkey and Greece.

As expected, war was declared within hours. The Turkish air force directed heavy bombing strikes over major Greek cities, with the emphasis on Athens. Satellite photos confirmed heavily damaged port facilities. Greek retaliation was as severe. The unexpected result on both sides was heavier damage to civilian centers rather than the well-defended military bases. At this there was an almost audible sigh of relief from the Pentagon, for they were expecting to need Greek and Turkish forces in the coming days. On that same day, Turkey announced that the Turkish straits, the Bosporus and the Dardanelles, were closed to all shipping until further notice. As it turned out, this was still not soon enough to halt the passage of a number of capital ships from the Russian Black Sea Fleet.

Due to continuing exercises by Russian divisions in Poland, East Germany, and Czechoslovakia, NATO forces were placed on Condition Two alert. Satellite photos showed reserve divisions mobilizing in the western sectors of the Soviet Union. Photo reconnaissance also pinpointed supply trains moving at an alarming rate toward the west in all Warsaw Pact countries. The CIA confirmed military contents.

Also that day, the Norwegian government requested U.S. satellite recon of its Svalbard territory, situated more than seven hundred miles north of the Arctic Circle in the Barents Sea. This was a relief to U.S. intelligence specialists, who had already recorded unusual happenings in the area. Communications with Norway's settlements on Spitzbergen Island had been dead for the past twelve hours. Indications were that heavy message traffic intercepted between Murmansk and Svalbard coincided with Soviet attack submarine activity in that vicinity.

D MINUS 5

ONE HUNDRED MILES EAST OF CHARLESTON, SOUTH CAROLINA

"American fighters approaching, Commander.... Range about three hundred miles, speed seven fifty."

"Their radar locked on us?" The pilot of the Russian long-range bomber was extremely cautious. Though he had reviewed this in his mind time and again, he was worried that something would happen, something that might ruin his mission.

"Yes, sir." The electronics officer paused for a moment, then added, "Not close enough to pick up a small object in the air.... A few more minutes, sir."

These huge, modern Soviet bombers often flew missions along the Atlantic Coast, always discreetly beyond U.S. airspace, but also always close enough to require an escort from American fighters. It was a game both for the Russian pilot and his American counterparts. The Bear-D bomber would maintain its altitude and speed and the course would be a carbon copy of all previous flights. The Americans would take station off either wing of the bomber, close enough to see the flight crew, yet distant enough to avoid any danger of a malfunction. They might stay together for an hour, sometimes less if the Navy or Air Force wanted to exercise other pilots and give them a chance to see what the enemy looked like. The pilots would waggle their wings and wave to each other. It was a game.

"Commander, they're within range now."

The Russian pilot gave his orders, anxious to release their surprise.

"Another thirty seconds, sir. We're not quite in position," the careful, assured voice of the navigator came back.

"You're sure?" Perhaps something would go wrong now, something to injure the mission.

"Fifteen seconds . . ."

"Fine," responded the electronics officer. "No doubt about it. They'll get a good echo on their radar, but they won't have the slightest idea what we're sending down to the water."

After a long pause, just as the pilot was going to question him again, the navigator remarked quietly, "Release." His final computer check indicated all systems would function normally.

The pilot exhaled with a long sigh, one that was easily heard over the interior communications systems. Both the electronics officer in his cubbyhole and the navigator in his shook their heads. How the hell would this pilot handle combat? they wondered to themselves.

The American fighter planes did pick up the object on their radars. They could not tell what it was, or why it was there, but their on-board computers told them instantly that it wasn't a missile—they were in no danger. As they closed in on the giant bomber, taking position on either wing tip, the senior American pilot reported the strange occurrence to his base. On board the Russian bomber, the electronics officer recorded that conversation with Norfolk. When they arrived in Havana, it would prove they had done their part of the job. Now the electronics officer thought to himself, Let's see if the technicians back home did their part. He carefully selected the correct U.S. Navy frequency, then waited patiently.

Half an hour later, at a small, obscure naval station on the Maryland coast, a chief sonar technician called his superior in Washington. "Sir, Bermuda station reports that

SOSUS hydrophone arrays at . . ." and he gave the locations between the Bermuda station and the Georgia coast, "are inoperative." The sonar technician went on to explain that the sonar technicians on Bermuda picked up an unidentified noise in the water, one their computers could not identify, just before the hydrophones went dead.

SOSUS is a system of listening points on the bottom of the ocean that can detect and classify literally every noise in the water. It is especially accurate in picking up and identifying movements of Soviet submarines, whether they are exiting a choke point from their own bases into open ocean or taking station off the U.S. coast. SOSUS is a critical line of defense, especially in detecting the possibility of a subsurface missile attack on the U.S. mainland.

THE SEA OF JAPAN

A brisk wind raised a four- to five-foot chop. Green water splashed over the bows of two ships, the spray splashing the sailors working on their decks. The Russian guided-missile destroyer had been tailing its American counterpart most of the day. The captain of the American ship, *Benjamin Stoddert,* also a guided-missile destroyer, wondered when the Russian would alter course and leave them alone. Since the Russian craft had been identified that morning, he'd very carefully selected his bridge watch, and now they were very tired.

On the Soviet ship, *Bodry,* her captain decided it was time. He rang up full speed, then called his engine room to insure that his chief engineer had personally assumed the watch. "We're moving in now. I want your senior men at the controls."

The chief engineer acknowledged the orders with a growl. He'd been called down to the engineering spaces to assume the watch three times now. The captain had changed his mind each time. Before they departed Vladivostok, they had gone over the operation with the type commander. Then the squadron commander had done the same thing. Once they were at sea, the political officer met with each department, not only for one more review but to place the operation in a larger, more glorious perspective. The chief didn't need any more of that bullshit.

On *Bodry*'s bridge, her captain took the course recommendation from his leading radarman to close with the American ship on a collision heading.

Stoddert's officer of the deck remained on the port bridge wing, watching the Soviet destroyer through his binoculars. Occasionally he would take a bearing on the other ship, then check its radar range. There was no doubt in his mind— steady bearing, decreasing range, *collision course*. He looked in the pilothouse. The captain remained calmly in his chair, reading a western. Once or twice he shifted position to scratch, but never once did he look out on the wing or ask a question.

The captain knew the way to manage naval officers was to give them responsibility. But out of the corner of his eye, he was watching that son of a bitch. He knew after many years when a bearing was steady, and he saw by the change in bow waves that the other captain had increased speed.

"Captain," the OOD finally called from the bridge wing after one more check on the bearing, "I think we have a problem." He spoke very calmly, almost matter-of-factly, even though his palms were damp and he could feel trickles of sweat running down his back.

"Just a minute, Jack. Let me finish this page." The captain never looked up.

The bos'n mate of the watch marveled at the two of them. He'd been watching the Russian and noted the change in the bow wave too, and the steady bearing. These officers were too much, but he was glad they were running *Stoddert*.

The captain finished his page, turning down a corner so he wouldn't lose his place, and meandered out beside the OOD. "What seems to be the trouble?" he asked, nodding his head toward the closing ship at the same time. "Does he want to give us a rough time today?"

"Looks like it, Captain," the OOD answered, his binoculars concentrated on the approaching ship. "No doubt he's on a collision course. Combat plotted it a couple of times."

"'Bout six to eight minutes, I'd say."

"Six is closer to it, sir, but I'll check combat again."

"No need to, Jack. Why don't you sound GQ. Button her up—and make sure you sound collision quarters too, so there's no doubt in anyone's mind. I'll be back in a minute. Going to the head." Instead, he called the chief radioman and bos'n mate to his sea cabin. The captain was following strict orders not to be intimidated. He was to inform Washington of his situation, then maintain course and speed.

The bos'n mate shook his head and muttered to himself, "Sure glad I'm with them." Then in a normal voice, "Want me to sound the alarm, sir?"

"Sure, Boats. Might as well not wait till the last minute," he added casually.

A short emergency message sent by the chief radioman to Washington was about to activate the camera in a "key-hole" satellite 150 miles above them. No human ear would ever hear as it shifted its axis minutely to focus on the scene below.

Bodry's captain looked up at the ship's chronometer. Pretty close to schedule, he decided. He knew that at approximately this time three other Russian ships were about to do the same thing.

The commanding officer of the Russian vessel insisted on retaining absolute control of his ship. He had no intention of any orders being mistaken in transition. His radar room reported ranges and bearings of the American every thirty seconds. It became obvious to him early on that the other captain had no intention of changing course or speed. The man must realize our intention, he thought. They have the right of way; the American would be a fool to react any other way.

Stoddert's captain meandered onto the bridge wing. "Jack, you move inside and stay right there," he said, nodding

toward the pilothouse. "Don't change your course and speed
the least bit. And," he added, "I'll have your ass if you take
even the slightest peek at him from now on." The captain
took out his pipe, dumped the dead ashes, and set it firmly
between his teeth. Leaning casually against the bridge railing, he watched the approach of the other ship, nodding his
response as each division reported its section of the ship
was sealed.

Bodry's course was set to pass barely off the American's
bow. Seafaring law compelled *Stoddert* to maintain course
and speed. The Russian was the burdened vessel and was
required to avoid collision.

At five hundred yards, the two captains could make each
other out with the naked eye. Neither gave the slightest
indication of concern. The Russian ship was slightly shorter
and just a bit lighter, but together they represented eight
thousand tons of metal hurtling at each other with collision
imminent.

The Russian was a superb seaman. At an invisible point
in the ocean, he hurled an order over his shoulder, dropping
his speed, and wheeling *Bodry* to port. She nestled in alongside the other ship with about ten yards to spare between
them. It was a perfect maneuver, enough so that neither
captain had to shift his stance to look the other directly in
the face. They remained devoid of expression, waiting for
one or the other to make the first move.

The wind remained steady. The ocean chop of their port
bows would give *Bodry* a slight push to within feet of the
other ship. Then the reverse action would push her away.
The slightest variation in wave size, any hesitation on the
part of either helmsman, any change in revolutions in their
propeller turns, could bring them together.

Bodry added a few turns to increase her speed ever so
slightly, her increase indicated only by a few feet every half
minute. Then she eased gently into *Stoddert*, bumping like
two racehorses in the final turn, their bows grinding together. As they rose and fell unequally, the sound of tearing
metal rose above the roar of the ocean washing between

them. The sea forced *Bodry* away for a moment, only to bring them back together more forcefully, the contact shaking both ships.

The captains stared at each other impassively.

Inside *Stoddert*'s pilothouse, the OOD gripped a stanchion tightly, his knuckles white. He was positioned beside the helmsman, whispering encouragement. Next to him was the bos'n somehow glad that he could finally perceive sweat dripping off the OOD's brow.

It was no different in *Bodry*'s pilothouse. The human reactions were similar, but here they also knew they were responsible for any movements, that the American would not initiate any changes. In addition, the political officer was behind them, leaning silently against the bulkhead, watching each sailor intently.

The two ships continued to bump dangerously into each other, and damage became more apparent with each contact. The Soviet captain finally accepted that there would be no winner; neither would give in. He gave the orders to increase speed. They would pull forward and alter course away from the American. But his order was reversed for an instant, just enough time for *Bodry* to drop back slightly, then be sucked by the wave action against *Stoddert*. As they bumped, a swell heeled the Russian over into the American.

Their railings and superstructures touched. The davits holding their motor whaleboats became tangled. With a grinding sound, *Stoddert*'s boat was ripped free and crushed against the bulkhead, then the steel davit of the Soviet ship tore through a bulkhead and an American sailor in the compartment behind it was instantly crushed to death.

At the same moment, the torpedo launcher on *Bodry* was ripped free. The launcher and four torpedoes were hurled into the water. The mistake in direction had been caught and corrected, and the Russian ship surged ahead, scraping the length of *Stoddert*'s hull as she hauled away to port.

Far above the two ships, invisible to both of them, the incident had been recorded and transmitted instantly to Washington. A simple electronic order was then given. With a quiet whirr, the camera perched 150 miles above changed its orientation minutely and began recording another such incident less than fifty miles away.

This time the Russians had been caught, their actions filmed. The film from outerspace was clearer than slides taken at a family outing at the beach. When the Russian news agency announced the American aggression and requested UN censure, the pictures would speak for themselves.

THE WHITE HOUSE

There was never a word from Washington about their SO-SUS system. In the Kremlin, it was an entirely different story. The Russians officially protested four separate incidents in the Sea of Japan involving U.S. and Soviet military ships. In each case, the Russians charged that American ships harassed Soviet units without provocation, causing damage and some injury to personnel. Anticipating this ploy, the White House authorized the U.S. Ambassador to the United Nations to distribute satellite photos to Security Council members to reinforce American charges of Russian aggression in each instance.

Well before the incidents in the Sea of Japan, however, the President learned that a relatively junior admiral had developed a series of unique war scenarios via the Naval War College computer system, scenarios that emphasized Soviet activity in another part of the world. The officer had become convinced that, while Soviet ground forces would attack with a blitzkrieg-type offense across Central Europe even before their naval supremacy was certain, defeat of the Russian naval forces in the North Atlantic and the Mediterranean would stop the ground war in its tracks.

No matter the variations he programmed, three objectives

continued to be paramount: 1) deny the Soviet Union control of the Mediterranean by means of the Sixth Fleet; 2) deny the attack submarines of the Soviet Northern Fleet access— via the Greenland–Iceland–United Kingdom (GIUK) gap— to our vital resupply routes to Europe; 3) neutralize the Soviet ability to threaten and/or carry out strategic nuclear warfare.

It was explained in more detail to the President that the Soviet Army would roll through Europe to the Atlantic coast unless the U.S. Navy and its NATO allies could support those three objectives. The point was not to allow the Russians to establish a second front on Europe's Mediterranean shores. If this occurred, NATO ground troops would be forced to divide their strength; that would insure their defeat, since the USSR had considerably more troops, aircraft, and armor. They could afford a dual front and NATO could not. Of equal concern would be resupply of NATO forces from the United States. Soviet doctrine was based on the belief that their strike forces could overwhelm defending forces so rapidly that they would capture or destroy most NATO military stockpiles long before the shock of their offensive wore off. NATO could survive only if the North Atlantic supply routes remained open. Therefore, the Russians would attempt to flood the North Atlantic with their formidable Murmansk-based submarine force if they were allowed to escape the GIUK. The final threat—the use of strategic nuclear weapons—had to be neutralized. The President noted that there was no solution offered for the last problem.

But he knew that if somehow these three objectives could be accomplished, Moscow would either withdraw or sue for peace.

The next day the President asked for the Admiral's service jacket. Rear Admiral David Pratt's record presented a picture of a rather different sort of officer than appeared in the forefront of the Washington scene. Most admirals that found their way into the Pentagon and then, if they were lucky, into providing military advice to the Oval Office, wore the wings of a naval aviator or a submariner's dolphins. David Pratt displayed neither on his uniform blouse, nor was he festooned with ribbons. His only combat assignments had been early in his career in Vietnam.

Pratt was considered a maverick within the military power structure. Though not an engineer, he was involved in more new weapons planning than any other senior officer. He was also a devotee of computers as the first line of defense, and offense, for the Navy of the future—and he committed himself up front when he felt he was right. That was a rare trait among those looking forward to a successful career.

The one final aspect that became apparent to the President was that there were occasional gaps in Pratt's service record—small, but there nevertheless—something not normally occurring with most flag officers. A little digging brought forth the fact that Admiral Pratt was a maverick in more ways than one: he had deep contacts in intelligence sectors, both military and civilian. And word of mouth elicited the fact that Pratt still consorted with an odd variety of men, some of whom had reached the top in covert-action specialties that the military did not freely admit to.

All in all, Pratt had intriguing possibilities. As far as the President was concerned, he was the right man for the job.

D MINUS 4

WASHINGTON, D.C.,
A HOTEL ON K STREET

Bernie Ryng glanced up for a moment when Pratt crumpled the latest Strategic Situation Report in his fist, jamming it in his jacket pocket. He chuckled as the Admiral growled to himself, then wandered over to look out the floor-to-ceiling window. Always grumbling about something, Ryng thought to himself. It's nice to see nothing has changed.

Pratt stared down into the jam of noontime traffic on K. The day was hot in Washington. He watched the secretaries in skimpy summer blouses and skirts hurrying alongside the young bureaucrats with jackets over their arms.

Pratt's gaze was riveted on a pretty blond whose mincing walk was attracting the stares of passersby, but in fact his mind was on his meeting with the President. It seemed just yesterday, but it was longer than that. It had been before the Russians had become serious.

Long ago, he had become inured to the fact that he would not be one of those admirals who would be invited to the Oval Office to rub elbows with the President and offer reassurance. Therefore, it was doubly surprising when the President not only brought him to the office alone, but then, after the interview centered on that part of his background that the official navy disclaimed, indicated that Dave Pratt was the man he wanted. In Navy circles, the term was called "reaching down." It meant that the man in power was overlooking the most senior officers and dipping into the batch of juniors for the man he wanted. It was an exceedingly uncommon occurrence.

"You're going to be in overall command, Admiral Pratt. While your major responsibility, when and if the shooting starts, will be in the Mediterranean, I'm going to ask you to put your actions where your mouth has been." Suddenly, all Pratt could think of was how many times he had been told that someday he'd regret opening his big mouth so much.

"I've reviewed the three-point program you outlined not so long ago." There had been a pause that seemed to last an eternity before the President continued. "And I happen to agree with you. Things may not occur exactly as you've presented them in your scenarios, but—" here he moved his head from side to side as if to show he was balancing each point, "—but I know of no other presentation that comes so close to what seems to be taking place right now."

The discussion had gone on for another half hour about the military aspects of the proposed Soviet offensive and the importance of the Mediterranean, but Pratt sensed there was really much more to come. Then the President had raised his eyebrows. "You remember early on I indicated you were to be in overall command? Well, I meant that in every sense of the word. We've got to keep the sea-lanes in the North Atlantic open, and that means keeping all those attack submarines from passing through the GIUK gap."

He went on to review the intelligence reports they were both familiar with—one noted that the flow of goods to Murmansk indicated the Soviet submarine fleet was being supplied for an extended deployment, that some of their vessels were already under way, and that the balance would probably follow soon. Another report mentioned a new development, perhaps a weapon, that no one really understood. And still another noted increased activity in the Soviet sector of the Norwegian island of Spitzbergen, raising the question of the movement of the Murmansk submarines in the GIUK gap. Finally the President concluded from the briefings that someone better act on the growing threat.

So, because of the scenario Pratt had developed at the Naval War College, this new overall command the President was giving him meant worrying about what was happening on Spitzbergen. That was when he decided that Bernie Ryng had to be included.

Pratt turned back to Ryng and scowled when he saw what the younger man was reading — *Morskoi Sbornik*, the official Russian naval journal. "Any sex in that rag, Bernie?"

Ryng looked up with a smile. "I guess you might say that, Dave," he answered, wiping rimless reading glasses on his sleeve, then holding them to the light. "Look at this picture and you might change your mind about these people." He grinned back at Pratt, savoring the opportunity to tease him even though he was a friend.

"Here . . . look." He held up the magazine for inspection.

"Just another ship." Pratt shrugged.

"Not just another, Dave. This one's a supply ship, and I also happen to know she left Murmansk two days ago fully loaded, and she had what looked like some new model torpedoes on her deck—that is, before they covered them with tarps."

Pratt turned back, a questioning look on his face.

"That's right. It was the sexy one in this picture. Of course, those high-resolution shots I saw this morning were much better."

"And you're interested because . . ."

"Right. Because I think this ship might just be anchored in Longyearbyen harbor in Spitzbergen when I get there." Ryng grinned again, very pleased with himself. The fleet types like Pratt didn't understand the intelligence types like him, and, of course, they felt the spooks didn't understand them. The hell with it, he thought. Be honest with Pratt. He's not a bad guy for an admiral and you probably wouldn't be here today if it weren't for him.

"I think, all things considered, Bernie, I'd rather be right where I'm going, right in the middle of the action." Admiral Pratt's actual orders were for the Mediterranean, to com-

mand a carrier battle group. Ryng was headed for Spitzbergen, the main island of the Svalbard archipelago, a
Norwegian territory six hundred miles north of Norway in
the Barents sea. It was the first of two choke points that
might prevent Soviet military vessels, especially submarines, from moving into the North Atlantic in time of war.
Ryng was to go in with a Navy SEAL team that was scheduled to depart in less than twenty-four hours.

Considering the situation now, Pratt knew he had been
absolutely right in asking for Bernie Ryng—and he had
told the President that. On the day Norway requested assistance in determining what was happening on their small
territory far to the north, Washington had also determined
that a guerilla-type unit should be inserted, since the Russians seemed to be concentrating so much effort on that
region. Pratt had explained to the President that a SEAL
team was by far the best solution—small, fast, capable of
both intelligence gathering and fighting. And in this situation, the best man by far was not the one the others would
pick. But Bernie Ryng was exceptional and Admiral Pratt
could work with him. In that case, the President had concluded, Pratt could relay his, the President's, orders to Ryng.
The Navy, bolstered by word from the White House, would
fully support Ryng and the intelligence man was to be told
by the Admiral to follow his own nose. Dave Pratt knew
Bernie would like that.

This meeting between Pratt and Ryng was a reunion of
sorts, a catch-as-catch-can affair. Pratt hadn't really planned
it that way; it just happened. Ryng had heard in the Officer's
Club the night before that Tom Carleton had been delayed
on his way through D.C. When Ryng tracked down Carleton, the latter told him that he had seen Henry Cobb the
night before. To his surprise, Cobb had mentioned he was
working for Dave Pratt. Though neither Ryng nor Carleton
had ever expected to see Cobb again, it all became even
clearer to them. Dave Pratt wanted the heavy hitters! They
had all been very close when they served with a riverboat
squadron in Vietnam, as close as any men could be who
owed their lives to each other.

Now Ryng looked at Pratt. "If those spooks up in that black-box room I visited this morning are right, I think I might find a bit of action myself," Ryng said. Studying Ryng, Pratt thought the latter could have been a native of the island he was heading for, with his fair complexion and longish blond hair. Bernie Ryng was one of those people whose age was hard to determine. His hair was thin, but not thinning. His complexion was fair and his expressionless blue eyes peered out over high cheekbones. As long as Pratt had known him, Ryng's features had never changed. He was of medium height and his build had remained the same. He never seemed to put on or lose a pound, and his physical condition remained superb. Most men his age had left the SEALs for less demanding careers. Pratt remembered that Ryng too had gone back to sea, but he soon drifted back into intelligence.

Pratt wandered over to the large window again, his hands fidgeting behind his back. "Harry Winters saddling up with you this trip?" Pratt asked, indulging in small talk.

"Sure. Where Bernie goes, Harry is sure to follow. Wouldn't want it any other way." He paused. "I doubt that you'll see any of them coming through that crowd down there," Ryng offered. He added, "Don't you ever relax?"

The Admiral turned slowly, a half smile on his face. "You been messing around with my wife?" The smile was quizzical, amused. "That's exactly what she said this morning, Bernie. Of course," he added, "she hasn't been reading the intelligence reports either." Dave Pratt had been awake since five that morning. He'd woken up in a cold sweat from a dream that had been repeating since he'd been ordered to a battle group command. It was the same each time. He could see the Russian cruise missiles bearing down on his carrier. They never became any larger, never seemed to be moving. It was just a surreal image hanging up there, aiming at him. But now that war seemed imminent, each dream brought them closer. They seemed to be gaining on him.

"This all reminds me of 'sixty-two," Ryng remarked. "I was still in school then. But I remember clearly that it was such a hell of a surprise when Kennedy went on TV to tell us how close war was and what the U.S. was doing. Obviously it had been going on for weeks in Washington, but there was never a peep. We were all fat, dumb, and happy, and then all of a sudden it was popped on us: hey, we may be in the middle of a war anytime now! I got a feeling it's going to be the same thing again for the civilians. Except this time, I don't expect there's going to be any chest thumping."

Dave Pratt nodded. "That's what I wanted to tell Alice this morning. Somehow I thought she deserved to know before I left." He sat down heavily, shaking his head sadly. "I wanted to send her up to Pennsylvania, to the mountains for the first few weeks I was gone. But can you imagine the shit I'd get if that ever got out?" Pratt was the perfect officer for the recruiting posters. He was over six feet, flat bellied, with short gray hair, a square chin, brown eyes under heavy dark brows, and his broad shoulders filled his uniform, giving it a tailored look.

"You'd get more than that, Admiral Pratt. You'd be commanding a desk out in North Dakota, the only admiral for hundreds of miles," a deep voice boomed from the doorway.

Neither man heard the door open, and the new sound startled them. Ryng, on his feet in a crouch before the speaker finished his first sentence, relaxed as he recognized Tom Carleton at the door. In contrast to the other two, Carleton was somewhat overweight, almost to the point of being dumpy. He always had been, even in the days upriver when they once survived for a week in the jungle on a diet of rice and *nuoc mam* sauce. Carleton tossed his hat and bag on a vacant armchair.

Pratt looked at Ryng. "Time to start an anchor pool on Tom's last hair. I'll put five down that says there're none left when he gets back."

Carleton's orders—written directly by Dave Pratt—were to take command of a guided-missile cruiser in the Mediterranean, part of Pratt's battle group. Short and chubby, almost bald, red-faced in the Washington summer heat, he appeared anything but a commanding type, nothing akin to Pratt. Yet this would be his third ship. Each of them had won awards for excellence. Now, taking command of the cruiser *Yorktown* was the ultimate honor. Pratt's carrier battle group was structured on the defensive capabilities of a computerized combat system named AEGIS, which was installed aboard *Yorktown,* the newest, most modern ship in the fleet. The system was sophisticated to the point where it could take control of the electronics and weapons systems of the entire battle group.

"Dave," Carleton said, "there're a lot of unhappy pilots hanging around the clubs mumbling about a nonpilot getting command of a carrier battle group. Better start checking your drinks." Turning to the other, he said, "Bernie, I figure every time I come back through the States, I'm going to find you in some padded cell, having scared yourself half to death with your latest assignment." He gave Ryng a bear hug, lifting him off his feet. "Hey, I thought you spooks were tough!"

"I've got a license to kill. Want to see it?" the blond man kidded him.

"Naw. I'd much rather drink. Come on, Admiral, where's the booze?" Carleton inquired of Pratt. "We've only got a few hours to tell a couple of years' worth of lies."

Pratt glanced at his watch. "Five minutes. I asked for a cart of bottles to be delivered here exactly at noon."

Carleton flopped onto the couch, placing his feet on the coffee table. Pratt had reserved a suite in the hotel just for this short luncheon, but after four years, it would be worth the price. "Say," Carleton asked, loosening his belt a notch, "think we're going to get to our duty stations before it all breaks loose?" The expression on his face was mock serious.

"I think the answer is yes." Ryng, the precise intelligence specialist, always had the right information. "We've got about five days, if our reconnaissance satellites are correct. The Russians aren't going to make a move until they know they can supply their second-echelon forces. They never do anything till they're absolutely sure. And then they're just going to let loose."

"I sure am glad I'm going where the action is," Carleton said with a grin. Out of the corner of his eye, he saw Ryng and Pratt shrug as they caught each other's eye. "What's so funny?"

"I'm trying to remember where I heard that before," answered Pratt. "It seems that . . ."

He was interrupted as the door swung open again. "Gentlemen, no need to get up. As you were." Commander Wendell Nelson entered the suite, both his arms in the air like a prize fighter. His immaculate summer white uniform set off his ebony skin. With a wide, bright smile, he added, "The party can now proceed." Damn, Ryng thought, nobody thought to tell me Nellie was coming. How many of us did they let Dave call up?

These are confident men, Pratt thought as he appraised the men around him. Carleton, spread out on the couch like a walrus and with his feet on that antique coffee table, would do that even in the White House; Nellie, always tried to be the life of the party, being the only black man in the group, and Bernie, sitting there quietly analyzing them all, would probably always be impassive and secretive. Pratt rose from his chair, grabbing Nelson's hand in his own and clapping him on the shoulder. "Have any trouble getting through the lobby?"

"There weren't any white men big enough to stop me today, Dave. I had such a head of steam up, I just bowled them over." Nelson reached automatically for a cigarette and shook hands with the others before sinking into the nearest chair. He was as handsome as Pratt and about the same size. He had high cheekbones that emphasized deep brown, intelligent eyes. He folded his large hands behind his head. "Where's the booze? I've never seen this group sitting on its hands before."

Pratt looked at his watch. "Any moment now it ought to be coming right through that door. As much of it as your little hearts desire, which is normally a quart apiece." Pratt cocked his head to one side, and the same laugh he'd always gotten from that remark came from each of them. They knew each other as well as they knew themselves, and their affection after four years was no different than it had been when their unit rotated back to the States in 1971. Now the youngsters, Carleton and Nelson, were commanding their own ships. Still absent was the baby of the group, Cobb. He had always been an enigma, though he had eased his way into their hearts. He frequently disappeared underground, and when he surfaced, this group seemed to be the only people he ever needed, and they tactfully never asked for details. He was the only one who acted totally independent, but he needed them as much as they needed each other. And Ryng—Ryng would always be the same, the famed SEAL team leader, drifting in and out of their lives from his world of special operations.

"Well, my dear Admiral, the next commanding officer of the U.S.S. *John Hancock*," Nelson responded, "will be taking off from Andrews in less than six hours, hopefully a bit drunk."

"Don't hold your breath, Nellie. I'm scheduled out then too—also hopefully a bit under the weather. Perhaps you'll have the honor of joining me." Pratt had written their orders, never expecting they would accidentally all be in Washington at the same time.

Nelson rolled his eyes humorously. Then he sat up straight, his face serious. "We going to make it in time, Dave? I'd hate to have the world blow while we're at forty thousand feet." There was no doubt in his mind, after the time he and Dave Pratt had spent together in Newport at the Naval War College, that it was Pratt who had gotten him *Hancock*.

Carleton's head bobbed up and down as he spoke. "No higher a personage than Bernie Ryng guarantees that we'll all make it. He's even cabled the Kremlin to slow down a bit so that we can be in position in time."

A knock on the door announced a Navy chief in immaculately tailored whites, pushing a cart loaded with glasses, ice, and bottles of liquor. Right behind came the very nervous waiter who had just been relieved of the cart. Coming to a halt before Admiral Pratt, Chief Petty Officer Henry Cobb removed a bottle of scotch, tossing it onto an empty chair. "I don't know what the others are having, but this ought to do me until lunch." The waiter gaped in amazement as the enlisted man walked up to the Admiral, throwing his arms around the taller man's neck. "David, my friend, how's the world been treating you?" The waiter had worked in Washington long enough to know that he'd never see that again—not to an admiral in uniform. There was no way he could have known that Cobb was really a civilian.

"Hank Cobb," Pratt answered. "Why was I ever so lucky to end up on the same carrier that you're heading for? I thought my final days were going to be easier." Pratt had specifically recommended Cobb for the most dangerous, and probably impossible job only because no other man could possibly pull it off. But until this morning, he had no idea how Cobb was operating or how he planned to travel. A Navy chief was as good a cover as any.

The chief grinned at the Admiral. "I read your orders in the *Navy Times*, called a buddy well placed in Norfolk, and asked if he'd cut me some orders to the *Kennedy*—just to protect you from yourself." The waiter exited the room quietly, deciding not to wait for the signature on the bill or his tip.

Henry Cobb would continue to turn up when he was least expected. That was the type of man he was. Years back, he had been part of Navy Intelligence, but it simply didn't work. Hank was too sophisticated for it. But even that wasn't quite the word Pratt really wanted when he tried to explain Henry to the President. Afterward, Hank had been transferred to Delta Group, and that had been a failure too. The group had been a force of men, while Cobb was much too independent—a one-man force.

Then the CIA heard about him and a deal was made. Overnight he was a civilian. Since Cobb was a linguist and Russian was his specialty, he had appealed to the CIA. And he was a man who could appear in just about any location at any time, getting there totally on his own, with no help from the desk, and pass himself off as a native. He was so successful in some of his more unsavory works, in fact, that he was discharged from the CIA. It would not do to have a man like Cobb traced back to them. And he liked that.

The idea of being an independent operative appealed to him. Though there were rumors that Cobb was for hire to anyone who could pay the price, Dave Pratt knew this to be absolutely false. In his own way, Cobb was a true patriot—as long as he could work on his own terms.

Henry Cobb was what one might call nondescript. Perhaps that was the reason no other organization had an exact picture of him. He was of medium height and build. His hair was short and brown, eyes brown, complexion medium, and there were no distinguishing features that would cause someone to remember his face. Only the other four men in the room would believe what Henry was going to do.

Cobb picked up Ryng's copy of *Morskoi Sbornik* and flipped the pages. "Hey, did you know this supply ship just left Murmansk and—"

"Believe me, Hank, I know."

Wendell Nelson was filling the glasses with ice. "Let's get into it, men. We may have to wait another four years to do this again. Say, Dave, you've been around this town for a few weeks. What's the word on the torpedo that hit the ferry yesterday? I don't believe a word I read in the papers."

"Don't ever," remarked Ryng sarcastically.

"He's pretty much right, Nellie. They interrogated that fisherman for quite awhile. He was no dummy. He'd seen those things before and could give a pretty good description. It wasn't anything we ever produced. It was a plant, and a damn good one. Like you say about the papers, they've already performed the roll of judge and jury and they've hanged New London without a trial. The only thing we haven't doped out is how the Russians managed to get it that close without anyone noticing anything unusual. They figure it might have been towed in by a fishing boat and dropped right where that poor guy fouled it in his gear."

"But whatever the answer," Carleton said, "their plan's working like it's supposed to—to turn the public against the Navy. Can't say I blame them, with that many dead from the ferry—not to mention all the noise the papers are making about those two Senators, Hodges and Hall, who were off on the ferry on that boondoggle. With the great stories I've heard about those two, I can imagine what they might have done if that ferry ever made it to the island. What a way to go," he laughed.

"And," Ryng added, "the thing was timed precisely right. Washington's about to start stamping and shouting about Soviet terrorism and aggression and our own papers are going to be raising hell about our torpedoing the Block Island ferry." He shook his head in disgust. "Perfect timing by the Russians while the American public hasn't the vaguest idea what's going on. Am I right?" He turned to Pratt.

The older man nodded in assent, absentmindedly sipping at the drink Nellie had handed him. "The President wanted to keep the Block Island thing under wraps."

Carleton eased his feet back onto the coffee table. "I know what Nellie and I are going to do for you, Dave. We're going to drive ships through knotholes. We're going to dodge missiles like the Lone Ranger. Then we're going to deal out justice to the Russian fleet. But what are these other two clowns going to do while we're in the middle of it?"

Pratt smiled. "I suppose you could say they'll both do what they do best. You see, I came into this through the back door. I'll tell you right now I wasn't waiting in line. As a matter of fact, there was no line." He eased back into one of the large, soft chairs and related how he'd been picked out by the President because of the work he'd done at the War College. "Nellie can tell you. We did a lot of the work together. I got the credit because I'm an admiral and he's junior to me. Ostensibly, I'm in command of the carrier battle group you all know about, but I also got to stick my nose in everything else too because of those strategy papers."

Each man was aware of the work Pratt was explaining. With the exception of Cobb, they all followed each other's comings and goings pretty closely. It pleased them that one of their own had been recognized, especially a good guy like Dave Pratt.

"The problem in the North Atlantic is supposed to be a

Navy problem. When the subs come out, sink 'em. But there's a first step—the Red's have to get their subs through the barrier we've set up." They were also aware of the minefield strung across the GIUK gap that could be activated only by the Soviet attack subs as they passed through. "Something's going on up north, way up in Spitzbergen. We haven't the vaguest idea what, but it has to have something to do with neutralizing our barrier. I suggested to the President that there was one man who could do the job quietly up there." He nodded toward Ryng. "It's a job for a SEAL team because it involves more than just snooping. Bernie and his boys can normally handle themselves in a good firefight, and that's what I told the man in the White House when he asked how to take the problem one step farther."

Tom Carleton shook his head, puffing out his chubby cheeks before exhaling. "It's not for me." He wagged a finger at Cobb. "And him?"

"Henry is going into the wine business." Pratt waited for a reaction, but the others outwaited him. "Russian wine. He has acquired a special taste for sweet dessert wines, the type from vineyards in the Crimea. It seems that the wine maker there just dabbles in the business as a hobby. His main job is head of the Strategic Rocket Forces of the Soviet Union."

Ryng whistled. "Assassination?"

Cobb looked up, expressionless. "A straight assassination would be too easy."

"There's a simple theory in Washington right now. I don't know which group developed it—and I'm not saying it's wrong—but the President is convinced that this next war, if we have to have it, must be the last. Now wait a minute," Pratt added quickly. "Part of the theory is not that we'll never have to fight again. Instead, the idea is both to keep ourselves from escalating this into a nuclear thing and also to do something that will permanently stop the posturing with nuclear missiles. If I could ever classify something as a 'mission impossible,' this is it. Our friend Henry Cobb is going to waltz right in and snatch the head of the Strategic

Rocket Forces from under the Russians' own noses. What do you think of that?"

"I'd say a snatch like that is impossible," Nellie remarked blandly.

Carleton looked over at him and nodded in agreement. "Me too."

"The President says it is too. But he asked me what the next step would be if we stopped the subs up north, and if we held our own in the Med. And I told him frankly that the Russian doctrine calls for nuclear weapons. First, they'll call our bluff, then they'll threaten, and then they'll use them to show they mean business." Cobb said nothing.

"Who came up with this brilliant idea?" Ryng asked sarcastically. Then he added, "Been nice knowing you, Hank."

"I have no idea. The day after we talked about the nuclear threat, he asked me if I thought grabbing this guy—Keradin his name is—would stop them long enough to think. I said that it might be a better idea to take him out. The President looked at me, you know, over the tops of his glasses, and said that was his feeling precisely. But the others arguing that morning thought that murdering the guy would make them so mad they'd just blast away." Pratt stopped for a moment and scratched the back of his neck. "But the more we talked about it, the better the idea of kidnapping sounded. You know," he leaned forward, "it might just put them off guard long enough to make them think. But first we'd have to neutralize them up north and in the Med." He got up and shrugged. "Anyway, the President was looking for the best man for the job." Pratt pointed at Cobb. "He'd heard Hank's name before, so I reinforced what he already knew."

"It's still impossible," Carleton said softly.

"Well," Cobb clapped his hands, "we'll never know until we try it, will we?"

There was no point, Pratt realized, in going over any more details of why Cobb would make this attempt. Dave Pratt had agreed because some of the studies justifying the idea stemmed from his own—that the organization controlling the Soviet ICBM arsenal might be weakened to the point of indecision if their commander was neutralized. Pratt had once emphasized three goals concerning the Strategic Rocket Forces: create confusion and vacillation within a system that relied upon one man; determine primary Soviet targets before they could make their initial launch, thereby instilling the threat of complete failure; and create disaffection within the Soviet high command based on the premise that their strategic system might have been compromised. Even if the kidnapping was near inconceivable, it was in Cobb's hands now.

For the next two hours, the conversation often returned to the days along the Mekong. Pratt had been a lieutenant commander in charge of the riverboat squadron; Carleton, just promoted to lieutenant, was his executive officer. Nelson and Ryng were both young ensigns, and Henry Cobb had been a petty officer in charge of one of the boats.

One of their final operations brought them closer to each other than ever. It was a raid deep into VC territory. Nelson and Ryng each led a division of boats; Pratt and Carleton directed the operation by helicopter. Ryng, his boat sunk in one of the early firefights, was pulled from the muddy water by Nelson. The boats continued upriver into a second, heavier action. This time the helo was shot down, crashing in the water near the river's edge. Carleton was thrown free of the wreckage as it hit the water. Hank Cobb, disregarding heavy fire from shore, leaped into the water, diving into the sinking wreckage to pull out Pratt.

The depleted squadron was attacked two more times as it retreated downriver. The final firefight sank Nelson's boat. The five men, injured now, were the only ones to survive. Somehow each helped the other through a week in the jungle. When Pratt could go no farther, Cobb and Nelson continued ahead and located a friendly village. Two days later they were rescued.

There was only one other event, a tragic one, that had united them even more. Henry Cobb had fallen in love with a Vietnamese girl. Unfortunately, they would later learn, she had once worked for the Viet Cong. She tried to escape them when she married Cobb. When the VC tortured her to death for falling in love with an American, they took turns caring for Cobb until he got hold of himself. Then, when they were sure he was once again himself, Ryng had gone with Cobb to where the girl's VC cell was located. The Saigon police counted twenty-two bodies the next day. After that, those in the group never mentioned her again, and Cobb never again, to their knowledge, became involved with a woman. It was his way.

At two P.M. the tray of sandwiches Pratt had ordered beforehand appeared. Half an hour later, Admiral Pratt called for his car to take four of them out to Andrews to catch their flight to Europe. Ryng would travel separately with his own team.

They shook hands on the steps near the front entrance of the hotel, knowing it might be years before they found themselves in the same town again. Admiral Pratt's car arrived, then went to wait discreetly at the corner, a hundred feet from the hotel's front door. The driver, a young sailor immaculate in fresh whites, stood patiently beside the vehicle.

Ryng was the only one who saw a delivery truck change lanes too quickly. It was then hit from the rear and knocked toward Pratt's car. The best Ryng could tell, the driver of the delivery truck probably stepped on the gas rather than the brake. It hit the Navy vehicle with tremendous force.

The explosion that followed was incredible, the thunderclap literally knocking the wind out of Ryng as he sprawled backward. Carleton landed heavily on top of him. Out of the corner of his eye, Ryng saw the automobile burst upward in sections. The bomb must have been directly underneath it. The gas tanks on both vehicles blew, spewing flames in all directions.

The carnage spread across K Street. Bodies and parts of bodies littered the street and sidewalks, some cloaked in burning gasoline. For a hundred feet in every direction people had been knocked off their feet. The glass was blown out of every building within his sight. And as Ryng knew would happen, the deathly silence that follows such a blast was pierced by the hysterical screams of the injured and the pitter-patter of small, gruesome objects falling around them like raindrops.

In a moment, Ryng and Carleton were on their feet, ahead of Pratt and the other two. None had been close enough to be hurt by the blast.

As Hank Cobb approached the scene, he simply nodded, never looking to either side as he strolled nearer. The bomb was a big, sloppy one. The word must have gotten out that Admiral Pratt was the boss. More than likely it was set for a time when Pratt would be well on his way to Andrews. Instead, it reacted to the impact of the delivery van. Cobb looked at the bodies sprawled all over K Street. Time to get on with my own work, he thought. I'd better get my ass out of here before anyone else gets hurt.

D MINUS 3

While Pratt was en route to Naples, the Turkish offensive reached a stalemate. Counterattacks by the Greek air force in the western half of Turkey offset further strikes against Greek military bases. The sinking of two Turkish troop transports off Cape Sounion countered an invasion force assumed to be headed for Piraeus.

While the public was distracted by the Greco-Turkish war, the activation of twenty-two reserve divisions in the western sector of the Soviet Union neared completion, with fourteen of those already in transit to the west. Though these reserves remained approximately 50 percent short of combat supplies, control of truck and rail systems was assumed by the military, confirming an earlier CIA release that most, if not all, of the Warsaw Pact nations had been placed under martial law.

The movement of shock divisions toward the west continued, following a north-south orientation directed primarily for the Federal Republic of Germany via Poland, East Germany, and Czechoslovakia. In concert, there was also a push south from Hungary, Rumania, and Bulgaria toward the Mediterranean. Moscow confirmed major exercises in these areas, claiming they were previously announced, ostensibly to test her satellite countries under such an emergency. The UN Security Council requested permission to send observers, but were answered with silence from Moscow.

Though subject to UN censure as a result of the previous day's Security Council ruling, Soviet vessels in the Sea of Japan continued to harass U.S. naval units, and at least one Japanese destroyer reported damage under similar circumstances.

While it was rare that the Soviet Navy would have more than one-third of their offensive units at sea at a given time, more than 60 percent of their Pacific Fleet conducted exercises in the Sea of Japan, extending the length of the Japanese islands. Similar exercises were also conducted by their Baltic Fleet within the confines of that sea. In the Northern Fleet, satellite reconnaissance showed that all but two submarines were under way. Since 80 to 90 percent of Soviet submarines were normally in port at any given time, this confirmed that not only did the Russians plan to reinforce the Fifth Escadra in the Mediterranean, but they likely were massing to cut off the vital supply routes to Europe.

Based on U.S. satellite recon the previous day, the Norwegian government now officially requested assistance from the United States to investigate the silence from their territory of Svalbard. Timing on the part of American intelligence had been critical, for if Norway had remained silent, the U.S. would have had to request permission to insert its SEAL team. Satellite photos revealed 1) little normal activity around the Norwegian settlement of Longyearbyen; 2) increased activity by Aeroflot at the Longyearbyen airport; 3) the supply ship with unknown deck cargo tracked from Murmansk was photographed anchored off Barentsberg, the major Soviet settlement on Spitzbergen.

A major resurgence of terrorist activities, coupled with leftist antiwar-antinuclear demonstrations, began to occur as predicted. Rioting broke out toward the end of the workday on D minus 5 in Tokyo, creating massive transportation jams. One of the consequences was that Japanese industry was brought to a standstill on ensuing days. Leftist organizations limited or halted all international transportation to and from Japan. Assessments at that time indicated that successful confrontation by these leftist groups could have brought down the government within three days. CIA contacts in most countries indicated that terrorist schools in Havana, Moscow, Libya, Pajkow in East Germany, Ostrava in Czechoslovakia, and Simferopol in the Crimea had apparently exported their student bodies by D Minus 6. Reports of these terrorists surfacing in various underground cells in West Germany, France, Belgium, Italy, the Netherlands, the Scandinavian countries, and Japan were confirmed by D Minus 4. A concentration of females from these schools in critical capital cities indicated an effort to subvert high government officials.

Insertion of terrorists on a major scale was a tactic that had concerned European defense chiefs during a meeting in Brussels the previous year. It was projected that about five days before launching an attack against the West, the Soviet Union might utilize this method to create civilian dissension, weaken government authority to call up reserve military units, and instill anti-American feelings in both the NATO countries and Japan. Combined with KGB disinformation campaigns, the tactic was highly successful. To counter this, the following units were alerted: British SAS, West Germany's GSG-9, Israel's GIRU 269, France's Gigene, Italy's SAST, Spain's GEO, and all of the Netherlands' marine corps spec units.

Six new satellites were also launched in the preceding forty-eight hours from remote bases in the Soviet Union. Four were identified as ASAT (antisatellite) units, each one settling in close proximity to U.S. reconnaissance satellite orbits.

WITH THE SEAL TEAM

"Wouldn't be without him." There was one man Bernie Ryng trusted over all others when he was sent out—Lieutenant Harry Winters. Harry was Ryng's protégé, if such a thing could be said to exist in their murky world. He was a mustang, a former enlisted man who had finally accepted a commission, and the only reason Winters ever accepted it was so that he could stick with Bernie Ryng. Ashore, they went their own way, but on any kind of mission, they were inseparable. They worked perfectly as a twosome, and when a larger group was needed, Winters always took charge of the other half of the SEAL team. Ryng could have had any executive officer he wanted. The volunteers were waiting in line. But Harry Winters was always there to lead men and deliver when the going got rough. Bernie wouldn't go without him.

The initial leg of Ryng's flight was to Gander, Newfoundland, to join up with Winters, who had brought the team there the day before with all the gear Ryng had requisitioned. Forty-five minutes later, they were airborne, this time for Reykjavik. After refueling, they headed up north, hugging the coast of Greenland.

When Svalbard was a thousand miles off the starboard wing, they turned due east. Leveling off below radar-acquisition level, they tracked on a homing signal from a trawler fifty miles off the island's west coast. It not only looked like a fishing boat, it was even experiencing a successful catch. Manned by the Norwegian navy, she was one of the small fleet maintained in that area for just such an emergency.

Ryng could sleep anywhere. Lieutenant Winters woke him an hour before arrival. There was just enough time to pull on wet suits. Watertight equipment packs were pushed out the cargo door, parachutes opening automatically as each cleared the craft.

With the deafening howl of engines and wind rushing by outside, there was never a reason for the eight men to communicate verbally. Anything important could be expressed by a tap on the shoulder, a soft jab in the ribs, a hand touching either side of the head—the silent language of men who trusted and depended on each other.

The green light above the door flicked on. Now it was their turn! Harry Winters, always the first out, stepped to the hatch, flashed his customary V sign, and was gone. Tradition was vital on this team; many in special operations become superstitious the longer they survive and Winters had given the victory sign in that same manner since the first day they had jumped as a team.

Martin Gable was next. He considered it his duty to give Winters, his underwater demolitions partner, a slap on the butt as the lead man jumped. Harry would always claim that Gable's "love pat," as he called it, reminded him to start breathing after his parachute opened. Gable flashed his usual smile at Mel Harper, his white teeth setting off his black face, and he was gone. Harper and Gable were demolitions experts whom Ryng had selected years before when he was instructing. Mel was short, Gable tall, and they became Mutt and Jeff to the team. Louie Chamas, radioman, corpsman, and language expert, followed after doing his version of the two-step, for luck, before he exited.

The team chief, Denny Bush, waved his arms to catch Ryng's attention. On the ground he was the team clown, able to imitate with precision every admiral they had ever come in contact with. Now, as Bernie Ryng watched with amusement, Denny pointed outside, then back to his chest, as if to inquire if he was next. Ryng had seen this before and nodded his head, pointing to the hatch. Denny looked out, shook his head, and backed away slightly; then he went through the same exercise again, this time with a smile, ending by pinching his nose as he went through the hatch like a kid jumping off a log into the water. His partner, Wally, followed without hesitation. Always the perfectionist, Wally did everything automatically. A former Marine, he'd transferred to the SEALs because he knew they were involved in covert operations and he couldn't imagine a military career without action. When he asked Ryng if he could join the team, he explained that he was not the type who could wait for someone to declare war. During his entire career, he had never been wounded, not even cut or bruised during training. He was the iron man.

Ryng's technical specialist and small-arms expert, Rick Carpenter, was second to last. Once again, tradition took over as he turned to Bernie Ryng and saluted with his left hand. Denny Bush had decided that the last man to see their leader alive before they rejoined on the ground should always proffer the left-handed salute, "to let Bernie know we care," he had explained with a laugh.

Bernie Ryng never looked about the fuselage for anything left behind. None of these men had ever made a mistake since the team was formed. He moved up to the position Rick had just vacated, grinning inwardly as he always did at the left-handed salute, and jumped after a silent, automatic count.

The fishing boat they made contact with took them around the north tip of Prince Charles Island, a long narrow strip of land just off the main island of Spitzbergen. The little island served as a good decoy. They ran south down the narrow channel toward the main harbor. There was little chance of running into any humans along that deserted coast, nor was there any radar.

The two main settlements on Spitzbergen bordered the

harbor that cut well into the mountains, which rose fjordlike on the southwest side of the island. Four months of the year, they were snow free because of the warm current that passed within a couple of hundred miles. The nearby current also thawed the tundra enough to make it almost impassably boggy.

The Russians lived in the first community, Barentsberg, situated at the widest part of the harbor near the entrance. The supply ship that had left Murmansk the week before was anchored off the town. About twenty miles farther into the harbor was the Norwegian settlement of Longyearbyen, which included the airport used by both groups.

The SEAL team landed across the harbor from Barentsberg. About a mile and a half up the coast, they were out of sight of the settlement. Less than five hundred yards inland from the shore, Ryng found a perfect spot to conceal their equipment. Then he split the team into two groups. His section would transit to Longyearbyen to investigate the Norwegian settlement. The second had to learn what was underneath the tarpaulins on the Soviet ship.

It was late summer in Spitzbergen, six hundred miles north of Norway in the land of the midnight sun. There was no total darkness, not even in the first week of September. In what would normally be the middle of the night, the sky and land still had an eerie luminosity. The sun, a golden spectacle on the horizon, cast long shadows that contrasted with the crystal reflection on the mountain glaciers. Ryng had to pass the Soviet base and make his way to Longyearbyen without the security of total darkness that the team had been trained to exploit. Even more difficult would be the other mission, aboard the Soviet ship. That problem was left to Harry Winters—he was trained to be innovative, and Bernie never doubted for a moment that Harry could pull it off.

The evening was a chilly thirty-five degrees when they separated. Dressed in dark trousers and turtlenecks, faces blackened, they blended with the long shadows and the darkness of the icy waters.

An electric motor, attached to high-capacity batteries that

would last them well into the next day, pushed their low rubber boat at about seven knots. Once past Barentsberg, Ryng was no longer concerned with detection. Nothing existed between the two settlements but cold, barren, snow-capped mountains. The only passage between them in the summer was by helicopter or boat. At night, even though they were the only floating object, they would never be seen darting through the shadows.

It was one-thirty in the morning when they came opposite the Norwegian town. Ryng could see nothing moving. Lights glowed in some of the windows, mostly in two larger buildings. He swung his binoculars around to the airfield. There the lights, even with the sun hovering on the horizon, were brilliant. In the glare he saw two huge Aeroflot planes. Continuing to scan the area, something in his mind—a sixth sense—made him swing back. He steadied himself on the edge of the boat, the glasses centered on one of the aircraft.

Lousy camouflage! There was no doubt about the exterior markings. Both military! He suspected that whatever was in the supply ship at Barentsberg was also connected with these two planes.

"What have you got here, Bernie?"

"Two Bear bombers, I think. Here, take a look." He handed the glasses to Denny Bush, the technical specialist.

"You're right," agreed Bush, handing them back. "But take a look at those pods under the wings. I never saw anything like that before."

Ryng shook his head unhappily. "Damn, I was hoping maybe you'd recognize them. I guess we'll just have to find someone who does know." Restarting the electric motor, he quietly maneuvered the boat across the half mile, slipping gently under a broken-down pier which was attached to an even more dilapidated fishing shack that had been left to the hazards of the frozen harbor for too many winters.

After concealing the rubber boat underneath, Bush unwrapped a waterproof packet and distributed weapons. Each man received a Browning 9 mm pistol with three clips of ammunition, thirty-nine rounds apiece. Ryng had selected this particular weapon for its close-in effect; he never allowed them to use a pistol at more than twenty yards. The team didn't work that way. Each man also had two knives. Bush, as usual, was most comfortable with his garroting wire.

Ryng gestured toward one of the lighted buildings. It was at the base of a rocky outcrop. "You and Wally go around that side," he whispered to Bush. "Rick and I will try the other. Don't bother with anybody yet." They all disappeared into the shadows.

Anyone looking in their direction might have thought the quick movements were simply his imagination. One man would dart across a patch of ground stealthily and swiftly. Then the other would move, always covered by the first.

Ryng knew from the satellite photos he'd gone over the day before that this was the town recreation hall. All the local events were held here—chess tournaments with the Russians, dances, holiday feasts. This was the center of activity for Longyearbyen, its heart and pulse in the long, dark winters.

He peeked through a window into a well-lighted room. It was jammed with men. Some were asleep on the floor, others rested with their backs against the wall. At one end, in the only chairs, sat two men, guns across their knees. Ryng recognized the weapons, brand new AK-74s, Russian made. He couldn't tell who the guards were—they had no uniforms—but they knew how to handle those guns. He could tell just by the way they held them. And even at 2:30 A.M., they were wide awake and alert.

He scurried back into the shadows. Rick was already there and Ryng nodded at him to speak. "Room full of women, all asleep, I think. Two men guarding them with AK-74s. One has tear gas grenades." Ryng hadn't noticed grenades in the room he had observed. "I wouldn't try anything with them, Bernie, not right away. They look sharp."

"I agree," Ryng said as they crouched in the dark waiting for Bush.

Rick's alert eyes caught Denny Bush darting through the shadows with Wally a second or two behind him. Then, so silent that only Ryng knew they were there, the two men settled bedside them. "Prisoners?" Bernie whispered.

"One big room," Denny replied. "Must be two hundred men in there, all young. A couple of them are tied up, probably troublemakers. There're four men guarding them. One's wearing a black beret."

So that was the reason! "That's why they don't need many guards," Ryng remarked under his breath. Russian marines! Some of the Black Beret units were almost as good as their U.S. counterparts. "How many entrances?"

Bush held up one finger.

"None in the back." Ryng hissed. "We only have to worry about one door then." He pondered for a moment. "There are supposed to be about a thousand Norwegians here. They may have some of them up in the coal mines, but there must be another few hundred around here. We have to find someone who can tell us what's going on."

"Wally and I can bring you a body—a live, warm one."

Ryng held his hand up to his lips. The transformer under his arm had vibrated twice. Winters, at the Russian town, needed to talk. Ryng extracted a small radio from under his shirt. "Go ahead, Harry," he murmured.

"We're back ashore all in one piece, along with one Russian sailor. We had to borrow him when we borrowed his boat. No opportunity to avoid him, I'm afraid. We did keep him alive. When he wakes up, perhaps we can learn a bit more about that cargo." There was a slight pause. "Very interesting, Bernie. Those things under that tarp look very much like torpedoes, but they sure as hell don't do the same job. No warheads. They're a hell of a lot bigger too, very long and thin. Harper says they're all fuel and high-speed engine from the looks of them. He also said he could be wrong but they sure as hell could be some kind of decoy. There's no way you can launch them out of torpedo tubes—too narrow."

"Okay, Harry. I think we may have something over here. Perhaps they're air launched. Rick and I are going to check that out and call back. We've found the community of Longyearbyen and apparently the Norwegians are all prisoners. Looks like we have some Russian Black Berets up here. I don't know how many. Send everything out on the SSB under the usual code. Stay loose for another hour. And, Harry, put together a little something special for that freighter. We still don't want it going anywhere from here."

"No problem, boss. Do you want it at the bottom of the harbor?"

"No. Put together something so it'll be about an hour or so out to sea before it goes off."

"Right, Bernie. We'll sit tight until we hear from you. Out."

With a motion of Ryng's hand, Bush and Wally drifted off into the shadows in search of their one warm body while the other two headed for the airfield.

Owing to the arctic climate, the island was barren. There were few buildings to provide cover. Darkness had always been a blessing in the team's business, but this time it would not come for another few months. So Ryng worked his way to the airfield using shadows and rocks and as much luck as possible, with Rick covering each movement.

Crouching at the shadowy edge of a maintenance building, they were treated to an unexpected display. Not more than two hundred yards away, one of the giant bombers was being armed. Ryng had to assume the torpedolike units that Bush had found on the freighter were the same objects being wheeled out under the wings. Forklifts hoisted them up to the podlike couplings they'd noticed from the other side of the harbor.

"What do you make of it?" Ryng queried.

"Harry's right. They sure as hell aren't torpedoes—not bombs either." Rick peered at the blackened face beside him. "I'm trying to remember any recent intelligence reports about something like that." He shook his head. "No weapon that I know of was even being developed in that shape."

"Must run underwater, but I can't figure out why." Ryng paused, his head cocked to one side. Both became aware of a growing engine noise overhead. A third Bear bomber was gliding across the harbor toward them. After landing, it taxied over near the other two. As they watched in silence, the loading of the first one was completed. Minutes later, an air crew appeared, paused outside the plane for a few moments, then swung up inside. The new one moved into line as the first departed.

"Come on," whispered Ryng. "It's getting brighter out. Time to hole up for the day."

Bush and Wally were patiently waiting in the deserted fishing shack where they had hidden the boat.

"I'm sorry, Bernie. That was all we could find." Bush pointed toward a body huddled in the corner. "That's why they must have forgotten him." Filthy clothes and beard and a lingering odor of alcohol suggested that the man had been on a prolonged drunk.

"Was he like this when you found him?"

"Yeah. We heard some noise from one of the cabins and found him inside on the floor curled around a bottle of Aquavit, snoring up a hell of a storm. Believe me, he hasn't said a word.

"Well, let's get him on the road to recovery. That cold water outside is a good starter. Got anything in the medical kit that could give him a jolt?"

Wally searched through his pouch for a small vial. "This'll probably do it. But it might kill him too."

"Tough. There's no choice—and he's not going to be missed," Ryng said.

With cold water and an injection of the drug, the man was functioning within fifteen minutes. He spoke no English, and much of whatever he said in his own language would likely have been incoherent to his own countrymen. Then Ryng tried Russian. The man's eyes lit up with fear. Unconsciously, he attempted to push himself backward, as if he were trying to pass through the wall. His lips moved but there was no sound. Again Ryng spoke to him, this time in a more soothing voice, realizing that all the man could see around him were four men in black clothes much like the Black Berets wore, their faces a menacing black. He explained that they were Americans. Abject fear modulated to uncertainty in the captive. To back this up, two of them dragged the man down under the shack, pointing out their rubber boat.

Back inside, the man's expression softened somewhat. His face was flushed from the effects of the drug, his pupils dilated. Either he understood or assumed they were going to kill him there and then. Perhaps it was Ryng's explanation of what might happen to his imprisoned compatriots if he didn't answer their questions.

The man was now willing to talk.

The Black Berets had arrived a few days before, he began. No one in the village was concerned, since the huge planes bore the familiar Aeroflot markings. They saw a group of men leave the plane, but they looked just like other Russians they'd seen from time to time. When the Black Berets arrived in uniform in two trucks in the center of town, it was too late. They appeared just after a shift change. One of the trucks went directly to the mines. As far as he knew, the same shift was still up there after three days. The rest of the town had been rounded up and placed under guard, one group in the recreation hall, the other in the warehouse at the town pier. Since he had been drunk at the time, he decided that's why they overlooked him. He'd gone out only once to find more to drink, somehow avoiding them by pure, drunken luck.

On Ryng's chart of the town, the man identified where the Black Beret unit was billeted. Bernie had half a dozen more questions to ask when he saw the man's eyelids start to droop. His brilliantly flushed face turned a deathly pale. Then his eyes rolled back into his head.

"I'm sorry, Bernie. All that booze in him and, look, he's no spring chicken." Wally shrugged. "Hey, he never knew what hit him."

Ryng removed his radio and pressed a button twice. Winters's voice came back. "Yeah, Bernie?"

"I've got what is probably an entire Black Beret platoon up here, Harry. They've been in town about three days. In addition to the locals being held at the rec hall, there's a shift stuck up at the mines and apparently the balance of the town is at the town warehouse. I'm not as worried about them as I am about those funny-looking torpedoes of yours. They're loading them on the Bears, four to a wing, and one of them's already off somewhere."

"We finally convinced the one we picked up to talk a little," Winters answered. "He was no ordinary sailor. Seems he was attached to the group that builds and services those things." There was a second of silence. "Bernie, this guy is very difficult to talk with. Very stubborn . . ."

"Have you tried a shot of that stuff you and Wally have in your kits? It worked here."

"Yeah, we have, Bernie. But this guy wasn't too happy about it. We had to put him out cold first before we could give him a shot. And you know Marty—never has been very gentle about those things. The guy was willing to talk when he came around, but it's very difficult to understand Russian spoken with a broken jaw."

"Shit, Harry."

"Now, it's okay, Bernie. Listen. From what I can gather, they're planning on sending just about every sub in the Northern Fleet down through the gap between Iceland and England. They must be up around here right now, or maybe even past here by now, if my geography is right. Anyway, they know damn well we got that choke point full of CAPTOR mines." CAPTOR was the designation for a mine that the U.S. had developed as a defense against Soviet attack subs passing through choke points, the somewhat restricted waters through which a ship or submarine had to pass to get to open ocean. Nothing could activate the CAPTOR except for the target they had been programmed for. When its tiny computer identified the sound from the craft's program—that of a nuclear attack submarine for instance—the engine activated. Immediately the mine became a homing torpedo, its one objective to silence the sound. Over the years, the U.S. had recorded the identifying sounds of every Soviet sub, and the CAPTORs now lying in wait were listening for the attack subs of Russia's Northern Fleet. Sinking them would protect the Atlantic frontier and the American supply convoys to Europe.

"I think these things are some sort of decoy," Winters continued. "Apparently they're designed to imitate the sub's sound. Could be the CAPTORs will just chase down a bunch of decoys so the real subs can waltz right through later."

"Harry, get all of this back to base on the SSB. Make sure they copy. Then schedule a pickup for us about twenty-four hours from now. Tell them we're somehow going to take care of the bombers here, and hopefully the troops too. You go back to that ship tonight and make sure she doesn't plan to travel far. I think when the shooting starts here, she might want to beat it out in a hell of a hurry. We'll meet you right where you're talking now. If we're not there in twelve hours, take off."

"Right, Bernie. Out." Winters never said a word about the cold water. The only way to attach a device to that ship was to swim, and these were arctic waters. Even with a wet suit, they could last only so long. He knew Ryng had considered that even before he gave the order.

ABOARD ADMIRAL PRATT'S JET
35,000 FEET
ABOVE THE ATLANTIC OCEAN

Darkness came quickly as Pratt's plane flew east. Cobb and Carleton slept most of the time, while Pratt was just the opposite. Once he committed his mind to something new, he found that body and brain could not relax. He sorted through reams of classified materials in his briefcase as the shortened night passed.

Nelson also experienced a sleepless night, but it was sheer emotion that kept him awake. He was about to take command of the only destroyer in the fleet whose name was raised in black script on the fantail. It was a perfect replica of the original *John Hancock,* a proud name and a proud ship. Nelson imagined how impressed his father would have been if he could have seen his son in command. Then he wondered what Tricia would have thought, but then he dropped that idea. She had divorced him. A woman with as much pride as her husband, Tricia Nelson could never accept second-class status in the Navy communities. Though he was sure she still cared for him, she divorced him to divorce *them.* At that stage of his life, career and success had seemed so much more important in this white navy. He wondered now.

They landed the next morning under the blazing Mediterranean sun in the humidity of Naples. Pratt would spend most of the day in briefings at Sixth Fleet Headquarters, then fly out to the carrier *Kennedy*, on station off Malta with her battle group. *John Hancock* and *Yorktown* were part of that group. Nelson and Carleton had already found a plane that would shortly ferry the mail out to the carrier. From there it was just a hop by helo to their ships.

Pratt was not surprised to learn that Henry Cobb would not be waiting for him. Instead, Cobb disappeared into another building which Pratt later learned was inhabited by ONI, the Office of Naval Intelligence. And when they found a bit of shade for a last handshake, Cobb announced that he had to run to make a flight out to *Saratoga*. That carrier, normally part of their battle group, was in the eastern Med, south of Cyprus.

"I promise I'll be back aboard *Kennedy* in two days, Admiral. I gotta get in the habit of calling you that again. There're some loose ends I have to wrap up out there, and then back to business as usual."

Pratt smiled as he grasped Cobb's hand. "Take care, Hank. Always keep your back to the bulkhead."

"Yeah, my friend." Nelson gave him a pat on the butt. "I'll be waiting for Dave to flash me that you're back on board—intact," he added.

With a wave over his shoulder, Cobb was gone, going off by himself as usual.

HENRY COBB

Once aboard *Saratoga*, Cobb slept most of the afternoon. When he was awakened, he ate a full meal, knowing he might not have another for a day or two. Back in his quarters, he donned a jet flight suit. There was no one to bid him farewell as the red sun disappeared into the Mediterranean. He simply climbed in the back seat of a jet after waving a greeting to the pilot, and waited calmly for the carrier and her escorts to settle on a new course into the wind. It was unusual for an entire battle group to go through such an evolution for just one flight, but this was a special mission.

The pilot set course just a few points east of north. It was not long before they passed over the southern coast of Turkey. The pilot never touched his radio, even though they were overflying a country at war. All that was required was a steady identification signal for military ground stations on a pre-established frequency. The flight had been cleared the day before from Washington. They landed at a small port on the southern coast of the Black Sea. The pilot refueled quickly and disappeared back to *Saratoga*.

A jeep took Cobb to a darkened pier. At the end, a small hydrofoil bobbed in the calm waters of the Black Sea. He was greeted by a man wearing the dark uniform of the Turkish navy, though he was American and spoke perfect

English. Extending his hand in greeting, he said, "Welcome, Henry. Somehow, someone picked the weather perfectly."

"All the way across?" Cobb asked Lassiter, shaking hands.

"As far as we can tell. When you get out in the middle, you'll find the normal swells but no chop. Just sweet summer zephyrs."

"Let's go then."

Lassiter gave a signal. Instantly the powerful diesel engines grumbled into life. At full speed on the calm waters, foils extended, they would be on the other side of the Black Sea, the Russian side, in three and a half hours, just before sunrise. Then Lassiter would be on his own in that boat. He didn't expect any problem, but one never knew. The odds were that the Russians didn't know that he'd taken their hydrofoil the night before. Everything on board was intact. His men were trained to respond to the Soviet radio codes every four hours. So, as far as Soviet Black Sea Fleet headquarters knew, this boat was still following its normal independent patrol assignment. But it couldn't last forever. Lassiter wanted desperately to be able to dump the hydrofoil at just the right time. That was highly preferable to hearing the final roar of MiGs diving on them.

Cobb's destination was the Crimea. Attached by a narrow spit of land to Mother Russia, it jutted out into the Black Sea. The Crimea contained the historic cities of Sevastopol, home of the Russian Black Sea Fleet; Yalta, where Stalin twisted the arms of Churchill and Roosevelt in 1945; and Simferopol, training center for the terrorists who had so exacerbated the current Greek-Turkish conflict. The Crimea was also the location of General Keradin's summer dacha, where the head of the Strategic Rocket Forces and his deputies were meeting that weekend. It was a strategy session, Cobb knew, just like those in Washington. However, DNI had explained to him personally that this was the *final* conference, the one that would decide at what stage they would launch and what the initial targets would be—if the Red Army did not own Western Europe within forty-eight hours after D-Day.

Lassiter and Cobb had worked together before. Neither one needed to speak until something important had to be said. Finally, Cobb broke the silence. "Where you going after this?"

Lassiter shrugged. "Depends if I still have this boat under my feet." He brushed away the hair streaming over his face. "You know what the Russians are planning with this little war they engineered here?"

"Sure. They want to clean out the Bosporus and Dardanelles—the choke points. Then they can come and go as they please over the next few days." The boat heeled to the side as one of her foils slid down a long swell. Cobb steadied himself with one hand on the railing. "It's all a matter of choke points, I was told. Keep 'em in their holes and we've at least got a chance."

"There's a hell of a lot of them already out in the Med."

"What they got out there so far we can handle," Cobb said. "I saw the intelligence reports and some satellite photos. They sent a carrier through the other day. There're still a lot of destroyers and cruisers in here, and just about all of the subs. The Montreux Convention doesn't allow their subs to pass through the Turkish straits. I suppose they're saving some of them to open the choke points and keep them open."

"Makes sense," Lassiter mused. "You know, Hank, I sure do love these little boats; turn on a dime, lots of power for your nickel."

"Sounds like fun. I wish you had a few more." He paused and contemplated the idea. "Perhaps I could hang around for an extra day or two."

"We might locate a few more by tomorrow night." Lassiter beamed.

They lapsed into silence. After a while, Cobb went below to change into his next outfit. When he came up again, Lassiter clapped his hands in amusement. Cobb was dressed like a Crimean peasant, the clothes authentic right down to the grape stains that a vineyard worker would have on his work clothes during harvest season. Keradin's dacha was also a working winery, and Washington had decided such an outfit provided the only means for someone to get close to the General.

WENDELL NELSON

John Hancock rolled gently in the Mediterranean swell. The hum of her engineering plant came infrequently to Nelson's ears. It was a sound that had so assimilated itself into his makeup over the years that he was already attuned to the ship he'd taken over just a few hours before.

It had been a quick and simple change of command. Nelson was escorted to the captain's cabin as soon as he'd stepped from the helo on *Hancock*'s fantail. Her CO went over the classified material in the captain's safe, then offered a rundown on the department heads and the condition of the ship. As soon as they finished, the captain called the executive officer and told him to make final preparations. There was little time for niceties.

Five minutes later, those members of the crew not on watch assembled on the fantail. Nelson read his orders. He turned to the former captain, saluted, and intoned the ritual words, "I relieve you, sir." He then became Commanding Officer of U.S.S. *John Hancock,* 7,800 tons of destroyer, as big as a modern cruiser—bigger than anything he'd ever ridden.

Now Wendell Nelson was reading the latest operation

orders, the details put to paper by the administrative types. These were law, the golden words passed down from Washington to Norfolk to the fleet command in Naples to the battle group at sea to the individual commanding officers. Throughout his reading, Nelson always came back to what all captains of all surface ships knew—the carrier was the heart of the battle group, the one element that could launch a devastating strike on enemy territory. It was the ship that had to be protected at all costs. Destroyers were expendable!

Hancock was an antisubmarine destroyer with surface-to-air missiles for point defense. She was part of the screen whose duty was to protect the carrier from submarine attack, to search out and kill Soviet attack submarines before they got within range of the carrier.

He finished his reading and carefully locked the material back in his safe. On top he placed the shrink-wrapped op orders that were only to be opened when Condition One was set—when war was declared.

Nelson ambled up to the bridge after a tour around the main deck of the ship. He leaned on the railing outside the pilothouse for a moment, adjusting his eyes to the darkness so he could identify the other ships in the screen. In the center, miles distant, he could make out the mass of the carrier *John F. Kennedy*.

Then he went into the pilothouse to the chart table and opened the night orders. The chief yeoman was efficient— Nelson's orders were already inserted in plastic to protect them from weather. And, he noted, they had already been passed around the wardroom, for the signature of each officer was already below them. It was a good omen, he decided—a good, efficient ship. He knew they'd do a fine job for him. The wardroom's initial surprise at a black CO gave him an advantage early on, he decided, remembering the night he'd been drinking with Dave Pratt and Bernie Ryng in some long-forgotten "O" club. Ryng had claimed Nelson's dark features were inscrutable, a perfect face for intelligence work. Pratt had agreed with Bernie. An inscrutable captain also, Nelson mused now with amusement.

He wandered out on to the bridge wing again and stared back over at the imposing outline of *Kennedy*. He was sure Pratt was on the bridge, surveying the new command surrounding him. I'm glad you're calling the shots, Dave, Nelson said to himself. We'll do all right.

TOM CARLETON

Like Cobb and Ryng, Carleton could sleep anywhere, and he took advantage of the long flight to rest himself as much as possible. But like Pratt and Nelson, he was also excited about his new command. He felt like a child wandering into a candy store clutching five dollars in his hand and with no one to tell him how to spend it.

Yorktown was the key to defending a carrier battle group from air attack. Her AEGIS fire-control system coupled with sophisticated detection and tracking functions could direct the weapons of the entire force. One-third of her cost was for the ship herself, the rest for an electronic installation unrivaled by any in existence. Tom had spent his last six months as a prospective commanding officer in schools and simulators. He'd commanded destroyers before and he was an engineer, but he had to relearn his trade, especially in accepting the reality that the commanding officer of an AEGIS cruiser no longer fought his ship from the bridge. Instead, he sat before a fire-control display system inside an electronics-filled space and communed with a computer to fight his ship.

It was a totally different Navy from the one his father served in during the Second World War. As a child, Tom had thrilled to tales of naval battles in the South Pacific. Today, Nimitz and Halsey and the rest of his great heroes from forty years before wouldn't have the vaguest idea of how *Yorktown* operated. Within microseconds, her radars and radios and computers could analyze intelligence from distant submarines or surface ships, planes hundreds of miles away, invisible recon satellites, and strategic and tactical details compiled at shore bases halfway around the world. And with all that data, her computers could then coordinate the weapons on those distant platforms.

And all of that hidden power was designed to protect the carrier in the battle group from missile attacks long enough to launch her air group to bring the war to the enemy.

For months, Tom Carleton dealt in a mysterious world of microchips and milliseconds, one where electronic gadgets made lifesaving or life-threatening decisions much faster and more accurately than any human being could. The system was designed to battle systems, not men. He also learned that this electronic gadget named *Yorktown* was only as good as the people who sailed her, that he was still only a valuable cog in her success or failure, as were each of her men. And it was his responsibility to make this marvel work when she was finally called on.

Current doctrine indicated that when it all began, the first salvo from Soviet forces would be awesome. His response, *Yorktown*'s, would have to be both instant and absolutely correct.

D MINUS 2

The President addressed a special meeting of the UN Security Council regarding the current military situation in Central Europe, and to speak for the censure of the Soviet Union for overt aggressive acts documented by recon satellites. The Soviet Ambassador refused to attend, indicating that any censure of his country would cause the Soviet Union's withdrawal from the international body.

Massive efforts were undertaken to evacuate as many American dependents in NATO countries as possible, but severe restraints on civilian air traffic limited selection of these evacuees. Special permission had to be granted for landings by American commercial aircraft at specific airfields in Germany, the Netherlands, Belgium, Spain, Italy, the Scandinavian countries, and England. The French government, not bound by NATO agreements, guaranteed protection to American dependents though Paris refused to acknowledge the activation of Soviet reserve divisions in eastern Russia or the fact that French military forces still were not under Condition Two.

The damaged SOSUS array off Bermuda was now back in operation after the emplacement of hydrophones. Similar damage had occurred over the previous forty-eight hours to arrays off Iceland, the Azores, Hokkaido, Adak in Alaska, and Seattle. In each case, escort aircraft were able to determine that Soviet bombers on routine patrols (i.e., following their normal tracks over international waters) released objects that apparently caused the arrays to go silent. Commencing early on D minus 4, all such Soviet patrols were intercepted on the perimeter of a three-hundred-mile circle around SOSUS arrays and escorted under accepted international rules. No further damage was reported.

Seagoing units of the Japanese Military Self-Defense Force steamed in company with units of the Seventh Fleet at the express request of the Japanese Premier. This overture appeared to be an effort to convince the Japanese public that the missile which damaged the *Haruna* on D minus 3 was definitely not fired by any American aircraft. Within an hour after the incident, Soviet-controlled propaganda identified the source of the missile as an American F-18 on routine patrol over the Sea of Japan. However, the memory bank of an electronic listening device aboard *Haruna* recorded the missile's lock-on radar signature as a Russian AS-5. This unfortunately did not have any effect on the rioting by left-wing students. Japanese government reports also indicated the insertion into their country of professional terrorists recently trained in Libya. Commerce remained at a standstill due to rioting and the effective disruption of civilian transportation services. Though it was obvious to the planners in the Pentagon that there would be no attack by Soviet forces in the Far East, these decoy efforts continued. They would have far-reaching effect on the future makeup of the Japanese government.

Due to the disruption of transportation in Japan, NATO countries gave unlimited authority to antiterrorist units in an effort to contain or at least limit damage to surface transportation networks. CIA white papers reported in the past that this would be the goal of Soviet planning before D-Day; though transport was harassed, military logistic movement was almost as steady as intended. The Russians had hurt themselves by being too effective in Japan too early!

An Israeli negotiating team, apparently sent at the behest of the United States on D minus 4, had success in halting raids by Turkey and Greece on each other. Israeli intelligence indicated to both sides (in a report prepared by their own intelligence agency) that the Soviet Union was responsible for terrorist activities that had fomented the military action over the previous three days. CIA reports anticipated that termination of Greek-Turkish activities would affect Soviet plans for controlling the Turkish straits, thereby likely requiring Soviet military action to control the exits from the Black Sea.

The U.S. CAPTOR blockade of the GIUK gap was reportedly in danger of breakdown by D minus 2. SOSUS reports, combined with infrared satellite intelligence, indicated that more than twenty CAPTOR mines had been activated by decoy units radiating an exact signature of a Soviet submarine. Since all but two of the submarines stationed in Murmansk were reported at sea and headed for the gap, it became clear to Washington that those submarines could exit into the North Atlantic via a destroyed CAPTOR barrier. The decoy devices were carried by Soviet bombers from a base on the island of Spitzbergen and deployed from the air. Upon entering the water, they moved at the speed of a submarine and radiated a signature that activated the CAPTOR listening devices. Though a submarine hunter-killer division had departed New London within hours of the first communication from Norway, most Murmansk attack submarines were projected to disappear into the Atlantic beforehand. At that time, Bernie Ryng's SEAL team had less than twenty-four hours to complete its mission.

Recon photos, commencing at first light on D minus 2, indicated Soviet shock forces in Eastern Europe were no longer involved in exercises of any kind. Offensive units were taking position near the western borders. Their political units had apparently already infiltrated government offices in Warsaw Pact countries, for communications from these capital cities to the outside world were limited at best. Computer projections now anticipated a full-scale attack across a broad frontier in no less than forty-eight hours.

SPITZBERGEN, THE HARBOR

Harry Winters knew, at the end of Ryng's last transmission, that there was little time to complete his end of the job. Bernie was not one to let grass sprout up around him. If the Russians were already sewing their decoys in the gap more than two thousand miles to the south, he had to move even in the inadequate cover of the midnight sun.

There was no chance, or even reason, to try to get back aboard the Russian freighter as they had done before when they had appropriated the supply boat. With one man missing, the Russians would likely be a bit more security conscious, and so a device would have to be planted under the hull. He couldn't use anything activated from shore. Considering the odds of a storm or fog or even the possible great distance were they to be interrupted for some reason, detonation would be too uncertain. It had to be an intelligent device.

The only problem was time. Once Bernie and his boys began to warm things up around the airfield, Harry knew it was probable that the ship would immediately get under way and move offshore. How long would Bernie take? He had no idea where Ryng might be at any given moment and over the years they'd learned never to bother each other at these times. Even though he'd never seen the field, Winters knew there was no way four Americans were going to sneak up on those Russian bombers in broad daylight, not with Black Berets guarding them. It seemed likely to him that Bernie might want to borrow some of the Soviet uniforms. That would take some time. Would he try to release the Norwegians beforehand? No way! That would only add to the chance of getting one of his own hurt unnecessarily and even compromise the objective of getting the bombers and the decoy torpedoes that had already been offloaded.

Two of Winters's men were experts at assembling the device he determined would sink the ship. There was no leeway for error. He gave Bernie three hours to get some sleep, another hour to waylay some Black Berets and borrow their uniforms, and another hour to carry out the mission. The first sign of action at the airfield would get that ship out to sea, or at least under way in the harbor. So he designed the timer for six hours from now, just to insure it held off until the ship made it to deep water.

Making the bomb, installing the timer, then waterproofing it was no problem. Any one of them could do it in his sleep, and each man could do the other's job with no hesitation.

The problem was getting out there and getting the damn thing properly planted so it wouldn't fall off on its own or be jarred loose by the motion of the ship. That's what took time and planning. But it could be done and done right.

Two hours later, Winters slipped into the water across the harbor from the freighter. Martin Gable was right behind him. The bomb was strapped to an electrically powered sled. Ryng had fashioned it years ago to glide through the water ahead of them, towing both divers and their gear. Winters realized that Bernie had considered the frigid water. He had made it a two-man mission because one man might not make it to the ship and back on his own. If neither was back on shore in three hours, the remaining two had been ordered to take off to the meeting place Ryng had planned for them.

It was dark under the hull and very, very cold. Their wet

suits were insulated and designed to survive forty-degree water for a period of time—but not over a long span of continuous immersion. Winters's flashlight settled on Marty's hands for a moment and held it there just long enough to see the difficulty the man was having. Each movement was slow and deliberate, an intense effort to insure that nothing could go wrong after the bomb was set. After each step, Marty would close his fists, squeezing them together rhythmically a few times to recover as much circulation as possible. Winters realized that if the hands already functioned in that manner, then the rest of the man's body could not endure forever. Once the cold took hold of one part of the body, impairment of other functions followed quickly.

The final step was Harry's—to install the timer. Totally absorbed, he forgot Marty, his mind wholly involved with overriding the ache in his hands as he set the delicate instrument. When he finally looked up, there was no Marty beside him. Flashing his light about the darkness under the hull, he caught sight of the man floating a few feet below, arms outstretched, fists still rhythmically clasping and unclasping, though now it appeared more a macabre, slow-motion ballet.

The spectacle was unmistakable. Harry had seen it in training films time and again. It was the final dance—that of a diver dying from the cold, his heart pumping more slowly, his brain functions dimming.

Winters floated down and held the flashlight to Marty's face. The man stared back blankly, head shaking slowly up and down to indicate that he knew what was next. It was understood, an integral part of their training.

Marty reached slowly for his belt, his fingers fumbling. Unable to make them do what he wanted, his fist opened painfully and with an index finger he gestured in slow motion that Winters should do it for him.

Harry grasped the belt, extracting a tubular plastic container no more than an inch in diameter. He held it out to his friend. Marty's fingers attempted to close over the object, but there was no way he could grip it. He pulled back his hand and with an effort opened and closed his fist. He desperately wanted to restore just enough circulation to handle the job himself. It was something that a man would want to do, hating to ask his partner to do it for him.

But eventually there was no choice. Time was against him and Marty knew it. At least one of them had to get back. And it would be impossible for a man in his condition to both give himself the injection and make sure his body sank before it took effect.

His head bobbed sluggishly, this time in sadness. Harry would have to do it. As Winters came closer, Marty clumsily patted him on the shoulder to show that he understood and that he was sorry. Then he rolled sideways.

Winters pulled off the top of the plastic container. In the artificial light, he could see the tiny needle reflecting sharply back at him. He put the object against Marty's arm, hesitated for a split second, then pushed. They were told it would take almost no effort. The experts were right. Before Winters fully understood how easily the instrument worked, he saw Marty's body tense and then relax. He was already dead.

Quickly, feeling the adrenaline pulsing through his own system, Winters released the tanks from Marty's back, puncturing the valve that would sink them. Finally he pulled the cord on the back of Marty's wet suit where the tank had been. It would insure that the body would sink—no chance of its coming to the surface beside the Russian ship. Martin Gable became the first American casualty of the operation.

Then he pushed the button on the electric motor and whisked away from the freighter. The return trip would not be that long. The sled had lost much of its burden. But now that he was motionless, he could feel the intensity of the cold, the numbing pain that came as his system wore down, the heart unable to pump blood fast enough to make the machine called the human body efficient enough to survive.

Winters checked off the interminable minutes it took to get back to shore—twenty, eighteen, fifteen, ten, eight, six . . .

Then the electric motor simply stopped. Unlike an internal-combustion engine, there was no stuttering or jumping or sputtering. All of a sudden, it just wasn't working.

He let the sled go, watching dejectedly as it slowly slid toward the bottom, the sun's rays penetrating the clear, cold waters and glinting off its surface. Then it was gone.

Winters took some preliminary strokes, kicked his legs. What was supposed to be a smooth bodily reaction, the combined efforts of arms and legs, was a clumsy thrash, like a fish flapping helplessly on the sand, Harry thought.

There was no way he could do it. It was beyond the function of his brain to force arms and legs to coordinate. It was beyond his mind to inspire his baser instincts to save himself. Winters knew there was no way he could make it back!

The one thing he knew he was still capable of was insuring that his body was not found by the Russians before the freighter got under way.

Clumsily, in the same awkward motions Marty had attempted, but failed at, Harry extracted the plastic container from his belt. As he did so, he found that his mind was acceding to what he was about to do. As he allowed himself to sink gradually, he decided that he would wait until the sunlight was barely discernible above, because he did not want to see himself do it. It was one thing to do his duty to a friend, quite another to do it to himself.

As he awaited the profound peace that all the books claimed would settle over him, the realization came that he was going about it all wrong! His orderly mind had slipped away for a moment. This wasn't the way he'd been taught. The classroom experience came back to him vividly. They had even done it in the tanks, step-by-step, even to plunging a phony needle into their flesh.

Step one: the tank! He slipped gradually out of the straps, each movement of his body a painful reminder that there was a definite purpose in this. His fingers fumbled for the plunger. They wouldn't close! You've got to! You've got to get through step one. With an effort he shoved and shoved until enough force was exerted. The tanks sank, only the bubbles showing where his former life-support system was disappearing.

Step two: the wet suit! He had to hurry. It was hard to hold your breath when your body was so cold, when each motion was painful. *Don't screw it up now for Chrissakes.* There was no way he could reach the cord in back, but there was another under the belt in front. His fingers couldn't grasp it. Finally, the heels of both hands pressed together, he yanked, and felt the flood of cold water against his skin. But it wasn't cold. It was hot, almost a burning sensation!

Step three: the container. He'd slipped it back in the belt when he remembered he had other things to do. *Step three, the container,* his mind screamed at him. Now the air— the last gulp of oxygen before he let the tanks go—was escaping his lungs. He could sense the bubbles on his lips. There was no way he'd allow himself to suck in any water, not Harry Winters! He had no intention of drowning, of causing his own death by the very element that he'd lived in and made a career of!

He couldn't bring his hand far enough around to push the needle against his arm. So, as the last breath left his body, he pushed it against his chest. There was a sharp prick, no pain. His whole body was already one big pain! He kept his mouth shut. The last conscious message to his brain was not to open his mouth—don't let any water in. Then there was darkness as the drug took him. Step four . . . *die.*

Harry Winters sank slowly to the bottom of the harbor— the second American casualty.

SPITZBERGEN, THE AIRPORT

Bernie Ryng's first notion was to knock off the horseplay. In a very short time, they'd be in the midst of a firefight. On second thought, it was better to let Denny Bush go ahead.

Bush, a black beret pulled down just above his right eyebrow, was conducting a mock inspection of the other two. Rick's beret was a bit too large, so Bush, the inspecting officer, had pulled it over his eyes. And Wally simply wasn't going to pass. The black uniform blouse was wrinkled and slightly soiled from the scuffle. "You look so sloppy, one would think you were wearing someone else's uniform," Denny scowled, his lips quivering in an effort to maintain a straight face.

It was too much for him. He turned to Ryng, saluting with his fingers at the edge of his eyebrow. "I apologize, comrade. These men are not ready for inspection. I will have them shot immediately."

It was good sport. Ryng appreciated the twinkle in Denny's eyes. Denny Bush was always the one to break up the party when they were ashore, or to find the bright side and loosen up the others when an operation neared the flash point. He was the type that cemented a group. Ryng commanded naturally, led by example, but his willingness to

let Denny clown made him even more of a leader in the
men's eyes. Every leader needed a Denny Bush.

"Very well, comrade," he answered, returning the salute
with an even more exaggerated one of his own. "Shoot them.
It's the only solution."

They were now outfitted in the Black Beret uniform of
the Soviet Naval Infantry. That would allow them to get
close enough to the planes to carry out their attack. The
bombers that were on the runway had to be destroyed and
the field left inoperable, and this would scare the ship out
of the harbor. It was Harry Winters's job to make sure it
never came back. Next, they would destroy the remaining
decoy torpedoes and eliminate any Black Berets in their
way. Ryng had no illusions about taking on an entire marine
platoon with four men, so the final objective was to get the
hell out of there.

Obtaining the uniforms was simple. Though it required
an extra effort to insure the clothes were neither damaged
nor bloodied, Ryng's team was skilled in that type of work.
They selected privates, men who would have no command
responsibilities and wouldn't be immediately missed. The
team moved fast, for a crack military organization like the
Black Berets wouldn't take long to realize more than one
man was missing. The uniforms themselves were impressive, black fatigues with naval insignia and striking black
berets with an anchor design on the left side and a red star
in front. Each man in his team spoke Russian. Ryng wouldn't
have selected a man who didn't.

Ryng checked his watch. Harry would be under that hull
by now, preparing his own little surprise. Time to move.
They'd already gone over the basics of his plan, and there
was nothing complex about it. Their explosives—antipersonnel grenades, Wally's homemade plastic pipe bombs,
and some with time delay fuses—were carried in cloth
satchels. Each man carried the Russian automatic rifles they
had taken when they appropriated the uniforms. Underneath
were their personal weapons.

A formidable little force, if I do say so myself, Bernie
thought. Not big, but I've worked with them enough to

know they're each worth four or five average infantrymen
and maybe three Black Berets apiece. He shrugged inwardly. We have the advantage of surprise. Maybe five to
one will be acceptable.

"Let's go."

Nothing else was necessary. No instructions. Each could
hold his own and look out for the other guy at the same
time.

They passed through what Ryng decided must have been
the town square when it wasn't buried in snow. The best
approach was the confident one. Look like you're heading
somewhere important, following instructions. Head there
as fast as possible, acting as if there's no time to pass the
time of day with anyone, and don't look back!

No one bothered them. One of the guards at the warehouse by the harbor waved and shouted a friendly greeting
as they passed. Ryng returned the wave and muttered something about stopping on their way back for a smoke.

As they came abreast of the maintenance building, where
the off-loaded decoys were apparently stored, Ryng spotted
an open vehicle. The keys were in the ignition. "We'll
borrow that when we're getting the hell out of here." He
pointed at Denny. "You drive." Over his shoulder to the
others, he added with a grin, "And why don't you all try
to be careful and not blow the damn thing up. I don't feature
running all the way back with a platoon of marines on my
heels."

"Makes sense," Denny agreed nonchalantly. He winked
at Ryng. "Maybe I ought to take the keys now."

"Don't worry about the keys, my friend. Just make sure
you drop anyone who wants to take it." Then to the others,
"We'll wander over by the shed and get an idea how many
are inside. And I want to know exactly where those aircrews
are." There were now three bombers pulled up one behind
the other on the field. "They know how to shoot too. Rick,
you find them for me. They can't be far. The crews last
night were supervising the placing of those decoys on the
wings, so these will probably want to also."

There were six Black Berets, each armed with the AK-

74s, inside the shed where the decoys were stored. Another dozen, unarmed, were preparing them for loading. Wally made a mental note that their weapons were stacked nearby. Rick found the aircrews in the rear of the building, relaxing at a long table over coffee and cigarettes. He saw nothing to indicate they were armed. That made eighteen marines, six of whom would have to be dispatched immediately, leaving twelve who would make trouble within seconds if they were allowed to pick up anything that would shoot. Ryng knew they could save the aircrews until last, but they couldn't take them for granted.

Back outside, Ryng explained, "We're going to wait until they start loading those two bombers. That'll get the crews out here and the coolies farther away from their guns. When I give the word, Wally and I will hit the shed. All I want to do is hold it long enough to blow the decoys. Denny, you and Rick handle the ones out here. Don't give them the slightest chance. More often than not, those flyers have pistols or other survival weapons in their flight suits. Take them first, then the work party. Then get those explosives inside the planes. I want them burning from the inside out. Then we'll scatter some time-delay grenades to keep their cleanup crews busy for a while—can't let them reopen the field," he added.

"Sounds simple," remarked Bush.

"Very," agreed Ryng, "if you believe no one else is going to come running as soon as the shooting starts."

TOM CARLETON

An overhead speaker in the *Yorktown*'s pilothouse crackled into life. "Permission granted to detach for maneuvering exercises. Request you maintain standard ECM and long-range AA guards per my Op Order 12–2. Over."

"Roger. I thank you. Out." Tom Carleton handled the transmission himself, since the maneuvering exercises were for no one other than him. The man he relieved hours earlier had assured him that his OODs were superb ship handlers, so it was apparent that only *Yorktown*'s new captain needed to be qualified in handling the cruiser.

"This is Captain Carleton. I have the conn," he called out to the bridge watch, following the Navy's time-honored tradition. The acknowledgment echoed back to him, then he said, "Right standard rudder . . . come to course one zero zero." He eased his well-fed bulk out of the captain's chair and moved calmly about the pilothouse to refamiliarize himself with the myriad dials and displays.

Before putting his ship through her paces, he would take her about five miles outside the perimeter of the formation. The process wouldn't be a long one. Carleton had commanded ships before, and he was a superb ship handler—any ship, any sea conditions. His purpose was simply to get the feel of *Yorktown,* to know before he gave an order how she would respond, how quickly she could accelerate, how she reacted in tight turns at high speeds. He had to know her personally not only under combat conditions, but also in close quarters with other U.S. ships.

Each vessel had a personality of its own. Though they were built following the same specifications, they were as different as human beings, each rudder biting just a tad differently, each mighty engine with its own quirk, each hull taking the sea with slight aberrations. Very few men could sense such minute differences. Most who could were commanding officers. Carleton was at home when he could feel a ship's personality through his feet or identify with her sounds through his pillow as he slept at night. But now there was little time to understand *Yorktown,* for everything pointed to the fact that she might have to fulfill her design obligations any hour now.

There were engine controls on the bridge. With a flick of the wrist, the powerful gas turbines could accelerate the ship instantly, the only limiting force being the drag of the water against her hull. Carleton first put the engines through their paces, increasing speeds slowly, then faster, then backing down, then forward again, full speed. He watched her wake, he felt her talk to him through his feet, and he learned very quickly how she would answer him.

Then he toyed with her rudders, turning sharply one way, then another, making Z's and O's, selecting various speeds— even backing down halfway through a turn. Such an action might be needed to avoid a collision or even be the last chance to confuse a homing torpedo, at least enough so that it might detonate in *Yorktown*'s wake rather than her engine room. He felt her cant as he increased her rudder angle, estimating in his own mind how she would respond when the seas were twenty feet and green water was breaking over her bow.

He spent over an hour gamboling about the Mediterranean, enjoying a luxury that he might not again have the opportunity for. She was magnificent! *Yorktown* outperformed everything he'd read in the designer's specs and the sea trials. Now it was time to go back to business as usual. Grudgingly, he returned the conn to the OOD and sat comfortably back in his captain's chair, his hands folded happily over his ample belly. For a moment, a very short one, he thought about his wife's cooking—it was almost as dear to him as she was. He imagined that, if he ever got a soft shore billet, that would be it! Lucille's food would fatten him up and they'd retire him permanently! He dozed off contentedly.

THE CRIMEA, USSR

A couple of hours before first light, Henry Cobb was paddled ashore northeast of Yalta, up the coast toward Alushta. Lassiter had shaken his hand, cuffing him playfully on the side of the head before Cobb went over the side into the rubber craft. It hadn't been necessary for Lassiter to repeat it as many times as he had, but he had to assure Cobb that he would be back in the same spot in less than twenty-four hours, then once more twenty-four hours later. If there was no Cobb by then, then the mission was a failure. Henry Cobb would be considered a casualty—an unreported casualty.

Cobb scurried up the hillside through the undergrowth to the winding road that led through the villages toward Yalta. A sliver of moon hung low in the sky, and the night was clear and black. He needed very little light to find his way. The track he would follow was imbedded in his memory. Days before, in the map room in Washington he had pieced together the satellite photos himself, recording each step he intended to take. If he'd had the slightest doubt about a potential obstacle in his path, he had had the photo blown up until he was sure what it was. Or if still hesitant, he would call over one of the photo interpreters and ask his opinion.

His was a photographic memory in many ways. But as Dave Pratt had once pointed out, they were very strange ways. Cobb's mastery of languages was incredible, right down to his ability to immerse himself in local dialect. He could have crossed a minefield blindfolded once he had the opportunity to study its layout. The structure of Kremlin hierarchy, the layout of each office, and the names of each individual could have been committed to memory in an amazingly short time span. Pratt often said that Henry could have made a fortune if his mind had been channeled in the proper direction, but the prospect of making money had never occurred to Cobb.

He followed the dirt road for a short distance, mentally checking off the identifying features he'd selected days earlier. Turning into the hills on a path that appeared to have been a goat track, he began an easy climb, now heading in the direction of the moon sliver that was hovering just over his objective.

Below him stretched the Black Sea, occasional lights bobbing in the distance signifying fishing boats. Farther away he could see the glow of lights in the sky, hinting at a large city, Yalta. This was where the gentry of the Communist Party came to play in the summer—senior officials, scientists, managers, prominent Party members, and, most important, the generals and admirals. Their dachas were scattered over the hillsides that looked down into the warm, blue waters of the Black Sea. This part of the Crimea was the playground of those who made the USSR tick.

His objective was the dacha of General Keradin, the head of the Strategic Rocket Forces of the Soviet Union, that element of the Soviet Army that controlled the ICBMs. With an order from one man, Keradin, the most terrifying attack mankind had ever known, and perhaps the last it ever experienced, would be launched. This man was so powerful, so respected by those few who were senior to him, that he could come and go as he pleased. And in the summer he chose to spend much of his time at his dacha in the Crimea, less than two hours flying time from Moscow. It didn't really matter where Keradin chose to locate himself, for the immense power of his command could be exercised in split seconds from wherever he happened to be.

General Keradin's dacha was not only his escape but his hobby. The sweet dessert wines of the Soviet Crimea were his first love, his way of escaping the terrible responsibility of his position. The hillsides sweeping up and to the north were covered with vineyards that faced the Black Sea and the summer sun. Though the dacha and its many guest rooms were designed to house a staff ready to launch missiles at a moment's notice, the real center of the estate was the wine-making barn, the heart and soul of Keradin's obsession.

It was Keradin's infatuation with wines that had precipitated a crash course in the art of winemaking for Henry Cobb. Whisked by a military jet to an Air Force base north of San Francisco, Cobb was met by the man who would be his teacher over the next five days. Very little surprised Cobb. Yet his host, the scion of a successful, family-owned vineyard, consistently astonished him during those days. As he struggled to acquire the knowledge that had come to one man in a lifetime, Cobb also learned that hatred spans generations. His mentor proudly acknowledged working for the CIA whenever he was in Europe promoting his rapidly growing industry. Cobb would later reflect that he learned more than he bargained for about his quarry during his whirlwind education.

The dacha was remarkably similar to his host's homestead in the Napa Valley. White plastered walls reflected the sun and allowed the inside to remain cool even on the hottest days. A veranda stretched much of the length of the building so that the inhabitants could come out to socialize in the sun or find enough privacy to be on their own. The only real difference was the many individual balconies on the second floor, much like a tacky motel, Cobb thought. These were where the staff slept, each with his own room, a nice gesture by Keradin to keep his people happy.

There was also a security force. It was composed of

military intelligence people from the GRU, and they were very good. The CIA also reported that Keradin was an extremely private man who did not appreciate the trappings of the military when he escaped to the Crimea. Moscow was one world, his dacha the other. And in the latter he insisted that the GRU maintain a low profile. No man could relax in an armed camp, and Keradin felt that his vineyard, far from the mainstream, was not a place that would be easily targeted by an enemy. He felt secure.

Cobb circled to the north, above the highest vineyards. Within yards of his final goal, he found the rock outcroppings that had been so prominent in the photos. It was not above the fence that surrounded the vineyards, but it slanted upward enough, almost like the lip of a ski jump, to make it the weakest point on the perimeter.

His one weapon was a razor-sharp knife in his boot. With this, he was able to cut a sturdy sapling from a nearby stand of trees. Carefully, he sliced off the branches one by one, close to the trunk. Then just as prudently, he smeared the whitened scars on the bark with dirt. After he was over the fence, there would be no way to dispose of it, and he wanted nothing that would attract the attention of the guards.

Back on top of the outcropping, he tested the strength of the sapling, making sure it would take his weight. To the southeast, he could make out the faint glow over the Black Sea that presaged the sun and a new day. Planting the staff in the hard ground below, he bounced lightly on his toes for a second, then vaulted gracefully into the air. It was not really a pole vault. He wanted just enough height to clear the fence, just enough distance to land far enough beyond the sensing devices that he knew were implanted two yards beyond the fence. As he reached the apex of his leap, he very deliberately cast the sapling backward into some rye grass growing a few yards from the fence. With luck, the grass and the dirt he had rubbed into the cuts in the bark would hide it from curious eyes.

As he landed precisely on his toes, he rolled forward before his heels could make full impact on the turf. Touching the ground first with his right shoulder, he rolled twice in an effort to absorb the impact and avoid setting off an oversensitive device near the fence.

He was in! Remaining on his knees, his eyes searched in every direction, using the faint horizon as a backdrop to ensure there were no guards nearby. He'd been right. The flashlights he'd counted from outside represented the only men who were there. As the CIA report had stated, they felt secure enough on this hillside that there was no effort to make the vineyard impenetrable, no anticipation that someone like Cobb would seek entry in this manner. Very unlike the GRU, he thought, remembering the difficulty he once had breaking their security in Moscow.

Now creeping into the safety of a row of vines, all he could do was wait for the sun to rise, for the workers to arrive so that he could mix among them and move about as if he were one of the peasant laborers. He knew the basic location of every building and every path, and the purposes of most of them. However, there were some buildings to the west, in the lower part of the fields, that mystified him. He had to quickly develop a feel for the movement of the day, the habits of the workers, the daily customs and routines of the dacha that its inhabitants followed without thinking. Acclimatization was one of Cobb's first steps wherever he went, and it was often what saved his neck in the first hours in a new place.

At a very early hour, when the sun had yet to heat the still air, the huge main gate was opened to allow the workers inside. Cobb noted both the security devices that were apparently turned off at this time and the location of the button that engaged an electric motor that moved the heavy gates. The guards had disposed of their rifles beforehand, their only weapons now apparently pistols. It was likely another of Keradin's efforts to avoid the tension of an armed camp.

The peasants shuffled up the dirt path to a large building where a man, whom Cobb gathered must be the foreman, addressed them for a moment. As he did so, the first breezes of the day came up to him from the Black Sea. They carried a multiplicity of aromas that indicated to Cobb that many of the grapes had already been picked and crushed. The timing couldn't have been more perfect, for this was the period that Keradin cherished most. They were about to harvest those special grapes, the most heavily sugared of all, that would eventually go into the finest wines. It could be a matter of days, though perhaps some were ready now, before they were ready for harvesting. Time was of the utmost importance to insure that the now-molding grapes contained just the right amount of sugar, that they had shriveled just enough to attain that magic essence the General treasured.

Keradin would be in the fields today, assessing the grapes himself, indicating those he wanted picked so that he might experiment. He usually wandered on his own, as shown in U.S. intelligence photographs. He would appear with a wide-brimmed hat shading him from the hot sun as he meandered through his vineyard, removing an occasional cluster of grapes from underneath the leaves to check their development, sometimes picking a grape to taste, other times slicing a cluster from the vine and dropping it into the picker's basket slung from his shoulder. Remembering the soft peaceableness of his own mentor, and the similarity of habits between the two men seemed incongruous to Cobb.

To thoroughly know the entire compound and its daily habits, Cobb would have to make himself a part of its routine as quickly as possible. As the workers moved up the hillsides, each with a basket slung from one shoulder and balanced on the opposite hip, he moved out of a row and picked up a basket that had been carelessly dropped nearby. His dress was perfect, though he noted that many of the workers' rough clothes were more stained by the harvest than his own. In a few moments, however, his own disguise was as blotched with juice as the others'.

The workers seemed to move with a numbing purpose, mechanically cutting, gently placing clusters of grapes in their baskets. They rarely talked, and this was fine with Cobb, though he longed to hear the local dialect to learn the oddities of local pronunciation.

As the sun climbed higher, the day quickly warmed,

waves of heat rising from the now dry ground. Rivulets of perspiration ran from under his cap, streaking his dusty features before they coursed down his back and chest. Pratt had once referred to him as a chameleon, and now Cobb adapted so rapidly to those around him that few would have recognized the movement of his head and eyes as he studied and memorized everything around him. Yet, with a natural expertise, he selected the proper bunches, separating them neatly from the vine with a quick slash of his knife and placing them gently in the basket to avoid damage to the fruit.

Three times he filled his basket and worked his way in the slow shuffle of the peasants to the dumping station near the crusher. Each time, he selected a different route so that he could learn every path, every fence, every root and rock. Most important of all, by watching the comings and goings from the main house, he could determine just what each room might be used for and where each door led. Through habit, he laid out a simple floor plan in his head. The estimated depth of a given room might certainly be questionable, but he learned years ago that his guesses were usually within reason. He also identified the servants and what seemed to be their responsibilities. All this could help him later.

Once again, he noted that security was lax at best. Once the workers had filed in for the day, the gates were closed. Though they and the fences were watched continuously by men dressed in civilian rather than military clothes, Cobb sensed that they did not consider themselves under the same pressures that existed in Moscow. A number of military men, almost none in uniform, drifted in and out of the main building. Cobb could have picked them out as military anywhere. It soon became obvious to him that General Keradin's staff was so highly organized, so professional, that a simple, relaxed system could exist, easily replacing the formalities of Moscow.

Cobb moved higher up on the hillside toward a row of vines that appeared more ready for harvesting. As he peered under the leaves, he could see that these grapes were almost perfect. Perhaps it was the soil, perhaps a deeper gulley between rows that held water for a longer period, perhaps even that these plants were a bit taller and caught the direct sun longer to produce a higher sugar content. These he would begin with in a moment.

He sat down on the edge of a cistern. Removing his cap, he mopped his forehead with a grimy rag he had found near the crusher. The cloth came away with a dark silt of sweat and dust. Neatly folding it, he wiped at either corner of his eyes to remove the clinging dirt.

A deep voice came to him at the same instant a shadow fell across his feet. "Well, it is a hot day, eh? Very good for the sugar. What do you think, eh?"

Cobb stiffened. For just a second, he had allowed his guard to slip. That was something he tended to avoid, even in everyday life. Perhaps the lack of sleep the night before was the reason. Whatever, there was no doubting that voice or that accent. He had listened to recordings of it over and over again. In person, General Keradin's voice was sharper, perhaps just a bit more friendly, since he was in his own vineyards.

He looked up at the familiar face that he had studied so often in the past days. It was shadowed by the wide-brimmed hat, but he recognized the bright, inquiring eyes above the high cheekbones. There was just the quirk of a smile at the corners of his mouth. "The sugar is very high along this row," Cobb responded, jumping to his feet, cap in hand in a gesture of humility.

"Oh?" Keradin raised a bushy eyebrow as he looked from the peasant to the clusters of grapes. He moved over by a vine, cradling a bunch in his hand, turning it one way and then the other. Selecting a few of the grapes, he held them to his eye, then popped a few into his mouth. His eyes opened wide in wonder. "You're right." He savored the sweet juice with his pursed lips. "I didn't know we had anyone in the fields who knew the correct moment," he added, turning back to Cobb. Keradin was a stocky man of medium height, rather nondescript in slacks and a short-sleeved shirt. But the confident eyes and authoritative voice was that of a military man.

"Yes, sir," Cobb responded. He bent down, exposing a cluster of grapes still shaded by the vines in front. "The sun won't hit these until afternoon, when some of the heat is already out of the rays. These," he continued, straightening up and pointing to another cluster, "have been in the sun since early morning. When they are this close, a couple of hours of sun makes all the difference in the world with the sugar. Tomorrow, or perhaps the next day, these lower ones should be ready."

"How long have you been working here?" the General demanded. "I don't remember you the last time I came down here."

"Only a few days, sir." Cobb inclined his body slightly from the waist in a sign of respect. "Just for the picking, sir. My family comes from Georgia, outside Kutaisi, where they used to make such wines as you make here—deep, golden, sweet." He paused, then added, "I work various vineyards as they need me, sir."

"I see." Keradin squinted in the bright sunshine. "Do you also know how to make the wines, how long the must should stay with the juice?"

"Yes, sir," Cobb nodded. "My family made this wine for many generations—first in Georgia, then here in the Crimea after the war."

"Ah! Perhaps you're what I'm looking for. I have been experimenting the last few years—three, maybe four, whenever I can get the time—for a special aftertaste." His eyes lit up. "Perhaps you understand what I mean: like the wines of Georgia?" He raised his eyebrows in question.

Cobb smiled ingratiatingly. "It is hard to be sure—without tasting, I mean. Everyone is looking for something a little different." Could this be the chance he had hoped for?

"Yes, yes." The General was nodding his head in agreement. "Maybe after you are finished here at the end of the day, you can come to the aging room with me. We could taste from the last few years. You will understand what I mean if we sample the different barrels. Do you think you could imitate something if we found the right one?"

"Yes, sir. It is possible." Was it all falling into place so easily? Cobb wondered. No. The guards, maybe even the foreman—there had to be one from the GRU. One of them would know he didn't belong. "But perhaps not, sir. It has been many years since I did that."

"What is your name?" It was not a question, really. It was an order from a man who was used to a direct response.

"Victor, sir, Victor Berezin. But perhaps it has been too long." It was a definite mistake, Cobb realized. Here, enclosed within Keradin's compound, there was no way to escape. Just a few questions from those men who wandered casually with pistols on their hips, and they would once again become the hated GRU, as efficient at eliciting information as they were in the heart of the Kremlin. He would have no chance to complete his mission. If only this had been a straight assassination, something simple and straightforward. Right now, with the knife that lay beside his basket, he could do away with Keradin and drag the body between some rows. He would not escape, of course, but the mission would be complete. But that wasn't what Pratt had ordered. Washington wanted this man alive if it was at all possible. "I think perhaps no, sir."

"Nonsense, Berezin. I will talk with your foreman, Kozlov." He turned on his heel. "I will send him for you about four," he called over his shoulder as he moved briskly down the hill.

Cobb stared blankly after him. What a price to pay for not being on his toes. If he had seen Keradin coming up the hill, he would have been able to disappear to the other side. Now, while he had been able to bluff his way for the time being, he found himself in danger. He hoped against hope that the General would not head toward the crushing shed, where he knew the foreman was working. He watched, the tightness in his stomach letting up slightly as he saw Keradin turn to his left at the bottom of the hill and go into the dacha. Cobb had no idea what his next step would be, but he had to keep a sharp eye out for when the man came back out of the building.

ABOARD U.S.S. *JOHN F. KENNEDY* SOUTHEAST OF MALTA

Dave Pratt felt the searing heat from the cigar butt clenched between his fingers. "Just what the hell do you mean, 'business as usual,' Commander Clark?" The heavy brows were knotted.

"What I mean, Admiral, is that they do this every day. At least as long as I've been out here, they have." The response was tentative, sensing a mistake had been made.

"We are in Condition Two. What that means is that at any time we are one second from Condition One, which means that those bastards will already have launched missiles, which means that, unless we have been on our toes, you will have the opportunity to count the seconds until you are either atomized or blown into little pieces." The cigar had burned its way down to his flesh. He could feel the finger blistering. "If you or—" he turned to glare at each of the officers in the room, "—or anyone else ever uses the term 'business as usual' again, you've just earned a trip back to the States. And," he added menacingly, "you can't imagine the fitness report that would follow if I survived what you all screwed up."

Commander Arthur Clark's eyes were fixed on the cigar in Admiral Pratt's fingers. As it smoldered next to the flesh,

Clark was sure the man would toss the stub in a butt kit. When he saw the skin color, then blister, he knew that things were definitely never going to be the same again aboard *Kennedy*.

Dave Pratt had been in his sea cabin when the initial warnings came over the voice radio. The Hawkeyes, flying patrol two hundred miles out, had picked up a Soviet flight closing on an attack profile. The Russians were utilizing satellite data to home in on the U.S. force and their target-acquisition radar was already in the search mode. At the same time, a transmission to four Soviet attack submarines had been intercepted; it ordered the Russian subs to close in a new formation, observed just recently for the first time during exercises in the North Atlantic. Their target seemed likely to be Pratt's battle group.

Dave Pratt knew the Russian forces wouldn't come this way—or they shouldn't. That would compromise the shock attack that would be their main objective, a blitzkrieglike lunge into central Europe. And when it started at sea, the skies would be saturated with the first salvo of Soviet missiles. This was an exercise, but Pratt was appalled that there was even one individual left aboard the carrier who could accept this as business as usual. The Russians would never be so complacent. They were using every minute to practice, taking every opportunity to see how the American battle group would respond. And when the exercise became the real thing, their approach would be exactly as they were doing now.

Casually, Pratt pulled one more drag from the remainder of his cigar, then tossed it away. As he passed through the hatch into his sea cabin, he called over his shoulder, "Report when the entire group is ready. I will treat this exactly as if it was *the* attack."

"If they make similar moves toward our fighters again, sir—"

Pratt cut off the questions. "That is considered an overt act in my book. Blow them out of the air." He restrained himself from slamming the door as he departed.

He sat down at the desk in his sea cabin, staring at the

bulkhead, his fingers drumming a solemn cadence on the metal surface. Out of habit, and perhaps with a dollop of nostalgia, he listened for the telltale sounds, the announcements coming over the ship's loudspeaker, the drumming of feet on the ladders, the sounds of engines warming up on the flight deck, but now such events were found only in the movies.

His sea cabin was deep in the interior of the huge island that was the giant carrier. It was one deck above the combat-information center of the ship, and right next to his flag plot. They were insulated against sound, against practically anything but a nuclear blast.

Dave Pratt stared hard at Alice's photo on his desk, the adrenaline of anger subsiding. Like his, her hair was graying, but hers did so gracefully. His had simply changed to a steel-gray color that matched his military personality. Alice was a lady, pure and simple, born to be a Navy wife, willing to be both mother and father to the kids. Pratt rubbed his eyes for a moment. Oh, how he wished he could have sent her off to the country away from Washington!

What he wanted more than anything else, as he forced himself to turn away from her picture, was to see how the command center would function. He was treating this as the real thing, and the Russians were too, and he intended to take them as far as they wanted to go without allowing them the slightest advantage. When they flew home to their debriefing session, he wanted them to report that the American battle group met them head-on and was just aching for a fight.

The buzz of the sound-powered phone interrupted his thoughts. "Admiral Pratt," he answered. He listened for a moment, then asked, "Who has air defense?" He was told that the *Yorktown*'s AEGIS system was now controlling the air defense for the battle group. Each ship's computer would be tied into the master, which could then assign targets, even control their firing if necessary. He was also told that *O'Bannon* had taken over the antisubmarine net. Pratt made a note to see about changing that to *Hancock*. He'd feel better if Nellie was coordinating it. "I'll be there in ten minutes," he concluded, returning the phone to its cradle.

His little scene with the men minutes before had turned the trick, Pratt decided. These guys were professional, well educated. They just needed a kick in the ass. They'd been through so many exercises in the past few months that the recent intelligence reports just hadn't sunk in. They thought they were to react when that first shot was fired, but he expected them to act faster, perhaps to squeeze off their own first shot just a split second more quickly. Anything that would give him the upper hand over the superior Russian numbers was what he was looking for. After that, he felt he could handle it. There were more of them, but he had the advantage when it came to equipment and manpower. Since Pratt knew time was short, the most vital gift he could give this battle group was his knowledge of what was about to happen—and his confidence.

He reviewed the organization in his mind once more, just to be sure that he could apply the notes originated at the Naval War College months before. He knew how he wanted to fight the group against each type of attack—air-to-surface missile, surface-to-surface missile, and submarine—and how to respond to one of them or all together. Most important of all, he had no doubt how he would coordinate the electronic warfare. That, he had decided, would determine the victor—electronic warfare, the magic of the black box.

Now he would see exactly how his staff reacted—both to the Russians and to his demands. He tilted his cap rakishly over one eye, once again the recruiting-poster admiral, and headed for the ship's nerve center.

His command post in the darkened, red-lit center was a well-padded swivel chair surrounded by a half-moon of electronic displays. In addition to a comprehensive picture of the Med, there was a display each for the air, subsurface, and surface scenes. It was easier to comprehend once your mind adapted to the futuristic environment. There was one color for your side, a separate one for the other. The shapes of the electronic images designated various ships and aircraft. Courses, speeds, heights, depths, distances, even time-

to-impact-after-firing appeared beside the images or above
the display boards. Continuous printouts of tactical information flowed from IBM machines in front of them. The
computer could respond to almost any question put to it,
but the inquiry had to be accurate, for it often concerned
objects closing the force at supersonic speeds. AEGIS took
command when man's decision-making could no longer
keep up with the weapons he had designed.

Admiral Pratt considered the location of his Hawkeye
recon aircraft in relation to the Russian bombers. Identified
as Backfires, they were electronically advanced, missile-
firing craft. "Are we jamming?" Pratt asked Clark.

Clark looked over from his position, brows furrowed
nervously. "You mean those closing jets?"

"Are there any others?" Pratt snapped.

"No, sir. Nothing within the zone."

"My understanding was that they were in an attack profile, using target-acquisition radar and with a satellite backup.
Why don't we just send up some balloons with arrows on
them to point to the battle group." Pratt's voice was rising
evenly, the pitch controlling the atmosphere in the command
post. "We should be jamming everything they can use.
There is no reason in my book—and that's the one you are
operating under now—for them to receive one pulse of
information from any one of their satellites. No reason that
anything should get back to their targeting computers except
whatever garbage we want to send them. No reason there
should even be a reason for them to activate the target-
acquisition radar in those missiles of theirs."

Pratt rose to his feet and placed himself directly in front
of the displays. He left no room for doubt that he expected
the attention of every man in the room. "Those Russian
aircraft are coming in because the Soviet Union has just
declared war on the United States. It will be awhile before
we get word. In the meantime, they are following the normal
pattern they have utilized in the past because we're so complacent about it that they think we'll just wait to see if their
pilots will wave when they go by. Before you know it, I'll
have to tell the computer to take over the decision-making

process for this entire battle group because the staff did not anticipate this war."

The faces looking back at him reflected shock. Perhaps I can convince some of them war *has* been declared, Pratt thought. Jesus, I hope so. I want to see their pale faces. I want to see the cold sweat on their foreheads. I want to see the fear in their eyes. I want them to think about their families back home and imagine that the ICBMs might already be in the air—even though this is still a drill.

"I want a direct voice order sent to that on-scene commander. Better yet, I'll do it." Pratt turned to his communications officer. "Which circuit do I want?"

"Twenty-seven, Admiral."

Pratt picked up the speaker in one hand while he punched in 27 on the black box. "Call sign?"

"Bulldog Two."

Pratt pressed the key on the mike. "Bulldog Two, this is Archer himself. Over."

"This is Bulldog Two. Over."

"This is not a drill. I repeat this is not a drill. Commence jamming on all Soviet frequencies as follows—satellite recon, search, anything else you can damn well find. Is that understood? Over."

"Roger, Archer. Will comply. Out."

He turned to Clark, who was obviously waiting for the next bombshell. "Who's controlling the intercept?"

"We have a flight of F-14s on the way, sir."

"I certainly hope so, but what I asked is who the hell is controlling the intercept?"

"They're reporting to Bulldog One."

"And what are his instructions?"

"They will track at a distance, sir."

"Like hell they will. Just as soon as they're within lock-on, they will commence a head-on attack, vectored in by Bulldog One. They will await a firing order from me." He nodded toward his communications officer. "Now."

"Yes, sir."

Pratt turned to the air-status board. "Take me out to full-scale on that board. Use a satellite picture if you have to.

There has never been a Russian attack designed against one of our battle groups that didn't have a second or even third flight directed at the same target. *Saturation,*" he bellowed, pounding his fist into his palm for emphasis. "Saturation is their doctrine." He continued to slam his fist down. "Attack from different angles and altitudes and fill the air with missiles. That's what they do. Don't wait for them—look for them! And while you're finding those other flights, I want to put our electronic-countermeasures plan into effect— jamming, deception, everything we can do to confuse their missiles."

He gave them time. There was no doubt they knew their business. It was just that they had never carried the exercises through to completion before. They had always assumed enough warning to react, but that wouldn't happen now. The Russians will keep the pressure up. Wear us down, Pratt thought. Put us at ease. Then, blam, and we'll feel just like Custer. But that's what he also liked about the Russians. They were predictable. They followed doctrine, making it easier to handle them. It was more a question of how well Pratt and his men could defend the battle group when the air was full of missiles. Could they limit the number of hits?

"Next—subsurface picture, Mr. Loomis."

"Yes, sir."

"You have four submarines closing—a wolf-pack approach, I assume."

"Yes, sir."

"You have them all tracked?"

"Three of them, sir. One has broken off. We still have him in the passive listening mode, but no course or speed." He looked more confident than Clark. "I expect a second to break off soon. *O'Bannon* has orders to detach two frigates as soon as the second one goes." Again, doctrine said a Russian wolf pack would do just that as they came in for attack. It also said that they never limited themselves to a frontal attack. There had to be one or more submarines coming in from another direction.

"Have you opened up your detection range in other directions?" Pratt asked.

"Yes, sir. No contacts out to fifty miles." Fifty miles was nothing for a forty-knot submarine!

"Run a line of sonobuoys every twenty-five miles just like they taught you in school, Mr. Loomis. You'll find them. Next!" Here his voice rose again. "I want you to put everything in the water you can think of that will make noise. I want those bastards so confused they won't have the vaguest idea where this group is or what we're going to do next. If we're keeping their aircraft busy, those subs will become useless so fast..." His voice trailed off.

He saw recognition gradually spread over various faces, some that had been unsure of his intent only moments before. They would react instantaneously should there be any indication the Russians had orders to complete their missions. No longer would there be a chance of a lost moment, a lost moment that might mean the survival or loss of a carrier battle group.

"*Kharkov*—where is she now?" That was the Soviet carrier that had been patrolling the southeastern sector of the Med for the past week. Her Forger aircraft ranged to only three hundred miles, and Pratt was determined to haunt her as soon as she showed any interest in closing the battle group. *Saratoga* had been detached with full battle group escort to keep tabs on the Soviet carrier, but Pratt knew that when the time came *Sara* would be the first to bear the brunt of the first salvo. *Kharkov* and her escorts would then once again become his responsibility. Quite possibly the Soviet carrier *Minsk* would also be out of the Black Sea to bother *Sara* by then.

"*Kharkov*'s still hanging offshore of Alexandria, Admiral, covering pretty much the same area as yesterday. This morning's satellite photos indicate that she's expanded her screen to include two Udaloy-type destroyers and one ASW cruiser. I expect that means she's getting ready to turn west."

"What kind of tail do we have on her now?"

"Two attack subs, one either side of an east-west heading, and satellite recon, of course."

Chin in hand, Pratt surveyed his display board. The screening force around *Kharkov* was above standard for a Soviet carrier group. That meant only one thing to him—they were planning to change from an antisubmarine group to an attack force. "Set up a scouting line, north-south orientation, running between Tobruk and Crete. They'll have some attack subs leading the way, and I'd hate to see them get past there before we locate them."

"Yes, sir. How about *Saratoga?* Won't she have to worry about that group too? I should include her."

"Message her, of course. But," he included Loomis in his gaze, "they have *Minsk* up there also, and I expect that's the one *Sara*'s going to have her hands full of, especially when they empty out of the Black Sea."

"Nothing's coming out, sir. The Turks have everything closed up," offered Clark.

Pratt smiled grimly. "Wanna bet?"

"Pardon, sir?"

"You want to bet on that? I'm saying that within twenty-four hours the Russians have the Turkish straits completely under their control. So much so," he grinned, "that they'll probably be charging the Turks tolls to use their own water-ways."

Clark looked down at his shoes, then back at Pratt. "I don't follow you, sir."

"Don't feel bad about that one. There was no way you could see the intelligence reports I got hold of the other day. That little skirmish with the Greeks was beautifully directed by our friends in Moscow just to put everybody a little off their feed. The outcome of the whole thing couldn't have been better for them. The Turks and the Greeks were supposed to wear down each other's military strength to the point that the Russians could waltz in long enough to drain the goddamned Black Sea if they wanted. The only things in their way are the choke points and the Greeks around the Aegean. They're both quite a bit weaker today . . . just what keeps the Kremlin happy," he concluded.

He turned back to his status boards again. "That's *John Hancock* out in that screening line with *O'Bannon*, isn't it?"

"Yes, sir," Loomis responded.

"Designate *Hancock* as OTC (Officer in Tactical Command) for that little scouting line." Now was the time for Nellie to try some of the new tactics they'd played with back in Newport.

"Sorry, sir, *O'Bannon*'s senior." Loomis hit some buttons on the computer in front of him. "Commander Nelson is next in line, though."

"What circuit are they on?" Pratt requested, his voice tired.

"Seventeen, sir."

Pratt punched the button for 17 as he hefted the radiophone to his ear. He got through to *O'Bannon* immediately.

"This is Archer himself. Request that tactical command shift to *Hanock* for duration of this exercise to experiment with new tactics." It was that simple. Give an order. It seemed, though, that he had to take over each time he wanted to convince his subordinates that he knew exactly what he was doing.

Pratt sat back in his chair to watch.

ABOARD U.S.S. *JOHN HANCOCK*

Wendell Nelson smiled inwardly when he heard Pratt's voice. Without moving from his chair, he called to his OOD. "Expand ship intervals to fifteen miles. Alter base course to one three five. They've been hiding a bunch of subs off the Libyan coast and there's no better time than now to set them loose." He lit another of his never-ending string of cigarettes and puffed quietly as he prepared the geographic picture in his mind. Easing out of his chair, he called over his shoulder, "I'm going into combat for a few minutes to show them a new trick or two. Ask the XO to report to me there."

It took Nelson just five minutes to show his executive officer what they were going to do, and not much more time for the watch to understand. It was another thirty minutes before the destroyers could launch their helos, and a bit more than an hour before the ASW aircraft from *Kennedy* were fused into the search pattern.

Nelson was back in his captain's chair in the pilothouse soon after the search began, cigarette in hand, his legs calmly crossed. There was no need for him to supervise the three-pronged sweep. He knew what it should be and he could visualize in his mind's eye how they were establishing

106

it as he overheard the reports from combat.

The system had been initially developed under his direction, by a team of Naval War College students using a computer in Newport. It was a complex geometric pattern based on time sequences of various screen elements on station, combined with the ranges of their sound gear. Their movements were programmed. ASW planes would establish a barrier of sonobuoys covering a fixed line. To one side of that line were the widely spaced ships moving at high speed, sweeping fixed, cone-shaped areas before them. On the other side were helicopters dipping their sonar in a predetermined area.

A submarine, if the captain and crew are in concert with their complex equipment, can avoid an active sonar sweep unless the searching unit is already on top of them. The intelligence originally programmed into the Newport computer identified each uncovered area, and part of the assumption was that the enemy sub would naturally head for those empty spaces. As the destroyers swept through the sonobuoy screen, the helos would hop to their rear, dipping their sonar in the open areas that had not been covered by the ships. The planes would then split up, each group sewing a line of sonobuoys on two sides to complete an imperfect rectangle approximately ninety by fifty miles.

Nelson impatiently listened to the reports. Occasionally he would go down to combat to check the electronic display of the search. It was remarkably accurate for a first effort, especially considering that there were more than five thousand square miles to be covered in less than three hours. If the subs were out there, he had to get them!

Within the next half hour, there were five contact reports, each one classified within moments as a submarine. Now for the hold down!

"This is Hedgehog." Nelson spoke calmly over the tactical circuit to his small force. "We will now commence the terror aspect of our new system." He rolled the word "terror" over his tongue as if he savored the idea. "Our friends down below are already surprised enough that we found them so easily. I want every unit to have a turn running attacks. At each instance, one destroyer will stand off to the side and explain over the underwater telephone exactly what we are doing. The subs each have someone who can understand English, and if they don't, I think they'll get the idea fast enough. We're going to make this part of the Med sound like Coney Island. I want anything in the water that will make noise. And I want grenades dropped at the right time to signify hits from each attack—whether or not you think your solution was correct. Every unit will take its attack solution as gospel and complete every step except for the actual firing. I want computer tapes from each of you after we finish. Should there be any reason to think our friends might do something stupid, I will be the only one to give the firing order. You will treat this as actual—not an exercise."

ABOARD U.S.S. *JOHN F. KENNEDY*

On the *Kennedy*, Admiral Pratt listened to the tactical circuit between his recon aircraft and interceptors.

"Bulldogs, Bulldogs," called the intercept officer on the circling Hawkeye, "your targets are dead ahead at one four zero miles, speed mach one point four, course two six five, two thousand feet above you, and they have no idea you're down there. Report your lock-on."

Almost in unison, the pilots announced target acquisition. Their on-board computers developed a solution that was then fed into their missile-control systems. Once fired, the Phoenix missile could be guided by the fighter plane until it acquired its target or the recon aircraft could override and take over direction.

"Stand by to fire, Bulldogs."

Pratt knew that the instant the F-14s locked on to the Soviet planes, a warning signal went off in the enemy cockpits, accompanied by an automatic jammer on the missile frequency. He also knew the Russian pilots had to be aware their missile jammers were only a partial defense, for the recon planes could guide the missiles onto target. He waited for the next transmission.

"Archer, this is Bulldog One. Targets have commenced

evasive action." There was a slight hesitation. "They must be damn sure our birds have been fired. Ho! They're on a roller coaster ride."

Pratt picked up the mike. "Bulldog One, this is Archer. When your Bulldogs have visual contact, I want them in on a wing-tip escort. I want those Backfires to understand they've been had." He paused for a moment as he surveyed the air-status board, searching for the next Russian flight. "Bulldog One, you're already painting the next group. You have F-18s reporting shortly. Follow identical procedure."

Pratt had no more than relighted his cigar when Loomis called out, "Admiral, *Hancock*'s got submarines coming out his ears."

Pratt punched the numbers for the 17 circuit again. "I give up," he growled. "What's Nellie's call sign?"

"Who?"

"*Hancock,* what's their call sign."

"Hedgehog, sir."

"For your next project, you can make a list for me, for everyone in here. This is driving me crazy." Though the communications officer would prepare a special call-sign board for the Admiral, he had the feeling that no matter what the situation, Pratt would still be growling about his call signs. "Hedgehog, this is Archer One. I understand you have made contact. Over."

"Affirmative, Archer. There may be one or two who've gone silent for a while, but we have everybody who wanted to make life difficult. I am prosecuting now. Over."

Dave Pratt relaxed at the sound of Nellie's soft, mellifluous voice. The man could maintain his calm under any conditions. "Give each unit a chance to conduct an attack, and have them do it over again if you have any doubts. Once you're satisfied, you may release airborne units. Keep contact if possible until they reverse course toward the Libyan coast. I assume you have your search-and-attack phases on tape. Over."

"Roger, Archer. We did make a couple of small changes now that we've seen how it really works. I think we can distribute to all ASW computers now. We're not going to have this chance again."

"Roger, Hedgehog. When you rejoin the formation, request you ferry over to me for conference. Out."

Admiral Pratt leaned back in his chair, stretching his feet out under the console before him and locking his hands behind his head. Christ, it was good to be out here! It was what he was good at, what he had trained for over the last few years, and it was what he was afraid might pass him by, perhaps fall into the hands of another man who simply did not have the background.

Then he thought of Ryng and Cobb, each off on his own, away from all the supposed security of the electronics world, operating purely by his own wits. Perhaps they were better off than he—even safer! But he sure as hell wished he knew what they were doing and if there was anything he could do for them. He could not communicate with them. Anything that came to him would be relayed—if anything came at all.

SPITZBERGEN

Ryng's eyes snapped shut with the initial burst from the automatic rifle. The reaction was instinctive, and he'd never been able to break it. His first time on the range the instructor had chewed him out, and Bernie never forgot the shock of that first moment—the feeling in the pit of his stomach, the chill running from his groin up through his spine, the shudder through his entire body. Then he had been all right.

This time was no different—it never would be. His finger squeezed and released the trigger in an instant, yet he was aware that his eyes were shut. There was the icy feeling in his groin, a chill like the cold blade of a knife that followed some primal nerve, shooting up his spine; then he shuddered involuntarily, the act shaking his entire body.

Then he was in motion again. That also was instinctive—anyone he might not have seen would have no chance of finding a target.

The Black Beret directly in front of him was spinning wildly as the impact of the bullets flung his body back against the wall. Another reflected a momentary look of surprise as his chest was stitched with the small, steel-cored slugs. Then his lifeless body jumped involuntarily in a neat

112

back flip. The AK-74 bullets, tumbling as they entered the body, were designed to be especially lethal.

The sharp, explosive crack of the guns echoed through the warehouse, increasing in magnitude as each succeeding round was fired. Ryng sensed rather than saw Wally firing. One, then a second, marine were blown backward by the deadly force of the bullets.

Ryng dove to his left, rolling, coming up with the gun at his shoulder, already aimed toward the third Black Beret. But there was no one in the spot he anticipated. Out of the corner of his eye, he saw Wally bouncing up from a similar roll, his target just where he'd expected. There was another short burst, and then there was only one left—Ryng's.

The warehouse was silent now. Only the sound of heavy breathing reached Bernie's ears, as well as the thumping from his own heart.

He glanced quickly for Wally, receiving a negative head shake for an answer. The last man couldn't have gone far. How many seconds had it been? Five? Ten? He had to have moved in fear. A dive and maybe a roll. He couldn't be more than ten feet on either side of where he'd started.

Ryng thought of using a grenade, but then reconsidered. Not in here, he thought. Too close. End up splattering themselves all over the warehouse.

He kicked over a table, shoving it viciously to where the marine should be if he'd gone to his left. That was it! he realized. There was a movement, maybe a head, a shoulder. Bringing the stock of the AK-74 to his shoulder, he squeezed the trigger gently, moving the barrel slightly to either side with his wrist. It was a superb weapon. It had little recoil, and it never climbed on automatic.

The last Black Beret had only a coffee table and the false security of some corrugated boxes for protection. The boxes shreaded. The table splintered. Ryng saw the man rise up, hands over his face, a cry of anguish mingling with the last explosive echoes.

Six up—six down! How much time? Ten, fifteen seconds? That left Denny and Rick outside with a dozen more marines, their rifles precisely stacked to one side, and two aircrews, probably with survival weapons.

As they raced out into daylight, Bernie Ryng was aware of a series of explosions. The neatly stacked rifles were scattered. The Black Berets who were about to load the bombers were caught in the open. They dispersed as best they could, some able to find cover, others falling to the automatic weapons fire.

One enterprising air crewman, crouching behind a bomber's landing gear, was returning their fire with a pistol. Perhaps it was the sharp, individual crack of each shot as opposed to the staccato chatter of the rifles that caught Rick's attention. More likely he knew he was the target. Whirling, dropping into a kneeling position, he brought the gun to his shoulder. The AK-74 was intended as a close-in weapon for crowds rather than one person. This was a well-protected individual and harder to hit.

Wally came to his assistance, firing until his clip emptied. Ryng recognized with anguish that one of his shots hit the Russian at the same time as Rick was hit.

Bernie saw the shoulder bag fall as Rick's body crumpled, the precious grenades rolling out onto the runway. Each one was critical if they were going to blow those bombers and the decoys.

Carefully, as precisely as a jeweler, Wally was picking off those Russians still without cover, moving closer to the planes as he did so. Ryng, running in a crouch, changed magazines on the move. He halted for a moment by Rick, saw death staring back at him, and scooped up the bag and the grenades in a single motion.

Denny had moved up to the first plane, leaping up the ramp into the fuselage in one fluid motion. Ryng covered him, counting the seconds, amazed so few could pass before Denny leaped back out, avoiding the ramp, his feet already in motion as he hit the tarmac, body crouched as he moved toward the second. He hit this one just as systematically as the first.

A foreign sound caught Ryng's attention—once again, the single shots of a pistol. He whirled, eyes off Denny's moving form, searching for the source. Wally, caught in the act of digging in his own bag for a grenade, was frantically bringing his rifle to bear on a Russian wildly firing from his hip with a pistol.

There was no match between a revolver and an automatic weapon at that range, unless the pistol was lucky. And it was. As the Russian was blown backward from the impact of a dozen slugs, Wally grabbed at his stomach. He doubled over in a curious slow motion, the shock lasting only a moment. Then he was erect once again, extracting the grenade he'd been after, yanking out the pin and lofting the grenade toward a scrubby hedge.

Ryng was riveted in stunned fascination as the hedge exploded in a cloud of dust and branches. It revealed four Black Berets immobilized by the blast. Wally sprayed them mercilessly with the AK-74.

Then a strange silence followed. No one was visible. Nothing moved. There appeared to be no more resistance.

Denny vaulted into the last bomber, breaking the momentary stillness, sowing the remainder of his incendiary bombs with the aplomb of a professional. It took less time than the first two planes. An expert at his trade, it was a matter of simply insuring that the time-delay devices came to rest within each fuselage where he wanted them. Experience already guaranteed what the effect would be.

How much time have we taken? Ryng wondered. Thirty seconds? Fifty? A minute? Two minutes? However long, as soon as their first shot echoed across the airfield, he knew Russian marines had dropped whatever they were doing. They would be automatically checking their weapons as they raced toward the field.

"I'll grab the jeep," Ryng called to Denny. "Blow the rest of those decoys." Wally ambled toward him with a weird sort of gait, his rifle slung with military precision from his shoulder, both hands pressed tightly against his belly, shiny, dark blood seeping through his fingers. He nodded toward the jeep, indicating he would get to it on his own. As he shuffled along, he occasionally glanced down at the blood, then over at Ryng with a confused look on his face. He'd never been hit before, no matter how exposed he'd been. Now Wally was terrified. There was a dull hurt but no pain, no sensation that would tell him that everything was going to be all right—or that this was the end.

Wally eased into the adjacent seat. "I don't know if I understand this, Bernie. It never happened before. I don't know...." His voice trailed off.

"Just hold on," Ryng answered. He shifted the jeep into gear. "Can't do a goddamned thing until we get back to the fishing shack." Then he recognized the anguish forming on the other's face as he moved his hands from his belly. Ryng was embarrassed that he'd been so unfeeling. "We love ya, Wally. Just hold on!"

Denny methodically placed his incendiaries around the decoys, moving as efficiently as he'd done with the bombers. There was never a lost movement when he was doing the work he loved. He leaped gracefully into the back of the jeep, slapping Ryng on the shoulder. "Hit it! I don't know what's in those things, but if they're explosives, it's going to be awfully messy around here in half a minute." They had made a decision beforehand—set longer timers inside the planes. They might catch someone poking around inside. But the decoys had to go first. As they raced away in the jeep, Denny methodically dropped his last fragmentation grenades behind one by one. They too had time-delay fuses which would make the Russians think a little before they went snooping around the planes.

Wheeling into the village, they heard the first explosion, followed by a second and a third, then a prolonged series of blasts. A column of smoke and flame roiled into the air. "Must be some special kind of fuel in those things. Look at the color of the smoke," Denny remarked almost casually. "If those were warheads, they would have just blown themselves apart, no smoke like that." He was very pleased with himself, grinning like a cat at his success.

They passed the building on the dock that held one of the Norwegian groups. Ryng once again waved to the guard in a friendly manner. He guided the jeep through the one main street, then turned off toward the old fishing pier outside of town.

The smooth gravel surface ended abruptly. Without warning, they were moving much too fast down a dirt path just wide enough for two wheels. The jeep bounced over a rock into the air, plunging down hard on the other side. Wally screamed with an unearthly wail, doubling over in agony, his body awash with the pain that had eluded him until then.

"Keep going," he moaned between his teeth, his head turned to Ryng. "Get this son of a bitch to that pier, to the morphine!" he shouted in the next breath, his features contorted through waves of pain. The comfortable refuge of shock had left him. Then the spasms of agony brought a merciful loss of consciousness. Denny reached over the seat and held his shoulders until they pulled up beside the fishing shack.

They laid Wally gently on the floor of the shack. Blood pulsed heavily across his stomach, steadily pumping life out of his body. Denny, the team medic, administered the morphine first, then listened to the heart, checked the blood pressure, and finally cleaned the wound enough to determine the damage.

"Forget it, Bernie. Gut shot, not a chance."

"Will he come around again?"

"He might. He's lost so much blood already, I wonder if he's got enough strength left to open his eyes." He felt the pulse. "Hardly enough left to take a breath, Bernie."

"Can you do anything for him?"

"Yeah. Another few hundred cc's and Wally Land will disappear without a thought in the world."

Ryng's knuckles whitened perceptibly. "We're down to minutes ourselves." There were only so many people on the whole damned island, and the Russians would know there were no Norwegians that could mount an operation like the one that had just taken place. They had just minutes to escape. Ryng nodded, his eyes avoiding Denny's. Wally Land's face was tranquil when they left him in the shack.

They crawled down under the old pier, making their way

between broken-down pilings and remnants of fishing gear
to the rubber boat. Their only purpose now was to escape—
to survive. They kept two automatic rifles, their pistols, and
a few fragmentation grenades. Everything else—food,
medicine, electronic gear—was dumped. Ryng kept his
radio.

They pushed off from the pier simultaneous with a
succession of explosions from the direction of the airport.
They could see tall, greasy tongues of flame erupting into
the sky—burning aviation fuel. So much for the bombers.
If Harry Winters was successful with that freighter...

The electric motor purred inaudibly. Christ, Ryng thought
impatiently, I could care less about how quiet the engine
is. All that matters now is speed. I'd take it big and noisy
and fast, anything to get us the hell out of here. Silently
and with agonizing slowness, the little motor pushed them
across the harbor toward the opposite shore. They would
follow the coastline as far as they could. If they were followed, then they'd just have to move ashore and somehow
get back to civilization overland.

The day was clear and crisp, barely a cloud in sight. It
was a perfect arctic autumn day. After months of perpetual
daylight, the harbor would soon begin its annual season of
darkness. How lovely it would have been to have conducted
this operation under that kind of cover, Ryng thought. But
then it would have been forty below zero, the arctic winds
would have frozen Denny's fingers as he tried to set his
bombs, and the harbor would have been frozen solid.

The familiar noise of a helicopter in the distance snapped
Ryng out of his momentary reverie. Perhaps if they had
been on land, they could have hidden, but there was no way
they could escape the helo that was moving slowly in their
direction. The rhythmic thrum of the engine swept across
the water, the bass-drum boom magnifying as it rebounded
between the peaks on either side of the harbor.

The helo swept back and forth in a zigzag pattern, unsure
of what it was looking for, what it might find. In the small
boat, the two men placed their rifles on automatic, laying
their extra magazines within easy reach. The AK-74 was

terrific for what they had done earlier, but it was next to useless against a helicopter—even with incredible luck.

Quite unexpectedly, a deep rumbling from the direction of the harbor mouth caught their attention for an instant. It started like distant thunder, a low growling on the horizon. Lasting no more than two seconds, the rumble became a thunderclap echoing up the harbor, oscillating between the peaks on either side. Beyond the harbor, rising in oily black clouds that rolled over and through one another, came the proof to Ryng that Harry Winters had completed his part of the bargain. There was no doubt in Ryng's mind that Harry had pulled it off.

"Harry . . ." Denny offered tentatively.

"Yeah," Ryng responded. "He's never missed yet." A low whistle escaped from his pursed lips.

"I hope he made it—" he began, but Ryng cut him off, gesturing toward the helo.

Ryng headed for the shore on an angle. A wide, glacial river poured into the harbor ahead of them. There would be no way they could cross that if they went ashore on this side of it. He had to get to the other side, and he needed time and something other than the quiet little electric motor that pushed them sluggishly along. It didn't seem so slow when we came in here, Ryng reminded himself, but no one was after us then. He looked over his shoulder as the helo closed in. It had spotted them.

They both recognized the telltale increase in pitch and knew without looking that they'd been seen. The helo banked as it changed course in their direction, lowering altitude to inspect what had been sighted.

The first pass was free. As the craft hovered just ahead of them, they fired together. It seemed a foolish venture, hand-held guns pumping small antipersonnel bullets into a huge metal machine. Three clips each were expended senselessly while the helo backed off to a safe distance.

Ryng swung the boat toward shore. They'd be easy targets on shore—but they were sitting ducks in the boat.

Raucous noise shattered the peaceful arctic calm. Either man could have described the developing scene if he had been blind. Once again the increase of engine revolutions, the thwack of the rotors. The helo was making another pass at them. They waited with loaded clips, bobbing along like toy ducks at a shooting range.

Even before the helo came within range of their rifles, the chatter of machine gun fire added a new dimension to the sounds of the harbor. Foamy trails, punctuated by tiny fountains of water, heralded the path of the bullets, racing first one way and then another. But Ryng realized they had one advantage. The machine guns were attached to a vehicle hanging in the air, swinging as if on a thread, making it more difficult to aim. The trails continued to sweep aimlessly across the water, leaving a white froth behind them.

Ryng whipped the little boat about frantically with one arm—anything to provide a harder target—while he fired wildly with the other. In the hail of bullets, Denny was transformed into a madman, emptying clip after clip when the helo came anywhere within range. As he expended the last shot in a clip, he would yank it out, inserting one clenched between his teeth, mechanically jamming another in his mouth even as he began squeezing the trigger.

Now a path of bullets swept erratically across their craft. There were two, maybe three, thuds as the bullets hit and passed through. The boat was intended to be self-sealing, and they held their breaths. It was! But it was built for occasional damage, not .50-caliber slugs.

The helo circled away, this time climbing slightly.

"Oh, shit! You know what that means," Denny hollered. "The heavy stuff—*rockets!*"

And as he uttered the final word, they saw the telltale wisps of smoke. One—two—three. They could see the rocket trails, make out the rockets themselves as they bore down on them. The first struck twenty yards in front, erupting in a cloud of water and shrapnel. The second passed close overhead, cutting the air with a howl in concert with the blast as it hit the water fifteen yards away. The final one was too close. It might have been a good aim or a lucky shot. In any case, the buzz of metal shards told Ryng there was no more time.

The hiss of escaping air added a new dimension to the sounds around them. Looking down, Ryng saw a large tear in the rubber, no more than an inch to the left of his knee. There was no way any self-sealer was going to solve that problem. Before he could call attention to it, Denny was reaching around him, jamming his shirt into the hole.

"That'll buy us a couple of minutes," Denny shouted above the sound of the helo making its next approach. "I hope to hell they're not developing a style up there. That last was too close."

This time the helo came in much closer. Now they could even hear the pop as the rockets were fired and the whooshing noise of the weapon as it raced at them. Above it all, Ryng heard the steady chatter of Denny's gun, clip after clip, working so rapidly that he functioned like a machine gunner.

Whump! A rocket burst directly in front, not more than ten yards away. A second exploded into the water within yards of Denny, the third passing well astern. Clouds of water poured down on them. The helo was bearing down now, diving behind the rocket fire, machine guns blazing. Ryng rolled into the bottom of the boat, hands over his head, knees drawn up. Operating only by instinct at that moment, trying to hide like an ostrich, thinking he couldn't be seen if his head were buried.

Then he looked up as the helo roared overhead, a perfect target, but Denny was no longer shooting. Ryng noticed a wisp of black smoke, then a rush of it from the exhausts behind the engine. The helo banked sharply, increasing altitude at the same time. The smoke! They'd hit it!

"Look at that! No shit, will you look . . ."

Bernie Ryng turned impulsively, overcome with joy. Just as quickly it became horror. He found himself staring in fear at what was beside him. Denny was as dead as could be. There hadn't been a sound, no shout, no thrashing to indicate he'd been hit. A shard of metal protruded in grisly fashion from his forehead. There was no blood. It was impossible to tell how deeply the chunk of shrapnel had penetrated, but it was enough to have killed Denny instantly.

Ryng rolled into a sitting position from the corpse. The boat was riddled with innumerable holes. Air hissed out, water sputtered in as it hopelessly tried to seal itself. The jagged tears were so deep that there was no chance the boat could float. Water was already lapping over one corner, its weight dragging the craft down.

The helo now hovered a few hundred yards off, still smoking. The engine was powerful enough to keep it airborne, but Ryng could sense the ragged sound of a machine struggling with itself.

There was only one option left. Ryng threw the last ammo bag around his neck and rolled off the shoreward side into the piercing-cold water less than fifty yards from land. He doubled over to pull off his shoes, then thought better of it. Once on land, he had a long way to go. He knew that the terrain was rough, all sharp stone and gravel, midsummer tundra that had defrosted down a foot or so. And there were innumerable rocky hills and cliffs along the shoreline.

The tempo of the helo's engine increased as it dove toward him, machine guns once again blazing. The line of bullets raced toward him. He dove, struggling against the double fear of icy water as a contrast to bullets. When his lungs burned more than he could stand, he surfaced, his face in the direction where he expected the helicopter to be. It was there, hovering like a bird of prey. He sucked down another breath and arched his body to dive again. But he stopped at the last minute.

More smoke was pouring out of the craft now, dense black clouds. It was in as much trouble as he was. Maybe it would have to turn back. The odds of any man surviving alone in this water much longer were poor.

Ryng struggled toward shore, his eyes never leaving the helo. Then he saw what he had never expected. The helo was making one last pass, but it wasn't shooting. He watched in numb curiosity, ready to dive until he saw an object fall from the side of the fuselage. As it seemed to grow in size, he realized from a distance what it was. A depth charge! The helo was equipped for anti-submarine duty. He thrashed frantically for shore.

The charge tumbled end over end, hitting the water with a huge splash, followed by a graceful waterspout.

Ryng's mind went blind with fear. Then he grabbed his knees, rolling into a ball. The ensuing explosion thundered through his head, driving the air out of his lungs, pressing inward, forcing water down his throat, into his eyes, creating pressure like a giant sledgehammer. Time seemed to stop from the pain. He had no idea if he was conscious—no idea if he was alive or dead.

Then he found himself struggling for shore. Was there enough strength left in him to make the beach? Would he crawl out onto the sand to die in agony, spilling blood across the sand from his ruptured guts?

Strangely enough, he had some energy left, though he could hear nothing but a ringing in his head. He splashed awkwardly through the water, but there was little feeling in his hands and feet. He rolled over onto his back, expecting to see his nemesis swooping down, machine guns blazing.

But there was nothing. In the distance toward Longyearbyen, he made out a smoky cloud descending toward the land. It must be, he thought. The damned helo couldn't stay up any longer. Then he realized the ammo bag, with his only weapon, was gone!

He turned back on his belly and pulled for the shore, not more than twenty yards away now, though it seemed like miles. Each yard closer to the beach became interminable. But his will to live won out. Only sheer determination got him the last few feet to the water's edge.

Dragging himself out of the water onto the beach was an even greater effort. There was some sand, but mostly rocks. Yet they were like a down pillow to him, so soft and welcoming after the terror of nearly drowning.

There was some scrub brush farther up the beach beyond the high-tide mark. He half crawled, half dragged himself into it, then fell forward on his face. It seemed natural to him that he should pass out. It would be his body's way of telling him that he had abused it past redemption. But he remained conscious. His first physical sensation as he lay there collecting his thoughts, mentally identifying the various parts of his body that were still intact, was from his stomach. It was churning violently.

Could this be the way it would be? Safety, then death? Was it now that the insides that he couldn't feel would suddenly turn on him? His body jerked in a spasm as he felt the sudden contractions of vomiting overwhelming him. But it didn't matter. He had never in his life been so overjoyed at being ill. Great quantities of seawater—not blood—came up.

As his stomach completed nature's job, he slumped down again in relief. The pressure from the depth charge must have forced all that water down his throat. He remembered the unbelievable weight on his head, his eyes. And he realized that the water must have been too shallow for the depth charge to do the job they'd intended. At that depth, the bottom must have deflected the blast upward. He vaguely remembered the tremendous waterspout. The explosion probably occurred right on the bottom so that it went straight back up rather than spreading out as it was designed to do. There had been only one blast. If they dropped any others, the water must have been too shallow to set them off!

He realized that if the water had been deeper he wouldn't have made it. Then the exhaustion rolled over him in waves with colors flashing on his eyelids. There was no way to fight it.

Bernie Ryng was out before his eyes closed, face down in the dirt and rock—but alive!

ABOARD U.S.S. *YORKTOWN,*
SOUTHEAST OF MALTA

Tom Carleton leaned back in the chair, touching the bulkhead under the console with his toes. Stretching his arms back behind his head, he yawned, squinting up at the ducts in the overhead of *Yorktown*'s combat information center. The vague glow of red lights in the darkened room cast indistinct shadows into the gloom above him.

This isn't where I should be, he repeated to himself once more. How many times have I said that in the last half hour? The bridge, *his* bridge, was two decks above his head. That's where the captain of a warship should be.

Carleton was seated at the console of *Yorktown*'s fire-control display system. In today's Navy, at least on an AEGIS cruiser, that's where the commanding officer fought his ship. He'd been through it all at school in the past year. There he'd been taught that today the secret to victory was the three C's—command, control, and communications—and it all hinged on a supersophisticated electronics system within his ship's hull that managed the defense of the whole damned battle group. But that didn't mean that he had to like it!

It seemed to him that he was encased in this console, part of the electronic organism. In front of him numbers and letters skipped efficiently across the display screen in digital perfection. Answers to any question he might ask the computer instantly appeared on that screen, and before him was a smaller screen which displayed what various elements of the fire-control system were doing at any given time, whether responding automatically to the computer or accepting orders from him.

But there was no longer that heady aroma of salt water, no whistling of sea breezes across the bridge, none of the familiar sounds. He was isolated within the machine, an intimate and important part, but nevertheless only a part.

"I have missile lock on, range one eight zero miles, speed mach three." The voice in his earphones droned on. They were going through a drill, but perfection was demanded along with repetition. Even as Carleton reached to question the time of arrival of the missile, another figure appeared on the screen, announcing the answer as six minutes. "Six minutes to impact of missile," came over the phones. It was just the same as when he'd served aboard his first ship, someone repeating what was already obvious. You could change the hardware, but changing the system was like pulling teeth.

As the minutes passed, more cruise missiles appeared on radar, emanating from numerous flights of Soviet Backfire bombers. What was now evolving was nothing more than the doctrine they had been trained to respond to—that of the first salvo. When the Russians attacked a battle group, they intended to fill the air with missiles, which was no different from saturation bombing forty years ago. It was a simple theory—some of the missiles would be intercepted, some would get through the defenses, and some would impact on vital targets. The Soviet objective was first to destroy the aircraft carrier, the major weapon of the battle group, then hit the AEGIS command ship, in this case *Yorktown*. That would destroy the nerve center of the battle group. After that, they could relax and take out the stragglers one by one.

At an expected, given point, the computer took over.

There was no way man could respond to the saturation attack, to the decoys, the electronic countermeasures, the counter-countermeasures—to the doctrine of the first salvo.

He watched the screen as battle casualties were indicated, both Soviet and American. None of the enemy's bombers would return to base, but that was of little concern to the Soviets. Attrition was part of the first salvo theory. On the other hand, not all the missiles were being intercepted either. The minutes and seconds to impact were displayed coldly and efficiently. The carrier took one hit forward, but it did not impair her ability to launch aircraft. Moments later, a second and then a third made it through. The carrier's flight deck was now incapable of recovering aircraft. There was heavy damage to engineering spaces. Its max speed was now eighteen knots.

One or two destroyers and cruisers were hit and sunk and now *Yorktown* was hit! Her after launcher was knocked out, there were fires in emergency steering, but her electronics were still functioning.

Carleton had been through these exercises before, but none of them had been so realistic. Before, they had always been in trainers, where they knew that soon the lights would be turned up and an evaluation would be conducted by their instructor. This time, however, he was at sea. There was the familiar ship's hum in the air and the deck rolled gently under them, but a computer controlled the entire exercise. It struck him that the computer did no better than the instructors on shore. Both of them made sure the battle group was inoperable before the exercise was over. This was a little more realistic in that Russian Backfire bombers were actually a hundred or so miles away from the ship, and the computer had brought a sense of realism that a shore-bound trainer simply couldn't provide.

Carleton heaved his bulk out of the soft chair and stretched again. Soon the coordinator from the staff would be over to evaluate the exercise. Anything they could imagine to improve the battle group defense would be considered, anything at all. Intelligence estimates left them with no more than two days—three at the most—to iron out any mistakes, dream up any viable tactic, anything that might be more effective when the first salvo became a reality.

THE CRIMEA, USSR
KERADIN'S DACHA

With a deep sigh, Cobb settled heavily on the edge of the cistern, carefully folded his dirt-smeared handkerchief, and mechanically mopped his brow and the back of his neck. There was an unpleasant sting of sweat and sunburn. The conditioning from his few days of toil in the California vineyard reminded him that a field hand's skin was often tanned and wrinkled by the sun. That little touch was something that had never entered his mind until just then. Plunked down by General Keradin's favorite vines, he realized that this simple part of his careful disguise could easily give him away.

The day had been long and hot. There was little air movement. Now, as the sun began to set, he felt a light, cooling breeze from the north. The really cool nights of fall were maybe four weeks off, but there was a definite change in the weather. And the grapes seemed to reflect it. They were plump and juicy, ripe for the picking. Those of prime interest to Cobb and Keradin were almost ready. In some instances, as he'd pointed out earlier in the day, those benefiting from the full rays of the day-long sun were just about perfect.

He picked up a wooden bucket and poured cooling water

over his head. Shaking it from his hair, he let the rest run down his back. He was so immersed in the cooling sensation that he failed to notice someone approaching until a long shadow stretched before him.

"Hello," the girl said in Russian. "I haven't seen you around the vineyards before." She was relatively short and well built, like many of the peasants he'd seen in the fields that day. Her long, rough skirt and her blouse were similar to the others. A colorful scarf covered most of her blond hair. Her face glistened with perspiration, little droplets beading on her upper lip. High cheekbones set off the loveliest blue eyes Cobb thought he'd ever seen.

"Hello," he muttered in reply, mopping the back of his neck. There was no time to become acquainted. Besides, he felt insecure enough that he didn't want to become involved in extensive conversations.

"Is there any water left in your bucket?" she asked.

Cobb shook his head, tipping it upside down to show it was empty.

"It's very hot. May I use it, please?"

He nodded, rising from the cistern and extending it in her direction. She waited hesitantly, then reached out to take it from him. Perhaps she had hoped he might dip it for her. The friendly smile remained on her face, though now it reflected slight disappointment.

There was no need for such rudeness on his part. It was a perfect way to attract attention. He smiled back. "Here," he said, lifting the wooden cover. "Let me get some for you." He took the bucket back and dipped it half full.

"Thank you," she murmured, raising the bucket to her lips. Her smile was most pleasant, Cobb thought, unlike the dull, sour faces he'd noticed most of the day. "Um, that tastes good." After drinking her fill, she knelt beside the cistern, bringing water out of the bucket with her hands and rinsing her face in a much more ladylike manner than he would have expected.

"Yes, it is," he replied. "At the end of the day, a nice relaxing shower . . ." He stopped. Not only did he not want to talk, but he was sure few peasants in this area had any idea what a shower was.

She looked up at him from where she was kneeling with an amused smile on her face. She was really quite pretty, he realized. The blue eyes above the high cheekbones twinkled when she smiled. "You are not from around here, are you?"

He shook his head. "Georgia—near Kutaisi," he answered, referring to the republic and city at the eastern end of the Black Sea.

She looked him up and down, still smiling, then rose slightly to sit on the cistern. "And not a field hand I should expect, at least not if you're used to showers after a day in the fields."

Cobb cursed himself for saying the wrong thing to the wrong person. "I was sent to a school once, to study the grapes. They had modern conveniences there." He grinned back at her. Perhaps it was a good idea to talk with her, to learn as much as he could from someone who seemed to have a knowledge of the area but was more sophisticated than the average peasant. "You're right. A lot of men had no idea how to use them. Some of us learned and grew to like them. Others dipped water out of the toilets."

She laughed at that. "I've seen the same thing myself." Then she looked at him more quizzically, tilting her head to one side. "But you don't talk as if you are from Georgia, either. We have had others from there before."

"You do not have the local accent either."

"No," she shook her head. "I am Polish." This time she studied him a bit longer, with an inquiring look on her face. "You really are a stranger here, aren't you?" Without waiting for an answer, she continued, "There are many of us here in the work party. We were students in Warsaw—until three months ago," she added bitterly. "Many of us were rounded up and sent to this damned country, and I don't know whether or not we're the lucky ones."

"Lucky?"

"I don't know how many are still alive," she responded,

her voice now deep and bitter, the sparkle gone out of her eyes. "We are forced labor," she added.

This was something Cobb hadn't expected. Nothing like this had been mentioned in his briefing. He had seen no indication that there were prisoners around Keradin's dacha—no guards or guns. "I'm sorry. I wasn't aware..." Perhaps this was the reason for those unknown buildings in the far corner of the compound. Neither he nor the photo interpreters were familiar with their purpose. He now realized they had been constructed in the last six months for slave labor.

This time when she looked up at him, there was anger in her eyes. "I suppose you are one of *them*—" she gestured toward the main house, "—spying on us." But the bewildered look on his face reassured her that this stranger was not one of "them." And after all she had learned about the peasants that toiled in this particular vineyard—they were the only natives she had come in contact with—she also sensed this stranger was not one of Keradin's men. "Forgive me. You're much too naive to be looking for an evening with me." It occurred to her that this man should be cultivated. Perhaps he could be her means of escape.

"An evening?"

She looked up at Cobb, her eyes squinting against the glare of the sun. Her gaze swept up and down his figure, taking in the clothes, stopping at his hair. She lifted one of his hands, which he quickly pulled away. "Perhaps I should just go back to the barracks."

"Barracks?"

She pointed down the hill to one of the buildings in the far corner. "That's where they lock us up at the end of the day, except when Keradin or one of his men wants an evening. That's what we call it—an evening. Then they send the foreman down with one of the guards to bring us back." She grimaced. "About the only good thing I can say for it is the shower." Now she grinned again. "Imagine that. After a while, you're willing to trade yourself for a shower. They like us clean, not like the smelly peasant girls." Cobb said nothing. Again her head tilted to the side. "If you had been around here even for a short time, you would have known all about that. The peasants won't pay attention to us." She pointed at the bucket. "They wouldn't even have dipped water for me."

"What's your name?" Cobb asked.

"Verra."

"That is Polish," he nodded. "Very pretty." Looking around to make sure that no one was paying attention to them, he continued, "I haven't seen any guards. I'm sure I would have noticed."

"Keradin doesn't want to make a big thing about it—not in front of the peasants. The foreman—a GRU in charge of security—works for him, along with some of the others. They keep a close eye on us. There's no way we could get away, at least not during the day, and they keep us locked up at night. That's when the guards come out."

She stood up then, her hands on her hips, and half circled him, studying both the man and the clothes intently. She had promised herself that the first time there seemed to be a chance, she would take it. Verra was not about to accept the existence offered to her at the dacha. She had only accepted it when the other choice was prison. Pursing her lips and nodding to herself as she stopped in front of him, she determined that the gamble had to be taken. "And you— what is your name?"

Down below, near the main shed, the foreman stepped out into the sun, looking up the slope. Cobb stood up, pouring the remainder of the water over his head. Hoisting his half-full bucket of grapes, he said, "Come on," indicating the foreman down the hill with a jerk of his head. "I'll teach you a little bit about grapes." He moved to the edge of the arbor, noting over his shoulder that the foreman still hadn't moved. "I'll tell you my name," he added when she hesitated.

She moved into a row above his so that she could watch both him and the foreman below. Good for her, he thought. She doesn't trust a soul. "You can call me Cobb."

"Cobb . . . Cobb?" She rolled the name over her tongue with difficulty. "That isn't Georgian or even Russian, is it?"

He was normally not a gambler, not at such an early stage. But there was no time for games . . . no time to analyze just how he could effect a smooth operation and spirit off the head of the Strategic Rocket Forces within the next eight to ten hours—and his last chance would only be one day later.

It was time to gamble. "No, Cobb is not Russian."

She looked down at him, studying his face closely as if looking for something that would answer a question. Like him, she moved slowly along the row of vines, clipping bunches of grapes and dropping them gently in her basket. Each time, she looked away only for a second, then her gaze fell back on his face again. Yes, she determined, she would take a chance.

"You have never been here before today?" It was a question and a statement.

"No."

She grinned at him. "You are right not to talk to anyone." She pointed at his clothes. "You look right, but I could tell when I sat down with you that you didn't smell right. Only a day or so of sweat." She wrinkled her nose. "You spend long enough here, you'll know what I mean. I think some of these peasants bathe only after the harvest. You had one of those showers you mentioned not too long ago. So don't talk and don't let them smell you."

"I've already talked with Keradin."

She looked up in surprise, then her face softened. "I think perhaps he's so comfortable here he wouldn't consider those little things. He pays others to worry about that." Her voice sharpened. "How long do you plan to stay here?"

"As little time as necessary."

"And you expect to get away just as easily as you came?" There was a tone in her voice that implied it wouldn't be that easy.

"I had considered that."

"If I help you, would you take me too?"

For just an instant, but long enough to resurrect the pain of memory, Cobb's mind flashed back to another woman who had asked that same question. It seemed so long ago. Those fifteen years were sometimes an eternity and other times seemed only a moment in time—and it had happened in a land so different from this one. But the other woman was just as beautiful in her own way, her hair long and dark, almond eyes just as penetrating, slender Asian body just as inviting. She had asked the same question and he *had* taken her. He had loved her beyond anything he had ever understood before, and Henry Cobb had made her his wife. Then his enemy had taken her away and tortured her before they killed her. After that, he had repeated the words many times after: "Never again!"

"You don't know what I'm here for," Cobb responded.

"I don't *care* what you're here for," she answered emphatically. "If I have even the slightest chance to get away from here, I'll do what I have to."

"I don't think you'd find my work very appealing." He was gambling now, gambling as he'd never done before. By now, Keradin would already have talked with his foreman about the new man who knew so much about the grapes. It was probable the foreman would say nothing to upset the General. More than likely, though, he would be looking for Cobb shortly.

"What I am forced to do is not very appealing."

"I don't follow you." He thought he knew what she meant, but he had to be sure.

"I am one of his whores," she spat. "He likes me. Keradin, he calls me one of his favorites." Her eyes narrowed and her full lips became a narrow line. "I will do anything that might get me out of here. I have even hoped that if I please him enough, perhaps he will take me back to Moscow with him. It would be easier to escape from there than this place."

Cobb straightened momentarily. "I'll take you if you help me, yes." He'd said it. Would he regret such a decision again?

Her expression changed now. She had figured out Cobb

long before he'd realized how weak his disguise actually was. The moment she decided he might be something other than what he admitted to, she had decided to take her chances with him.

"I'll do what you want." Her expression changed again. "But I wish I could cut off that son of a bitch's balls before we go." Her tone was vicious—definitely a woman to have on his side.

"You just may have that opportunity." Cobb grinned at her. "But not until you're given permission. I think I'll need more help than I realized."

"You are quite brave to come in here like this—and most foolish to think you could get away with it for long. Who are you really, Cobb?"

"Does it matter right now?"

"Later, maybe, yes. Right now, no. Anything would have to be better than servicing that beast."

"Is he really a beast?"

"No. He is a very brilliant man—and very dangerous. He shows a certain amount of respect for the women he uses like toys. But," and she looked hard at him, "I am a lady, not a field hand."

Thank God he'd met this girl. Without her perhaps he'd have had no opportunity to get to Keradin. "I'm going to need more help than you want to offer," he said tentatively.

"Will it get me out of here?"

"If I get out, you will. But we must do it tonight."

"It has to do with Keradin?"

He nodded. "Keradin and you."

She smiled grimly. "I guess one more of his evenings won't be the end of the world. Perhaps," she offered, "I can stall him long enough and you can move fast enough in whatever you want to do that I can postpone him indefinitely."

"That would be up to you. I'm afraid I can't help in that regard."

"Are you going to kill him?"

"On the contrary. I'm going to take him with us."

"Take him?" She spat. "He will go with us—with me?"

"I'm afraid that's part of the deal. I need your help. But apparently you need mine more."

She said nothing, moving down the row of vines, selecting and cutting at random. "You are an American, Cobb?"

He nodded in answer.

"A spy?"

"Not really. Does it matter?"

"No. Once again, it doesn't matter. But I like to know who I am forced to put faith in. How do you want me to arrange this little tryst?"

"How does he choose?"

"We think just when the spirit hits him. He usually comes to us, or sends one of his men at the end of the day or after dinner, perhaps when he has had a little to drink."

"Is your basket full?"

"Enough so, I guess."

"Come on." Cobb jerked his head in the direction of the cistern. They went over to it, and he dipped the wooden bucket, filling it to the brim, and handed it to her. "Pour this over your face and chest—not in your hair. We don't want you looking straggly. Just enough to appeal to him."

She did as she was told. The cool water cleansed her face, bringing color to her cheeks. And the water over the peasant blouse accomplished exactly what he had hoped. It clung to her tightly like a second skin, emphasizing a better figure than he'd assumed earlier. She looked down at herself, blushing. "This is what you want?"

"Let's hope it's what General Keradin wants. Come on. He said he'd be there now."

Her movement down the slope accomplished what he had hoped. She moved with a sensuous gait that was appealing even at the end of a workday in her soiled peasant clothes. She was, Cobb decided, a most desirable woman.

"Keep it up," he said admiringly. "You may be your own best ticket out of here. Stay well ahead of me. We don't want anyone to get the slightest idea we've even seen each other."

He would have to trust to pure, dumb luck as far as Verra was concerned. He'd told her only to get Keradin into his

room as early that night as possible, that he'd take care of
whatever would happen. If nothing did, then she was no
worse off. At least no one would know she had ever spoken
with him. But as he trudged tiredly down the slope, there
was the foreman, slightly withdrawn from the others as he
stood near the crushing shed, hands on his hips, waiting.
The man seemed not to notice Verra as she passed by.
Keradin did see her and without hesitation was at her side.
She seemed to be cementing her part of the arrangement
with little effort. However, Cobb's end of the deal appeared
to be in trouble as the foreman moved out to intercept him
before he could dump his basket.

The foreman, a product of GRU training, was most unhappy at that moment. General Keradin had inquired about
the new man, the one who knew so much about the time
for the sweet wines. The foreman's knowledge of grapes
and wine making had given him this once-in-a-lifetime opportunity to work for the head of the Strategic Rocket Forces,
one of the most influential men in the Kremlin. But his
future success depended more on his security measures than
it did on his skills with the grape. The peasants he employed
were prized for their closed mouths. The workers were
allowed out of their barracks only during working hours,
and they never spoke out of turn. There were no labor
problems at Keradin's dacha.

"I hired no such person, General," he'd responded earlier. "I believe it was my assistant who canvassed the neighboring villages for more help during the harvest." It was a
weak excuse, for the foreman was supposed to know the
name of every person in the compound, every event that
occurred. "At times like this, with the grapes so close, I
make sure we put on some extra men for a day or two," he
said, shrugging knowingly. "Sometimes we have luck, I
guess, and someone like this Berezin appears. But, General,
please let me talk with this man first—it is my responsibility."

Now when he noticed Keradin in conversation with one
of his women, the foreman moved out to intercept Cobb.
"I want to speak to you," he hissed quietly, grasping the

other firmly by the arm. "Give your basket to this man to empty." And when they were out of hearing of everyone else, he demanded, "Who brought you here?"

"I came in this morning with the other workers, sir." Cobb remained as respectful as he felt a guilty peasant might act, one who was poverty stricken and willing to do almost anything for a job. "I have had no work for so long. My children are hungry. Some people said there might be work here during the harvest."

"What people?"

"Oh, just people I talk to." He named some of the neighboring villages where he was sure some of the field hands lived. "Please, sir, I thought that maybe if I came here, showed you how hard I work, you might be kind." He was whining now. "Let me start at low pay."

"You should know that's not the way things are done around here." He maintained his grip on Cobb's arm, the pressure increasing.

"I know, sir. I know." Cobb remained subservient, eyes blinking nervously, hands wringing. "My children, they need food," he repeated. "Please. I will show you how hard I work for beginning wages."

Keradin's conversation with Verra had finished. He watched appreciatively over his shoulder as she sauntered away in the direction of the barracks and then, beaming, he came over to the two men. "Well now, Kozlov! Have you been working on some problems?" It seemed obvious that the General's immediate interest centered either on Verra or his wines, and his foreman was not quite sure that it was in his own best interests to change his optimistic mood.

"Sir," responded Cobb in his best whine, his head down, groveling superbly, "I don't think I know that much about the wines. I have forgotten much—there is so much difference here."

"Nonsense. Up there," he pointed toward the top of the hill, "you knew exactly what you were talking about." His voice hardened perceptibly. "Come!" It was an order. To the foreman he added, "Do you prefer to join us?"

Kozlov had released Cobb's arm when the General came

over. Now he looked impatiently at the peasant with the hangdog appearance. "Yes, sir. I would like to see just how much he does know for myself. But first I would like to make sure that all the workers have left and that the security is set for the night. I will join you within half an hour."

Cobb was well aware of the unhappiness underneath the calm demeanor of the foreman. It was now a matter of buying time. Thankful for the small amount of breathing space, Cobb still knew that he would have to account for himself to Kozlov when Keradin left to prepare for his evening in the dacha.

The cellars were cool and clean. Keradin may have only taken to wine making as a hobby, but his cellars were those of a professional. The equipment was modern, as up to date as that back in the Napa Valley. They sampled a number of wines selected by the General, discussing the maturation of the grapes, the blends, the aging process.

What General Keradin was looking for was just what Cobb's mentor hoped to create in Napa. It would be the closest he could come to the great sauternes without developing a poor imitation. To do so would have been to come up second best. To be successful was to produce a new taste, one in the manner of a sauterne, but also unlike it. It had to possess a nose and an aftertaste that could hold its own. That would appeal to the connoisseur, not an imitation. As they talked, Keradin couldn't have agreed with him more.

The foreman caught up with them eventually, and remained on the fringe. Arms folded, withdrawn from the discussion, Kozlov studied Cobb closely. Cobb sensed the foreman could spot trouble a mile away—that he was sure Cobb was not only not from Georgia, but that he knew too much for a peasant in that part of the Crimea. Yet he said nothing to the General, wisely keeping any suspicions to himself.

Back out in the yard again, Keradin turned to Cobb. "So, tomorrow you stay out of the fields, eh? First thing, we sample the juices from today's crush—see what we have. Maybe we wander up there—" he gestured toward the arbor where they'd first met, "—pick some grapes, experiment a little, eh?"

"I would be honored to help, sir," Cobb responded.

"Good. You go home to your family tonight, get yourself a good sleep." He gestured to the foreman. "See that he gets some money to give his family. You have my permission to pay him in advance. Take good care of our Berezin." And with that, Keradin was off at a brisk pace toward the twilight-obscured dacha, whistling in anticipation of his evening with Verra.

Cobb, hat in hand, had not quite decided his next move.

"What are you thinking about, Berezin?" It was the foreman. Grabbing Cobb's shoulder with a beefy hand, his fingers dug into muscle at the base of the neck. He knew how to inflict pain. "I think we should have a little talk—in private." His hand maintained its painful grip as he turned Cobb around and walked him in the direction of the crushing shed. "Come into my office."

Once inside, with the door slammed behind them, the foreman spun Cobb around, shoving him against the rough wall. "So you call yourself Berezin. What is your real name? Berezin isn't Georgian. Your accent is more northern—Moscow or Leningrad maybe—not Georgia."

"I don't understand, sir. I . . ." Cobb's feigned innocence never had a chance. The foreman caught him in the side of the head with a stunning blow. The noise alone was enough to stun him; the impact knocked him off his feet. Before he could gather his senses, he was jerked to his feet and pressed against the wall.

"You don't seem to understand," the other snarled. "No one—*no one* makes a fool of me. And today the General must have thought me to be an idiot. We'll just stay in here until we know a little more about you."

It was all Cobb could do to remember his alias. He took a deep breath. "My name is Berezin. I . . ." The remaining air whooshed out of his body as the foreman buried his fist in Cobb's midsection. He doubled over onto the floor, his legs kicking spasmodically, gasping for air.

"When you're ready, you may get up. Then we will start

again." The voice seemed to come through a tunnel, echoing through Cobb's head, and he tasted bile, choking on it as he gasped. There was no way, Cobb realized, that he could go through this and still execute his plan that night. He got to his hands and knees.

"Now what do you think, my Berezin friend? Shall we talk?"

Cobb wiped at the blood running down his chin. His words came in gasps. "What I think . . . is that it won't matter what I say." He waited. There was no reaction from the other man. "I was brought up in Georgia. I don't know where my family name came from," he added quickly. "I can tell you about our grapes, our vineyards, our wines. . . ." He didn't see the blow coming this time, a brisk open hand to the side of the head that was as hard as a closed fist. Cobb went down again, ears ringing.

"I am sure you can tell me many things I don't need to know about your wines. Anyone can be trained to do that." The foreman had seemed relatively calm up to that point, but now anger was evident in his voice. "I want to know who sent you here. Nobody, not even the high and mighty in Moscow, makes a fool of me in front of General Keradin." He pointed his index finger at Cobb, then jerked his thumb upward, indicating he wanted Cobb to get to his feet. "You could be from anywhere, but I suspect someone sent you to break security, someone who wants to see me sent off so that they can have this job."

He went on, but Cobb barely heard what he was saying. The fact that the foreman thought he was being tested more for a breach in security than actually being compromised from the outside was Cobb's ace in the hole. He had passed the test as a Russian, but not as the little old wine maker. Well, play Kozlov's game, then!

"You are much wiser than anticipated," Cobb began.

"This has been done before, you realize. I have been able to see through it each time. General Keradin is well taken care of, my friend. No one is going to compromise his position." The words were spoken with arrogance and cruelty by a man who had succeeded in a mean world. Cobb had heard tales of GRU spying within the ranks, of how underlings sought to overthrow superiors by any means possible. Only the wisest, cruelest, most suspicious survived to retire. "All I want to know," the foreman said, "is who sent you in."

Cobb lowered his eyes, sensing he might have a chance if he played the part of the enemy within. The foreman took a step in his direction, stopping when Cobb raised his hands in a gesture of peace. "You place me in a difficult position," Cobb spoke slowly, still gasping. "If anything happens to me, you will of course, be considered responsible. If I am allowed to leave, you will be considered a fool. If I tell you who wants your position, then I will be a dead man."

It was a chance Cobb had to take. If he kept talking, perhaps the foreman would relax his guard. "Let's talk about how we can work together. After all, General Keradin is much taken with my knowledge of his wines."

The foreman looked at him with disgust. "You turn on your seniors now; you will turn on me later."

"I too want to work with Keradin. I took this assignment to meet him, believe me. I want to get out of Moscow. My life is wine. I have no interest in your job. A life of peace . . ."

"I can't believe someone would send you." The foreman shook his head in disgust. For a second, he turned his back to Cobb, wandering toward the small, single window. "Imagine . . ."

That was the foreman's last word as Cobb sprang across the space between them, covering the distance in an instant, his arm already raised. He brought it down, his hand flattened sideways like an ax head. The blow caught the foreman in the back of the neck. As he slumped sideways, Cobb grabbed him, twisting his head back. The neck snapped with a sharp crack. Cobb released the body. The foreman was dead before he hit the floor.

Cobb peeked anxiously out the window. No one was around. He dragged the body behind the foreman's desk. Knowing there had to be a weapon of some kind, he went through the drawers. In one of them, he found a Makarov pistol, fully loaded. He tucked it inside his shirt.

Outside, the shadows had merged into the blackness of night. A cool breeze blew in off the Black Sea, pushing the lights of magnificent yachts safely into the arms of this Russian Riviera. He pulled his cap low over his forehead and exited into the darkness. He hoped no one had business in the foreman's office that night. The light was off, the door locked as he slipped out. Perhaps, just perhaps no one would miss the foreman for the next few hours.

Cobb already knew where he would hide until he judged the time was right to move. There could be no possible reason security would ever inspect the crusher. He climbed easily up the side and slid over into the catch basin inside. If for some unknown reason someone did want to look inside, Cobb would be able to hear them climbing up the side.

Feeling gently with his fingers, Cobb found the side of his face swollen from the foreman's blows. He sat up cautiously. His stomach also hurt. Stretching slowly, Cobb grinned to himself. He would feel just fine in no time. The foreman would never feel a thing again.

He peered cautiously over the top of the crusher. Nothing—no one. He looked toward the Black Sea. Safety! Lights blinked back from the water. The glow of Yalta, off to one side, offered comfort, especially to the powerful few in the Soviet Union. Like the foreman of Keradin's vineyard, they had willingly done anything to achieve the good life.

Tonight, if he was successful, Cobb would change that good life for another well-rewarded Russian citizen. But he would only accomplish that if another person, one unknown to him until today, was able to pull off her part of a sensitive plan, one he had conceived in just a few brief moments. This was not out of the ordinary for him. His existence depended on his reactions. He succeeded in the job because he was the best there was. He relished the spirit of the hunt. But Verra was joining him in a spirit of hatred, as well as trust that a complete stranger would do everything in his power to bring her with him. After the degradation she had suffered, she had nothing to lose.

Cobb felt for the pistol, extracting it from his shirt. It was warm with the heat of his body. He checked it again, just as he had done before allowing himself to doze for an hour. The Makarov would be used only as a last desperate measure. Their weapons would make short work of him and Verra if they were caught. Perhaps if they confronted only one man or two, it might buy him time. It might buy time for the girl.

Verra. Cobb dreamed about her. She had changed from a peasant girl, covered with dust, clothing stained with grape juice at the end of the day, to a beautiful woman in an evening gown. He imagined her sweeping down a long staircase, jewelry glittering, hair upswept, long gown covering all but her shoes . . . and there at the bottom of the staircase, waiting for her in full uniform . . . was Keradin. Though the shock in the dream had jolted him awake for a second, he realized then, as he did now, that she was as beautiful in reality as she had been in his dream. The peasant clothing she had worn that day was nothing more than a uniform. The elegant way she carried herself, the manner in which she spoke, even her desire to emasculate Keradin, made him realize that she was indeed the lady she claimed to be, a lady who would seek revenge if she was violated. She would be a worthy partner—and he had not realized how much he needed a partner until she clarified that for him. He forced the memories of another time and another woman in Saigon from his mind.

He slipped out of the crusher silently. Sticking to the shadows, he moved toward the dacha. The plan he had roughed out that afternoon as they trudged down the slope to the crushing shed was to have Verra seduce Keradin. She had to make sure that she got Keradin to his room no later than two hours after sunset, and then Cobb intended to take him when he was naked. Somehow a man was obviously weaker and much easier to control that way.

In a few minutes Verra had detailed where the guards were normally stationed at the dacha, the location of Keradin's bedroom, and which others were adjacent to it. The separate barracks where the slave laborers were housed were considered the major and only source of trouble by Keradin's guards. They had control over the neighboring villages and saw little chance of trouble from the outside.

That afternoon when he shuffled down the hillside, kicking up dust with tired feet, Cobb saw something he could use—a discarded wine barrel lying on its side not far from the balcony outside Keradin's room. If she was as equal to her part of the bargain as Cobb anticipated, Keradin would hear no noise. She promised that the sliding glass door would be ajar.

There was a quarter moon that night, not enough light to be seen by, not even if he were within ten yards of someone. Only the white walls of the dacha stood out. It was a country home, a retreat. There had never been a need for spotlights or illumination alongside the single-lane, dirt road, and no traffic existed at night this far from Yalta. This was true country, a place where Soviet officials could relax.

The main house, facing the Black Sea, was lighted primarily in the main dining area where, Verra explained, all the parties took place. It was there, each evening, that Keradin and his staff would bring the women they chose from the barracks. Alcohol—vodka, wine, and brandy—flowed, and sumptuous meals were served. After dinner and brandy, one by one they would drift up to their rooms. Cobb could see some of the rooms lit now. In the one to the left of Keradin's, the light was extinguished as he watched. Having sex, no one would be listening for strange sounds.

Creeping up to the wine barrel, he rolled it, slowly and quietly, toward the balcony outside Keradin's room.

Less than ten feet from the balcony, Cobb heard a door open at the far end of the building, by the dining area. Leaving the barrel, he slipped back behind a setting of small bushes lining the front patio area. A man walked out onto the front deck, stretched, then stepped down onto the lawn, unzipping his fly. He looked over in Cobb's direction, spying the barrel. He meandered toward it, his hands still working at his fly. Looking up at the balcony outside Keradin's room,

he obscenely extended a finger in the General's direction
as he relieved himself on the barrel. When he was finished,
he spat in Keradin's direction and extended his finger again.

All is not well among the chiefs, Cobb thought, trying
not to think about the barrel he had just appropriated. Remembering the foreman's suspicions, he wondered at the
hatred and distrust among men who worked so close together. The man wandered back to the front porch, taking
his time, looking from side to side. He stopped, turned, and
looked back at the barrel as if he hadn't remembered it being
there. Muttering something under his breath that Cobb could
not hear, he finally sauntered back inside.

Cobb waited to make sure the man did not return to
consider the barrel further, then slipped out from behind the
bushes. He rolled it toward the balcony, awkwardly trying
to grasp it only at the top end, the still-dry part. But he
quickly admitted that he couldn't get a good hold on it that
way. What's a little used vodka? he thought.

He turned the barrel on end at one corner of the balcony,
then crept backward to survey the building once more. The
lights were now off on both sides of Keradin's room. That
meant that one was being used and the other . . . more than
likely they were also indisposed.

Standing on the barrel, he grasped the edge of the balcony. Silently swinging up with his feet, he knelt momentarily on the edge, then pulled himself up slowly, peering
over the railing. There was a light on inside, but curtains
were drawn on this end. He pulled himself very carefully
over the railing until both feet were planted on the deck.
Then he dropped to his knees and crawled to the other end
of the balcony.

Just as Verra had promised, the sliding glass door was
ajar, open about three inches. He could hear voices inside.
Listening, he identified both hers and Keradin's. The sen-
tences were short and sharp. Her voice rose, followed by
his. They were arguing—and that wasn't part of Cobb's
plan. She was supposed to keep him occupied, not angered.
He put his ear close to the opening and listened.

Keradin had an extraordinary sexual imagination, especially when describing his own prowess. But tonight, whatever he suggested, Verra would not go along. Soon Keradin was whining, wheedling, but she would still not cooperate.

Obviously, Cobb realized, Verra was distracting him so he wouldn't be watching the curtains. Stealthily, not moving the cloth more than a centimeter at a time, he pulled back the curtain until one eye peered into the room. Indeed, Verra had insured that Keradin was indisposed. He was buck naked. In his hand was a camera that looked very much like one of those instant developers which were so hard to obtain in the Soviet Union. It was easy to understand what he had in mind and obvious why Verra was protesting.

It was also obvious why she had become the General's favorite. Her hair was swept up. She was perfectly made up and she wore expensive, ornate jewelry. But that was all. Cobb was sure he had never seen a more gorgeous woman.

She was sitting on the edge of the bed. The General was a few feet away from her with his camera, trying to convince her to pose. She would have nothing to do with him. While he pleaded, she looked down at the floor or in the direction of the curtain as if she was hoping Cobb would burst through in that instant and come to her rescue.

But Cobb waited. He had to be sure that Keradin was totally occupied with his own pleading rather than with where her eyes were roaming. Once Cobb was satisfied, he moved the curtain ever so slightly when she looked in his direction, just enough so that she would know it wasn't the evening breeze. She saw the motion, he was sure, but gave no indication of it. She looked down at the floor again, then back in his direction. Again, Cobb moved the curtain, this time keeping his eye there. She saw it, nodded slightly, and looked back at the floor.

What the hell do I do now? Cobb wondered. The argument renewed. It was finally settled when Keradin agreed that he would pose for her first and then she would reciprocate. A clever girl! Cobb thought.

She offered a number of suggestions for poses, each of

which met with an argument from the General. But when it was made clear that her poses would be definitely determined by what he agreed to, the man had no choice. First the General placed a bedside table on top of the mattress. Then he climbed precariously on top of it, his head scant inches from the ceiling. Verra tossed him his hat, which he put on after much discussion. Cobb was about to enter at this point when he thought better of it. The man was still in a position where he could move fast.

The next pose was more to Cobb's liking, with Keradin lying on his back on the table. This would be it, Cobb thought. When the General appeared the most uncomfortable, Cobb moved quickly into the room, sliding the door shut behind him with one hand, the other holding the gun steadily on the prone General.

Keradin remained motionless, his eyes moving from the girl to Cobb and back again.

"There were a couple of times I wondered," she said, still standing in the same spot with her camera. "It seemed you were never going to show up."

"I appreciate your professionalism," Cobb answered. "Nice pose."

"Can I cut his balls off now?" she hissed.

Keradin's eyes settled on Cobb. Still no expression. He was a tough man.

"No, not now, not unless we have to. I would like him in one piece. But if there's the slightest doubt, then, yes, you may." He made sure the General absorbed that.

"He's dangerous, you know," she said.

"He doesn't appear to be now." Cobb grinned. The General said nothing, still motionless. It seemed best to keep him in that position for the time being. Cobb turned to Verra. "Put on your clothes."

As she dressed, Keradin's eyes never left Cobb, watching his every move, waiting perhaps, Cobb thought, for me to do something dumb, perhaps leer at the girl. One should always enjoy a beautiful woman's nudity—but the alternative here wasn't nearly as pleasurable. He must realize that I am not the little old wine maker he thought he'd found, and certainly not an enemy from Moscow. They wouldn't do it this way.

Once dressed, Verra went through the General's clothes without a word from Cobb. Neatly hung over the chair was the man's holster, belt, and gun. "What do you want to do with this?"

"Strap it around my waist, gun over the left hip, butt forward. You can have this one when we're ready."

In the General's dresser she found a slender but deadly looking knife in an ornate sheath. Removing it, she stroked the blade thoughtfully looking Keradin up and down as she did so.

"Are you planning to kill me?" Keradin inquired. He spoke in a normal voice, though his eyes were now on the knife.

"Not unless it's absolutely necessary," Cobb answered. "As far as she's concerned," he inclined his head toward Verra, "I'm going to try to convince her not to either. I can't swear that I can keep her from using the knife," he added.

From the look in Keradin's eyes, he seemed to share Cobb's concern. "May I get up and get dressed?"

"You may get up, very carefully. Roll off that table, slowly, onto the bed. Once you're there, I'll tell you when you can stand up."

The General did just as he was instructed, bouncing slightly as he landed on the mattress, rolling over, then watching Cobb silently.

"Good. Now slide toward me until your feet are on the floor." It was an odd sight, the naked man moving as though he were fully clothed, seemingly unconcerned with his own nakedness. As his feet touched the floor, his hand snaked out, grabbing a leg of the table still on the bed. In one fluid motion, he was on his feet, heaving it in Cobb's direction. But Cobb was a split second ahead of him, and ducked. The table passed a fraction of an inch from his head, crashing against the wall. As Keradin lunged toward him, Cobb stepped slightly to one side, slashing the gun barrel across

the man's cheek. Keradin looked up from the floor at Cobb
with an astonished look on his face. He felt the welt on his
cheek and stared at the blood that covered his hand when
he pulled it away.

"Someone will come—all that noise," Verra said, the
first sign of fear in her eyes.

Cobb looked down at the General. Behind the pain in
his eyes was a triumphant expression, as if Keradin knew
he had won, whether or not Cobb had knocked him to the
floor.

"The knife," said Cobb. "Use it if you have to."

Before Keradin fully understood what was implied, Verra
was on her knees beside him, the blade of the knife nestled
in his crotch. Honest fear shone in Keradin's eyes.

Cobb waited. The response was quick. There was pounding at the door. Voices outside called Keradin's name.

Cobb dropped to his knees, whispering close to the man's
face, "Answer them. Laugh, tell them it's all right." Keradin
looked stubbornly at him. Cobb turned slightly to Verra,
then back to the General.

"Everything is all right," Keradin answered. "Nothing to
worry about."

"What happened?" a voice responded, not satisfied.

"It is very personal, tell them," Cobb whispered. "You
can explain everything in the morning. You're having a
wonderful time and it will make a funny story." Keradin
hesitated again. Cobb got to his feet. "If he doesn't do what
he's told by the time I count to three," he said to Verra,
"he's all yours."

Keradin looked down at the knife. Verra moved it slightly,
enough for Keradin to get the message that she would enjoy
carrying it through. "I will have to tell you all about it in
the morning," Keradin shouted. "You'll all be amused. But,
please, I am occupied now." He finished with a suggestive
laugh.

Outside the closed door, male laughter answered. Voices
called a pleasant good night to the General as they drifted
down the hallway. Keradin looked down at the knife. Verra
hadn't moved it. He looked up at Cobb.

"A deal's a deal." Cobb grinned at her appreciatively. "I can't let you scare him to death. I still have a job to do." She removed the knife, slipping it back in its sheath and dropping it inside her blouse. Cobb had the General's gun holstered around his waist. He handed Verra the Makarov. "Remember, if there's any problem, anything that he could have saved us from, the first shot is for him." He looked at Keradin. "You understand?"

The General nodded. "Where are you taking me?"

"It doesn't matter. Put on your shoes and socks."

The General indicated the rest of his clothing hanging over the chair.

Cobb shook his head. "You're traveling incognito tonight. All I'm worried about is your feet." He indicated to the girl. "Make a little roll for him—shorts, shirt, pants—just in case there's a delay. I wouldn't want to lose him to pneumonia. He'll carry his clothes himself and like it." And to Keradin: "Remember, the first bullet will be for you. But if I have time, even just a few seconds, I will let her use her knife. Any questions?"

Keradin shook his head. Cobb explained to both of them how they would get out of the dacha and away from the area. There was no reason to explain yet where they would go afterward.

Even the most jaded observer would have found humor in the departure of a well-dressed woman, followed by a naked man, followed by a peasant. After lowering themselves from the balcony to the barrel to the ground, they walked to the main gate. Verra's knife was once again pressed against the General to assure his silence.

The gate was the easiest method of escape. Electrically controlled from the inside by the guard, it could not be opened from the outside, and apparently security had not considered the possibility of someone escaping from the inside of General Keradin's compound. As a result, there was only one guard there, whom Cobb had watched for a while from his position inside the crusher. He was by himself and likely bored. Cobb disposed of him quickly. Having seen earlier where the controls were, he opened the gate just the slightest bit to allow them to slip through. Taking the guard's body with him, he dumped it in the bushes on the opposite side of the road. He knew that sooner or later the man would be missed, the gate found ajar, and then Keradin's absence would be noted. However, it seemed unlikely to him that they would be discovered missing in such a short time, and assuming luck was with them and Lassiter appeared as planned, things should turn out well.

The naked General preceded the other two, following directions as Cobb dictated them, taking the same path Cobb used when he came into the area. The road between Yalta and Alushta was mainly dirt, and it carried more horse- or ox-drawn carts than motorized vehicles. At night, it was deserted. Only peasants ever used it, and nowhere but home existed for them after dark. Twice the General indicated how chilled he was becoming, but each time Cobb decided that he would be more obedient if he was cold.

They left the road close to the spot where Cobb had climbed up from the sea the night before. "Give him his underwear for the time being."

"Why?"

"The undergrowth—he'll hurt himself."

"So?"

"He'll slow us down. We don't have time."

"For what?" she persisted.

"We are not staying in the Crimea, believe me."

He could sense her happiness even in the dark. "That's all I wanted to know. I thought—oh, forget it," she said, handing Keradin his underwear, then giggling at the ludicrous sight of his putting it on.

Cobb led them down through the underbrush, halting at a point about fifty yards above the water's edge. Here he had a view of the shore to either side, yet they could not be detected by anyone who chanced to wander nearby.

For the first time, Keradin spoke. "May I ask where you are taking me, and why you are doing so?" Since the moment Cobb had appeared quite suddenly in his bedroom, the General had heard only Russian spoken. He knew nothing other than that Cobb, supposedly a Georgian, seemed to know a great deal about wine. Though the girl was Polish, it was obvious that this man was not. They left no doubt about their willingness to kill him, if necessary. Even worse, from Keradin's point of view, was the man's willingness to set the girl loose with her knife. If he were to die, he far preferred a bullet.

"It's not important where you're going," Cobb told him. "That you'll see for yourself."

"Are you holding me for ransom?"

"You'll see. But I don't think your friends want you back anyway. They'd never know how much you might have spilled to us. Better alive with us than dead with them."

The underbrush was covered with a light dew. The dampness in the air added to the chill. "May I put on some clothes?" Keradin persisted.

"No. I want to make it as easy as possible for her to operate on you if I decide it's necessary. Did I tell you how good she is with that knife before we left?" Keradin said nothing more, but his teeth chattered. Cobb had no idea whether it was the cold or the prospect of Verra's knife.

They waited silently. Verra's eyes never left the General. Keradin looked up every few moments but eventually gave up when he realized she was as alert as ever. The minutes passed with an agonizing slowness for each of them. The girl was anxious, the General apprehensive, Cobb just a slight bit concerned that Lassiter might have run into trouble.

But a half hour before midnight, he saw the light come on briefly out at sea then search the water as if a fisherman were putting something over the side. Before it was extinguished, it blinked in their direction three times. To an observer on the beach, it would have appeared casual. Keradin, who had been following Cobb's eyes, saw it and murmured to himself. He knew he was going to sea.

They relaxed for a few more moments before Cobb said, "All right. Down to the waterline. We have an appointment." Soon a small black boat appeared out of the darkness. Its electric motor made no noise and neither Keradin nor the girl knew what to expect until it loomed before them.

A man in the bow jumped gracefully out to hold the boat for them. It was then that Keradin heard Cobb speak another language for the first time.

"English," the General growled.

"No," Cobb responded quietly. "American, courtesy of the U.S. Navy," he added, pointing at the small craft. "Get in."

Lassiter perched on a stool in the hydrofoil's wheelhouse moments later as the larger craft slipped out to sea. He pointed at Keradin. "Is that guy in the shorts really him?"

"He sure is," Cobb answered.

"Doesn't look like a general to me." Lassiter got up and circled their prize. Keradin, who affected a haughty air, refused to acknowledge the other. They had just boarded a Soviet hydrofoil, and as they had come alongside, Keradin had the faint hope that perhaps a mistake had been made— until he heard someone hail Cobb in English. To his knowledge, no one in Moscow was aware the Americans had comandeered a Soviet boat.

"And the lovely lady, Cobb—who is the lovely lady?" Verra was still wearing the dress she'd worn to Keradin's dacha that evening. In Russian, he remarked, "Cobb has done some pretty strange things since I've known him, but he never found someone like you before. I expect you'll be wanting to change into something a little more in keeping with our trip. I'll have one of my men take you below and see if they can fit you out."

She still had an eye on Keradin. "I hate to let him out of my sight."

"Well, ma'am," Lassiter continued, "I don't think you have to worry about him at all. You see, even though we still seem to be in the Black Sea, he's just got himself into American custody. The only Russian you're going to find around this boat is the General himself. Everyone else is as American as you can get—just like your friend Cobb here." Lassiter talked like a boy just off the farm. His accent and demeanor were easygoing, as if he were welcoming someone to the country fair. "You leave him up to me and I promise you that nothing good's going to happen to him. A couple of my boys will hog-tie him for you, just to be sure."

When Keradin and Verra had gone, Lassiter's expression changed. "Cobb, my boy, I hate to be the one to tell you this, but the best-laid plans of mice and men..."

"We're not crossing," Cobb interrupted.

"Nothing to cross to. That lovely little Turkish village you landed in when you flew up from *Saratoga* is no more. No landing field, no town, not even a dock to tie up to. All gone, blown into tomorrow. I don't think they were onto you specifically. Otherwise, your friend the General might have been a little better informed about us. But I think their satellites gave them the message that American aircraft were landing there. What better reason to blow it up?"

"Okay." Cobb pulled up a stool in front of the chart desk. "Where do we go from here?"

Lassiter pointed at the chart. His finger settled on the western end of the Black Sea. "New orders came through from *Sara*—from Pratt, I suppose. We're going to have to make it back by boat. They figure the Russians have airspace control all the way to the Turkish straits and they don't want to lose your general. I'm hoping to refuel at Istanbul." He clapped Cobb on the shoulder. "Then you're in for the ride of your life. NATO really would like to have Keradin in one piece."

D MINUS 1

Pratt postured with a rash of plain language messages directed to the Pentagon to convey his optimism, knowing Moscow would intercept them. Battle group preparation was at a pinnacle. French and Italian naval units were making a magnificent contribution, beyond anything Pratt had expected. Soviet Backfire bombers, testing the readiness of the Americans, had been led by the hand and then shocked at their own inability to either surprise or penetrate the early-warning screen. Totally original antisubmarine tactics had baffled Russian attack submarines lurking in the Gulf of Sidra. And his final message revealed that his man had apparently been successful in removing the head of the Soviet Strategic Rocket Forces alive, though he was not yet in American custody.

The picture in Washington, however, was not so rosy, with the United States and much of NATO presented with an entirely different set of circumstances. KGB disinformation had progressed beyond the USSR's wildest dreams. The Japanese government, after the resignation of the Premier, demanded the departure of the U.S. Seventh Fleet; they claimed it was making a target out of their country. Terrorist activities in the major cities of NATO member countries had succeeded in frightening the general populace, if not their leadership. Industry and business had ceased to function. Transportation was at a standstill. Citizens feared to leave their homes after the threats of assassination and bombing became a reality. As reserve forces were activated and U.S. Military Police appeared in the streets to reinforce local police and militia, newspapers and left-wing organizations called for a halt to war preparations. Evacuation of U.S. dependents further heightened the crisis as the European media hinted darkly that the American intent was to make Central Europe the *only* battlefield.

Washington needed proof that General Keradin was actually in American hands. Soviet television had already countered with television photos of Keradin that morning attending a meeting of the STAVKA, the Main Military Council, and there was no way to prove that the pictures had not been taken previously. At the same time, Moscow announced that their Strategic Rocket Forces were prepared to launch missiles on both NATO countries and the North American continent at the least provocation, with satellite photos and intercepted radio messages from the Soviet Union confirming their state of readiness. The only option for Washington was to counter, bringing the American triad—ICBMs, Trident submarines, and nuclear bombers—to an equivalent state. Only if General Keradin could be delivered into American hands at the appropriate moment and displayed to the world did U.S. leaders feel that the strategic nuclear forces of both countries could stand down. It was absolutely critical that both sides limit the confrontation to conventional weapons.

In the North Atlantic, American naval convoys plowed on toward Europe, surrounded by antisubmarine forces and preceded by specially trained packs of hunter-killer subs. There was still no firm indication whether or not they would be intercepted. First-light photographs of the Svalbard region through partial clouds revealed damage to the Longyearbyen airfield and the Soviet bombers that had been there at the time; but there had been no further communications from the SEAL team, and no final confirmation of how many of the Soviet decoys had been destroyed. Even then, some may already have been delivered along the GIUK gap to counter the American CAPTOR defense line. More Soviet bombers were in the air on the way to Svalbard. If those decoys still existed, and if those bombers could get them to the GIUK gap, there was a good chance the Soviet subs could get through to the U.S. convoys.

Only the political and military leaders of the Soviet Union, NATO, and the U.S. knew how critical the situation was. Actions over the next twenty-four to forty-eight hours would determine the fate of Europe and whether there would be a nuclear barrage. The citizens of those countries knew nothing but the terror that comes of not knowing.

ABOARD U.S.S. *JOHN F. KENNEDY*, SOUTHEAST OF MALTA

Admiral Pratt tentatively picked up the stub of his cigar from his favorite ashtray, with its solid-brass base made of an old five-inch shell, a going-away present from the chief petty officers on his first destroyer. That ashtray traveled the world with Pratt, and today on the eighty-thousand-ton carrier, it remained his pride and joy. Perhaps, he often thought to himself, it's a symbol of the old and the new, the guns-and-guts Navy versus the microchip Navy. The guns have become missile launchers, the guts have become brains—but it still takes a human being to manage either one.

Wendell Nelson studied the cigar along with Pratt. He's not going to light it, he thought, not without burning his nose—it can't be done.

Pratt touched a match to the tip of the cigar, his lips pursed. The end glowed, a flame caught on the dried ends, then smoke issued from the Admiral's mouth. He beamed. "So it works in practice, Nellie."

"Sure as hell does," the other agreed. "But I wouldn't want to try it again before the first real shot. Otherwise some smart Russian skipper is going to run that through his computer." He sipped cold coffee from his mug, gesturing at the graphic printout from *Kennedy*'s computer. "And it's so simple, a fresh-caught sailor could run it if I spent ten minutes with him."

"No complaints from the other COs?"

"You know how it is. No one wants to try something new without playing with it in a trainer on shore first, but when the Russians provided us with a couple of live subs, they went along with me."

Pratt lay the display back on his desk. "I'll have copies run off and heloed over to each commanding officer. I want you and Tom Carleton to run a class for all COs first light tomorrow aboard *Yorktown*."

"That is one thing that might rub a bit." Nelson paused. "I don't think some of those senior skippers were too happy about me taking command of that screen."

"No problem," Pratt said. "When you get back, your XO will probably already have a copy of your new promotion. You're a full captain for the time being, a four striper, the only one in the screen outside of Tom."

Nelson grinned. "They'll be shouting discrimination."

"That's the other thing, Nellie. When you read the small print, you'll see it's only temporary. I couldn't convince the powers-that-be in D.C. Maybe after it's all over, they'll make it permanent."

"Maybe there won't be any Wendell Nelson after it's all over."

"In that case, I'll *insist* they make it permanent—sort of an honor for the deceased hero." Pratt chuckled through the cigar smoke. "Think how happy those survivors' benefits will make the wife and kids!" He immediately knew he had made a mistake. Tricia had divorced Nellie. She had the kids. But Nelson never blinked an eye.

"Too kind . . . too kind. Will you shed some tears at my funeral?"

"I would, Nellie. I really would. But I figure if they get you, then they're more than likely going to get me too. . . ." He was interrupted by a knock. "Come."

Tom Carleton entered the stateroom. As usual, he looked anything but the captain of a ship, especially *Yorktown*. His tan uniform blouse was wrinkled; his belly protruded over his rumpled work pants, and he managed only a pale imitation of a salute as he fell into the couch across from the desk, his legs sprawled straight in front of him.

"How's she going, Tom?"

Carleton beamed. "She's everything the designers claimed—and more. I can't thank you enough. She drives like a tin can and she'll fight like a whole goddamn fleet. No kidding. When we put that system in automatic this morning—Aw, what the hell am I telling you for? You already know what she did."

Pratt nodded. "I was watching in plot. It's kind of hard for an old sailor like me to believe it all." He put the cigar to his lips, winced, and dropped the wet remainder into the ashtray. He sighed, rubbing tired, red-rimmed eyes. "That's why I asked for you two." He picked up a sheaf of messages, weighing them in his hand for a moment, then dropped them back on the cluttered desk. "I expect any of the others could probably handle the job. If the Navy has qualified them, they can run those ships, but there's hardly a soul familiar with that stuff we've been fooling around with in Newport."

"Newport" meant the War College, the think tank where select officers studied global strategy and tactics. There were also war-gaming facilities that lent reality to war scenarios dreamed up by men like Dave Pratt. The Navy power structure claimed the Russians were predictable, and they were in many ways. But no man was that predictable if he was reacting under actual wartime conditions—or if he was losing. That's what Pratt had assumed when he began to play with new tactics. The ships under his Mediterranean command were capable of much more than was required from them under published tactics. The Soviets were expected to attack, and they expected the Americans to wait for the attack, then defend themselves. Pratt's theory was to dig them out before they could possibly gain an upper hand. Computer simulation was the trick.

Pratt loved to call himself an old salt, a grizzled old man of the sea ready for retirement after one more tour. But in reality, he was anything but that. That's why Washington had sent him to *Kennedy*, and that was why they let him take Nelson and Carleton and why they let Pratt choose their ships.

The Russians were experimenting with innovative submarine tactics. Pratt saw what those new tactics were for. When he went to Washington, senior admirals shook their heads. That was not the way they saw the scenario, nor the way they wanted to see it. Pratt went back to Newport and ran his ideas through the computer. The results confirmed that the Russians could do what he projected. The computer also agreed with Pratt on how they might be stopped.

"How're the others doing?" Carleton asked.

"We're halfway there. The base at Svalbard has been damaged. We can see that by satellite, but we don't know how badly. The British have been chasing every sub near there and seem to be holding them off, and I think our own attack subs have set up a barrier to stop anything that gets by our CAPTORS. We already have convoys coming across the North Atlantic that have a chance of making it now."

"And Bernie?" Nelson asked.

"Not a word, Nellie. Satellites have picked up some Soviet movement in the mountains across from that base he was after, but we don't have anything else for sure. The Brits are looking out for him."

"Cobb?"

"He got in and somehow got out with his man. Only Henry could manage that. *Saratoga* forwarded just one message that said they were still in the Black Sea. Admiral Turner also said something about his man picking up Cobb, the Russian, and some woman in an evening dress."

"That means it couldn't be anyone else but Hank," Carleton remarked, shifting his frame on the couch. "Now it's our turn."

"*Saratoga*'s group will catch it first. We may learn something from that. I just hope to hell they can recover Cobb and Keradin and get them here. Then that only leaves us...."

"And the soft underbelly," finished Nelson.

"The soft underbelly," Pratt echoed to himself. He went over to the bulkhead and flipped a switch. Background light glowed softly through a plastic covering. On its surface were blown-up prints of film from recon satellites. Their appearance reminded Nelson of X-rays in a doctor's office—though the body in question was the Mediterranean. One set involved satellite photographs of the surface. Each island, each group of naval ships, even small fishing boats were delineated accurately. Photo interpreters had neatly identified each item on each photo.

The second set was of more interest. It contained infrared readings of what was under the surface of the Mediterranean. Like X-ray cameras, infrared satellites actually looked within the body of the ocean for telltale signatures of submarines. Not all could be located, but enough had been detected to show where the Russian wolf packs were located. Unless they were on active patrol, they tended to congregate either near land or the surface to facilitate communications.

"Leave anything to the imagination?" asked Pratt.

"I can't imagine why there would be the slightest possibility of us losing if we know so much, except . . ."Carleton let that pass. They each knew that the Russians could provide almost the exact same intelligence on their own forces.

It still came down to three things: if Bernie Ryng had been successful and the Russians were cut off from the North Atlantic, if Cobb came out with General Keradin and was able to deliver him in one piece, and if Pratt's battle group could control the Med, then the Soviets might pull back to their own borders, or at least halt their advance. It sounded very simple considered in that regard; it was extremely complex from the point of view of the three men in Pratt's office aboard *Kennedy*.

WITH A U.S. NAVAL PICKET FORCE

Later that day, the ordeal of Admiral Pratt's battle group began two hundred miles to the east of *Kennedy* and about one hundred miles north of the Libyan port of Benghazi. It was here that the guided-missile frigate *Oliver Hazard Perry* was assigned as a picket. She was one of the ships intended as a primary submarine barrier and to provide early warning—if U.S. Hawkeye recon aircraft were knocked out. *Perry*'s basic task in early warning was to engage any Soviet submarine that was intended to take over and direct guidance of air-launched Soviet cruise missiles as they closed their targets.

Perry clearly understood there were enemy submarines in the vicinity. She was the southern element of a four-ship picket squadron, steaming at loose intervals of ten miles, the space between them covered by their own ASW helicopters.

The first indication the little ship had that she was under attack was from her own radar. An object suddenly appeared on her screen, about twenty miles distant on her port bow, traveling at high speed. It was a missile breaking the surface! Launched by a submerged submarine, it appeared sporadically on radar as it flew close to the surface.

Perry's captain instantly ordered his chaff canisters fired in an effort to throw the missile guidance off course. A second missile painted on the radar scope from a separate location. Another submarine!

Her captain understood his odds of steaming alone. He had no antimissile defense other than decoys, or a lucky shot from his one gun mount. His last-ditch effort would be to shoot the missiles down with his Phalanx close-in weapons system. This was a Gatling-type gun atop the hangar that spewed three thousand rounds per minute automatically at an incoming missile. But its range was less than a mile— seconds in the world of missiles. Phalanx would continue firing until its radar informed its computer there was no more missile—or it would keep firing until impact.

Perry's captain turned her stern to the incoming missiles; it would open Phalanx for unobstructed fire. The chaff canisters were reloaded and fired again.

Perry waited. Her crew waited. Her captain waited.

The first missile went awry, the guidance system unable to pinpoint the target. The second missile was more persistent. The ship's single gun mount automatically fired in the direction of the missile—a futile gesture. At fifteen hundred yards, Phalanx opened fire with an incredible racket. A steady stream of bullets raced out, directed by a radar system locked on to the missile.

The noise was so ear shattering, so undeviating, that any member of *Perry*'s crew within eye contact stopped what he was doing. If the missile was shot down, it was a once-in-a-lifetime experience. If the missile impacted, it didn't matter anyway.

At approximately thirty to forty yards distant, the bullets from the Gatling gun exploded the missile's warhead with a tremendous blast. Fragments sprayed *Perry*'s stern, hangar deck, and upper deck, cutting down any man who had stopped to watch. Metal chunks tore into the after one-third of the ship. As *Perry* reeled from the detonation astern, the radar on Phalanx lost its target. Automatically, it ceased fire, mechanically returning to its original position even as metal fragments glanced off its small radome.

Perry's casualties were primarily personnel. Nothing impaired the ship's ability to fight. Her captain wheeled her about and brought her to flank speed to close her attackers.

Aboard the Soviet submarines, the targets were obvious—four American ships, most likely frigates from the sound of their single shafts. Both subs immediately commenced reloading tubes to fire a second set of missiles; their alternate tubes contained torpedoes. It seemed, at this range, to be similar to shooting fish in a barrel. The Americans apparently did not have their helicopters in the path of the submarines. By reloading quickly the Soviets could destroy the targets before they came within torpedo range. Only the two closest American frigates provided any immediate hazard to the submarines—and these were easy targets.

Perry's captain deployed his helicopter in the direction of the missile launch. Within minutes the helo was dipping its sonar in the area where radar had first spotted the missile breaking water.

Contact almost instantly! Two contacts! Three . . . four. The sonar operator was confused—too many different sounds. Decoys! That was it—the minute the Russian submarine heard the initial ping of the sonar, it released decoys. Which was the real target? Which was the phony one?

There was only one way for *Perry* to tell—get weapons in the water! As *Perry* closed, her own sonar picked up contact. One was strong and solid. No doubt about it—classified submarine!

Even as the helo prepared to drop her first homing torpedo, *Perry* came within maximum torpedo range of the contacts. Saturation—that was the best way at this stage. They had no idea how many subs were in the vicinity. Splash! *Perry*'s captain could see the first torpedo fall from the helo. Splash! A second in the water.

Solution complete. Ship's torpedoes ready. Fire! Leaning over the edge of the open bridge, her commanding officer saw three torpedoes leap out of the starboard tubes at short intervals like sprinters, hitting the water with tremendous splashes. One skipped on the surface for an instant, the others dove immediately.

Her commanding officer brought the little ship parallel to the sub's course. Can't close them too much—too good a target.

The helo was on the way back to the ship, her torpedoes expended. He'd launch the second helo with two more torpedoes before retrieving the first. What a hell of a chance he'd be taking, slowing down and maintaining course until he could launch one, bring one home.

But the word came to the bridge with a sudden finality—the hangar doors had been jammed by the near miss of that first missile. They'd have to start cutting—fifteen to twenty minutes before they could get the doors open and clear the deck for launch.

But they couldn't wait! There were at least two enemy subs out there. *Perry* was the only ship prosecuting contacts yet. Other helos were coming in. Someone had to maintain the attack.

There was a report of more missiles breaking the surface. Then, in much less time than anticipated, there was an explosion a few miles off their bow. One of the missiles had locked on to their sister ship's incoming helo, knocking it out of the air. *Perry* was the only one that could keep the subs busy. Her captain turned her directly toward the underwater contacts.

By now, at least one of the torpedoes should have hit, he thought. His binoculars steadied on the horizon above where the subs should be. Nothing. Sonar continued to report multiple noises in the water. Screw beats—submarines, decoys, *Perry*'s sister ship approaching from astern at flank speed. Then a report of an underwater explosion, then a second. Only two! The others must have run off.

Sonar was incapacitated by noise, clutter. The underwater explosions blanked any possibility of determining whether they'd gotten a hit. They were, after all, nuclear attack subs capable of outrunning a torpedo.

Only one thing left to do. Run down their throat. The missiles were for long-range, standoff-type weapons. Close in, they'd have to use torpedoes.

Off their port quarter, there was a rocking explosion,

one that echoed across the water, definitely not from a torpedo hitting below the waterline.

Perry's captain swung his glasses around. He saw only smoke and flame from the direction of their sister ship. She'd taken a hit from that last missile. Now *Perry* was all alone.

No sooner was he aware of that than another voice came over the speaker from sonar—more torpedoes in the water from the submarines! In the confusion, had they streamed their own decoys? Yes! The gunnery officer had seen to that automatically with the first contact. Her NIXIE buoy was streamed astern, creating more noise for a homing torpedo than the ship's propellers.

But *Perry* had nothing else to attack the subs with. No standoff weapons, no depth charges, just her own torpedoes, and he had to reload the starboard side now. His attack would be made with the remaining port torpedoes—three of them. Then he had nothing—nothing until he could launch his second helo!

He came about to tow NIXIE along the track of the incoming torpedoes. As he looked out over the surface of the water, staring in the direction of the unseen torpedoes, various reports arrived on the bridge—another ten minutes to free the hangar doors, about the same time to reload two of the empty torpedo tubes. The third had been damaged by the launch!

The effect of the underwater explosions was diminishing. Sonar again had a definite submarine to port, operating at high speed. New sounds—like a boat breaking up. They *must* have hit one of the subs—one of the five torpedoes must have hit one of them! Other sounds—high-speed screws, more torpedoes approaching from port.

Perry's captain overheard the telltale sounds through the speaker from sonar—a high-pitched squeal increasing in intensity as they drew near. He waited—an explosion astern, water bursting hundreds of feet into the air. One of the torpedoes had homed in on NIXIE! Where was the second? There was no squealing of screws nearby. Both must have gone off at the same spot—the decoy!

The water was once again turbulent. Nothing could be detected by sonar. The captain turned his ship in the direction of the last contact. As soon as he found that sub, he'd fire. There was no logic in giving the Russian any chances. Who could tell which sub had fired the last missiles—the one that had been hit or the one he was after now? If it was the former, he might expect another missile breaking the water any minute. Or was he too close to his quarry? Those subs were faster than his frigate; one had had a chance to run while he'd been evading them. In five minutes, going in opposite directions, the subs might be ten miles apart. One of the subs' computers could feed a solution into its launching system and another missile...

Radar contact port quarter—on the screen—off the screen—high speed—another missile! The damned sub had opened the range while *Perry* was evading! At that range, it would take about a minute to impact.

Sonar gave him a course for the submarine. It had apparently fired a missile, then changed course to come in for a torpedo attack, if necessary. The sub was closing in again! The captain brought *Perry* on a new course to intercept, leaving his Phalanx open.

Even as they settled on the new course, the Phalanx opened up with a deafening roar. Four minutes until they could put the second helo on deck—only one starboard torpedo tube loaded. The second would take longer because maneuvering was delaying the loading.

The shattering sound of the Gatling gun was cut short by the impact of the missile in *Perry*'s midsection. It detonated under the torpedo room. The port-side torpedo tubes were blown over the side; the automatic 76 mm gun was damaged; the nearest gas turbine under the blast was disabled; fires spread quickly on three deck levels. The captain could see nothing of his ship from the impact point on back—he had no idea whether or not she would be able to continue the attack.

He called for the rudder to be put over—*Perry* responded. But with only one engine functioning, his speed had been cut considerably. The torpedoes he had planned to use while they finished reloading the starboard tubes were gone. He had only one torpedo ready, and one helo that he had no idea whether or not he could launch, and a ship that was burning badly.

What he still had was sonar contact, and he conned his ship down the throat. He intended to take the second sub with him. Closing was difficult. His speed was diminished and *Perry* had been holed below the waterline. As he moved through the water, he was forcing the ship to fill faster than it normally would have. He was shortening her life—the weight would slow her and lessen her maneuverability. But that was his last concern at the moment.

Sonar had a solution: they could fire their remaining torpedo! He brought *Perry* to the recommended firing course. He saw his own torpedo hit the water, porpoise for an instant, then dive.

"Sonar reports torpedo running smoothly. Sonar reports other torpedoes in the water." The Russian submarines had also fired at least two tubes. They waited.

Perry was now leaning heavily to port, smoke pouring astern. But she still was able to make about ten knots—she might still have a chance. The captain eased her on to a new course, directing his bow toward the oncoming torpedoes, and waited.

The first hit was *Perry*'s. It was definite. The cheering from sonar spread to the bridge. But the last report from sonar was of torpedoes closing. The sonarman had been making his report just before their own hit. Now they would hear nothing after the explosion in the water; they would not be able to track the incoming torpedoes.

Wham! Perry's bow rose out of the water from the impact, the explosion of the Soviet torpedo lifting her, shaking her 3,500 tons like a child. When she settled back, the bow, from the missile launcher forward, was gone. There was no need for a second torpedo. Flames licked back over the forward section of the ship. Before the captain could give orders to abandon ship, the missiles in the forward magazine exploded. What was left of the little ship plunged like a rock.

A helicopter from one of the two remaining frigates arrived on the scene moments later. It found *Perry*'s sister ship still burning. It found remnants of *Perry* herself. And in separate locations, it identified what were later considered remains of two submarines.

Oliver Hazard Perry had begun the legend of the Battle of the Mediterranean one day prior to D-Day!

SPITZBERGEN

Ryng was aware of an internal struggle. It was the body's automatic reaction to returning consciousness... get those eyes open... identify your surroundings... let the rest of the body know where it is.

One eyelid opened slightly. A sliver of light penetrated, but something else held firm. He reached up tentatively. The eye was crusted. Cautiously, he rubbed, gently removing whatever held it partially shut. He removed his hand. Light flowed in, creating a sharp pain. He blinked, closing his eye, then opening it slowly until the discomfort subsided.

Ryng knew instinctively that he must locate his surroundings before moving. But nothing registered. Nothing. Sand, gravel, pebbles. A breeze blew something that brushed his face. He rolled the eye up. A bush of some kind.

Svalbard! That was it! Spitzbergen—that island in the middle of nowhere. Longyearbyen! Russian bombers. Black Berets. Their boat. Theirs? That's right. Denny? Forget it. Denny's dead—no head left. I'm alive.

Why? Rockets... machine guns... depth charges...

Hold it! That's it... depth charges. That's what happened. Son of a bitch! It came back now... flash...

flash . . . flash! The tremendous kick in the guts . . . shit, no! All over. That's what happened. I swam for it. Helo disappeared for some reason . . . smoke! That's it! That's why I'm still alive. The son of a bitch couldn't stay up any longer . . . maybe thought I was dead. But, a signpost in his unconscious flashed—I survived!

Smell returned. And with it his stomach churned, for he was lying in his own vomit. It wasn't just salt water. That's why his eyes were stuck shut—must have been face down in the stuff!

Cautiously he rubbed around the other eye, gently blinking it open. Christ, they stung. Why the hell shouldn't they? Salt water, gravel—what a hell of a paste.

He rolled slightly to search for the sun. Forget it! Almost twenty-four hours of sun up here—no way to tell the time.

He was about to get to his knees when something in his subconscious rebelled. Listen!

There it was, only louder now. The realization came quickly. Only one thing made that steady, monotonous tone, that thrum, that relentless beat as it drew closer. He couldn't see it, but he knew without a doubt it was a helicopter.

No dummies, those Soviet marines! They knew better. They were trained just like he had been. No body, no proof of death. Bring back the body and that job's finished, then get on to the next body.

That helo that had gone down smoking must have informed base that they were dropping depth charges, using their last available weapon because they'd seen a body still moving down there. They'd all know there was no reason it should survive a depth charge. But that they were also the type that knew, just like he would, that you never trust to luck—or even probability—that your enemy is dead if your enemy had just done what Ryng's team had. Bring us a body, their leader would say, or just part of one. An arm or a leg will do. But bring back something to prove we don't have to worry for the time being.

Whump . . . whump . . . whump. Now he knew where it was—almost overhead. They hadn't seen him or the change in rotor beat would have indicated that they were hovering.

But they were covering that forsaken beach very slowly, looking for any trace that would either prove he was dead or tell them where he'd gotten to.

Ryng rolled his head, staring up. He was looking through the branches of the scrub brush. He put his head back down, satisfied that he was under some sort of cover for the time being. He felt the ooze as he rested his head on the ground, but there was no point in moving. Even as the stink came back to him again, he knew he would be crazy if he moved another muscle.

Almost on top of him now. He could feel the draft of the rotors. He caught the first movement of the bush above him, then the increased shaking as the helo passed directly overhead. Dust churned up around him, assaulting his eyes, working into his nose and mouth. Instinctively, he moved both hands over his face, covering it as best he could without moving the rest of his body. He would be harder to see through the dust, but he was damned if he'd do anything that would give them the slightest chance. There wasn't much cover around him. The brush was about the only thing he remembered that gave any shelter as he crawled up that beach. But when? Minutes, or hours ago?

Don't move, he ordered himself. No automatic reactions. Don't roll over. Don't pull your knees up. Don't do a damned thing but cover your face. Save those senses 'cause you're going to need them later. Blow it now, and all you'll know is lead. The last sound you will hear, Mr. Ryng, his brain repeated again and again, is your own scream. So just take your shit like a man and in a few moments they'll move on and you can take inventory. In just a few moments, you'll find out whether you can move, whether you're going to have a chance of getting your ass out of here, or whether carrion-eating seagulls are eventually going to lead them to your body. Again and again, the same voice repeated itself, just as he had trained himself to do years before, letting the mind take over, letting it control the body. Sometimes it made the body do superhuman things and sometimes it taught the body to stop.

The helo drifted away, moving on down the beach slowly

in a crisscross pattern. Ryng rolled over now and peered out. The water was twenty-five yards away from where he lay. Must've been a hell of a crawl, he thought. Why no trail? He dug at the ground. Nothing could leave much of a path in this crap. It was hard—sand and mud packed together. Like the silt that came from under glaciers, he realized, only this stuff had had time to harden. There was gravel too, and some pebbles, but no rocks. They likely had been ground into those few pebbles by some past glacier.

Inland, away from the water, no more than another 100 yards away, the mountains rose up sharply from sheer cliffs. Nothing grew on them; nothing could grow between the climate and the vertical surface. That's what made it so easy for that helo. The space between the water and the cliffs, which no man was going to climb, couldn't have been more than a 150 yards. It was simple to swing the bird back and forth. No need for a search plan. Just cover every inch of ground.

It was also no place to stay. He looked toward the west, where the safety of the open ocean should be, where the remainder of his team was supposed to meet sometime. But he had no idea when. He had no concept of time, how long he'd been unconscious.

There were two items that occupied Bernie Ryng's mind at this stage. The first was wholly instinctive—survival—and was the first order of business. But the second meant almost as much to him, for he was a military man and order and discipline was vitally important. He had been sent on a mission by a man he loved and respected and who was depending on him. It was vital that Dave Pratt know that much of the mission had been carried out. The decoys that had already been unloaded at Longyearbyen airport had been destroyed. The aircraft intended to carry them would never fly again. Most important, the ship that carried those decoys to Spitzbergen, and still had much of that cargo on board ready to be unloaded and taken to the airport, had been sunk in deep water. That last element was the most critical, the factor that North Atlantic strategy would be based upon in the coming hours. He had to get that information to Pratt.

Ryng reached inside his shirt, searching for the chart of the harbor area. What he extracted was a soggy mess, still neatly folded but decidedly wet. With the care and precision brought on by years of training, he unfolded it gently. Open it to the first fold, he told himself. Stop. Pat it flat out. Make sure no edges are tucked under that are going to tear on the next fold...

As he followed each step of the process, a chill came over him. He shivered involuntarily. His shirt and pants were damp but not wet. That meant he'd been out of the water long enough for the combination of body heat and air to evaporate much of the water. But then again, his uniform was designed to dry quickly for just such occasions.

Not more than two hours, he determined, otherwise he might be even colder, his body temperature lower. Then hypothermia. That would be his greatest enemy. This time of year, a fifty-degree day was balmy. But at least the sky was clear, the air dry.

The chart lay flat in his lap. He saw where he was and what he would have to do. The map was printed to withstand immersion. And now he silently thanked some cartographic clerk back in the States who'd made sure the job was done right when he transposed the satellite data onto the chart.

Ryng saw the glacial stream that came down near where he now sat, the one they'd seen from the boat before the helo attacked. He stood up to check—a couple of hundred yards away. Using his thumbnail, he marked the rough surface to the meeting point. Twelve, fifteen miles, no more. Nothing like thumbnail navigation.

A couple of miles down the beach, he saw the helo turn out over the water and head back toward its base. But don't kid yourself. They're not going to give up that easy. Maybe they'll go back, but just maybe they'll swing out and then dash back to see if they fooled you. Remember, there's no such thing as a dead man until you have a body—or a piece of one! Grab your ass and lead on out of here, but remember that body they want. Better yet, think about a separate arm or leg!

The next instant when he raised his head, the helo had reversed course, returning to his side of the harbor, just as he'd suspected!

With that he started out, moving from one clump of scrub to the next, mindful of the helo which now seemed intent on searching a section of water a few miles farther on. "Thank God you had the good sense to keep these shoes," he muttered outloud to himself. He could feel the sharp pebbles through his soles, some smooth like bullets, but others, rolled the wrong way underneath all that ice, were sharp as arrowheads.

At the glacial stream, he stopped to check the helo. It was still zipping back and forth on some inane path in an exercise that didn't make sense. The stream wasn't at all deep. It was a miniature flood plain, a delta at the base of a tiny glacier now receded back into the mountains. This time of year, it exuded a steady flow of water, but not enough to cut a deep trench.

Gingerly, he stepped out, his eye already on more scrub fifty yards away on the other side. He lurched forward, his foot sinking up to the ankle. Taking a second step, he again sank in. Pulling, the rear foot made a sucking sound as it escaped from the grayish-brown silt. Wherever the water ran, the damn stuff was just mud, he thought. Each step was an effort, the mud clinging, pulling relentlessly at his shoes. It would take twice as long as he'd estimated to get across. If the helo came back . . .

He struggled on, trying to move faster. But he could only move so fast. The last half dozen hours had taken their toll. No one could put his body through what his had already done and cut through this stuff like a sprinter.

The water and the mud were cold—ice cold, glacier cold. He could feel the creeping numbness in his feet. Perhaps it would be easier if he couldn't feel anything. Just plod along, steady pace, no discomfort, perhaps eventually move faster.

He was finally halfway across. No wonder I wanted to get the boat to the other side of this crap before they attacked, he thought. He'd forgotten to look more closely at his map to see how many more of these little streams there were.

Too many and he might as well kiss it all good-bye. It was taking so long it was more like crossing a river.

He looked back out to the helo. Same place. No, wait a minute. He remembered the peak he had been sighting it against. The helo was to the left of that now. As he staggered along, muddy step after muddy step, he watched its perspective change. Damn! He's headed back this way.

He thought of his tracks and then he thought of a wounded animal in the snow. No shit, Ryng, you should have waited until he got low on fuel and headed back for a drink. Now you've got yourself in a hell of a fix! He felt his heart beat faster, partly from exertion, partly from fear, as he attempted to pick up the pace, one sucking, muddy, numbing footstep at a time.

The helo wasn't racing back. No need to. No one on that godforsaken coastline was going to go anywhere fast. He knew it. They knew it. Shit!

He faltered and stopped for a minute as one of his shoes began to slip off. It would be foolish to leave it behind, just on the off chance that he might get away this time. He stopped, reset his foot in the muck, gripped with his toes, and lifted. The foot came out with the same sucking sound, the shoe still on it, covered with mud, only the small amount of sensation he had left in his feet convincing him that the shoe was still there.

Checking the angle on the helo, he saw it closing in steadily but still not quickly. Perhaps there was a chance to make it. With ten yards to go, he literally dove toward the scrub, arms stretched in front, waving in the air.

And then he was free, his feet suddenly released from the mud. It threw him off balance, and before he could catch himself, he was pitching forward, no longer held up by the thick silt. Putting his hands out, he covered the last few yards on all fours like a crab, rolling under the brush. Breathing with deep, racking sobs from the exertion, he pictured tracks across the mud of that stream pointing out his frail hiding spot—just like landing lights.

The beat of the rotors were sharper than when he awakened before. Now all his senses were alert. Not only did

he know where he was and what he was trying to do, he
also knew that he'd now covered all of three hundred yards
and was cowering under a bit of scrub brush like a dog
waiting for the whip to fall. The deep breathing helped. The
oxygen, the blood racing through his system, all of his
muscles active for a few brief moments, each of these were
warning him, making him more alert. Moments before, he
had been thinking hypothermia, that slow reduction in the
body's temperature until all feeling and caring disappeared
and you gave up. Now there was no intention of giving up.
Just don't be so damn stupid next time—if there is a next
time. Don't try to outthink a helo, Ryng. If you let it go
away, it'll let you go away.

And then it was directly overhead, the rotors again beating the dust and pebbles into his skin with a deafening roar.
It banked slightly, passing within yards of the cliff, then
swung back over him, crossing the stream toward his first
hiding place, then again sweeping back over the stream.

This is it! Ryng thought. It's following the goddamned
wounded beast, the blood in the snow. But it passed overhead again, moving down the shoreline, then out over the
water.

Ryng waited, his body immobilized, his brain still unable
to ascertain why the helo hadn't gone into a hover directly
above him before blasting wildly with its machine guns.
Then the sound drifted farther away. He turned his head.
Off over the water, he could see the helo headed in the
direction of Longyearbyen. He could tell by the sound of
the engine that it was traveling close to full speed. It wouldn't
be back—at least not until it was refueled.

He sat up amazed, shaking his head over his good luck.
Then he stood, searching the stream. There were no prints!
Looking more closely, he saw that the water, an opaque,
milky mixture from the detritus that flowed from the glacier,
had quickly covered his tracks. Already the silt was beginning to fill the holes where his feet had been.

With the knowledge that there was no time to ponder his
good luck, he turned west, moving off at a good pace. If
he were hiking under normal conditions—on flat ground,

no mountains, no streams, no tundra—he could cover the distance in five or six hours. He was in good enough condition, but there *was* that slight problem of mountains and streams and tundra, not to mention the beating his body had taken recently or the probability that helicopters, perhaps more than one, would be back. And there was another problem—the fact that he had no weapons.

As he traveled, sometimes changing his pace to a trot, he reviewed the time that had passed since landing on Spitzbergen. He decided it had to be mid- to late afternoon, and that he had anywhere from eight to ten hours left before the others were picked up by the Norwegian boat.

An inlet lay ahead that cut into a narrow valley. Ryng wanted desperately to get away from the narrow beachhead he was now covering. Its 150-yard width offered very little protection, a thought that kept him looking over his shoulder in the direction of Longyearbyen every minute or so. His chart showed a stream, a real one this time, that coursed out of the mountains to this inlet. It appeared narrow and deeper than the glacial runoff that had almost trapped him.

It was a few miles from the spot where the last helo had passed over him. There was no mud or silt to form a plain in this one, or at least it was hemmed in by the natural gully of the stream. Ryng fell to his knees, cupping the water and sipping slowly from his hands. Not too fast—his stomach was empty. Then he bent farther over and splashed the water over his face, onto his head, and down his neck. He could feel the caked mass in his hair breaking up under the make-shift bath and thanked whatever had saved him for also being sure that nobody saw him looking like that. The water was cold, but the exertion had warmed his body to the point that his earlier chill was gone. Ryng knew that if it had been a few weeks later, or one more of those arctic storms had come over the island, that his odds of getting away would have been very slim indeed.

After sipping some more of the water, he extracted the chart from his shirt. It was as accurate as Naval Intelligence could make it. As soon as the Norwegians had reported strange happenings in their territory, intelligence satellites had been repositioned to photograph the entire island. Highly specialized cartographers had then compared the photos to the latest charts in stock. It was a necessary exercise because they could detect annual changes in a particular area—in this case, the terminus of glaciers and the places where a man could and could not pass freely.

The stream he now sat by would be of no use. It worked quickly back into the mountains in a series of sharp falls. And at this point, the coast of the harbor narrowed even more than its current 150 yards. The cliffs facing across toward the Soviet base became sheer—impossible to climb.

He would have to cross the stream a few hundred yards up, then turn into the higher country. While the cliffs facing the harbor were impossible, their reverse side was much gentler, sloping into a series of glacier-scooped hanging valleys. Water runoff from the receding glaciers allowed some vegetation that would provide cover from time to time. Ryng could make it almost in a straight shot, except for the last peak, which was part of a westward-facing range— toward the ocean and safety. That one was steeper and would involve climbing in snow on one side and likely a long slide down the other, for he would briefly find himself crossing year-round snowfields.

As he slipped the chart inside his shirt, a growling in his stomach reminded him how empty it was. There was little chance of finding anything to eat. Svalbard was so far north, merely a thousand miles or so from the North Pole, that only a few species of animal life could survive here. Although polar bears, reindeer, and sea birds seemed to thrive in the harsh climate, Ryng had nothing that could kill one. Better to forget the hunger and concentrate on getting the hell out as fast as possible, Ryng realized. If he didn't get to the meeting place in time, he could plan on a most unpleasant stay.

For the next half hour, he climbed a slope toward the first valley. The climb was gentle at first and then steeper as he came near the lip. Once over the top, there was another gentle slope where he could again pick up his pace without tiring himself. There were no trees, nothing that might provide a hiding place when they came back searching for him—which was another aspect to worry about. There was no longer the early warning of the helo coming across the broad harbor. The peaks would blot out the sound, and he would know nothing about them until a helo cleared a peak and came down toward him. They had the advantage this time.

As he progressed, he planned each few hundred yards, determining where he would duck if he suddenly heard the telltale sound of that engine. Unless they were lucky, they wouldn't spot him instantly. There would be time, however short, to run for cover—unless he was directly in their line of sight as they came over the top.

The terrain varied between the hard surface of gravel and dirt and the softness of ground cover that Ryng decided must be tundra. He had never been in such a place before and his knowledge of what the terrain might be was limited to what he had read in books and training manuals. The land provided a cushion in spots, giving slightly as he moved along. It was almost like walking on a mattress.

What he wasn't prepared for, however, was the water underneath the vegetation. Quite unexpectedly, his foot sank through. Water squished icily around his feet, the ground shaking like jelly. Each step became more difficult, forcing him to head toward a side where the gravelly, hard surface could be seen again. But as he moved toward the solid ground, he found that he was also crossing a more dangerous area. Now his feet broke through with each step, sometimes sinking halfway up his shin before he could pull out of it. He had read about the tundra before and how during the warm weather it could melt down for a few feet. It would become almost impassable at that point. Now Ryng knew exactly why.

And as he struggled for the edge, he heard the ominous sound of rotors again. Looking up to his left, he saw a helo just clearing the ridge above him. As the fuselage came into view outlined against the clear sky he could see the rockets on either side, the machine gun pods suspended farther out. If it kept on the same course, it would pass right in front of him. Should he simply throw himself face down in the quaking tundra, lying out in the open, hoping not to be seen yet realizing what a simple target he provided? Or should he try to run for it, stumbling across the remainder of the bog, trying to get to the shelter of a boulder at the edge?

He decided to run. Struggling against the suction of the bog, adrenaline coursed through his system. He somehow knew that if the helo turned at all in his direction, he would have to dive forward, hoping the unfriendly tundra would somehow cover him, close over him until the helo passed over.

It was like a goddamn dream. No matter where you go, Ryng thought, something always chases you, and no matter how fast you try to move, something drags at your feet so you can't get away fast enough. It didn't make any difference to Ryng whether it was thick, oozing silt or a bog in a hidden valley. The result was the same. He couldn't move fast enough and there was a helicopter searching for him and the people in it wanted him dead and they had more than enough in the way of weapons to make him dead. The thought passed through his mind again that all their commander needed was a body, *or even a piece of a body,* as evidence, and that made him frantic enough to push beyond normal bodily limits.

The helo remained on the same course long enough for him to make a last desperate plunge out of the bog. He slid nose first behind the boulder, which was large enough to conceal him. If the helo came toward him, he could huddle close enough and crawl around the rock if the craft came down to circle and inspect.

And that's finally what it did. It came down low enough so that Ryng wasn't sure whether they saw the prints he'd made or not. Unfortunately, this time there was no colored water to cover his path. In his anxiety to escape the cloying vegetation, he had torn it. Tufts of roots and gnarled vegetation stuck out in every direction. From his vantage point, it was like a well-marked trail. The helo slowed, and perhaps the occupants did see that the ground cover had been disturbed by something. They hovered for a moment, then slowly came over by the boulder, passing on the opposite side, then swinging out and heading back on the side where Ryng had been cowering. Snakelike, he crawled around the base, always placing it between himself and the eyes in the helo.

After another pass over the tundra, the helo skipped up over the peak and disappeared from Ryng's view.

He waited, somehow sensing they had been disturbed by the change in the ground cover. If he had been in the cockpit, Ryng would have known that they were concerned, that they had seen the torn bog, and that they would report it when they got back to base. But having been on Svalbard for less than a week, the two men in the helo temporarily dismissed the situation—probably a bear. They knew there were bears on the island, but they had no idea that they remained on the other end, preferring the perpetual snow cover or ocean to the barren rock and human population to the south. But when they reported the tracks later, the base commander would know that no bear would have been in that spot, and he would be in the next helo.

LONGYEARBYEN

Back at Longyearbyen Airport, smoke still drifted from the wreckage of the Soviet bombers. Colonel Mikhail Bulgan removed his black beret, unconsciously wiping his forehead as if he were perspiring before he replaced it. He was deep in thought, studying the cartographic map that his own intelligence staff had provided the day they had been airlifted from their Pechenga base to Spitzbergen. Alongside the chart, staring back at him, was a photograph of Bernie Ryng. It was no more than a mug shot, the same type that appears on passports. This one was an I.D. photo from Pentagon files.

There was no doubt in the GRU's mind that Ryng was the leader of the SEAL team. The exact time he had left the U.S., and how he had gotten to the remote island, were still items they hadn't determined. But that information wasn't necessary. That they knew who he was and how he operated was all that Bulgan cared about. The Colonel would have given almost anything to have such a man on his side, and he hesitated momentarily at the idea of killing such a talent. On the other hand, men like Ryng were not the kind to change allegiance or to allow capture. Exterminating Ryng was Bulgan's duty to himself and the Motherland. Though he had no idea of the efficacy of the decoy plan, he knew

that Ryng had succeeded where he, Bulgan, had failed.
Getting Ryng would be his last act as a Soviet officer—
and it would be an act of satisfying revenge.

So it was a matter of finding and doing away with the
man. Bulgan knew Ryng would have done the same to him.
A large red cross marked their last contact with him—
thrashing in the water just off the glacial stream entering
the harbor. A few miles past that, the shoreline turned into
sheer cliffs. There was no man, especially one on the run
and without the necessary resources, who would attempt
those.

Bulgan knew what he would do—and he considered
himself almost the equal of Ryng. The file indicated that
Ryng was no mountain climber. But he was an escape artist
if ever there was one. American training included traveling
long distances without sustenance, yet Bulgan knew Ryng
could find something if it was available. Obviously the man
was unarmed, or at least should have been after being thrown
from his raft. It was likely that Ryng escaped with only his
wits. But the GRU emphasized that unless the man was
wounded, he still had an advantage over most other men.

The Colonel traced a path on the map with his finger—
up a streambed, then left into the hidden valleys that rose
in an easy progression toward the final range before the
Greenland Sea. Once on the opposite side, the down side,
Bulgan knew that Ryng might very well have protection.

Colonel Bulgan was a hard-looking man. In an American
uniform he would have resembled a U.S. Marine with his
close-cropped hair, square jaw, and well-muscled, fit body.
In many ways, he thought like a Marine, and that was to
his advantage in this case.

The thrum of the rotors outside interrupted his thoughts,
and Bulgan rose to greet the returning helo. As he watched
the craft settle outside his command post, he knew immediately by the still-loaded weapons that they had found no
sign of Ryng. Damn! Not only had the man succeeded
admirably in his mission, he had ruined Bulgan's.

Inside, the two men showed Bulgan where they had been,

carefully transferring their rough marks onto his larger chart. They studied the recon photos closely, comparing chart terrain to satellite view. Colonel Bulgan could see how inexperienced men could have been fooled by Ryng, even with the limited hiding spots. But he also knew that his assumption about Ryng's path was probably 90 percent correct. It was going to take a man with similar training and temperament to ferret out this American.

Bulgan used his dividers to cover the projected course to the peak, then marked off the distance on the chart. He guessed roughly how much distance Ryng could travel each hour, marking in current time where he thought the man would be. Once he checked, then rechecked the assumed track, he again closed his eyes, unconsciously removing the black beret and running his hands through his hair. In his mind's eye, he determined where he would like to trap the American. When he was sure, he marked that general area with a red pencil and again checked off the distance.

In about six hours, give or take half an hour, Ryng should be beginning the climb on that last peak through the snowfields. There were no places to hide there. It had to be an open climb, some of the time working sideways to avoid perpendicular cliff faces. Bulgan yawned and stretched, then gave orders to his aide to awaken him in four and a half hours. He wanted a helo ready then. If Bulgan had realized that the ship with the remaining decoys had blown up outside the harbor and that there was no chance at all to resurrect the Longyearbyen mission, he never would have allowed himself the final luxury of a nap.

ABOARD A HYDROFOIL
ON THE BLACK SEA

The run across the Black Sea to the Bosporus entrance to the Turkish straits would take about eight hours—and 90 percent of their fuel supply. The last three hours would be in daylight and more dangerous. Lassiter explained to Henry Cobb that the only advantage they had was that they were riding a Russian boat in a Russian sea under Russian air cover. Once they approached the Turkish coast, a Soviet boat would be in unfriendly waters. War, though not yet declared, was a foregone conclusion as far as the Turks were concerned.

The last message to Lassiter explained that the Turkish government had been advised that their boat would be approaching Turkish waters early that morning and that it would be refueling at Istanbul. Somehow, Lassiter explained, he doubted that every single gunner in the Turkish military had been informed that a Soviet hydrofoil flying an American flag was to be allowed to pass without a second look. It just didn't make sense, considering all that Turkey had been through over the past few days and considering that much of the trouble had been due to the Russians' interference.

During the night passage, Soviet aircraft would swoop

down to missile range, breaking off each time Lassiter's electronic identification system would provide a friendly response. Turkish aircraft did not yet have the luxury of closing in on them. Though there was no declared war, the Soviets would chase the Turks back whenever they approached Russian airspace.

First light brought with it the sight of land, a low, hazy line to westward. The only one at all rested was Keradin. Since Lassiter spent almost all of his time in the wheelhouse, it was up to Cobb and Verra to keep watch over the Russian. When a turn came to rest, sleep was almost impossible. Lassiter insisted on the fastest speed consistent with arriving in one piece. He was unconcerned if the boat disintegrated thirty seconds after they finished with it, so they were able to maintain about forty knots an hour. The constant vibration, the roll of the boat from side to side as it slid down the swells, the bouncing to bring it back on course, each made sleep a wish rather than a reality. Cobb was used to going for two, even three days without much sleep but this was a test of his endurance. Even with an earlier nap, the hot day in the vineyards had done nothing to improve his strength.

As they approached the coast, Turkish jets came out to meet the Russian fighters that seemed to have escorted them. This time they did not scare away. No doubt the Turks' aggressiveness was a surprise to the Russians. To Keradin, it was even more of a surprise as he was allowed on deck to see the midair missile exchange. There was no way to determine who was winning, but the fight allowed Lassiter to bring their little boat to maximum speed as he rocketed for the safety of the Bosporus channel ahead.

As their Soviet flag was lowered, Lassiter made a thing of showing Keradin his pleasure in dropping it over the side. In its place, an American ensign appeared, a large one so that, as Lassiter explained, there would be no doubt about who owned the boat now.

The entrance to the Bosporus is at the far western end of the Black Sea. It is a natural strait dividing Turkey and narrowing in some sections to less than a half mile wide.

It is defensible from both sides and at the moment the Turks still owned those defenses.

Cobb yawned, trying to stretch the tired ache out of his muscles. "I'd like to keep our Russian friend on deck," he said to Lassiter. "Sort of rub his nose in it a little. Got anything aboard that we might use to keep him in one piece?"

"As a matter of fact, I have just the thing for you." Lassiter laughed. "It seems the Russians are very discipline conscious, even in little boats like this one. They've got a little brig up forward, not much bigger than a head. Even comes equipped with handcuffs, chains—that sort of thing."

"How about if we hook him up to the mast?" He pointed just outside the wheelhouse to the stanchions anchoring the electronics mast. "It'll give him a bit of a tether if people start shooting, but it'll also relieve one of us from watching him." He grinned. "And it'll let him see the new world he's going into."

"Going to put any clothes on him?"

"No more than he has now. A man in his underwear somehow isn't as brave. Besides," and he tested the air with a wet finger, "it's going to be a lovely day. He could use a bit of sun. He's a little pale."

The General displayed a weariness, or perhaps it was resignation. Something about captivity can alter the features of even the strongest person. His jaw no longer jutted out. His eyes no longer played the game of trying to hold Cobb's. There was no chance of escaping. It was evident that they wanted to keep him alive now that they'd gotten him this far. For the most part, Keradin would have preferred death now that the chance of escape was so slim.

Keradin peered down at the shackle on his ankle, studying the three feet of chain. "I see you are most thorough," he addressed Cobb. His mouth was a thin line. "May I now have some clothes?"

"Are you chilly?"

"No. But a man needs a certain amount of dignity. I am a general in the Soviet armed forces. I would expect you to treat me in the same manner and extend the same courtesies that I would offer you as a prisoner."

"I am," Cobb growled, fingering the side of his head where the foreman had hit him the evening before. "Be glad you have your shorts."

The General scowled back without a word.

Henry Cobb could afford to present a cavalier attitude before Keradin, for the most difficult part seemed to be complete. He had accomplished the near impossible and removed the General from a supposedly secure position. But this man—so vital to American strategy—must now be kept alive and turned over to Pratt's people as quickly as possible. Cobb did not pretend to understand the fine points of the plan, but he knew intuitively that the loss of such a high-placed man was intended to put the Soviets off balance at a crucial point in this crisis. Since Dave Pratt had entrusted Keradin's return to Cobb, Cobb would do his damnedest to deliver Keradin.

Lassiter had the crew fully armed at this point. Somehow, Cobb noted, they had come up with some pretty fair armaments, considering the nature of the operation—old fashioned bazookas, modern antitank weapons, some wire guided rockets, and an assortment of grenade launchers and mortars. Lassiter did not trust a soul. That was why he, like Cobb, was a survivor.

They sped down the Bosporus, weaving constantly. This satisfied Cobb, who did not take the idea of being a target lightly. He operated furtively. This open-air approach was not to his liking. At every bend, he expected a surge of weapons fire to sweep the deck. But the passage was a safe one.

Within half an hour, the distant hills of Istanbul rose through the morning haze. As they came closer, the farms on the shore gave way to small factories, then to smokestacks, then to a combination of new construction interspersed with dwellings put up before the United States became a nation.

Istanbul is called the City of Seven Hills, once surrounded by nearly impregnable walls built down to the water. It's Old City surrounded on three sides by water and thus well fortified, stands on the Golden Horn. The New City, to the northeast and across the Galata Bridge, is not nearly so fascinating.

Their boat slowed to a crawl to navigate through the heavy commercial traffic of this major seaport. Slender, graceful minarets towered above the mosques of the Moslem city. They were to fuel at the Sirkeci Ferry Pier. It was directly ahead as they exited the Bosporus into the widening Sea of Marmara.

Lassiter was the tour guide. He pointed out the first hill atop the Golden Horn, which ended in Seraglio Point. The Ataturk Monument and the Topkapi Palace were to their left. The waterways of the ancient city bustled as if there were nothing of concern, no recent war with Greece, no Soviet planes gradually encroaching on their airspace, no fear of the Russian warships that continually passed on their way to the Mediterranean. The small Russian boat flying the American flag was a fearful-looking craft with her assortment of weapons displayed on deck. She was given a wide berth as she stood half a mile off the pier. Lassiter intended to drift and watch for a while.

Verra, her eyes continually wandering back to Keradin, remained close to Cobb. "It's beautiful," she murmured sleepily. "I've never seen anything like this, never traveled before."

Cobb smiled. Now that he had a few moments with nothing to concern him other than eventually getting back to *Saratoga*, he studied her more closely. She was young— young enough to be his daughter—but so grown up after being at Keradin's vineyards. And she was tough too. She had to be to come out of that experience the way she had. Verra was relaxed. Her face had softened considerably from the vixen who had wanted to emasculate Keradin on the spot. She would have too, Cobb acknowledged, smiling. He felt an affection for her, much different than he imagined a man would have for a daughter. It was something he had not felt for a long time, something he had long ago told himself he should avoid.

He pondered the idea for a second, imagining a life he

knew he wasn't cut out for, studying the wisps of hair that blew over her face as she stared, fascinated, at the ancient city. Cobb, he reminded himself, you're getting too old, too old to handle sleepless nights because you're letting a kid, a female kid, turn your head. There's work to do, my friend, much work before you can think about such things.

His mind drifted back to other operations—steamy jungles in Vietnam, midnight landings in rubber rafts in the Caribbean, one in South Africa, another in Libya, and then the drinking afterward, disdaining sleep in the heady excitement of close-in fighting, and finally coming out of it all alive! There were moments now when he knew he wasn't functioning on that level. This time he wanted to get it over with, get it done, and get the hell out with his skin intact. And a kid, a female—no, a woman in every sense of the word—was occupying his mind.

"Why are we waiting out here?" she inquired.

Cobb pointed at Lassiter, who was still surveying the docks through his binoculars. "After you've been in this business long enough, you tend not to trust anyone or anything but yourself. That's where we're supposed to fuel." He pointed straight ahead to the pier, easily identified by the Sirkeci railroad station looming over it. "The Turks expect us. Our own people spent hours explaining how we'd be in a Soviet boat with an American flag. But anything can happen. An old philosopher friend of ours, Bernie Ryng, once said, 'Never trust a soul and you'll live to tell someone else the same thing.'"

"Do you believe that?" Verra asked.

"Absolutely." He did not mention that Ryng, the perennial bachelor, had also said that there was no place for women in their business, that you saved them only for when you needed them.

"Do you trust me?" she asked him.

Cobb looked down. She waited calmly for his answer, her eyes never leaving his. Even Ryng would allow him an occasional lapse. "Yes. I trust you, but I also had an alternate plan if you turned on me." He shrugged. "We'll never know if it would have worked, will we?"

"I don't know you, but I trusted you," she whispered. "And you brought me out of there."

Cobb smiled. "That statement from the great Ryng did not include every single person on the face of this earth. You may always trust me. If you ever meet the great Ryng, please trust him too. And," he gestured toward Lassiter, "that is a man I trust, so you can stick with him also."

"Just the three of you?" She smiled. "Only three men in the whole wide world?"

"There are others, some old friends of mine."

"Will I get to meet them?"

"I don't know if I want to share the likes of them with you." Now what the hell did he mean by that? She didn't belong to him, and he didn't belong to her. "Yes. I hope you will," he concluded.

The boat rocked in the gentle wavelets created by the heavy flow of traffic off the Golden Horn. Wafting across the harbor were a variety of aromas similar to those that had fascinated Cobb in so many other seaports. Each one was different, each had its own special appeal.

Lassiter dropped his binoculars and gestured for Cobb to come up with him. "Here, sweep those docks starting about a hundred yards to the left of our pier. Then go to the right, up to about the Galata Bridge."

Cobb closed his eyes. He squeezed them tight, then opened them, pressed against the lenses. They adjusted quickly. He first saw what he expected, a variety of craft tied to various piers, trucks outside warehouses, stacks of goods on pallets—Wait a second—fire trucks, wisps of smoke here and there, uniforms. Must be military. Not a lot of smoke, not enough to cause concern, but nevertheless, he could locate at least three distinct spots where light smoke was driven to the north before it rose far into the sky.

"What do you make of it?" Lassiter asked.

"If there was much of a fire in any of those locations, they're pretty much out now or they never amounted to much to begin with. Looks safe enough to me now."

"Yeah. It does to me too. But how often do you have that many fires all near the same spot, namely the one we want to refuel at?"

Cobb knew Lassiter wasn't looking for an opinion. "Not every day, Cap'n."

"We're gonna' ease in. I want everybody ready, but I don't want them to look like we're going to sack Turkey either. I never trust anybody."

Cobb jerked his head in Keradin's direction. "What about him?"

"Looks fine to me." The General was leaning against one of the mast stanchions, his arms folded casually, attempting to look as dignified as a man could chained to a mast in his underwear. "He'll make people think we mean business. And if we have Russian problems up there, he'll either keep away unfriendly fire or draw it—one or the other."

Cobb again looked through the binoculars. This time he had a better view of some armed craft similar to their own. At first he thought they were tied up to the piers, but now he could tell they were idling nearby, the exhaust from their engines clearer now at this range. "What do you make of those gunboats in there?"

"Turkish patrol craft. Built right here in yards in the city. They're pretty well armed, and as fast as this, but they keep them pretty close to home, I'm told. Guard the capital city, that sort of thing."

"They're sure as hell not tied up."

"Here, let me take a look." Lassiter studied them through the glasses. "All the more reason to be careful. They must be waiting for something."

They were now no more than a hundred yards off the pier. They could see line handlers waiting for them to come alongside. "Yeah. . . ." Lassiter's face was grim as he sniffed the smoke in the air. "Perhaps they're screwing with us."

"Perhaps." Both men were standing easy now as the hydrofoil idled slowly along the piers, far enough away to make room for a fireboat directing a stream into one of the warehouses. Cobb watched army regulars stack their weapons and move in to assist the firemen. Maybe this was the right time, he thought. Wait until everyone's having the time of his life being a volunteer fireman, then move in.

"What the hell?" Lassiter recognized the sound at the same time Cobb did. It was a rushing noise, a splitting of the air for just an instant by something moving at high speed. Then the warehouse in front of them erupted. A section of the roof peeled back as if an invisible fist had punched it straight up in the air. It tottered precariously for an instant, held by a gust of wind, then tumbled backward onto the street, crushing soldiers and firefighters alike. The outward force of the explosion sent flames, until now unseen, gushing out along the ground. It was like a colossal flamethrower, and everything in its path was ignited—vehicles, firemen, soldiers, and surrounding buildings.

A second and then a third blast followed in rapid succession. In less than thirty seconds, the building was leveled. Their bos'n had already rammed his throttle forward. As their boat leaped ahead parallel to the piers, they were showered with sparks. Simultaneously, two other buildings were hit by similar blasts.

"Son of a bitch, look!" Cobb shouted. Lassiter's eyes strained in the direction of his pointing finger. He saw the flash half a mile beyond Seraglio Point, then the telltale stream of flame. "Missiles—that's what they're using."

Lassiter saw the white wakes of the oncoming craft before he could pick out the boats themselves. "What—"

"Missile boats. Small ones. They're great little weapons for something like this, aren't they? High speed, fast attack in and out. Unload your weapons and get away as fast as you can. I guess they don't like the idea of our taking Keradin with us. But I wonder how they figured out where we took him. Why here? Why wait until here?"

"Simple," Lassiter explained. "They intercept a couple of our plain-language radio reports. Use their satellite photography. Check with headquarters in Yalta about that fast little boat that seemed to be going balls-to-the-wall toward

the Bosporus, and find out that none Yalta knows of is
supposed to be doing same. Then they start checking fleet
lists. Do you want me to go on?"

"How dumb of me to ask."

The roar of engines came to their ears now as a squadron
of boats bore down on the docks. Cobb could see their deck
guns now, spouting flame as they poured small-caliber fire
into the waterfront. Missiles from farther out continued to
pass overhead, striking deeper into the city.

Out of the corner of his eyes, Cobb saw a direct hit on
a mosque, the minaret tilting slowly, then a cloud of dust
and smoke as it hit the ground. He was aware of Verra
hanging tightly to his arm.

She looked up at him, fear on her face. But when she
spoke, her voice was steady, her words rational. "You didn't
tell me about all this yesterday in the vineyard." She managed a smile. "Perhaps I was better off—"

Cobb never let her finish. "Get below," he shouted above
the din. "You can take him with you." He handed her his
pistol.

She turned to Keradin, who was still shackled to the
mast, but it was obvious the man had understood Cobb's
order. He shook his head firmly from side to side, though
he said nothing. He was a proud man, Cobb knew—and
now perhaps suicidal. There was no time to argue. "Forget
him. Just get the hell below."

Already their bos'n was turning their own boat to meet
the attackers. Cobb identified two hydrofoils gracefully
banking from side to side as they zigzagged toward their
target, deck guns blazing. Neither had yet seen Lassiter's
boat. Instead their fire was concentrated on the army troops
pouring onto the docks.

Then the small arms on Cobb's own boat came to life
and their brief moment of anonymity was shattered. One of
the hydrofoils, detecting return fire, banked gracefully in
their direction. A hundred yards distant, it turned again,
running parallel but in the opposite direction to their own
course, its weapons concentrated fully on them. Neither was
an easy target at high speed. The shells from the other craft

passed overhead, but Cobb knew they might not be so lucky when the other boat came back to match their course. It was obviously faster and more heavily armed.

The hydrofoil reversed direction, turning in a tight, hard circle. Settling now on their course, it resumed fire. The man nearest to Cobb abruptly flew backward, arms and legs extended seaward as he was slammed into the deckhouse. Lassiter stared in fascination as the structure around him began to splinter.

"For Christ's sake, will you get down!" Lassiter heard Cobb's voice at the same time he felt the hands on his shoulders yanking him backward and down. He hit hard, his head bouncing against the deck. Before he could blink, the bulkhead above him disintegrated in a shower of metal splinters, peeling inward like a tin can to reveal the men in the pilothouse.

Turning his head to the side, Lassiter felt Cobb, before he was sure who it was, crawling forward past him. At the same instant, his eyes flew from Cobb back to the interior of the pilothouse. The bos'n appeared in the middle of a slow pirouette, his hands grasping at the back of his head. Then he pitched through the hole in the bulkhead, sprawling across Lassiter's legs. Lassiter yanked himself from underneath the corpse.

Cobb was now inching forward on his belly, both arms out to the sides as the boat slewed to the left, then headed sharply to the right. Another sailor, clothes blood-spattered, had the wheel. The boat settled on course for an instant, then heeled sharply as the wheel was thrown over to avoid a burning pier.

"Reverse course!" Cobb was shouting above the din, frantically pointing at the pilothouse. But Lassiter was not about to move. Machine gun bullets splattered the bulkhead above him. He tucked his head, turtlelike, into his shoulders.

"Reverse, reverse," Cobb insisted, looking over his shoulder.

Lassiter was well aware of the danger they were in. But he was also even more sure of the aim of the other boat's machine gunner, and pointed up at the bullets splattering a

foot above him. He knew what to do. Reverse course, change
direction of the boat—he understood that. The bullets trailed
down the side toward the stern. Without another thought,
Lassiter drew himself onto his knees and launched his body
through the shattered bulkhead, landing at the sailor's feet.
Pulling himself up to a crouch, he saw another boat coming
at them from the bow. He grasped the sailor's arm, shouting
as he jerked his fist in the opposite direction. The boat heeled
sharply in reply to their rudder.

The spray of machine gun bullets that had passed over
Lassiter's head had also swept their bow clear of gunners.
The boat charging at them behind a steady flow of shells
was now unchallenged, maintaining both a closing course
and a steady rate of fire.

Cobb appeared now in front of the pilothouse, moving
in a crouch toward one of the guns. Reaching it, he stood
just long enough to shove away the gunner's body. Then
he slid in behind the small armor shield, checked the ammunition belt, and, satisfied, commenced fire on the oncoming boat.

Their wheel was over tight, the boat reversing course
just as Cobb wanted. The attacking boat was unable to slow
down, and as it passed, Cobb and another gunner stitched
it with deadly accuracy.

Lassiter admired their shooting and cheered above the
din. The deck of the passing craft became a helpless target
for an instant, its gunner now unable to return Cobb's fire.
The pilothouse glass of the opposing vessel burst out. One
of Lassiter's men fired an antitank missile at close range.
The other boat's bulkhead disappeared much the same as
that of their own boat moments ago. But this time when
Lassiter looked closely there was no one upright inside. It
was pilotless. The boat slewed one way, then the other, its
speed still full. For some inexplicable reason, it turned sharply
to the right. As it leaned hard into the turn, it also headed
directly for one of the piers. At full speed it jammed beneath
the dock, shearing off the upper deck. There was a flash,
an explosion, and both the boat and the dock disintegrated.

Lassiter recognized a screaming beside him that increased

in pitch. He turned, feeling the man at the wheel clawing blindly at his arm. Blood covered the man's face. Lassiter pushed him away roughly, grasping the wheel himself.

A powerful explosion near the stern jolted him. The boat shuddered convulsively. Lassiter could feel they were losing speed. Then he saw the first boat, the one that had been turning only a second before, begin to bear down on them. In seconds it made a pass, guns bracketing them. Catching sight of her empty missile canister, Lassiter realized what had hit them.

He had no steering control. In the next instant, it was also obvious that they were slowing so much that they had no power. They were dead in the water with their attacker bearing down on them! Sporadic fire from weapons still functioning did nothing to slow down the oncoming boat. A steady stream of fire encircled them.

Cobb, his ammunition expended, watched helplessly as the killer bore down on them. There was nowhere to move or hide. All he could do was fall forward, face down on the deck. He saw Lassiter do the same in what was left of the pilothouse. Yet in the most revealing location, Keradin stood, arms folded, seeming to welcome death.

But as suddenly as the incessant pounding had begun, it ceased. Cobb waited. There was no reason the other boat should stop firing. He counted—one...two...three ...four...five. Nothing. He looked up cautiously. A section of deck was bent upward in front of him, blocking his vision. He got to his knees, crawling slowly as if his executioner were waiting on the other side. Peering out at where the other boat should be, he saw a flaming hulk. From stem to stern, the Soviet boat was in flames.

Looking to the rear, the answer became immediately obvious. A Turkish boat, one of those that had been dockside when they had first come by the piers, was cruising slowly no more than a hundred yards off their bow, pouring small-arms fire into the hulk that seconds before had been bearing down to finish them off. Her missile canisters on the port side were empty. She had made a direct hit on the Russians' fuel tanks.

The Turkish boat turned in their direction. Pulling within range of her fire-fighting hoses, she arched a stream of water toward them. Sailors on her deck were pointing at them, but Cobb could not understand what attracted their attention. Facing amidship, he saw Lassiter's huge U.S. flag still fluttering atop the mast. And at the base, still chained, stood the defiant Keradin, arms folded, smoke from their burning boat occasionally shrouding his head. No doubt the Turks were sure that he was the brave little craft's captain.

Verra! She was still below, and they were sinking stern first. He had to get her! How long had they been involved in the running battle? No more than three or four minutes.

He covered the space to the pilothouse in a few steps. It was a shambles. Three bodies sprawled on the deck. Lassiter was one of them, a hole in his chest, a surprised expression on his lifeless face. A bloodied sailor was leaning against the remains of the control panel. "I hit the button for auto washdown—nothing. Those tanks can go any second now!"

"I'm going after the girl," Cobb shouted. "Smash that chain." He pointed in Keradin's direction, handing the sailor his pistol. "I want him more than ever now. If he tries anything, shoot him in the knees."

Cobb leaped for the hatchway leading below the pilothouse. At the base of the ladder, he saw Verra struggling to climb up. Her face was covered with blood; one arm hung at her side. The boat shuddered and heaved to port, taking an instant angle of almost twenty degrees. She stumbled against the bulkhead, falling to her knees.

"I'm coming," he bellowed, taking the rungs three at a time. Kneeling, he wiped her face with a towel she had been carrying. There was a deep cut on her forehead, the skin hanging over her eye. With his fingers, Cobb pressed the flap of skin back against her forehead and wrapped the towel tightly around her head. Her left arm was broken, no doubt about that, but it and the head cut seemed to be the only injuries.

She mumbled something about a shell ripping out the outer bulkhead where she'd been but her words were distant, incoherent. "Never mind now," Cobb said sharply. "We're sinking—understand?"

She looked up at him through cloudy eyes and nodded.

"There's a Turkish boat coming alongside. We'll try to get on that. If we can't, we have to jump. Do you hear me?" he shouted.

Again she nodded, mumbling inaudibly.

"I'm going to stay with you like I promised. You're not going to be left." He pulled her good arm around his shoulder and stumbled back up the ladder. It was difficult going. The angle of the sinking boat seemed to increase with each rung. Nearing the top, a sailor leaned down and, putting his hands under Verra's arms, lifted her bodily through the hatch onto the deck. As Cobb stumbled to the top and leaped through the hatch, the boat heaved again, the bow slowly rising into the air. She was going to go down by the stern!

The sailor had released Keradin. His gun never waivered from the General, who watched with disdain. It had been made abundantly clear to him that they did not intend to lose him at this point, or allow him to escape on his own. Keradin also was quite sure of the sailor's promise to shoot him if the opportunity presented itself. He had decided once again to take his chances.

The Turkish boat could not come closer, fearing for herself if either of Lassiter's tanks blew. With hoses playing at the flames on the stern in an effort to slow their advance to those outside the demolished pilothouse, the Turks gestured frantically for the survivors to jump. Nets had been lowered over the side.

Cobb stared grimly at Keradin. Again he reminded himself that they had come too far to take a chance on the General's either escaping or dying now. Cobb led him to the bow of the boat, waving his arms wildly to draw the Turks' attention. When he was sure they were watching, he turned the General slightly and caught him firmly on the side of the jaw with a roundhouse punch. As Keradin staggered backward, Cobb pointed first at him and then at the Turks, hoping they would understand his intentions. Then he pushed the General over the side, again gesturing at the spot where the body had hit the water. Two Turkish sailors immediately leaped over the side and swam for Keradin.

"Give me a hand when we're in the water," Cobb shouted to a sailor. Then, facing Verra, he wrapped his arms tightly around her and without a word, jumped over the side. On the surface, the sailor was beside him. Each slid a hand under her arms and struck out for the Turkish boat.

From its deck, they witnessed the death of Lassiter's craft. She slipped by the stern deeper into the water, bubbles swarming furiously around her, flames reaching the tip of the bow. Then the boat and Lassiter were gone.

ISTANBUL

Cobb studied Verra's features closely. Even with the bandage covering part of her forehead, he admired how naturally lovely she was. Her hair, blond and soft looking, had been pulled back by one of the nurses and tied in a ponytail. Her face was definitely Slavic, cheekbones high and accentuated even more by the rainbow bruises on the side where the stitches had been taken. Her mouth was wide, her lips full, slightly parted now as she slept. Christ, how he hated to leave her.

He held her hand, occasionally stroking it as he had been doing since he came in to sit with her. Tough! That's what she was—tough to be able to hold up so well after what she had been through over the last fifteen hours.

Her eyes fluttered open, looking first at him, lips opening slightly in a smile, then scanning the room. "Cobb..."

"Right here. I've been here, right beside you, since they fixed you up."

"Where are we? Who...?"

He hushed her with a finger to her lips. "Shh, it's all right. We're in Istanbul. You're in a hospital. You got a busted arm when that bulkhead caved in on you, and they stuck a couple of stitches in that cut on your head. But other than that, you're fine. A few days and—"

"Do we have a few days?"

"Sure you do. An attaché from the American Embassy has already been over. He'll take good care of you until you're able to—"

"Cobb, no. You promised you'd take me away."

He hesitated. "You'll be in American custody."

"And you—where are you going?"

"I have to get back. Lassiter's dead. And Keradin—I have to get him back to my boss who's on a carrier somewhere near Malta. I've got another boat, a loaner from the Turks. It's still too dangerous to fly with Keradin until we're back in our own airspace." He brushed her hair back from her face. "Our other carrier, *Saratoga,* will provide air cover on the rest of the run. She's east of Cyprus now."

"Why are you going back on your promise?" Her eyes above the classic cheekbones were damp. She pushed his hand away. Her expression was sheer disappointment.

"But you'll be under American control here."

"If the Russians decide they want Turkey, they will take it very quickly. There will be no questions about that, no time for American officials to worry about an injured Polish girl." She turned away from him. "Maybe twenty-four hours from now, when you are back secure within your airspace or whatever you want to call it, I may be under their control again." She turned back, expressive eyes narrowed, half accusing, half imploring. "Is that how you keep your promises, Cobb? I kept mine."

He remained silent, caught in her gaze. "I don't know how we'll get you out of here."

"I'll walk out. I don't need your help, just your word."

"It'll still be dangerous, even with air cover. They could—"

"I'll take my chances, Cobb. Keradin seems to have done just fine taking his."

He remembered the Russian General standing stoically behind the wheelhouse, exposing himself to fire, welcoming death as a release from captivity. Cobb smiled at her. "He's almost as tough as you. Okay. I guess at this point I can arrange anything."

"Thank you." Her face softened again. "I don't know how to thank you . . ."

He patted her hand again and smiled back. "Later. My boat's ready and I've got some volunteers who are willing to fill up my crew. I told them I was just waiting to say good-bye to you as soon as—"

"Never mind, Cobb," she insisted. "I'll manage." She sat up, dangling her feet over the edge of the bed. Her head hung down for a minute. Then she looked up at him, smiling painfully. "You know, Cobb, it hurts a little." She pointed first to her head and then to the arm tightly strapped to her ribs with a sling. She took a couple of deep breaths. "There. See? All gone—or almost." She stood up. The ridiculous hospital gown the nurses had half wrapped around her fell open. "No secrets, eh, Cobb? I guess there's no need— after our little episode in Keradin's room." She looked around. "My clothes?"

"I suppose they burned them. What was left of them was covered with blood. We'll find something."

"How about Keradin?" she asked, wincing slightly as she walked back and forth. "Did you give his back yet, or do you still have him running around in his shorts?" Her face brightened with a malicious grin.

"General Keradin is now dressed as a Turkish sailor."

She turned, her eyes again slightly narrowed. "If you were me, Cobb, you would not offer him the slightest comfort." Looking away, she said, "Forget it. He's your prisoner, not mine. Please find me some clothes. I want only your promise." She broke into tears.

Cobb went over to her, turning her around slowly. She looked up at him, tears running down her cheeks. Tentatively, she placed her free hand on his shoulder, blinking back her tears. Cobb pulled her to him, his arms encircling her, and said, "I'm sorry I ever thought about leaving you here, breaking my promise."

"Shh," she whispered in his ear. "Just hold me for a moment. I was afraid you might not take me after everything you saw at the dacha."

He kissed her lightly. "Never entered my mind. Here, let me go find something for you." There would be time to be together later; there was none now. He released her very slowly, gazing into those deep eyes. He was not accustomed to the emotion he felt. Perhaps he was just tired. Perhaps that was why he was experiencing this odd and very warm feeling.

D-DAY

Through Pentagon intelligence reports, the President was fully aware of the dawn meeting in the Kremlin of the STAVKA, the Main Military Council. He also knew that the purpose of the conference was to make final recommendations to the State Committee for Defense. But these recommendations were a foregone conclusion, for the meeting was simply to determine any final alterations to their operations plan. Since the Soviet leadership preferred efficiency and constancy, the President anticipated there would be no changes.

Of those seen entering the Kremlin that early morning, the Soviet Navy was noted to be heavily represented. The intelligence report reinforced Admiral Pratt's earlier assessments for those in Washington who supported his views. Admiral Chernavin, the Commander in Chief of the Soviet Navy, was in attendance along with Admiral Milchaylovskiy, Commander of the Northern Fleet, Admiral Khovrin, Commander of the Black Sea Fleet, and General Colonel (Aviation) Mironenko, Commander of Naval Aviation. General Keradin's second in command, General Colonel Melekhin, surprised the President when it was learned he attended the meeting, because intelligence reports predicted

weeks before that Melekhin's status was weak and that he
would likely be purged.

While the White House was not privy to the minutes of
the STAVKA, much of the discussion in the meeting could
be predicted. The Commander of the Northern Fleet couldn't
report how many of his submarines had broken through the
American CAPTOR barrier. His submarines were under
strict orders not to report to Murmansk until they commenced their attacks, since the first radio signal would give
away their position. The weather over Spitzbergen had
cleared enough so that the devastation of the attack on the
Longyearbyen airport was known. But the White House
knew that the STAVKA was at a loss concerning the where-
abouts of the freighter carrying the balance of their decoys.
Another flight of Bear bombers was approaching Longyearbyen even as the STAVKA was meeting, but those in the
Kremlin still did not know that reinforcement was futile.

Admiral Khovrin would report that the majority of his
Black Sea Fleet, including the carrier *Minsk*, had now passed
through the Turkish straits and the Mediterranean Fifth Escadra was at full strength. He would also point out that
harassment in the Aegean Sea by the Greek navy had indeed
delayed plans somewhat, but he was confident Admiral
Konstantin, now commanding the Fifth Escadra, was a superb on-scene commander. What that really meant was that
he would follow orders from Moscow without question. The
entire scope of the coming confrontation had already been
specified, for that was the Soviet command system—cen-
tralization of command, all orders to front-line units on land
and at sea issued from the Kremlin where the full strategic
picture could be evaluated. There was no localized decision
making of a strategic nature in the Soviet military. It was
unheard of that a shot could be fired without direction from
Moscow. Of course, in the heat of battle the responsibility
fell on the shoulders of the on-scene commander, in this
case, Admiral Konstantin. If Moscow's strategy failed, it
would be his fault.

The Pentagon also reassured the White House that the

previous day's face-off between Soviet aircraft and their American counterparts would make little impression on General Colonel (Aviation) Mironenko. He was absolutely convinced there was no possible way the U.S. Sixth Fleet could withstand his first salvo. The Americans would wait until it was too late (he had once written for *Morskoi Sbornik,*) and then his follow-up attack, combined with sub-marine- and surface-launched missiles, would destroy the survivors. The American Chief of Staff assured the President that it was preferable to have Mironenko believe this right up to the end.

There was confidence in the White House that the supply routes to Europe could remain open. Though final information remained sketchy due to the lack of a final report from the SEAL team sent into Spitzbergen, the Pentagon now projected that approximately 75 percent of the U.S. convoy ships would survive the passage. The President, more than any other man, maintained absolute confidence in Admiral Pratt. Pratt, through his own efforts, had learned more about his foe, spent more time in developing original strategy, and certainly deserved to command the main force. Perhaps a major reason for the President's confidence was simply that there was no other man to do the job.

The final piece of the puzzle, one that could only be speculated on, was an unknown and purely theoretical factor—General Keradin of the Strategic Rocket Forces. A major Soviet effort had been made to locate and recover him in Istanbul. Word had come in hours before from Pratt that the undercover man, Cobb, had succeeded in escaping the Turkish port and was now en route to *Saratoga* with substantial air cover as protection. But that was no guarantee that the Russians wouldn't once again learn where Keradin was and try to kill him. And, the President suggested, once we have him under our control, can we be sure that that will have the desired effect? Would the Soviet leaders' dis-like of General Colonel Melekhin as Keradin's replacement, coupled with the instability created by a new face in the command system, allow the U.S. that extra bit of time to prevent a nuclear exchange? Much of the answer to this question also hinged on Admiral Pratt's defense of his battle group and its ability to destroy Admiral Konstantin's Fifth Escadra.

SPITZBERGEN

Bernie Ryng had to make up his mind which was the most dangerous—the suddenly treacherous soft spots in the tundra surface or the arctic terns. This time of year, the birds nesting on the tundra were invisible, blending in with the arctic growth until he was almost on top of them. Then they would swirl angrily into the air, squawking their anger at the sudden disturbance. Though they settled quickly to the ground as he passed, they could serve as a signpost to his location if a helo were to slip over the nearby ridges to either side. Even an idiot, thought Ryng, would know there was almost nothing in the area to upset the birds, nothing but a man.

Most of their eggs were already hatched, but some untended nests still held the rich food that Ryng knew would offer enough sustenance to last him until he crossed the peak. He'd never been a fan of raw eggs, and these had an odd, brackish flavor to them, but they were small enough to slip down his throat quickly. A little pressure on the soft, tangled vegetation at his feet was enough to form a puddle of drinking water to wash them down. His stomach growled back at the unusual food, but Ryng paid little attention to it. He'd eaten much worse in the past.

Perhaps five hours had passed since the last helo had chased him under the boulder in that first hidden valley. That bothered him. It meant that someone was thinking the way he was. There was no need on the Russians' part to waste fuel or ammunition. If their plans had been for a short stay on Spitzbergen, their supplies would necessarily be limited. Why wouldn't one of those Black Beret officers do exactly the same thing as he would? Figure out your quarry, then wait for him at the most logical spot.

Ryng glared up at the peak in front of him. It was not especially high, but the path to the top was not a straight line either. He pondered his choices, mapping a course in his mind as his eyes searched out secure hiding places. The course became gradually steeper as it progressed, but not once did he allow himself to be positioned where he could not seek cover. The snow line began about halfway up. Once he reached it, he would be a perfect target. His blood photographed against the whiteness would provide perfect proof to Moscow that Bernie Ryng had been had.

While he rose to begin the final ascent, that little voice echoed through his mind, quiet at first, then more insistent. If they've been letting you travel this far and this long, Ryng thought to himself, don't you think they might have a plan? Do you really think a Black Beret officer would be dumb enough to let you go on your merry way without having something in mind? Ryng looked back up at the peak. The voice made sense. Don't you think they have maps and photos equal to your own? he continued to reason. If you were chasing one of them, would you let him hop from shadow to shadow, or would you plot a logical track and wait until he gets to the snow? Why do it the hard way when there's a nice, easy way to do the job without wasting precious fuel?

Right, Ryng answered himself. I have to stop at the snow line and wait. He'll be there, surer than shit, about the time he figures I'm far enough into the snow to thrash around like a scared rabbit. Just don't pass the snow line, Ryng.

Wait there until they come for you. Then take your chances.
In the snow, you won't have any.

Colonel Bulgan stood to one side of the helicopter, his
eyes fixed on the peaks across the harbor. He tried to pick
out the exact one that Ryng would now be ascending, but
they blurred together in the whiteness of the mountain range.
The Colonel had changed after his nap and was now outfitted
in fresh black fatigues. Grenades and clips for his rifle hung
off his uniform. His AK-74 was cradled in his right hand.
Bulgan had no expectations of using it from the helo, but
he would feel more comfortable with it if they had to settle
down for any reason. It was only revenge now, revenge for
a failed mission. He would pursue this vendetta if for no
other reason than that this American had ruined his career,
perhaps even the all-important North Atlantic strategy.

The Colonel looked at his watch again, then at the careful
track layed out on his map. Ryng would be about to enter
the snow, if he had not already. It was time now. He jerked
an arm in signal to the pilot and climbed into the helo.

ABOARD THE CARRIER H.M.S. *ILLUSTRIOUS*, THE GREENLAND SEA

Admiral Sir Jonathan Harrow, O.B.E., had always been more than comfortable in making complex decisions. Yet right now he was involved in the most difficult one of his career.

According to the best NATO estimates, it was little less than hours to D-Day. However, that point in time had already come and gone aboard his flagship, H.M.S. *Illustrious*, an antisubmarine aircraft carrier. *Illustrious* and her escorts, now positioned approximately two hundred miles west southwest of Spitzbergen, had been under attack by Soviet submarines for the past six hours. *Illustrious* had taken a torpedo in her forward engine room two hours before and had only just regained normal operating speed.

Admiral Harrow's escorts, along with the carrier's helicopters, had been prosecuting subsurface contacts until he sometimes thought that the entire attack submarine contingent of the Soviet Northern Fleet had surrounded him. But he knew better. Most of them were already to the south, heading for the open waters of the North Atlantic. He was sure those harassing him had been detached to insure his group did not turn south.

Now Admiral Harrow again extracted the message from

his shirt pocket and reread it. He knew there was no choice. Land-based aircraft would never get to Spitzbergen on time, at least not without a challenge by Soviet forces. He had no choice but to obey orders. He called the commanding officer of *Illustrious* over to him and gave the orders that would launch the five Harrier attack fighters that comprised the tiny carrier's air defense complement. Admiral Harrow also advised that he would speak to the pilots in the ready room in five minutes. It seemed that, in addition to the priority target, an unknown airfield on the southern end of Svalbard's largest island, they should keep a lookout for any other provocative incidents. An American SEAL team, backed up by armed Norwegian fishing craft, was also operating in the area. But there had been no confirmation whether or not their mission had been successful. His was a desperation mission if they'd failed.

Thirty minutes later, *Illustrious* turned into the wind to launch her Harriers. They orbited once over their ship before disappearing in the direction of Longyearbyen airport. Admiral Harrow had explained their mission, adding that there were no friendly aircraft in the region and that there were more Bear bombers, likely under fighter escort, headed toward the island. He silently wished them well as they disappeared to the east. Now *Illustrious* was alone, her meager missile defense the only protection from air attack. Harrow wondered who might be crazy enough to take a SEAL team into that godforsaken place.

SPITZBERGEN

Ryng wished he had a cigarette even though he hadn't smoked for years. It would give him something to do with his hands. If he had been able to save even one weapon when their boat was hit, he'd be cleaning it now, or at least insuring that it would function perfectly when needed.

Instead, he was perched on a small, flat rock, snuggled close to a boulder that would initially keep him out of sight of any helicopter coming over the range to the east. The snow line was about a hundred yards above him.

It was a good thousand yards to the summit, more than half a mile. It wasn't as steep as some of the territory he'd covered in the past hour, and he had already picked out his course to the top, but it would be slower going than he liked.

Ryng waited. A tempting voice in the back of his mind kept saying, Aw, go ahead, because once you get over the top it's downhill all the way. But another voice, the one developed through years of training, was the one he followed. It told him that the odds for the downhill side were very long indeed if he tried to make it now.

He waited—waited for the hum of the rotors that would presage a helo coming over the peaks to his right, a hum that would be followed by the louder beat as the craft closed in on his position.

How the hell do you fight a goddamn helicopter armed with rockets and machine guns? Throw rocks at it? Ryng glanced around him. There were rocks, but nothing else. He picked one up and threw it in disgust. As it landed and bounced down the hill, a small cloud of birds rose at the intrusion. As quickly as they flew into the air, they settled down with irritated squawking at the disturbance. Stay quiet, he told himself. Disturbing those birds is like waving a handkerchief.

It wasn't long before the sound came to his ears. Ryng watched patiently as the craft came close over the snow of the adjacent peak, skirting first along the top of the ridge above him. It didn't bother with the valley area below him. That convinced Ryng that this time someone who knew what he was doing was riding shotgun.

For some reason, the helo swept the area to his left as it approached the snow line, keeping low, hovering whenever it neared a shadowed area. Each time, the birds rose whether in defiance or confusion, forcing the helo to rise and drift off to avoid fouling its rotors.

That's one idea, Ryng thought—piss off the birds and maybe they'll do the work for me. The more he thought about the idea, the more feasible it became, considering that he had nothing whatsoever to defend himself with. Now, on the opposite side of the boulder from the helo, he collected a small arsenal of rocks, heavy enough, he thought, to upset nesting birds, light enough to be somewhat accurate.

Time to waste some of his ammunition. He threw half a dozen stones as rapidly as he could down the slope to his left. He hoped that the disturbed birds would draw some fire.

It worked too perfectly.

With a roar, the helo banked in his direction, swooping toward the rising birds. Ryng saw the telltale smoke from either side as two rockets were fired into the slope above the frantic birds.

Wham . . . wham. The rockets burst fifty feet above the

spot, sending an avalanche of rocks down through the area. The loose surface would wipe out anything in its path as it increased in mass.

Smart—but not so smart, Ryng said to himself. Went for the quick kill without checking first. Maybe he figures I still have some protection. On the other hand, he's just used up half his rocket load—only two left.

As he watched, fascinated by the small craft's firepower, the helo circled at a slightly higher altitude. Then the air was shattered by the multibarreled machine guns. Something obviously had attracted the helo's eye. Whatever it was, a deadly hail of bullets sprayed the area.

Ryng thought about the snowfield. He would have been just about at the top of this point. Christ, there wouldn't be enough of me left to color the snow!

The air was filled with birds circling and turning in fear above their nests. There was no longer any way the men in the helo could use the bird population to find him. The helo was forced to a higher altitude to avoid fouling the birds. Anything that will do the trick, Ryng thought, trying harder to make himself one with the boulder that was his only protection. Now they have a problem too.

The helo dropped farther down the slope, moving away from his position and the birds. Had they given up already? Not a chance. They've got time on their side. They'll let everything settle down, then move in again.

The son of a bitch knows I'm here, Ryng realized. He didn't mess around in the lower valleys. He came right up near the snow line and fired at the first thing that moved. Being the object of a hunt when there was nowhere to run was not Ryng's idea of fun.

The helo swept back and forth below him, dropping farther down the slope then working its way back in his direction. Ryng looked around, determining where he might shift to next if there was even an inkling that he might be spotted. It was then that he realized he hadn't been so damn clever after all. He'd selected the largest boulder in that section of the slope below the snow line. Could there have been a more obvious place to try to hide?

The helo, moving back up the slope in his general direction, decided the same thing. Its zigzag movement halted and the bulbous nose dipped slightly as it settled on a course directly for his hiding place.

Frantically, Ryng searched about him. There was nothing else big enough to use as cover, nothing that would serve as adequate protection if they opened fire with machine guns, and nothing at all if it used rockets. This was the only place, and Ryng, thinking exactly like Colonel Bulgan, knew they would be on top of him in a matter of seconds.

The helo did not circle around the large boulder to search for its quarry. It headed straight in.

Nearby birds rose from their nests, but this time the helo hovered about seventy-five yards away horizontal with Ryng's position.

What the hell were they going to do? As he mulled over that question, the answer became evident. There was a tell-tale wisp of smoke from the left pod. Ryng had seen rockets fired before—he had even used them himself—but he had never had the misfortune of being the target. He had no more than a second to ponder the sleek missile racing in his direction before his reflexes took command. He buried his head in his arms.

Wham! The rocket hit the boulder directly with an ear-shattering explosion. The concussion rolled over him at the same instant, sucking the air from his lungs, the blast bouncing his body into the air, then smashing it back to the ground.

Ryng was unable to move, even to lift his head or draw a breath into his agonized lungs. The silence that followed the blast was broken by the sound of small rocks dislodged by the explosion rolling down about him.

The heavier ones were what jolted him back to the real world, the world of a helicopter moving in closer, its rotors piercing the air. Ryng struggled for air, desperate to return oxygen to his system before he blacked out. He could feel himself going, eyes clouding as his feeble chest spasms failed to supply the needed air. He arched his body into the air, let it fall to the ground, then increased the rhythm until the impact forced his body to react, to suck the crisp mountain air into his lungs.

He was breathing again, painfully, but breathing nevertheless. The acrid smell of high explosives came to him. Ryng sensed, even before his eyes recorded the fact, that the helo was swinging out to the right. It swam before him as his eyes focused on the approaching perspex canopy. It was close enough to see the one remaining rocket and the wicked machine gun, its multiple barrels almost in line with him.

On his hands and knees, hugging the ground, Ryng scuttled backward like a crab. The cloud of birds constantly fluttering between him and the helo seemed his only hope, but they flew to either side as the craft came closer.

Just as he ducked back, the machine gun opened fire. They had seen him! The ground erupted. Hundreds of bullets ricocheted in every direction. He felt tiny shards of stone rip into his skin like a thousand little pins. Instinctively, he covered his eyes. As the noise of the gun-burst subsided, the only thought that came to him was how one-sided it all seemed. It was an alien situation to Bernie Ryng, being unable to shoot back.

As he chafed at the problem, he was also aware of the movement of the helo, now maneuvering above and behind his boulder. He backed around, and again the guns pounded away at the spot he'd just left. The one advantage he knew he had was that the helo could not easily shoot down on him from its position between the boulder and the snowfield. But he couldn't crab his way around this boulder forever either. Sooner or later he'd make a mistake when there was no room for even one slight error. A ricocheting bullet could solve the enemy's problem, and the odds were good that if they fired enough, sooner or later one would get him.

The thrust of the rotors saturated the air with dust and feathers. The mess penetrated his eyes and nose, and when he choked on it, it got in his mouth too. Through the haze, he could see the helo floating off to the other side, literally following him around the boulder. The guns let loose once more, kicking up the earth to either side as the craft bobbed in its own air currents.

Ryng slipped in the gravel as he skittered backward, sliding momentarily with the curve of the slope into the open. Frantically he rolled back to safety as the helo drifted into view. Shards of stone sprayed over him, penetrating his skin.

It was fast becoming a losing game for Bernie Ryng. There was no way a man could long protect himself from the hovering monster. Only instinct and the reactions he had left had protected him so far.

Now the copter was downhill from him again, with more room to raise or lower its target angle. It swung back and forth in the air as if suspended on a string, persistently firing short bursts whether or not he was in sight. The Russians, Ryng knew, understood the odds of the stray bullet as well as he did.

It was between the bursts of the helo's machine gun that he heard another sound, something new added to the cacophony around him. Only, this was different, something alien to this snow-peaked, arctic hellhole. It was the screaming sound of a jet engine, and it was accompanied by a piercing shriek that he had rarely heard. The latter sound was followed by a tremendous burst below and to one side of the helo. It was much louder and many times more intense than the rockets that had been fired at him.

Ryng looked up to see a jet fighter spiraling into a high turn. He knew instantaneously that it was a Harrier fighter, recognizing vaguely the British colors on its tail. The explosion must have been an air-to-ground missile. Where the jet came from, or how, never entered his mind. Just the fact that the confrontation had evened out was all he cared about.

As the possibility began to overtake him that it might be a one-shot deal, a second fighter screamed down. Though its missile also missed its mark, Ryng was overjoyed to see that it came closer than the last.

He stared into the sky, wondering whether the first would return, and saw three others circling in a tight formation above. This was more like it. Now the helo was facing roughly the same odds as he had moments earlier. The odds that a third or fourth guided missile would miss its target were remote, and he waited with joy as he saw the first plane diving on its prey.

The pilot of the helo was no fool. Only by hugging the ground, hoping to confuse the missile guidance with the surface clutter, could he hope to survive. This time the helo began a series of wild cuts and dives, much as Ryng had been forced to do to avoid its deadly fire.

Whoever was piloting the first jet seemed to have little concern for his own safety. Since the Harrier could move at exceptionally slow speeds for a jet, it came in very low, picking a path that seemed to Ryng to be sure suicide, seeming to fly directly at the helo for a moment. As it pulled out of its flat pattern, climbing away from the mountain at the last minute, another missile was released.

There was little the Soviet pilot could do at that point. He lifted the copter straight into the air, perhaps hoping the missile would lock on the ground. But that was not to be as the heat-seeking missile locked on the helo's engine exhaust and detonated at the rear of the craft.

Ryng rose to his feet to watch the helo cartwheel through the air, leaving a trail of black smoke. For a second, he thought it might recover. Then it pitched onto one side, careening into the hillside just below the snow line.

The second jet swooped low overhead, waggling its wings in recognition as Ryng waved back. Flying at a slow speed, it passed over the peak toward the sea and waggled its wings. Turning, it retraced its path, again passing over Ryng with a waggle, before flying over the mountaintop again. Then the two jets climbed with a roar to join the other three. Ryng was sure they were continuing on their way to pay a visit to the Russians at Longyearbyen. Of course there was no way word of the success of the SEAL team could have gotten back to the British. These Harriers were an inde-

pendent last-ditch attempt to destroy the Russian base at
Longyearbyen.

The question, he noted to himself, is, Where the hell did
they come from? There was no way they could show up
like the cavalry unless there was a carrier offshore, and that
second waggle must mean I have a chance if I go over the
top and slide down the other side to the beach. Just like
that! Nothing made sense, at least not since this whole mess
started when he and Denny were hit in their rubber boat.
From that time on, he had been able to miraculously escape,
each time figuring that the next round would be the last.
Time and again, the idea of survival had been pounded into
his skull, the idea that people could survive against the most
amazing odds, but they had to want to live or there was no
reason to run, or to fight back. Just keep at it as long as
you have the ability to spit in their eye, they said, and you
may just get out of it.

And he had. Or at least for the time being he had. But
there was no time to waste. There must be other helos, and
when this one didn't return, they would send out another.
And then his odds would plummet way down again. Forget
it! He had no intention of taking any chances. Ryng, his
stamina somehow regenerated, turned toward the peak and
trotted off uphill into the snowfield on the path he'd selected
before the helo had intercepted him. Though it was only
half a mile to the top—if what he saw was indeed the top—
it was a twisting path and could take half an hour, maybe
an hour or more. He had no idea how hard or how deep
the snow really was.

What Ryng also didn't know was that the instant Colonel
Bulgan had seen the Harrier diving at them, he had known
the end was not far off. In fact, he decided that the American, Ryng, probably had better odds from the beginning
than Bulgan had right now. Bullets only went in the direction
they were fired, hopeful that their target would get in the
way. Missiles preferred to seek out their target.

While his terrified pilot skewed the helo wildly about, perhaps afraid to realize how near the end was, Colonel Bulgan very carefully prepared as best he could for the inevitable. He plucked the grenades from his uniform, tossing them out the door to his right. No need to have one detonate under him if he survived the missile or the crash. Then he crammed the AK-74 under the seat, wrapping it tightly with his life jacket. Perhaps it might still function afterward. Then he cinched the safety straps even tighter around his chest until they seemed to stop his breathing. The last thing he remembered—about the same time the missile impacted—was grabbing the pilot's life jacket and covering his head with it.

More than anything else, the life jacket did the job. It not only saved his head from the metal that flew about the cabin, but it protected his face and lungs from the searing heat. Finally, as the helo hit the ground on the pilot's side, it protected his head when the seat ripped away from the deck and he hit the instrument panel. The other saving grace was the pilot. The man's body was under Bulgan and absorbed the impact.

The crackling of flames so close, so very close, came to the Colonel's ears. He opened his eyes. Half in and half out of the fractured helo, Bulgan moved tentatively. The flames hadn't reached him yet.

He moved his arms. They were free. His left wrist hurt like hell—it must be broken. The other was all right. He moved his legs one at a time. Both seemed to function. He heaved himself up on an elbow and a sharp pain bit into his side. Rib, he thought—maybe a couple. Check those out later. You can move. Go!

With a superhuman effort, knowing his body was free, he threw himself out onto the ground, rolling as he did so to get away from the helo. Then he realized his mistake. The rifle was still in there. He had to take the chance and go back. Without it, the American was sure to get away. And Colonel Bulgan felt a deep personal desire to get Bernie Ryng for ruining his mission. He ran back to the burning craft, peering into the shattered front cockpit.

There it was! It had been under him. As quickly as he had leaped from the helo, he grabbed the AK-74 and jumped back from the heat of the flames. As he did so, there was a popping sound as flames engulfed the entire machine.

Bulgan patted his pockets, feeling for his ammunition. Would the weapon work? He went through each function, finally squeezing the trigger and listening to the satisfying click. Perfect! He slipped an ammo clip into the gun, cradling it against his body with the bad arm. He would have to fire with one arm and it would be awkward, but he was sure his quarry was not armed.

Looking up, he saw Ryng working his way through the snow. Bulgan knew the man would never think to look back. He brought the gun up to his shoulder, attempting to bring Ryng into his sights. Instead, the barrel wavered back and forth across the rapidly moving figure. Realizing that the odds of hitting the man from this distance with an AK-74 were almost nil, Bulgan slung the weapon over his shoulder and headed up the grade at his best possible speed.

It would have to be a close-up shot, one with the rifle on single fire, and probably one where he could lie in the snow for a decent aim. There would be no second chance. The pain in his side increased as his breathing deepened in the cool, thin air.

ABOARD U.S.S. *SARATOGA*
FIFTY MILES EAST OF CRETE

Admiral John Turner, *Saratoga*'s battle group commander, spoke quietly, dark circles under his eyes conveying sleepless nights. His voice was steady, almost emotionless, as he described a litany of events that presaged an imminent Soviet attack on NATO. "You were wise to get out of Istanbul when you did." He slid a sheaf of messages across the metal desk to Cobb. "That attack on the city as you arrived apparently had everything to do with General Keradin. It was also another diversion while they moved a lot of their remaining heavier surface ships to the western end of the Black Sea, waiting until Istanbul fell. Then they moved 'em through. About twelve hours and the whole of their Black Sea Fleet steamed into the Aegean—less time than that until Turkey fell."

Cobb was unsurprised. The scenario, as he had learned back in Washington, prophesied exactly the moves the Russians had made so far: Turkish ports on the Black Sea immediately neutralized; fast motorized forces crossing the Bulgarian border to the north, one group driving southeast in a pincer movement in concert with Soviet marines landing to the east of Istanbul, the other advancing in tandem with tank divisions aimed at Gallipoli. NATO indicated that the

Turks, weakened by their short tiff with the Greeks, would fall faster than initial computer projections.

The second part of the Russian scenario called for destruction of the carrier battle groups in the Mediterranean. The closest, and thus the first, would be *Saratoga*'s group.

Admiral Turner's voice droned on. "I think my first responsibility is to get you and General Keradin off this ship, and I think your young lady deserves some land-based medical care."

"Could we grab a few hours sleep, Admiral? It's been two days since we've really had any rest." The passage from Istanbul had involved too many hours, including a refueling stop at the island of Samos. Much of the run through the Aegean had been in the dark. The winds had slackened enough to maintain speed, but it was still rough enough to prohibit sound sleep. They had come alongside *Saratoga* in the early morning hours, just as the sun was rising. Verra, seasick and in pain, had been sent to sick bay. Cobb was fed and then had reported to Admiral Turner's quarters.

"I'd like to give you some rest, son, but I intend to come into the wind in about an hour. I'm going to launch relief for our Hawkeyes out on the perimeter, and I'm going to launch every fighter I've got except for my own CAP."

Cobb looked up, caught by surprise. He understood what that meant. "I take it that we're pretty close?"

"Too close. Satellite recon picked up a new launch yesterday from their Tyuratum Rocket Center. As far as we can determine, they put up antisatellite systems and something is flying around up there that has a nuclear instrument of some kind aboard. And," he sighed, "we have a flight of their Backfire bombers approaching their initial launch point now. We know they won't fire right away, not at that range, because they couldn't get a hit on us. But..." His voice drifted off.

The description was accurate, Cobb realized, as accurate as could be. Knock out our early-warning satellite system with ASATs, send in a flight of Backfires with antiradiation missiles to knock out the Hawkeyes, then launch cruise missiles once their own satellites had a guidance solution for them. Those would be targeted for *Saratoga*'s battle group. But a nuclear weapon in space? That didn't figure. The Russian scenario didn't call for a first launch of anything nuclear unless the U.S. gave an indication they would.

"Have we sent in—or has NATO sent in—any requests to use nuclear weapons?"

"Nothing. That wouldn't come anyway until we had an idea how long we could hold them on the ground in Germany."

"How much hardened gear do you carry?" Cobb was referring to electronic equipment designed to withstand a high-level atomic detonation. Such a burst could knock out all communications, radar, and launching systems.

"I think you understand why I want you off to *Kennedy*." Turner's face was grim. "The Air Force has already launched F-15s. They're going to try to take out whatever it is up there. But who knows if they'll be on time. We could end up being sitting ducks in a matter of hours." Again his voice drifted off. Then he got to his feet. "So when I come into the wind, you folks are on your way. It may be the last chance I'll have to get you off, and your Russian friend seems to be a key."

"He's very important, Admiral."

"That's what Pratt told me. So my first responsibility is to get you off of here in one piece. Be ready in half an hour. An escort will pick up you and the girl in sick bay. General Keradin will already be aboard the aircraft."

Cobb stood. "I wish you luck, sir."

"I sincerely hope that luck holds." Turner grinned wryly. "If it doesn't, it won't take long for them to go after their next target." They both knew that would be the second carrier battle group—*Kennedy*'s.

The fireball was not brilliant, not what military people had been trained to expect. But even in the early morning sunlight, it caught the eye like the flash of a camera. Cobb was in the copilot's seat at the time, talking with the pilot while they awaited clearance for takeoff. He noticed it immediately, but said nothing. It was, after all, a blast at 150 or more miles in the sky, and could easily be mistaken for any number of natural occurrences.

The pilot looked at Cobb out of the corner of his eye. "Notice that?"

Cobb nodded, saying nothing. He put on the extra set of headphones to listen to the air-control net. There was dead silence for a moment. Then he heard the voices, normal at first, then more anxious, calling on the net. First they asked for radio checks, then requested those who answered to call the long-range planes on other frequencies.

But Cobb knew what the response would already be. Nothing. It was not a large burst as megatons went—probably no more than one or two, but at that height—two hundred kilometers, the computers projected—the damage would already be taking effect. The Air Force F-15s hadn't gotten to it in time.

There would be no burst effect, nothing that would bring the launching of ICBMs in retaliation. There would be no loss of equipment or lives, nor even wounded or radiation victims. Instead, the victims would be the heart of the American offensive and defensive machine—electronics. The atmospheric ionization caused by the detonation of an atomic weapon at that height, well above the atmosphere, would halt all medium- and long-range communications for ranges of possibly 1,500 miles for up to two hours. Line-of-sight radio communications would not be affected, but satellites were out of the question, as were all air-defense and airborne communications. The electromagnetic pulse (EMP) could also damage solid-state electronics. Virtually all susceptible computers and sensors would be inoperative and even radar and microwave transmissions might be mute for as long as an hour.

It was long enough, Cobb knew, long enough to get in that first launch against *Saratoga*'s battle group. The computers could only assume so much, but to his knowledge, no programs had ever been developed coordinating EMP with the Soviet Backfires launching their cruise missiles. Would they launch just before or just after the blast? How might the missiles be affected. Was it all timed so that Soviet submarines would pop to the surface and take control of the missiles, guiding them the last short distance to target?

Cobb didn't know. Neither did Turner, nor Pratt. No one really did. And the computers were inoperative.

"What happened?" the pilot asked Cobb.

"Perhaps you'll be able to tell your grandchildren that you saw the first atomic blast of the war—and survived it."

The man blanched.

"Doesn't affect you or me or anyone in the whole group. Not directly, anyway. But you can't believe how screwed up the nervous system of this whole damn battle group is now." He thought of what would follow. "Come on. Call up control and let's get out of here. Pretty soon there *will* be something that'll hurt you pretty bad." It didn't require a genius to do the simple mathematics necessary. Air-launched cruise missiles would be arriving in half an hour or so, give or take a few minutes. The Hawkeyes would do what they could, but they were a long distance from the carrier, they couldn't communicate, and they couldn't use the satellites in the way they were intended to, and the group's own early-warning system was useless at this stage.

The pilot requested permission to take off. It was Admiral Turner's voice that granted it. And then he added, "We'll do what we can to hold 'em off, Cobb. Give Pratt my regards."

Cobb learned much later how well they did.

The effects of the atomic blast had not been as severe as expected. *Saratoga*'s Hawkeyes had done their job. They intercepted the Backfires before launching. An acceptable number of Soviet aircraft had gone down.

But there were fighters joining up with the Russian bombers, and the Hawkeyes took a beating after that. The assumption the Soviet submarines might take over control of the cruise missiles on their final run was correct. When they surfaced to do so, Turner's helos and antisubmarine ships went after them. That accounted for the accuracy of another batch of missiles. But a number continued toward their target.

The ships undertook countermeasures, using everything they could to decoy the incoming missiles. That accounted for another batch. Sea Sparrow missiles accurately brought down more. But there were more than a dozen that survived all phases of the battle group's defense.

Saratoga was actually the first ship to be hit. A missile impacted aft of the island on the starboard side, just below the elevator. Fires ignited on the hangar deck. A second missile hit just below the angled flight deck on the port side. A large section of deck ruptured. More fires erupted. The third missile penetrated the hull plating, detonating in the after engine room. The watch there died almost instantly, either from the blast or from escaping high-pressure steam. *Saratoga* was now operating on three shafts.

As the carrier was fighting her own battle, other ships in the group also came under fire. The frigate *Gallery* disappeared in a belch of flame as a missile exploded in her torpedo storage. A surviving captain of one of the nearby ships reported that within sixty seconds almost nothing remained of the little ship.

The stern of *Deyo* disappeared to the waterline.

The bridge of *Macdonough* was cleared by a direct hit. When her executive officer took command, he was told that the blast took out the bridge, the combat information center, and three decks below, and that the fires were out of control. Three minutes later the torpedoes in the ASROC launcher blew, and he watched the forward third of the ship drift away.

According to the computers, the first Soviet launch had been more effective than projected—perhaps even by them. It had never been considered that they would take advantage of the effect of a high-altitude nuclear blast. The computers also said that an aircraft carrier should be able to survive at least four cruise missile hits. *Saratoga* was trying to survive three. Fires in her hangar threatened fuel and ammunition. The angled deck was useless, as was the elevator that had been hit. There was no chance of getting the after engine room back on line. She could likely float after more than three direct hits, but was it worthwhile?

On the bridge, Admiral Turner explained to *Saratoga*'s commanding officer that Soviet doctrine called for a second, equally devastating launch.

ABOARD U.S.S. *YORKTOWN*

The initial assault on *Saratoga* and her battle group was taking place even as the commanding officers of Pratt's battle group were meeting aboard *Yorktown* about four hundred miles to the west to make final plans for their defense. The radical nature of the attack—the creation of an electromagnetic pulse—had not been expected by most of those men. Only Carleton and Nelson were unsurprised; one of Pratt's original projections had been based on the Soviet fleet attacking before ground forces moved into Germany. It was based on the persisting Russian concept that NATO forces in the North Atlantic and Mediterranean would have to be neutralized. If they were not, then NATO ground forces in Europe could be reinforced, control of the air could not be guaranteed, and a prolonged ground war would likely mean acceleration to the nuclear level.

The Russian hierarchy would accept nuclear war only if it was to combat a last-ditch NATO nuclear effort. Once the Russians thought the flow of battle in Europe was to their advantage, they would call for peace talks as their divisions swept across Central Europe to the Atlantic coast. By the time a cease-fire would actually be effected, NATO would no longer be a threat.

"They're ahead of schedule," Nelson whispered to Carleton.

"Probably want their General Keradin—dead or alive. But I never expected they'd go for the nuclear stuff this early."

One of the other COs stood up to ask Pratt's staff man a question. "Just what does this EMP thing mean now from a strategic aspect? I mean we all know what it does technically, but they weren't expected to go for anything like that this early. Does this mean they'll set one off over us too?"

"They don't have to set off another right away," came the answer. "All of us use the same satellites, whether it's *Saratoga* or *Kennedy* or NATO headquarters." He shrugged his shoulders. "Washington anticipated something like this could happen, and they've got some more recon satellites perched at Vandenburg right now. For all we know, they may already have launched. On the other hand, the Russians also launched some maneuverable killer satellites yesterday. We send one up; they go after it. If they can't catch up to ours, they launch another ASAT; we send up our F-15s to fire antisatellite missiles at their antisatellite satellites . . ." He shrugged again, to Nelson's amusement. "What we do is we go back to doing the same thing we did at Okinawa forty years ago—radar pickets. This time it's Hawkeye aircraft and guided-missile frigates, and they're facing the same threat—a cruise missile is just like a kamikaze."

Another staff officer appeared in the back of the briefing room, whirling a finger in the air to indicate "speed it up." It would be hours before their own group was attacked, but Pratt's plan was to disperse the formation even farther in case of nuclear attack. Pratt then intended to launch his own attack.

He had asked Wendell Nelson to impress the role of submarines on both Tactical Action Officers and captains. Military use of the waters beneath the surface had changed radically since World War Two, the last time subs had proved their worth under actual wartime conditions. In those days, a submarine was actually an air-breathing creature, able to submerge only for short periods of time. Now they were truly submersibles, capable of navigating the strange subsurface world for extended periods. A true silent service, they traded in stealth and surprise. Their preferred environment was the open ocean. Effectiveness within the straits and narrows of the Mediterranean depended completely on their individual performance. Because subs from both sides were forced to pass through straits to gain access to the Med, the initial element for achieving success was to sever contact with the inevitable shadows that tracked them. The submarines would present a challenge when the confusion of combat released them.

The reaction of the COs to Wendell Nelson was markedly different than the previous day. He was no longer an upstart—he was accepted as a full four-stripe captain in the forefront of radical antisubmarine tactics, and the traditional white attitude had become colorblind in the face of the Soviet threat. When they left, each commanding officer had access to antisubmarine tactics never before used. They felt they now had an even chance against Soviet numbers.

As they waited on the stern of *Yorktown* to be heloed back to their ships, the action reports from *Saratoga* filtered in. The second Soviet strike had been as bad as the first. Three more tiny frigates sunk, two Halsey-class destroyers badly damaged, one sinking, a guided-missile cruiser gone, *Yorktown*'s sister ship, *Essex*, in danger of sinking, and *Saratoga* had been hit four more times. Large deck carriers were supposed to be able to survive four cruise missiles— she had taken seven and was still afloat. Her flight deck was buckled and in shambles. She was dead in the water, engine rooms flooded, fires ravaging much of the inner hull.

Pratt announced later over the main radio net of his battle group that when *Saratoga*'s commanding officer asked for volunteers to try to keep her afloat, no able man would leave her.

The legend of the Battle of the Mediterranean was growing.

THE WAR IN SPACE

Russian reconnaissance satellites over the Mediterranean suffered the same ill effects from the nuclear blast as the Americans'. That was accepted by the Soviets. But timing was also to Soviet advantage, for they instituted a new series of launches from deep in the Soviet Union at Tyuratum, scheduled to achieve orbit after the old ones were rendered ineffective. Launches from Vandenburg Air Force Base soon followed. U.S. launch vehicles had been stockpiled for such an event; replacement recon packages were ready on the launchpads.

Anticipating the use of killer satellites was a specially trained squadron of Air Force F-15s armed with two-stage, warhead-carrying rockets. It was not difficult for the engineers in the United States to determine which were the killer satellites, and once identified, it was up to the F-15s to climb to maximum altitude and fire their rockets into space. In the vicinity of its target, each rocket could maneuver with tiny thrusters to achieve lock-on. At 17,000 plus m.p.h., they disintegrated the Russian weapons.

The Soviet ASATs were actually orbiting satellites—but with one difference. They could maneuver in space, placing themselves in proximity with their target. Once in killing range, explosive charges propelled metal balls in the direction of their targets—which would be unable to maneuver. The outcome was much like the grape-shot used by sailing ships two hundred years before. Everything in its path was destroyed.

Unlike the action on the surface of the Mediterranean, the war in space was not initially harmful to human beings. Once the computers took over, it was artificial intelligence versus artificial intelligence. The intent of both sides was to deny the enemy the use of intelligence and communications at the most critical moment—when their forces were racing toward each other. The winner, according to the computers, would be the one that had the latest intelligence concerning the location of the enemy and the most advanced weapons systems employed at that moment.

Consequently, the space battle was not prolonged. Though both sides planned for the event, there were only so many rockets that could be positioned on the launchpads, only so many navigational, reconnaissance or offensive weapons that could be placed atop the delivery systems. In the end, the space war—the first war of the future, the war that would shed no blood—was over in a matter of hours. The available machines had been exhausted.

Once again, it was up to the human intellect to determine the outcome.

ABOARD U.S.S. *YORKTOWN*, SOUTHEAST OF MALTA

Until the attack on the *Saratoga* battle group, Russian warships hung back. They remained close to friendly shores under the protection of their own air cover. Their mission was to advance under the envelope created by air-launched and sub-launched cruise missiles. The cruisers and destroyers were to mop up, to finish off the stragglers. Then they would move on the soft underbelly in support of amphibious invasions. A second front, if Russia controlled the North Atlantic, would be the kiss of death for NATO.

The picture beneath the surface remained murky for both sides. The objective of an attack submarine was to neutralize the aircraft carrier or any other capital ships. Often, this could be accomplished in conjunction with cruise-missile attacks by either surface ships or aircraft. But timing was vital, especially in the few short, crucial hours of actual combat. A submarine surfacing preliminary to the attack would be a sitting duck; after the attack, it would be unable to assist, its element of surprise compromised.

To get into position to attack the surface force, a submarine was required to dispose of its own natural enemy—another submarine capable of equivalent stealth. Opposing groups of hunter-killer submarines were positioned in front of both Pratt's and Konstantin's battle groups. Their mission was to deny the other's submarines the opportunity to break through into an attack position.

It quickly became a one-on-one situation that day. With detection capabilities greater than the range of their weapons, submarines attempted to outmaneuver each other to keep out of range, at the same time searching for a position to fire on the enemy. It was a prolonged, desperate cat-and-mouse game that could end only when one was sunk. In such engagements, the water would suddenly be full of torpedoes, each one intent on seeking out the target inserted by the mother-ship computer in its memory bank. A torpedo would attack on its own as long as its fuel held out. It was a deadly game—its outcome remained unknown to those who fought on the surface.

Tom Carleton looked from the shiny slick in the bottom of his coffee cup to the dim red lights above him. The last sip had been cold, the powdered cream at the bottom rancid tasting. The dregs reflected the reddish glow.

The status boards reflected the strategic situation in a ninety-degree arc from the Baltic Sea to North Africa. A second board displayed the area that he was specifically concerned with, the Mediterranean, and the enemy forces that would affect *Yorktown* and *Kennedy*'s battle group in the next few hours. The Soviet carrier group that had been off Alexandria the previous day was close to striking range—but not quite. Their job was not to initiate the attack on the American battle group. Both the Americans and the Russians knew that *Kennedy*'s group was much too strong, their attack aircraft superior to anything the Russians could yet launch from a carrier. But they should not retain that superiority after the initial salvo of cruise missiles—and that's what the Russian group was moving up for now.

Saratoga's group was no longer effective—what remained of it. An ASW squadron had been sent to their aid in an attempt to keep Soviet submarines from sinking the survivors. Though *Saratoga*'s group had been battered, they achieved what Admiral Pratt had most hoped for. They had absorbed the combined ravages of two cruise-missile salvos and submarine wolf-pack attacks, and enough of the ships were still afloat that they were keeping more units of the Soviet Navy busy than the enemy had obviously anticipated. That meant that the Russians were behind schedule. The elements of their fleet were not proceeding at the pace that Moscow had planned—and that was critical if the efforts in the Mediterranean were to coincide with the movement of the ground forces in Central Europe.

Saratoga had also contributed through the efforts of her attack squadrons. Their targets had been the closest air bases within the Iron Curtain; their purpose had simply been to take out as much Soviet airpower as possible and to destroy runways and base facilities. They had been successful. With assistance from the Air Force, they might have been overwhelming, but the latter had been withheld to support NATO ground forces in the event of attack. *Kennedy* had been much too far away to recover those few *Saratoga* aircraft that returned. They had either made their way to the few safe fields that were left within range, or they ditched. Their success had also verified a second factor that was accepted but never mentioned—once the shooting began, there would be no carrier for the surviving pilots to return to.

Carleton mulled over that as he studied the projected flight pattern of the air groups recently launched from *Kennedy*. He preferred to take his chances on the surface. Each pilot understood that his mission was essentially one way—that the Soviet battle plan was to eliminate the carriers first, and that delivering his weapons and escaping the Soviet defenses were just the beginning of his problems.

Carleton considered the location of the Soviet Backfire bombers. They had been launched from untouched fields deeper within the Soviet Union and there was a bit more time for planning than *Saratoga* had been given, but their numbers were still impressive. It was what had been called a "maximum effort" in World War Two, an all-out attempt to achieve their goal in one attack. Either to allow the conflict in the Mediterranean to be drawn out for more than twenty-four hours, or to concede the prerequisite of the first salvo, would imperil the Soviet thrust into Germany.

With the exception of his visit to Pratt's quarters aboard *Kennedy*, Tom Carleton's time on *Yorktown* had been spent in a small section of the cruiser. He allowed himself enough time on the bridge to become familiar with the watchstanders and to learn the eccentricities of his ship. The balance of his time had been spent in his cabin, one deck under the bridge, or in CIC (the Combat Information Center) two decks below his cabin. If *Yorktown* and its AEGIS system were the central nervous system of the battle group, CIC was the brain. It was as desirable and necessary a target to be eliminated as the carrier. The Russians would learn that soon if they were not already aware of it.

"Fresh coffee, Captain?" It was one of the radarmen. "Just brewed a fresh pot."

Carleton looked in his mug again. "Can you swab this one out?"

"No problem, sir. Cream or sugar?"

He remembered the rancid aroma from the dregs of the cup. "No thanks, son. Black." An acid rumbling in his stomach reminded him how long it had been since he'd eaten. Except for a courtesy call on the wardroom, any food he'd taken had been on the run. "Wait one, son. I know it isn't your job, but could you give my steward a buzz and ask him if he'd send a couple of sandwiches in?"

"Don't worry about a thing, Captain. Any of us are more than happy to do anything we can for you." He smiled, then added seriously, "It's good to have you here, sir. We've all heard a lot about you." With that, he was off.

Carleton wondered for a moment at the last comment, then let it pass. There was so much to do, so little time. He saw the blinking lights on the boards indicating the approaching wave of Soviet Backfires. Not too much time until they crossed the line, the imaginary line delineated by the computer when the Russian bombers conceivably could launch their missiles. He knew they wouldn't. At that distance, the computer projected only 1 to 3 percent hits. But as each minute passed, the success ratio improved.

"There you go, Captain." The radarman appeared at his side with a steaming mug of coffee. There was also a doughnut in a napkin.

Carleton sniffed the aroma appreciatively. "Where'd you find this?" he asked, gesturing with the doughnut.

"Came up from the crew's mess, sir. The cooks have been baking like crazy since last night. Figured they probably wouldn't have a chance today. Hope you don't mind. We're not allowed to eat 'em in here, but the chief said he thought you might be careful."

"I never considered that, son. If there's no food in here, I'll be glad to have my sandwiches outside. I could use a little air anyway."

"If it's all the same, sir, everyone sort of hopes you'll stay in here—unless you really want to go outside. It makes everyone feel pretty good today to have you around."

So that was it! It was no secret. There probably wasn't a soul on the ship who didn't know that the next couple of hours would make all the difference in the world to them. The captain of the ship was a father figure. Until he proved otherwise, he could do no wrong. They were putting complete faith in a man they'd never heard of until a few days before. Then rumors about him generated stories that each man would accept as gospel.

"Okay, son. If you insist, I'll break the rules. And the next time I have a few bucks in my pocket, I'll drop some in the kitty to cover costs." He looked more closely at the mug. It wasn't the same one he'd handed the sailor. This one had the seal of *Yorktown* on one side. Hand-painted on the reverse was "Captain Thomas H. Carleton, U.S.N.— Commanding Officer—U.S.S. YORKTOWN CG-48— Honorary Radarman." It was his ship, all right!

"Hope you don't mind, Captain."

"Not at all. I hope you'll let everyone know right now it's a real honor for me."

It felt good. There was something special about commanding a ship—nothing like it in the world. He wanted *Yorktown* to be his for a long time.

The disposition of the battle group spread before him on

another board. Surrounding *Kennedy* were the nuclear cruiser *Arkansas,* two double-ended guided missile cruisers, *Yarnell* and *Dale,* and the two Spruance-class destroyers, *Radford* and *Stump.* Wendell Nelson was to the south, toward the Gulf of Sidra, with seven more Spruance destroyers. A combined NATO force, made up of ships from Italy, France, and England, covered the northern flank. The small Italian carrier *Garibaldi* had reinforced this unit for antisubmarine purposes. To the east were the picket ships, groups of two to four units whose responsibility was both early warning and first-line harassment of the superior force aimed at the battle group.

The initial flight of Backfires had just now passed over the Black Sea into Bulgarian airspace—eight hundred miles distant. A small initial launch of new, untested missiles could be expected at a range of about five hundred miles, when they were over the Aegean Sea nearing Greece. Even then, the odds for these missiles were slim. But the idea was that the Backfires, already harassed by the Hawkeyes and *Kennedy*'s fighters, would maintain a gradually increasing saturation effect.

The picket groups were not under fire themselves. Attack planes from *Kharkov* were combining with wolf packs to make life difficult for the easternmost group. The American losses would be heavy out there, but if they could limit the effectiveness of the Soviet attack subs, *Kennedy*'s group had a fighting chance.

Carleton was tempted to step outside and enjoy the fresh air when his sandwiches came. Instead, he circulated around the darkened room, talking with the sailors, offering the support they were looking for. Then he slipped up to his cabin and penned a short note to his wife. It had become a habit whenever tension set in.

A change of clothes and a quick shave took only moments. To a crew as sharp as this one, a freshly pressed appearance would make all the difference in the world to morale. He also decided it would be a good idea to say a couple of words to them.

ABOARD U.S.S. *JOHN HANCOCK*, ONE HUNDRED MILES NORTHWEST OF BENGHAZI, LIBYA

Wendell Nelson convinced only the captain of *Nicholson* to call him Nellie; the others, though more at ease with him now, remained formal. He and *Nicholson*'s captain were the last members of the old "black shoe" Navy, the ones who had come aboard during the Vietnam era. They had cut their teeth on remnants of the old steam-boiler fleet or chased through steaming jungles in riverboats. Though they were educated in the weapons of the eighties, they were inured to the older traditions.

Nelson was of their generation, but he was different; he was tight with this new admiral; he was tall and handsome and looked like a Moorish god in his whites; he made statements such as: "Be goddamn happy you have pilots who can fly helos off your fantail, because if you didn't, the first sound you'd hear would be the detonation of a warhead fired by a submarine you didn't know was there—and it would be the last thing you'd ever hear," or, "Thank your lucky stars that you've been set loose from that battle group, because you don't have enough protection on board to keep yourselves from being blown out of the water with that first salvo," or, "You don't have to think about the tactics I'm

246

going to use—just follow directions. The computer will save your ass."

They understood Wendell Nelson, grudgingly accepted his truisms, and would follow him. But that didn't mean they had to like him. They accorded him the respect that Navy regs required and let it go at that. There was no time for comparing notes to see if they could present a united front. Each commanding officer was hidebound to his ship, responsible to his men, and would fight his ship to the maximum of his ability.

Nelson stretched, then patted his breast pocket and was reminded that he had run out of cigarettes. There was no way he could function without them, not now. He sent the bridge messenger to his cabin for three more packs. There was no telling how long it might be before he was able to get back down there himself.

There was a bit of the old Navy buried deep within Nelson. He preferred to spend as much time on the bridge as possible. Hell, he loved it. He could operate from there because his was a three-dimensional mind, one that could develop an absolute picture of his strategic environment. He could either picture *John Hancock* as the center and see the air, surface, and subsurface situation, or he could withdraw himself. He would place his mind in a remote location and develop a holographic image. In it, there was no ocean surface on which his ship sailed, nor a darkness that hid submarines. Rather, the surface was an invisible plane, the air above and the water below equally clear. He could visualize the whole picture; he was omniscient.

It was in that manner that he would function as a squadron commander, coordinating two divisions, each operating independently of the other. If the computer projections and Nelson's mind functioned in concert, those two divisions would actually be sweeping the Soviet wolf packs in closer to each other than was judicious. Then he would destroy them—if they didn't get him first.

Nelson thanked the messenger for the cigarettes, lit one immediately, and meandered over to the chart table. One of the quartermasters had set up a separate chart for him to insert latest-estimated-position reports. He erased the old locations, pinpointing the Soviet submarines that he was to take out.

He had no concern for those that were to the west of Malta or to the north in the Ionian Sea. They were covered by the NATO forces that Pratt had established. *Garibaldi* and her mixed-nationality escorts seemed in control up there. The submarines that Nelson targeted were proceeding from the east in advance of *Kharkov* and other Russian surface forces, or from the Gulf of Sidra to the south. The frigates were only a picket line, a stopgap measure to slow the advance from the east. Nelson estimated that as many as a dozen Soviet subs might penetrate that line after disposing of the frigates. With the eight that were coming from the south, it was indeed a formidable force. There were no friendly submarines to move ahead of him to counter them. The last order Pratt had given to his own submarine commander was to move eastward, placing himself between the Soviet carrier group and *Kennedy*'s.

Nelson compared these subs to a pulling guard, leading the sweep around the end. Their mission was vitally important to the success of Soviet strategy. If the full force of that all-important first salvo was to achieve maximum effect, these submarines were the key. The Backfire bombers depended a great deal on them, the attacking surface forces depended on them, the entire strategy of achieving an initial blow that the Americans could not recover from depended on their success.

Pratt knew exactly how Nelson's mind functioned, how the man responded to a threat. The Admiral envied Nelson's ability to envision the threat by completely withdrawing and establishing that objective mental picture of his. He knew of no other man capable of succeeding in this particular case.

Nelson lit another cigarette from the butt of the one he had just finished. He sketched some more on his chart, then called his executive officer over. "This is where we're going to chase them." He pointed at an imaginary spot about a hundred miles north of Benghazi, Libya. "Have the communications officer prepare a message designating *Nicholson*'s CO as northern division commander. I want him to move the remaining frigates gradually down in that direction. They'll either chase the subs in their sector in his direction or draw them down there. I'll take any help I can get."

The executive officer looked at the chart for a moment with a touch of uncertainty, then back at Nelson. "Admiral Pratt still has tactical command of those pickets, Captain." He was one of those not yet able to figure out how his commanding officer could assume such responsibilities.

"You're right. Send another message to Pratt and tell him I will assume command of those frigates immediately."

"Uh . . ." The XO couldn't swallow that one. In his Navy, junior officers were not in the habit of telling an Admiral what they were assuming command of. But the XO simply couldn't think of what to say.

"Just send it, and watch what happens. Okay?" Nelson pushed his baseball cap back on his head in a jaunty manner and grinned at the XO. The meaning of his expression was obvious. It said in no uncertain terms, I know what I'm doing and I know my bounds.

"Right, Captain."

"And when you get the comm officer set, zip up the ship for the duration. We're just about in missile range and they have a better idea where we are than we do them. I'm going to need you to run this ship." It was the way he wanted the XO to see him—a man above the other captains, but also a man who trusted his subordinates, one who would give them all the responsibility they could handle. The XO was a good officer—Nelson had checked his credentials before he'd ever gotten together with Pratt in Washington. He could have asked for another XO, but this man and his ASW training were superb. What the hell, thought Nelson, I might not be too excited about having me for a CO either. But I needed a go-between with the crew, and they understand this guy. A crew needed a known entity and the XO was it.

"Contact!" The voice report echoed across the bridge from sonar a split second before the warning bell went off. A missile was locked on *John Hancock!*

ABOARD U.S.S. *JOHN F. KENNEDY*, SOUTHEAST OF MALTA

When Admiral Pratt settled into his chair in flag plot, the displays before him were accurate within seconds. Commander Clark had been made a staff officer because of his brilliance in strategic concepts. Once Pratt made him understand what was expected, Clark was able to deliver. From the moment he entered the room, Pratt knew there would be no necessity for sharp language again. The only element missing was the satellite picture. But that was balanced by the fact that the Russians were no better off in that respect.

Clark eased into the chair next to him. "The Hawkeyes are having a rough time of it, Admiral."

Pratt's eyes shot up to the board that displayed the air battle taking place four hundred miles to the east, well to the south of Crete. Colored symbols representing friendly forces were minimal. "Status?" He struck a match to light the stub of cigar between his teeth.

"Our Hawkeyes picked them up as they passed over Bulgaria and commenced jamming, just in case they decided to fire a few early shots to keep us off guard. But it wasn't too long after that the Hawkeyes got caught in a pincer between MiGs coming down from the north and some fighters that I guess were sent up by *Kharkov*. That's one I guess we didn't expect. Anyway, our fighters arrived on station a few moments after it all started. Our boys hadn't been able to do much about fighting back. All they could do was jam and evade, and you know how well they can do that."

"Cut the shit, Commander. How many did we lose?"

"Two of them, sir. They were apparently too close together. We were listening to the net and the controllers were vectoring our Tomcats in when they went off the air."

Pratt interrupted. "That's max range for the Tomcats. They should be in closer." The cigar remained unlit. He tore off his last match.

"We still have recon aircraft out there, Admiral." It was Clark's turn, his first since Pratt had come aboard. "I gave the orders for them to haul ass out of there, sir, because we wouldn't have had any Hawkeyes left if—"

Pratt extended his hands in a gesture of acceptance. "Okay. Okay. No need to outdo my act. I would have done the same thing. Those Russian fighters didn't have much time on station either, did they?"

"Very little. It was pretty quick, I guess—old-fashioned dogfight for a second. We lost two, claim four of theirs downed, though I think our men in the rear seat tend to exaggerate. But they accomplished what we sent them out for. The other Hawkeyes got away, and we still have a pretty good air picture as a result."

"Very good, you mean," Pratt mused. "That's what I was looking for before." Now he slapped his pocket, looking for more matches.

"They've tried barrage-jamming our picture, but we're restationed so that LINK is working properly now." LINK was the process by which the recon aircraft were able to transmit the tactical picture back to *Kennedy* and *Yorktown*. It also allowed the controllers in the Hawkeyes to vector the fighters to a target or even to take full control of the craft from the pilot.

"We've been able to take about five or six Backfires out of the picture, but, Christ, they just keep coming, one flight after another."

"That's the idea. Simple mathematics. It doesn't matter

to Moscow how many planes they lose or how many missiles we knock out as long as enough of them get through. They never designed the goddamn things for perfection. If half a dozen missiles break through on us for every fifty they put up there, I'll bet they'd call that a successful attack."

Clark pointed at one of the boards. "It looks very successful then, sir." He handed Pratt a pack of matches.

The attack was successful indeed. The red enemy symbols on the board, each representing a Backfire bomber closing in on their force, were numerous, merging into a single red blob in some sectors. And converging on the intercept point a little over a hundred miles from the battle group were the Hornet fighters, the last source of long-range defense before Pratt's battle group would have to undertake its own defense.

Pratt viewed the situation dispassionately. The perimeter was already over—the pickets had done their job and now it was up to Nelson. He saw that Nelson's ASW forces had now come under attack. Their success would be measured in a matter of minutes. If their tactics were successful, the Soviet submarines would neither be able to control the cruise missiles nor launch an attack of their own on the battle group.

The Soviet cruise missiles would be launched shortly. Then it would become an electronic war—missile versus missile, countermeasures versus countermeasures, men versus black boxes. Clark had seen that electronic countermeasures had been instituted before Pratt entered plot. Each ship in the battle group constantly radiated signals that would confuse the incoming missiles, fool the enemy radar into thinking that there were more ships than really existed, that small ships were really carriers, that the carrier was a series of small targets. But Pratt knew there would be more missiles than targets. There were men in those aircraft and submarines who understood American battle group dispositions well enough to know where the carrier was located and which ship was an AEGIS cruiser.

ABOARD U.S.S. *YORKTOWN*
WITH THE KENNEDY BATTLE GROUP

Tom Carleton made a tour of *Yorktown* after his shower. Since she was secured for action, the PA system was used whenever a hatch was opened to another compartment to allow entry. This served two purposes—many men actually had the opportunity to shake their new commanding officer's hand before they went into battle, and nothing could have done more for morale than to see the captain apparently as confident as if they were about to take an extended liberty.

By the time Carleton was seated at his station in CIC, his appearance was no different than when he left. He was one of those men who could put on a freshly pressed, custom-fitted uniform and ten minutes later appear as if he'd slept in it. His slacks were rumpled, the buttons on his shirt strained over his more-than-ample belly, and his belt had once again eased itself below his midsection. He was definitely not material for recruiting posters. But nothing in his outward appearance could have adversely affected the crew of *Yorktown*. He understood what sailors respected and what they reacted to—and they were on his side.

The computer could have told Carleton how long it would take for the two opposing forces to meet. *Kharkov* and her escorts were a little over two hundred miles to the east.

Both groups were making about twenty-five knots, closing in at more than fifty miles each hour. In four hours, they would be on top of each other. In two hours or less, though they would not yet be in sight of each other, they would be within shipboard missile range.

The proximity of the opposing surface forces to each other would have meant a great deal in the early stages, if they had been the main elements. However, there were submarines capable of moving much faster than the ships on the surface that could alter the situation at any moment. Some of the subs had not been detected since the satellite-intelligence capability had been lost. The overwhelming influence in the modern theater of war was the air-to-surface missiles. At any time now, they could be on their way with some probability of a hit. As each second passed, the odds increased that the initial missiles of the salvo would be launched.

The link with perimeter aircraft disclosed a large number of Soviet aircraft breaking through the barrier. The picture was revealed clearly on both *Yorktown* and *Kennedy*. Though Pratt and Carleton were in direct contact, their responsibilities differed considerably. The Admiral was in charge of overall strategy. Carleton was to coordinate the defense of *Kennedy*'s battle group.

The red light on Carleton's console winked in concert with the buzzer that sounded through CIC, and within seconds of the warning that the attack had commenced, a voice in the darkened room announced to no one in particular, "Missiles away!" It had begun.

There was a perceptible sigh in CIC, a collective release of tension. The waiting was over. Now they could act.

"Time to impact—twenty-four minutes." The voice was cold, impersonal. It was the speaker's job to announce the information, even if others could note the time simply by pushing a button.

A tactical signal came over the primary voice net for all ships. On their direct line, Admiral Pratt said, "Tom, I'm shifting the screen around, moving everybody a bit. No reason to make it easy for them. I want you to act independently. There are two of their Alfa-class subs out here that we've completely lost." Those were titanium-hulled attack subs, extremely fast, unusually quiet, and their hull alloys did not distort the magnetic field—making them even harder to locate.

"Probably went silent," Carleton responded.

"That's exactly what my man Loomis figures. They could pop up anywhere."

Carleton gave his executive officer free reign to conn the ship. The ship's movements made no difference to the computer as long as it continued to provide the necessary functions to back up the system's operations. Able to detect and track a couple of hundred targets at a time, it now would face its greatest test. The Soviet Backfires were filling the air with missiles, some fired from maximum altitude, others from lower levels. Some of the bombers swooped down to sea level to release their missiles below the acquisition level of most shipboard radars. And there were a select number of bombers in each flight that retained their weapons. They would continue to close in on the group, conducting evasive action so that some of them might get close enough to fire at point-blank range—close enough to penetrate the security envelope that allowed ships' computers time for a target solution for their own defensive missiles.

Dale, one of the perimeter anti-air-defense ships, was the first to come under fire. While the carrier and the AEGIS cruiser were primary targets, it was imperative to eliminate a ship like *Dale*. She carried dual missile launchers fore and aft and she could reload the rails of one launcher while the other took the target under fire. She was a guided-missile cruiser that could handle herself under pressure.

Three incoming cruise missiles were locked on *Dale*. Sea Sparrows slid onto her rails. Her fire-control radar relayed guidance data as each one was fired. While these small antimissile birds raced for their targets, the launchers returned to load position. Two aircraft were coming in low on the water, intent on the main body to the rear of *Dale*.

Again she fired, this time with Standard missiles locked

on the Soviet aircraft. The launchers automatically snapped
back to reload. Sea Sparrows slid onto the forward rails,
Standards to the rear. *Dale*'s radar was cluttered with targets
now. Computers determined the threat level as she fired—
reloaded—fired—reloaded—

But now an equally dangerous threat presented itself to
the cruiser. ASW helicopters had been prosecuting a contact
about thirty miles off *Dale*'s port bow, which eventually
escaped. When contact was regained, the sub was seen to
be closing in on the cruiser at high speed. As a radio warning
from the helos came to her attention, the ship's sonar established contact. Within moments, the telltale sound of
high-speed screws signified torpedoes in the water.

While maneuvering to defend herself from torpedo attack, *Dale* continued to fire her missiles. There were hits.
They could not be seen with the naked eye, though smoke
was visible soon after, but radar confirmed when a target
went off the screen. *Dale* was one of many ships launching
a hail of missiles, and only the computers would ever know
which missile and which ship achieved success that day.

Dale was the first ship in her group to be hit. A missile
slammed into her stern between the after launcher and the
fire-control radars, detonating on the second deck. The blast
decimated engineering spaces, and almost instantly the ship
was out of control, her starboard shaft bent, steering control
lost. Fuel oil fed flames that threatened the magazine below
the aft launcher.

As damage-control parties fought the flames, attempting
to get through to after steering, a tremendous explosion
shook the hull as at least one torpedo exploded the NIXIE
decoy. But another passed by, undeterred by the explosion,
to strike just aft of the bridge below the Harpoon missile
canisters. One of the missile engines ignited, sending the
vehicle careening into the rear of the pilothouse. The torpedo
blast destroyed the engine room that controlled the port
shaft. With both shafts damaged, *Dale* gradually slowed
until she was dead in the water. A second torpedo blew up
in her bow. There was no longer power for the weapons.

As she settled quickly, heeling to port, the abandon-ship order was given. A second missile dove through her pilot-house, the blast detonating the warheads remaining in the ASROC launcher. Fires swept back through the survivors. *Dale* had done her duty.

ABOARD U.S.S. *JOHN HANCOCK*

"Missiles away," the report echoed through *Hancock*'s CIC from one of the helos even before it painted on the radars. Two more voice reports followed, each from a different location.

The submarines had initiated the action. That was to be expected. They could detect and track a surface ship well before they themselves were ever located. That was to their advantage. Once they were found out, they had no other choice but to run.

Nelson had four ships in line at broad intervals. They were at high speed and each ship had a helicopter working in tandem with it in much the same pattern Nelson had taught them the previous day. It was the equivalent of eight ships, as far as Nelson was concerned. That made it even, perhaps gave him a slight advantage, because the subs had no idea where the helicopters might be until they heard the ping of the dipping sonar. If a helo was lucky and lowered his sonar near a submarine, a homing torpedo could be launched well before the sub could piece together what was taking place.

But on the other hand, a cruise missile launched from beneath the surface also presented a formidable advantage.

There were four of these missiles now rocketing toward the surface ships. The lock-on warning buzzer indicated *John Hancock* was a target. Chaff rockets were automatically fired to draw the missile off target. Deep within the ship, a computer fed continual solutions into the missile-defense system. First *Hancock,* then *Conolly,* then *Spruance* fired Sea Sparrows at the oncoming missiles.

A submarine-launched cruise missile is intended to fly at low level, low enough to deter radar acquisition, or at least make a fire-control solution complicated. They are not exceptionally fast as missiles go, but they are persistent, designed to correct their course against the actions of their target. They are difficult to defend against. Only one of the Sea Sparrows met with success.

Three missiles bore in on the destroyers now. An anxious *Conolly* fired a second missile—too late. Her Phalanx system opened fire; this time she was lucky—the hail of bullets destroyed the warhead within a hundred yards of the ship.

Spruance had less success. Her radar lost contact with the incoming missile only for an instant, but the time lost in reacquisition delayed the Gatling gun just long enough. When it did open fire, the missile was diving for *Spruance*'s flight deck. It penetrated through officers' quarters, exploding in the ship's laundry. The force of the blast blew upward, unseating the huge ASROC launcher that allowed the luxury of firing torpedoes from a distance.

The last missile was drawn off her target by the chaff and exploded harmlessly, well away from *Hancock.*

Two of the helos were able to pinpoint one of the missile-firing submarines. They released torpedoes less than a minute after the missiles had broken surface. The run time was quick. A resounding underwater explosion rewarded them.

Conolly's helo reported a solid contact close to its sonar but was experiencing trouble with the torpedo-release mechanism. Within moments, the mother ship fired her ASROC as a backup. The rocket-propelled torpedo, keying in on the ship's helo, hit the water less than half a mile from it. Immediately the homing device locked on the target and moments later a second submarine had been hit.

There had been eight Soviet subs divided into three wolf packs. One sub remained on the port bow, two directly ahead, and the helos were bothering them. The intact three-sub pack on the starboard bow had apparently now raced out to the starboard beam of the approaching destroyers. In a one-two-three effort, they launched missiles, then sonar showed them closing in for a probable torpedo attack.

On the port beam, the remaining submarine of the two-boat pack was able to break into torpedo range of *Spruance*. Unable to use her ASROC, the ship was forced to recall her helo to her defense. As the craft's sonar lowered onto the water, the first sound that came was that of torpedoes. The water was seemingly filled with them, the high-pitched scream cluttering the entire scope. The first hit *Spruance* on the port side, exploding into the forward engine room with a force that knocked the outboard turbine engine into the other. Blazing fuel wiped out the entire crew in that space. Still reeling from the force of the first torpedo, a second struck amidships. The hits were so close that the port side of the ship opened to the sea for more than fifty feet. Watertight compartments, intended to limit flooding, were ripped open by the pressure. Immediately, *Spruance* listed heavily to port, her speed cut to only a few knots to slow the flooding. She was out of the battle.

Nelson saw that the integrity of his line was breaking up. The Soviet tactics were obvious; they intended to separate the ships, isolate them. One submarine, the one that hit *Spruance*, remained to port. The hell with it! Two more were dead ahead but were dodging helos. The immediate threat was to starboard—still three of them out there. They had just launched missiles and were now closing in!

He wheeled his three remaining ships to starboard. In a ragged column, they raced down the throats of the closing wolf pack. *Briscoe* was point and the only ship not yet required to defend herself. Turning slightly to port, she fired her Sea Sparrow launcher. The closest incoming missile had been diverted by chaff and was flying an erratic course. The Sparrow brought it down. *Conolly*'s Phalanx activated as the next missile raced directly at her. She had turned to starboard to open her radar-controlled gun. The missile burst at forty yards, showering the superstructure with debris. The interior of her pilothouse was shattered. *Conolly*, with no control from her bridge, steamed blindly away from the column.

Nelson ordered one of the helos in ahead of them to cover for the damaged ship. *John Hancock* and *Briscoe* continued at flank speed toward the submarines. At maximum range, they fired rocket-propelled torpedoes from their ASROC launchers. In concert with the two ships, the one helo in front also dropped its remaining torpedo.

Before the ship's torpedoes even hit the water, their sonarmen identified high-speed screw noises. The Soviets had torpedoes in the water ahead of them. Doctrine said that each sub would fire a spread of at least two torpedoes—as many as six could be heading toward the ships.

The second helo coming into the area was vectored over a sonar contact by *Hancock* and, without taking the time to dip her sonar, dropped another homing torpedo. It was contrary to everything Nelson had learned, but he had once run a program to determine hit possibilities in such a case; the chances weren't much less in this situation than in a controlled attack. There were at least three submarines down there making noise that would attract a homing torpedo.

An explosion astern of the damaged *Conolly* accounted for the first enemy torpedo; it also meant one less decoy. A second blast lifted the ship's stern clear of the water. Seemingly before she settled, a third torpedo struck under the forward gun mount. The resulting explosion was a combination of torpedo warhead and the forward magazine. Nelson heard the bridge report that *Conolly* had neither a bow nor a stern; what remained was swept with flames. Two ships left!

The sea ahead of them erupted. *Briscoe*'s lookouts reported wreckage boiling to the surface at the same time her sonarmen reported secondary underwater explosions. A submarine had been hit! The second helo, arriving on station, had just reported torpedoes still running when another undersea blast occurred less than a mile away. A second sub!

Two destroyers and one submarine were left in that sector. But there was no way to locate it. No sonar could penetrate through the underwater mess to locate the last sub. And nothing was more dangerous than a high-speed submarine, one that knew it was free to move for a period of time without detection.

Nelson wheeled the two remaining ships about, reversing course. The sub had the upper hand for the time being. There was no reason to offer two perfect targets. Only *John Hancock* had a second helo available. She couldn't recover, but Nelson could launch the remaining one. It had been armed and was ready in one hangar, and now he ordered it rolled out for launch.

As best they could determine, there were four submarines left against two destroyers. Each wolf pack had been hurt. Now the packs were independent, no longer able to present a united front. The initial part of Nelson's plan had worked.

"Missiles away." The buzzer echoed the voice, once again indicating that at least one missile was locked on to *John Hancock*. The source was in the vicinity they had just left. The one remaining submarine persisted! These must be its last missiles, unless the sub could reload tubes under trying conditions faster than Nelson anticipated. If only *Hancock* could get through this. . . .

Nelson overheard the report of Sea Sparrows launched. He heard the report that they failed to bring down any missiles. Shortly thereafter, he could hear the thump of the automatic five-inch guns vainly pumping shells in the direction of the incoming missiles, hoping for a lucky hit. Then *Hancock* hummed to the shattering noise of the Phalanx system pumping three thousand rounds per minute at a point the fire-control system determined would intercept the missiles. There were two distinct explosions. One, Nelson was sure, was a hit on a missile. The second followed so quickly that the two were barely distinguishable—except that *John Hancock* reeled from the impact of one of them.

The missile struck to the rear of the ship, perhaps near the aft gun or the Sea Sparrow launcher. It did not penetrate the lower decks of the ship before blowing up, but detonated on impact. The explosions that followed were Sea Sparrow warheads still in their launcher, and a combination of the helo on the flight deck and her torpedoes. The after section of the ship was shattered and fire raged out of control, fed by the fuel in the helo. Yet *Hancock* continued on her way, her engineering spaces untouched, her steering gear still functioning. Her only defenses were forward—a single five-inch gun, the remaining torpedoes in her ASROC launcher, and her Harpoon missiles which were useful only against a surface ship. She no longer could defend against missiles—her Sea Sparrow and Phalanx systems were destroyed.

There were still submarines ahead. One of the helos had regained contact but no longer had weapons to fire. Nelson sent *Briscoe* to its aid. Using the helo to pinpoint the approximate location of her contact, *Briscoe* fired ASROC torpedoes, hoping to home in on the submarine before it went deeper to reload its tubes. They assumed it must have been a stern chase, the submarine running and diving at the same time, but the torpedoes were faster. Sonar soon confirmed a sub breaking up. That left three submarines. The Russians' undersea attack had been neutralized. Three subs could still fight, but their strategic capability had been destroyed.

Briscoe came back alongside *Hancock* to assist in the fire fighting. Now Nelson had to make a decision. Should he shift his command to *Briscoe*? To the north, *Nicholson* had three destroyers and three frigates, all with helicopters—a more formidable force than Nelson had started with an hour before. From the position reports, Nelson was positive the Russian strategy had been for both forces to join, probably forming a southern submarine line to act both as decoy and secondary cruise-missile group for the Soviet surface forces as they swept toward *Kennedy*'s battle group. *Nicholson* was experiencing some contact, but the reports seemed to indicate that those submarines intended all along to head south toward a meeting point. If they did not attempt to break through *Nicholson*'s line, they could also be isolated.

In the end, there was no argument that could keep Nelson aboard *John Hancock*. The battle was to the north, an hour or so away. His ship could no longer fight a meaningful battle or defend herself. He was the overall commander. His XO could handle the ship. He was highlined to *Briscoe* to see his part of Pratt's war through to the end.

ABOARD U.S.S. *JOHN F. KENNEDY*

Admiral Pratt had seen such attacks before; some had been even more overwhelming than this one. But they had all been simulated. Sometimes NATO prevailed; other times the Russians had won. Some said it was all a matter of throw weight—the explosive power launched at you at a given time. Those who felt the U.S. would always win were absolutely sure it was a matter of tactics—if those tactics were coupled with superior American technology. And there were those few who said these arguments were unnecessary if the enemy were removed from the face of the earth before he could attack.

Dave Pratt knew it was a combination of the first two, plus a dollop of luck. During war games, his computers could destroy his entire battle group if the Soviets were allowed an unlimited number of Backfires. But that would never be the case because, after warning of the initial launch, his own forces would rise to the attack, and the Air Force would set about destroying Soviet air bases and their re-supply system.

As he analyzed the development of the attack, Pratt quietly congratulated himself on his initial determination a few weeks before. If he were willing to accept heavy losses at

sea, there might definitely be a chance of turning back the
crucial land battle for Central Europe.

The nuclear cruiser *Arkansas* was his next ship to face
Soviet missiles, although the number of missiles that might
have been targeted for her was much more than ever came
close to hitting her. Some were drawn off by the chaff that
affected their homing radars, others were decoyed away
from the real target. *Arkansas* brought down at least six of
them herself, but there were those that got through. The
first dove deep into the bow, the explosion lifting the forward missile launcher out of the deck. When fire threatened
the magazine, her captain ordered flooding. The increasing
weight of the water began to slow her forward progress. A
second missile struck aft just moments later, passing through
the hangar deck. The blast damaged the steering gear, and
now *Arkansas* was forced to steer with her engines. Burning
fuel threatened the after magazine, and the captain was
forced to flood there also. The huge nuclear-powered cruiser
was now unable to operate her main battery, the formidable
dual missile launchers. She was limited to two automatic
five-inch mounts, less firepower than a tiny World War
Two escort.

Arthur W. Radford, out on the antisubmarine screen,
located the first submarine to break through. Her first warning came through sonar, the scream of approaching high-
speed screws. As her captain threw the rudder over in an
effort to evade, two torpedoes hit close amidships, about
fifty feet apart. The explosions were simultaneous—*Radford* broke in two. She never had the chance to fire a weapon.

The first hit on *Kennedy* was on the port quarter, disabling
the elevator. The fires there were quickly controlled and
might have been insignificant if a second missile had not
penetrated the hull on the same side. The flow of water to
the fire hoses was instantly cut off. Then the first fire began
spreading, igniting a helo poised to go up to the flight deck.
Fuel tanks exploded and burning fuel spread to ammunition.
In moments, a conflagration shrouded the after section of
the hangar deck, and a third missile slammed into the starboard side under the island. With power to the upper levels

cut, Dave Pratt found himself in darkness in flag plot. *Kennedy* was suddenly very alone, unable to monitor the battle outside. Luckily her engine rooms remained untouched, and she was able to continue under her own power. Yet in the real world of electronic warfare, she was proceeding blindly toward the enemy.

ABOARD U.S.S. *YORKTOWN*

As Carleton had explained earlier to Dave Pratt, *Yorktown* was everything they had designed her for — and more. Without AEGIS, there would have been no doubt about the outcome of the Battle of the Mediterranean. The Soviets' first salvo was intended to eliminate resistance, and the ferocity of the effort could only be understood by those who had studied Soviet strategy. With the exception of the use of atomic weapons to end the war in Japan, never before had so much explosive been used at one time by mankind.

As the Backfires crossed the southeastern Greek islands, Tom Carleton ordered AEGIS into automatic. Then electronic warfare devised by man took over man's battle. The computer was able to search and catalogue hundreds of contacts at one time; it was fed information on aircraft and air-to-surface missiles by the giant fixed-array radar. Secondary radars catalogued all surface contacts, and sonar delivered data on the undersea picture. The computer also received information from Hawkeye aircraft hundreds of miles out on the perimeter, from individual ships in outer stations, and would have accepted everything sent to it by recon satellites.

Once an object was recorded by the computer, it was

then identified as either friend or foe and appeared on the appropriate display console or status board. The next step was threat evaluation—to determine which of the hundreds of catalogued targets offered the most immediate threat to the battle group. AEGIS would then select the appropriate weapon, whether on board *Yorktown* or on another ship attached by Link to the battle group. Once the weapon was fired, AEGIS remained in touch with the situation until the threat no longer existed.

AEGIS instantly processed every bit of information within electronic range, notwithstanding the electronic countermeasures presented to it. The Soviets utilized jammers of their own, responding to search radar by returning dual or triple images where only one existed. As the Soviets came within range of the battle group, they launched their own antiradiation missiles which homed in on search and fire-control radars.

Electronic warfare has little concern for blast effect—its basis is purely deception, the creation of countermeasures and counter-countermeasures. Damage—and unimaginable loss of life—occurs as the result of a simple failure, the failure of a microchip, the failure of a circuit to open or to close according to design.

These thoughts coursed through Tom Carleton's mind as he watched the scene develop in *Yorktown*'s CIC. AEGIS's computer system faithfully recorded successes and failures faster than the human mind could assimilate them.

The initial hit on *Yorktown* did not seem overly serious at the time in comparison with what might have been damaged. The starboard Phalanx exploded a missile warhead an instant before it hit the ship. It was aft, just behind the number-two engine room, where damage could have been critical. Yet an explosion that close does inflict damage, and in this case, the explosive force tore into the hull at water level, opening up the generator room and damaging the number-three generator. Damage control isolated the area immediately.

When an electrical failure occurs on an AEGIS cruiser, there is a load-shedding feature that transmits power requirements to the remaining two generators. If one generator fails, the system sheds electrical demand by various sectors of the ship to avoid overload. In this case, Carleton noted with relief, there was only a momentary dimming of the AEGIS system before it continued normal operation. Those parts of the ship requiring electrical power would be quickly brought back on line through crossconnecting by the damage-control parties.

Yorktown continued on her way, steadily closing the enemy forces, steadily managing the battle with her powerful computer.

The second hit, however, was more critical. This time there was no last-minute save by Phalanx. A cruise missile plunged into the bow, destroying the three upper sonar equipment rooms. *Yorktown*'s ability to detect submarines was lost in an instant, but this was not critical to the battle group; other ships could relay the ASW picture. Of greater import was the fire that the blast generated. Within moments, the high-temperature alarms went off in the magazines below the forward five-inch mount. Damage control reported to Carleton that they were unable to control the fires in time to save the magazines. He was forced to order them flooded.

It was at this stage that a quirk of luck, or nature, occurred that threatened to change the outcome of the battle. Though *Kennedy*'s battle group was sustaining heavy damage, *Kennedy* was still moving east toward the enemy surface force. The carrier, though still burning, could still recover aircraft—*Yorktown*'s AEGIS still controlled the defense.

A Soviet Alfa-class submarine, one of those that had been worrying Admiral Pratt for more than twenty-four hours, was the cause. They are the fastest and quietest of the Russian submarine armada. Their titanium hulls make sonar detection extremely difficult. They are the deepest diving submarine known and they are highly automated. This particular submarine, *Odessa*, had escaped contact more than thirty-six hours before. Diving deep, she avoided the infrared capability of the recon satellites. Finding security under a layer of extremely cold water that defied sonar detection, she cruised slowly and very quietly under *Kennedy*'s battle group.

Odessa's captain was a brave man. He had no knowledge of what was taking place above him—only that the enemy was above, that his listening gear was so full of explosions that he could not differentiate targets, and that his operation order stated that a massive attack on the American battle group should now be under way. The only chance he had to make a contribution to the battle was to bring *Odessa* as close to the surface, and the battle, as possible. He brought his boat to as fast a speed as he could attain at a maximum up angle. His torpedo tubes were loaded, his men ready to fire the instant the submarine had a target. Perhaps the captain was too anxious or his diving officer's attention was diverted by the action above. Whatever the cause, she broke the surface of the Mediterranean in the midst of the battle group like a whale breaching. American sonars had heard *Odessa*'s rush, but the act was so fast, so unexpected, so brash, that before they could react *Odessa* had fired six torpedoes—four from her forward tubes, two from the stern tubes. Then, as quickly as she had appeared, she dove. Again her captain attempted the impossible. Achieving a critical down angle, he combined speed and rapid flooding of his tanks to escape. It was dangerous. The extremes he exercised were beyond those in the submarine manual.

Odessa's noisy dive was easily tracked by two destroyers to the rear of the carrier protecting *Kennedy*'s flank. They fired rocket-propelled torpedoes from their ASROC launchers well ahead of *Odessa*'s position. The submarine was faster, but the homing torpedoes had the lead time and she was an easy target. The submarine never came out of her crash dive to prove to her builders how much an Alfa-class submarine could exceed engineering standards. Two torpedoes fractured her pressure hull and *Odessa* continued on her last dive at full speed. Increasing water pressure ripped her into pieces, compartment by compartment.

On the surface, chaos ensued. Each ship was streaming its NIXIE decoys but *Odessa* had fired at the two major contacts that had appeared on her attack computer—*Ken-*

nedy and *Yorktown*. Two of the torpedoes from *Odessa*'s forward tubes swerved slightly off course to attack the carrier's decoys, but the others raced directly into *Kennedy*'s hull. The first struck aft, opening the after engine room to the sea. Fuel storage tanks ruptured, feeding the flames that erupted. Burst fire mains once again cut the water to the damage control parties on the hangar deck above.

The second torpedo hit below the carrier's island, penetrating through the voids into the fuel trunks before exploding. The blast raised a fireball almost to *Kennedy*'s bridge. She was now operating on just her port engines, her speed cut drastically. Water engulfed electrical switchboards, and critical sections of the ship began to lose power.

Electricity had returned just moments before to Pratt's flag plot when once again the power was lost. This time, smoke filtered through ventilating shafts into the darkened space. Nothing is initially so terrifying on a ship as darkness combined with smoke. In this case, Pratt's flag plot was buried in the interior of the island. There were no ports to open. No matter where a hatch was opened, there would be only darkness punctuated by the smoke-narrowed beams of battle lanterns.

Kennedy's captain called down to Pratt. "Admiral, we have fires out of control on the hangar deck from midships aft. Damage Control reports a danger to ammunition storage because they have no pressure in the watermains there. I'm flooding midships now to contain the fires in the engineering spaces."

"How much time to return to full speed?"

"We're not going to, Admiral. We've lost the starboard engines. Shafts are likely warped." The captain hesitated. "Admiral, you may want to think about shifting your flag."

Pratt considered for a moment, then responded, "I'll bring *Yorktown* alongside."

There was a pause, then, "Admiral, perhaps you'd better come to the bridge. *Yorktown* appears to have taken a hit too. Can't tell what it was. Too much smoke now."

One of the stern torpedoes from *Odessa* had hit *Yorktown*. For an unknown reason, the depth setting had been high.

It burst as it hit the hull at the waterline. The blast opened the number-one engine room to cascading seawater. The turbines, though they survived blast damage, were immediately shut down as the water rose toward them. *Yorktown* proceeded at reduced speed on her starboard shaft.

What had been missed initially on the first report to Carleton was the structural damage the explosion caused to the forward generator. The pumps were unable to keep up with the rising water. Before the generator could be shut down, the water got in and the generator short-circuited, burning itself out. As the one remaining generator began to overload, it also began shedding power to various spaces.

The red lights dimmed in CIC. The hum of fans, previously unnoticed, attracted attention as their motors began to slow down.

The interior communications speaker by Carleton's place echoed into life. "Captain," came the frantic voice of the engineering officer, "we're down to one generator. I've got to cut off something up there. The AEGIS system's drawing all the power." His high-pitched voice cut through the silence of CIC.

"Not a chance."

"Captain, if I don't, I'm going to burn the son of a bitch up. Then you got nothing."

Carleton was familiar with the tone of voice. The man was responding now to his training, following the damage-control book by the numbers. If you follow step one, then the following happens. Follow step two, such and such happens. That was fine, but only for exercises.

"What do you have to shut down to keep us going up here?"

"Practically everything, Captain—shut down the gun mounts, the missile launchers. Hell, I don't even know if I can keep the starboard engines running if I concentrate on the electrical system."

"Just keep turning things off until you're safe." All he really needed was AEGIS. Though his own magazines were getting low, there were still enough ships in the area. As long as AEGIS could keep them firing . . .

"Captain . . . I'm losing power here." It was his CIC officer, his voice cracking. He hesitated, moving from one location to another, checking his instruments. He turned to Carleton, barely visible in the dimming red light. *"We're going to go out of automatic."* He spoke each word separately and distinctly, the fear of failure imminent.

Carleton hit the button on the IC communicator in front of him. "Cut everything," he bellowed into the box. "Go dead in the water. I don't give a shit what you do, but don't cut us anymore up here."

"I'm doing everything I can, Captain." There was a pause, the sound of machinery in the background the only indication that the line was still open. "That's it, sir. Losing way . . ."

A voice cut into Carleton's thoughts from another speaker. "Captain. Bridge here. We're losing steerageway. The compass is out of sync." There was another hesitation. "Captain . . . we've lost everything up here."

It was at that moment that Carleton recognized Dave Pratt's voice above the disciplined commotion in CIC. The Admiral was requesting an assessment of casualties. Carleton responded directly himself, then Pratt asked: "Tom, have you still got full control with AEGIS?"

"Affirmative, Admiral, but we're dead in the water for the time being. I have no idea if we'll get a second generator back on line."

"I'll take my chances, Tom. I've lost the picture completely here. There's a helo waiting for me on the flight deck now."

Yorktown did have to use her engines briefly to maneuver enough to clear the smoke from her stern so that Dave Pratt could be lowered from the helo. With the missile damage and the fires still smoldering below, there was no way they could land.

The remainder of the Battle of the Mediterranean would be directed from a ship unable to maneuver.

SPITZBERGEN

Ryng found the going much easier in the shadows. There the snow was harder than the crystallized slush melted by the sun's limited heat. In shadows, he slipped occasionally where ice had formed or where small, unseen projections caught his feet.

He did not look back. His one goal was to get to the other side of the peak before another helicopter came looking for the first one. If Harriers had flown in from the direction of the ocean, there was the possibility of help that way.

A new sound came to him as he neared the top. At first it was a low hum, steady, occasionally increasing in pitch. The closer he came to the peak, the louder, deeper, and more resonant it became. Whatever it might be, Ryng had little concern. Rather than frightening him, it seemed to draw him toward the peak, to what he was sure was freedom from the chase.

The last hundred yards he could see multicolored snow crystals caught in the sun's rays as they swirled around the bare rock at the top. They were propelled by a steady wind rolling off the ocean and reaching a crescendo as it blew through the rock and ice formations to create that strange yet welcoming sound. Here the snow, constantly moving, was deeper and softer, and the last few yards were the most difficult as he struggled through the drifts.

From the top, he gazed out over an angry gray, white-capped ocean. The reverse of the long slope he had just climbed was much sharper; the snowfield swept down at an acute angle, and jagged rock outcroppings peered through a much thinner snow cover. The constant wind blew much of the snow on that side over the peak, to drift where Ryng now stood and eventually to add to the year-round glacier that he had climbed that day. Below, the surface was smoother and less steep, like the inside of a coffee cup.

Shielding his eyes with both hands, he slowly searched the horizon for any sign of life, even the smallest fishing boat, but nothing was apparent. Ryng shrugged to himself. What the hell—life had to be better down there than it had been here for the last nine or ten hours.

He was determining the best course down when a little puff of snow to one side caught his eye. With the steady blowing, it was a strange sight, a little geyser of white crystals leaping skyward for a moment, then being carried away. Everything else was so smoothly sculptured by the constant wind.

Then a second puff—this time beside his right leg. Without a moment's hesitation, Ryng dove face first into the snow to his left, burrowing into the coldness.

A goddamn bullet! That's what it was—a bullet. Christ, there was no warning sound, nothing to tell him what that first puff of snow was, what with the goddamned howling wind. He was lucky, just plain, half-assed lucky, that whoever had the gun was a lousy shot.

Ryng didn't move until he knew where the other man was firing from. He waited thirty seconds, counting softly to himself to counter the thudding of his heart. Then with his head covered with snow, icy water trickling down his neck, he slowly raised his head, careful not to make a sudden move. His gaze began directly below, moving slowly up, stopping at each shadow or rocky outthrust to see if there was any movement. As his eyes reached near the top, he saw the source. Even prone in the snow, the black uniform stood out like a sore thumb.

Christ! Ryng cursed. There was no way that person could have gotten where he was—just about in line with me on the ridge—unless he'd gotten out of that helo. Always cover your tracks, Ryng thought. Always look over your shoulder. Never take anything for granted. This joker now doing target practice on you had to come from that copter—wrecked or not. Somehow he got out of that mess and kept right on at what he was supposed to do in the first place—make sure Bernie Ryng never screws with the Black Berets again!

Those guys are good, Bernie, the voice in the back of his head continued, good enough to almost blow someone like you right off a godforsaken, snow-covered mountain peak in the worst goddamned place you've ever seen. No one would ever know, during that split second before it was lights out, that the reason they finally got you was because you were stupid!

There was another puff of snow a couple of feet to his left. Christ, it was eerie—no damn sound at all, just little puffs of snow from a bullet that could blow his skull apart. The guy was shooting where he expected his quarry to be. Ryng knew there was no way he could be seen buried in the snow like this. For the first time since he'd covered himself with it, he realized how cold he was. Snow melted around his ears and down his neck, the wind adding to the chill. There was no way he was going to spend much time lying here. Before he knew it, he'd be too damn cold to move properly. He had no desire to lie there and feel the numbness overtake him. And knowing Ryng wasn't armed, the other man wouldn't waste much time waiting for him to surface.

Ryng began to roll through the snow in the direction of the ocean. Very cautiously, his arms and legs straight out, head down, he rolled. As he came to the edge on the reverse slope, he peered quickly back at his pursuer and saw a black-uniformed individual slogging through the heavier snow, an AK-74 slung from his right shoulder, one hand on the trigger guard. The left arm appeared to hang uselessly at his side.

As Ryng began to roll downhill faster, his arms and legs flailing helplessly, the Russian spotted him. Through clots of snow, Ryng saw the flame from the gun muzzle and knew the weapon must be in automatic. Only a lucky shot would get him now, he knew, as he increased speed.

Bang—pain in his shoulder. Was he hit? Ryng felt his body spin around, his feet heading downhill, and he realized that he'd hit one of those jagged rocks. No bullet, but he felt the warmth of blood from a tear in his shoulder. Then his feet hit another object and he felt his body surge forward in a somersault. Head over heels, he pitched downhill, out of control.

The raw snow ripped at his bare skin like sandpaper. He grazed off other rocks, unable to see or avoid anything in his path. Then, for a moment, he was airborne, shooting off a little precipice and dropping down onto a steep slope where the snow was shaded and hard. Here he slid even faster, this time on his back, head down, too fast to roll or see where he was headed.

Abruptly, he was out of the snow. Gravel and loose rock now ripped at his body, and he felt the shirt tearing off his back. A new sensation of pain rolled over him. Ryng knew he could not afford the luxury of allowing the pain to over-whelm him. As he skidded to a stop, his arms and legs flailed for any kind of grip that might give him the chance to roll onto his belly.

With a groan of pain, he flopped onto his stomach, searching the slope above for his pursuer, then spotted the man in much the same state as himself. The black uniform stood out through the shower of snow where the Russian had also fallen down the steep pitch. In front of the man, bouncing end over end, was the AK-74. There was no way the man and the gun would get together faster than Ryng could get to them.

Groggy from the fall, Ryng drew himself onto his hands and knees. His shirt and pants were shredded, blood seeped from a myriad of cuts and scratches, and the pain from deep bruises made every movement agonizing. Forget the pain, Bernie, the voice reminded him. Better you get to that rifle before the other guy, or you won't have a prayer in this world. Somehow he was on his feet and lunging toward the spot where the Russian and his gun were headed.

But there wasn't going to be a gun for either of them.
As he neared the intersection of dirt and snow where the
other man would land, the weapon hurtled on past. It would
just be the two of them, and Ryng had no doubts whatsoever
that it would quickly be just one.

When Ryng was within fifty yards, the Russian finally
halted himself. Lying there just as battered as his adversary,
Colonel Bulgan forced himself to suck in deep breaths. The
pain, especially in the injured wrist, was agonizing. His
head and face were torn by snow and gravel and throbbed
intensely. The gun, he knew, was out of reach. He just
hoped the American had no better chance at it than himself.
Rolling onto his one good arm, Bulgan looked around,
reorienting himself. Then his eyes fell on Ryng.

The American was stumbling toward him. In Ryng's
mind, it was a charge; he was driving like a fullback. To
Bulgan, it seemed almost comic until he remembered who
this man was. Then he rolled onto his knees, balancing
precariously as his head swam with pain. At twenty-five
yards, the Russian stumbled to his feet, his good arm cocked,
the other hanging uselessly at his side. He lowered his head
and reeled toward the American.

To Ryng, the situation was bizarre. The Russian intended
to butt him as they came together. But try as he would, it
seemed impossible to avoid the Russian's crazed charge.

They came together with a thud, Bulgan's head hitting
Ryng's chest at the same time a fist caught the Russian in
the side of the head. They both went down, each rolling
away from the other, then back to their feet.

With a roar, seeing the other man's left hand was useless,
Ryng charged again. He swung wildly, catching the other
with a grazing blow to the shoulder. Bulgan hissed like a
snake, catching Ryng with a wild swing to the forehead.

But it was not really a contest. One man crazed with
pain had the advantage over the other with only one good
arm. Twice, Ryng caught Bulgan in the jaw, snapping his
head back each time.

Bulgan staggered, blood now flowing from his nose and

ears as Ryng hit him twice more in the face. Ryng then lunged for the kill. He spun the other around, catching him first in a head lock, then applying the pressure backward to snap the man's neck. He could feel elbows flailing back at his ribs, but that was a useless effort. The Russian was already too weak, and now his air was cut off. Ryng applied the pressure, but the Black Beret's torso was thick and tough and he was straining for his life.

As he reached the critical point, Ryng felt the body begin to relax in his arms, and for a reason he would never understand, he relaxed the pressure. But as soon as he relaxed, Bulgan's elbow stabbed into his stomach and his heel crashed down on Ryng's instep. Give him an inch and he'll kill you! Ryng thought, plunging back into the death struggle.

With a quick effort, Ryng snapped the man's neck, and Bulgan's body went rigid, then slumped in his arms, a permanent dead weight.

The body slid to the ground. Without looking back, Ryng trotted down to where the rifle had landed. Useless! The stock was broken, the barrel bent.

He again searched the horizon. Nothing. Wait—there was something there. Smoke. A black smudge where sea and sky joined. He thought he could make out thick clouds billowing upward, but it was too distant to be sure. More often than not steady black smoke at sea meant a ship was burning. But whose?

There was nothing to do but wait. Sharp bluffs to the south kept him from setting out toward the original meeting place. It seemed to him that the Harriers might have radioed his position back to their carrier when they took out the helo. If some intelligent soul put two and two together, they might figure where Ryng had come over the peak and where he'd come down to the shore. If they knew enough about him to allow the Harriers to take a moment off from their mission, someone must have the word out that he was worth rescuing. No telling how they'll do it; they could turn up any time. And if he wasn't available, no one was going to wait for him. With that, he moved off downhill at a good pace, aware now of the pain which seemed to take over every muscle and every joint in his body.

At the base, there was a narrow beach below a shallow rocky escarpment. Ryng saw the path down to the beach, but he chose to remain above it, giving himself a better vantage point for anything that might turn up.

Now inactivity brought on a chill. The air was cold, though probably not as cold as it had been for the past ten hours. But up until now he'd been in motion, or maybe his adrenaline had been pumping so hard that he was unaware of the temperature.

It couldn't have been more than fifty degrees out, if that. More than likely, it was probably a nice day for this far north. Moreover, to have no rain this time of year, not even the normal cloud cover, had been to his advantage, allowing him to survive this far. He had no intention of giving in now.

Considering that no one knew exactly where he was, or even if he was alive, he looked for a way to protect himself. He had nothing to eat, his clothes were in shreds, his body raw and bruised, and any change in the weather would kill him off within twenty-four hours.

Ryng set about searching for material to build a shelter, but that was fruitless. Because of the land's proximity to the North Pole, there were no trees. The ground cover of the tundra did not cling to the hillsides, and mosses and lichens were the only plant life. Only polar bears and reindeer ranged the islands, and the arctic terns and puffins nested according to their environment. Man was not meant to live here. The land was cold, gray, and barren.

Wandering the edge of the cliff, Ryng soon satisfied himself that there was no driftwood below of particular value. After all, there were no wooded islands in that part of the world and nothing afloat other than fishing boats. Accepting the fact, he determined the next best plan was to find some shelter from the wind. He located a rocky enclosure by the cliffside, providing a full view of the horizon. All that was left was to wait, conserve what little energy remained, and hope. There was no going back over the top.

He was not surprised when he awoke somewhat later.

He knew he had only dozed, but there was no telling for how long. There was little change in the position of the sun at this latitude, whether he had slept an hour or five hours. He felt cramped and moved to stretch his muscles. Pain washed over him as he made the initial effort. He seemed to have bruises on top of bruises. Where scabs had formed over scratches and cuts, they cracked open and blood seeped onto his skin. His head throbbed.

For a moment his eyes would not focus. The tender skin at the corners cried out when he rubbed at them with raw fists. The smoke on the horizon came into focus first. It was thick and black and it stretched across the sky to the north, gradually thinning as the winds dispersed it. Whatever it was, Ryng assumed there was big trouble, for fires at sea that lasted this long were probably out of control. Was it a ship in distress? Was that what was supposed to have rescued him?

His eyes crisscrossed the ocean. To his right—to the northwest—he saw what seemed to be a spit of land. Remembering the island that had been offshore when they landed, he assumed he was now to the south of that, probably closer to the entrance of the harbor than he'd expected. Dividing the ocean into sections, he returned his gaze to each one three times, rechecking to make sure he hadn't missed a thing.

There! His eyes flicked back to a spot on the surface. He blinked. Nothing. Wait! There *was* something along with a flash of white! There were whitecaps with the steady breeze, but this one speck remained on the surface, moving. Ryng cupped his hands to his eyes, squinting as if they were binoculars. He focused on that spot and now the ethereal became solid. There was no doubt in his mind. He'd seen periscopes before. Now the speck rose higher, circling the compass, he assumed, checking both the surface and the air. Then more apparatus appeared, radar and electronic gear probably, probing the airwaves for any foreign electronic signals that might mean disclosure.

He waited, pausing between each breath until he realized the ache in his lungs was self-induced. Whose submarine was it? Would he be able to identify it from that distance? Then taking his hands from his eyes, he realized it wasn't that far away—a mile, maybe a bit more. Whoever the crazy son of a bitch was, he was taking that boat into shallow water—a very dangerous move if war was still imminent.

Then the periscope was followed by the sail of the submarine. There was little wash around it; the sub was almost dead in the water. As the hull came into view, he knew it wasn't American. U.S. subs carried their sail well forward. It wasn't Russian either—their sails were generally more sleek, closer to the hull on the nuclear boats, and by the shape of the hull, he knew this was nuclear. What the hell, he thought. The only others operating around here must be British. He rose from his position, slowly, painfully, realizing full well that no one was going to see him there.

He watched people come out of the sail onto the tiny deck. They fumbled with something for a few moments, then he saw that they were handling a rubber boat of some kind. In a few moments, it slid over the side. A man climbed in it, fumbling near one end. Soon the rubber craft pulled away from the mother boat, moving quickly enough to be propelled by some kind of motor. As mysteriously as it had come, the submarine sank below the surface with a slurry of bubbles and froth.

Now is the time, Ryng decided after watching the boat bob over the rough offshore chop. There was no reason such an occurrence could take place in this nowhere land unless someone was taking the trouble to find out if he was still alive. Maybe the Harriers had reported that the Soviet helo was firing at something other than puffins, and in that location, an intelligence type would have to put two and two together and figure that someone on the SEAL team that went into Longyearbyen might have escaped. There could be no conceivable reason to think otherwise.

He descended the cliffside, the path curving back and forth until he was on the narrow strip of beach. The wind blew in off the arctic water, lifting the foam off each crashing wave, depositing the icy droplets on his bare skin. He shivered, occasionally at first, then in spasms as the boat grew in size. He wrapped his arms around himself, rubbing his hands up and down his body. But it offered little warmth at this stage. He could no longer feel his hands.

As the boat drew closer, he thought about his episode with the Black Beret hours earlier. Was he delivering himself into the hands of the enemy? He wasn't sure. But that wasn't any Soviet submarine that he'd ever seen before. In the end, there was no telling who was at war with whom... who was an enemy and who was a friend. But whoever was about to land on the beach probably wanted to find him. Ryng had no choice but to believe that.

He was welded to the spot as he watched the little boat approach the beach. The operator, he saw, wore a black wetsuit; only his face remained uncovered. At about fifty feet from the water's edge, he lifted the motor and picked up a paddle to finish the trip to shore.

What the man in the boat saw as he stepped into the surf to pull his boat the last few yards was an apparition of a military man. The man's uniform was in tatters. His skin was covered with ugly colored bruises, and there seemed not a square inch where blood wasn't either oozing or dried. The face was swollen, one eye half closed. Seemingly fixed to the spot, Ryng stared back unblinkingly, his hands rhythmically moving up and down his arms in what seemed an effort to keep warm.

"Commander Ryng?" the man inquired as he pulled the rubber boat out of the surf.

Ryng nodded, the rest of his body still planted in place, only his eyes moving over the man and then to his boat.

"Lieutenant Commander Hargraves, Number One, from Her Majesty's submarine *Churchill*, sir. We thought you might be waiting for a ride."

Again, Ryng nodded. This time he blinked his eyes, then rubbed them with his hands. "Her Majesty's submarine?"

"Right you are, sir. And our captain wants to extend his gratitude for the whole of the U.K. when you come aboard. Ah—shall we go, sir?" he asked, pointing at the rubber boat. "War waits for no man," he added.

"Are we at war?"

"Not officially, sir, at least it hasn't been declared—though we're told the Russians have moved into the Fulda Gap. But, as Admiral Harrow said, the war in Europe will start on D-Day. The war out here starts whenever one or the other wants it to, and our's started yesterday."

"And . . ." Ryng's eyes turned to the black smoke on the horizon.

"*Illustrious*, sir. Our group was the only one in the area when the Russians moved their submarine flotilla out of Murmansk. So it was us sent out to pick off what we could in case your mission was unsuccessful."

"My mission?"

"Aye, sir. Our group was under heavy submarine attack, lost two escorts, and *Illustrious* took a hole yesterday. Admiral Harrow thought it best to explain how the whole NATO plan was developing, and he mentioned about the American SEAL team, I guess so none of us would feel we were the only ones out here."

Ryng gestured toward the smoke. "More torpedoes?"

"There might have been one or two more. But it was missiles that did her in—from those big Russian bombers. They came in a couple of hours back, after Admiral Harrow was forced to commit his Harriers to that Russian base here, we were told. They weren't sure whether or not you got your job done. Didn't leave any real air defense. They were abandoning *Illustrious* when I left the submarine. Probably have to sink her soon's everyone's accounted for." Ryng still hadn't moved from the spot. "I think it best we get under way, sir. Our captain isn't terribly excited about these shallow waters."

Ryng moved stiffly toward the rubber boat.

He hoped his report would not be too late, that he and Denny and Harry Winters and all the rest had pulled it off.

AFTER THE FIRST SALVO

Soviet doctrine was having a rough go of it that day. According to computer projections, refined by months' worth of strategic alternatives, more Backfires should have penetrated the outer ring of Admiral Pratt's defenses. The actual loss of the aircraft was of little concern to Moscow; it was the loss of the missiles these aircraft were to deliver that forced them to generate revised scenarios as the day progressed.

To achieve a satisfactory success ratio, the cruise missiles first had to survive approximately 250 miles through the antimissile defense of a battle group; even to arrive at that launch point, a fixed number of Backfires had to survive. The success of the first salvo would be based on the number of missiles that remained in the air through to the primary zone—the initial thirty to forty miles from the center of the battle group. That was why the leaders in Moscow were reprogramming even before their missiles were launched. The optimum number of bombers simply hadn't made it to launch point.

Of equal concern were their subsurface forces. The computer could not generate revised projections in that sector, for the fate of the submarines would be unknown until it

was all over. If the submarines were successful, if they
penetrated the ASW barrier Wendell Nelson had established, then the diminished effect of the Backfire attack
might possibly be balanced. The intelligence they had hoped
for in this respect was limited, but a sufficient amount came
through to Moscow to make them believe that enough of
the NATO forces were still afloat to leave the situation in
doubt.

Kharkov and her escorts were proceeding toward *Kennedy*'s battle group at maxium speed when they sustained
their heaviest attack that day. It was conducted by *Kennedy*'s
heavy-attack squadron of Intruders, a follow-up to the earlier
attack from the *Saratoga*. Admiral Konstantin aboard *Kharkov* had expected the air attacks and was satisfied that the
damage had been no worse. The carrier had taken five hits,
only one considered serious, a two-thousand-pound bomb
forward that had destroyed her cruise-missile capability.
While fires still smoldered forward, she continued to operate
her aircraft.

There had been a cruiser, two guided-missile destroyers,
and two frigates lost, but they were expendable. What concerned Admiral Konstantin was the limited intelligence on
the American submarines. He knew the Egyptians and the
Israelis had allowed American attack submarines to hover
in their protected waters. The loss of satellite intelligence
had severely constrained his knowledge of their movements
both ahead of and behind him. They could be a potent force,
a possible turning point.

Now Konstantin was approaching the outer range of his
surface missiles. Shortly he would bolster the air attack with
his own missiles and, hopefully, those of his submarines—
at least those still able to provide reinforcement.

The intelligence from NATO's northern flank was disturbing. It was not so much the reports arriving in Moscow
as the lack of them. Communications had been successfully
jammed in that region for more than twenty-four hours.
Reconnaissance satellites had been neutralized by an unexpected source, possibly laser-beam systems that the Russians had not anticipated. Murmansk's northern submarine

force instituted radio silence within five hundred miles of the American CAPTOR barrier. The only intelligence the Russians gained was from the underwater disturbance in this area. The CAPTORs had been activated—but by whom or what remained a mystery. American resupply convoys continued with minimum harassment. Moscow was aware that numerous American submarines were still operating in that area, which could mean that the Soviet force had been delayed, destroyed, or that an undersea battle would soon develop.

With a certain reluctance on the part of a number of members of the State Committee for Defense, preliminary orders were transmitted to the Strategic Rocket Forces. Their hesitation was based on a mistrust of General Colonel Melekhin. He was not of the old crowd, like Keradin. Melekhin was young; he had advanced rapidly because of his political connections. Yet there was a concern among the older members that he was trigger-happy—that he was willing to act possibly on his own rather than under their strict orders. They saw the Strategic Rocket Forces as a threat in itself, not as a weapon that would be placed in action as part of an overall scheme. Many of the older members envisioned the awful specter of retaliation. They saw this war simply as an opportunity to expand the Motherland's boundaries, and they could not accept the idea of ICBMs raining down on their country. They would rely on Melekhin if it became absolutely necessary, but their final hope lay in the fact that General Keradin had yet to surface. His disappearance had created dissension and an inability to use the Strategic Rocket Forces as they had once anticipated.

With that in mind, Moscow determined that the final phase should commence in the Mediterranean slightly ahead of schedule. The American carrier battle groups had taken a beating, but they still retained the capability to defend themselves. The orders were given for the lead ships, with *Kharkov*, to open fire with their missiles on the perimeter defenses. Those would be the ASW ships under Admiral Pratt's command which were already hard pressed by the persistence of Soviet missile submarines.

A cruise missile launched at a surface ship by a submarine or another surface ship can be a formidable weapon if properly employed. Skimming the surface of the ocean above the speed of sound, it is extremely difficult to track. Quite often, the first warning of its approach is given when its homing device locks on the targeted ship. By then, it is often too late to effect any defense other than the last-ditch one—Phalanx.

A signal was transmitted to the Soviet submarines. They were to surface to assist in the control of the first missiles. With midcourse guidance, the range of the missiles from the surface ships would be tripled. The Russians were concerned about the longer range of the Harpoon missiles aboard the American ships. Exposing their remaining submarines was a desperate move.

For those submarines, surfacing could be a deadly strategy. Their natural element was underneath the sea, and it was there that they enjoyed a true advantage. On the surface, they were simply slower, unwieldy ships no longer able to utilize secrecy as a major defense—they were fish out of water.

It was a surprise to Admiral Pratt's beleaguered ASW ships and aircraft when the subsurface contacts they had been so intent on holding down to deny use of their missiles appeared on the surface. The purpose of this illogical exposure was not immediately evident. Fire-control solutions, whether with torpedoes, missiles, or even guns were executed with ease. The quarry was attacked and destroyed, one by one.

The purpose of these subs' committing certain suicide was not apparent until missile-warning detectors were activated in *Kennedy*'s battle group. The Soviet missiles wreaked havoc with the perimeter force. It took little time for the Soviet submarines' radars to lock on their targets, transmit the fire-control information to the missiles, and, if they had survived that long, to dive.

New guided-missile frigates like *John Hall* or *Stephen Groves* had little chance against the huge warheads. They were literally blown out of the water. Larger ships, Spruance-class destroyers like *Caron* or *John Rodgers*, survived the missiles, though severely damaged. But the combination of missiles and then torpedoes finished them.

Dave Pratt realized in *Yorktown*'s CIC that the two opposing forces—the Soviet subs and the American perimeter defense—were now neutralized. There would be little more contribution from them to either side. The Battle of the Mediterranean was drawing to a close. How it ended would be based on which surface force survived. If Nelson's sweep to the south proved effective over the next hour, and the Soviet submarines in that area were prevented from launching missiles, it would come down to an old-fashioned face-off between the main elements of two battle groups, just as had occurred generations before during the Second World War.

The undersea battle had run its course. The combatants in the air war had been exhausted.

ABOARD U.S.S. *BRISCOE*,
HEADING NORTH
TOWARD THE MAIN BATTLE GROUP

Wendell Nelson had been correct. The Russian submarines heading in his direction reversed course directly into the sweep line coordinated by *Nicholson*. It was a textbook execution, even more effective than the first one Nelson had demonstrated two days previously. The three destroyers and three frigates in *Nicholson*'s squadron each were flying helicopters. This doubled their force effectiveness, likely outnumbering the submarines they faced, and the helos were phantoms to the subs, appearing out of nowhere, unpredictably, when least anticipated.

The Soviet submarines' speed advantage was negated by the tactics Nelson had refined back in Newport. Not one of the subs was able to gain time or position to fire its cruise missiles. It became an action of attrition. Over a forty-minute period, five submarines were sunk by homing torpedoes. At the same time, two of the three frigates, somewhat slower and unable to survive if even one shaft was damaged, were sunk.

As *Briscoe* approached from the rear of the battle, unrecognized by the desperate submarines, *Nicholson* took a torpedo forward. In a series of violent explosions, first in the magazine under her forward gun mount, then as flames consumed the warheads in her ASROC launcher, *Nicholson* was blown apart in sections. As flames swept the remainder of the ship, a final blast in her fuel tanks sent her to the bottom.

Nelson ordered *Briscoe* into range with her ASROC-launched torpedoes. He was positive they had caught one more submarine when a tremendous explosion rocked *Briscoe*. She had been detected after all. The torpedo had not been deterred by her decoys. Instead, it struck aft, and in a series of explosions, the ship lost steering gear and both screws. Helpless, *Briscoe* wallowed in the swells, flames sweeping into the after magazines. Damage control lost water pressure. Though her forward weapons were capable of continuing the fight, *Briscoe* could no longer maneuver. Fires, now out of control, soon swept through her electrical system.

Once again the confrontation had been fatal for both sides. Out of the force that Wendell Nelson had taken south for Admiral Pratt, two destroyers now turned north to rejoin the battle group. Nelson transferred to his third ship that day, and headed north aboard *Samuel Eliot Morison*, one of the few guided-missile frigates to survive.

Wendell Nelson found the last few rungs of the ladder to *Morison*'s bridge suddenly very steep. He'd never been aboard one of the little ships. Were they really built so oddly or was exhaustion sweeping over him?

Morison's captain extended a welcoming hand as Nelson ambled slowly into the pilothouse. "I know this isn't the type of luxury you're used to . . ."

Nelson smiled wearily. "Captain, if this little fellow can stay afloat for the remainder of the day, that's enough luxury for me." He let the commanding officer's hand go, sagging tiredly against the chart table. "You know I hate to admit it, but I didn't even see the name on the fantail when you came alongside for me, or it just didn't register."

"She's the *Samuel Eliot Morison*, sir."

Nelson's eyebrows rose for a second. Then he smiled faintly. He had read literally every word written by the famous naval historian *Samuel Eliot Morison*. Now he had been saved by the ship given the great man's name. He stepped out on the bridge wing, leaning on the railing, and stared out at the horizon. Finally, he turned to the commanding officer, who had moved beside him. "I owe you one sometime, Captain, because I didn't get your name either, and it's one I want to remember."

"Two days ago I was sure you were going to have me relieved. I was the one who argued so much with you at that commanding officers' meeting about your new tactics. My name's Bill Stritzler."

Nelson smiled wanly. "It's been a couple of years for me since that meeting—or it seems like it. Did you execute those tactics?"

"Yes, sir. They worked beautifully—especially since we depend on our helos."

"Any idea how many submarines you might have gotten?"

"I like to think we were involved in three of them."

"Well, Bill, when we get back home, your penance for arguing with me that day will be to write a paper on your tactics. You see, I lost two ships in one day and you've come out smelling like a rose. Either you're damn lucky or damn smart, but I think we might make a good team." Nelson extended his hand.

Stritzler squeezed the proffered hand. "Were you ever a skeptic, sir?"

"Always."

"I'd love to work with you, Captain." He looked more closely at Nelson. "You look exhausted, sir. How about stealing a couple of hours in my bunk?"

"I had that in mind. And while I'm napping, why don't you have some of your men paint a few submarines on the bridge wings like they used to do forty years ago. I think Admiral Pratt might like that when we join up."

"I'm afraid I don't know where Admiral Pratt is, sir."

"Call me Nellie—Pratt does. Where is he, then?"

"We don't know yet. Just before we made contact down here, he was shifting his flag from *Kennedy*—her fires were out of control."

"See if you could find out for me." Nelson yawned, then added, "I'll take you up on that bunk now."

Wendell Nelson did not sleep as long as he'd hoped. He came to slowly. Opening his eyes, he found Captain Stritzler shaking his shoulder. "Have you located Admiral Pratt?" he asked groggily.

"No, but I think I have something equally interesting down in the wardroom, if you'll come with me. Some fellow with a gun claims to know you, and none of my people can get near him. He and some others were spotted in a raft a little while ago. He told us their plane was shot down. If you can talk with this guy," Stritzler added as they descended the final ladder, "I think we'll be even."

The sight in the wardroom stopped Nelson cold. As he pushed through the door, the first person he saw was Henry Cobb, shirtless, bruised, his battered face fixed intently on a man who sat across from him. Cobb had a pistol in his hand aimed at the chest of this bedraggled man who stared helplessly down the barrel. The gun never wavered, nor did Cobb look up. An equally battered blond girl was asleep on the couch at one end of the wardroom, covered by a blanket.

"He won't talk to anyone, won't give us the gun, won't let us do anything with his prisoner. The girl was unconscious when we took them aboard. That one," said Stritzler, pointing at Keradin, "doesn't seem to understand us. The one with the gun kept asking us to get Pratt for him. We still haven't located Admiral Pratt. When I mentioned your name, said you were a friend of Pratt's, he said he'd speak with you."

During Stritzler's explanation, Cobb had never looked up. He remained in the same position, the gun unwavering. Then, without turning, he said in a monotone, "That's right, I've got to talk with Pratt."

Nelson stepped over to him, placing his hand on Cobb's bare shoulder. "Is that Keradin, Hank?"

Cobb looked down at the black hand resting on his shoulder. He put his own over it and squeezed. "Yeah, Nellie, that's him." The gun in his hand began to shake. He gently rested it on the table. There was no reaction from Keradin. "Nellie, would you keep an eye on him for me? Can't let him get away. We've come so far." He looked up into Nelson's face. "It's been so long since I slept..."

"They'll take good care of you here, Hank. They've done the same for me."

"Wait a minute." Cobb rose, half turning, his eyes searching the room. "Verra... where's Verra?" He spotted the girl on the couch. Gesturing toward her, he said, "Without her, we wouldn't have gotten Keradin. We're a team, her and me. Never thought I'd say that—a team..." Then he looked back at Nelson, eyes widening. "Nellie, is there a doctor on board this thing? She's got to be..."

An officer standing to one side said, "She's all right, sir. She's just sleeping now. Exhaustion."

Cobb sat down beside her and began to stroke her head, smoothing her hair back from her face. He looked once more at Nelson. "You son of a bitch, Nellie, I never thought I'd be so happy to see you. Now, would you please get ahold of Dave Pratt?" He pointed at Keradin, who had fallen asleep upright in the chair.

Nelson turned to Captain Stritzler. "It's time to break radio silence. Do anything you can to find Admiral Pratt. If you can't, I know who to get to at NATO. If there's a key to stopping this whole damn thing, it's sitting right there." He gestured toward the sleeping Keradin. "That's what will stop them from the big launch."

There was a strange balance between fear and confidence in both Washington and Moscow. Because the battle reports were no more accurate in their initial states than they were over four hundred years before at Lepanto—neither side had yet adjusted to the loss of their reconnaissance satellites—each remained confident. The fear was generated by the ready status of their ICBMs. Though they had reached this plateau of readiness in the past, never before had it been the culmination of a major battle, a decision that might create a winner and a loser.

The nuclear posturing that was part of peacetime bravado had degenerated into a realistic threat—perhaps a certainty. Washington was aware not only that the Strategic Rocket Forces were in a countdown, but also that the STAVKA had recommended this and the State Committee for Defense had so ordered it. The only alternative was to commence the same process, insuring that the Russians too understood that the posturing was over—that Washington was responding in kind.

For those in control in Washington who could not conceive of the final orders, these were frantic moments. Not only did they not know if General Keradin was dead or alive, or even if he remained in American custody, but they had no idea whether Admiral Pratt remained in command. He had left *Kennedy,* ostensibly to shift his flag to *Yorktown.* The latter was apparently afloat, for they knew AEGIS was still in control.

The safety of hours—those hours before the Russians concluded they had only one choice . . . those hours before the Americans concluded they must retaliate—had now become the uncertainty of minutes . . .

ABOARD U.S.S. *YORKTOWN*

The Harpoon missile has a range of sixty nautical miles. With more than five hundred pounds of high explosive in its warhead, it delivers a blast ten times that of a five-inch gun shell. It can wreak havoc on a large ship; it is devastating to a small one.

Admiral Konstantin's missiles were not quite the match for the Harpoons in Pratt's battle group. As the Soviet force raced at flank speed to close the range, their ships took hits that gradually cut down their firepower. Fifteen minutes after the Americans opened fire, it was finally returned, but with little authority.

The unseen battle beneath the sea was uncompromising. To those on the surface, only sonar reports of underwater explosions and submarines breaking up gave evidence of its intensity. Nor would a soul below ever witness the weapons of his own destruction. For an instant, seconds at most, it would suddenly become apparent to each man that there was no longer a chance to outmaneuver the torpedo bearing in on his metal coffin. There would be an explosion and the submarine would careen downward. For those who survived the blast or the water that poured under tremendous pressure into shattered compartments, perhaps the lights would blink out one by one or the air would gradually fail. Then there would be the sound of the hull collapsing, eggshell brittle against the increasing pressure as the sub spiraled deeper, until there was nothing.

Few of these hunter-killers survived the day. In the confines of the Mediterranean, their presence was known and expected by their opposite numbers. They neutralized each other. Their fate would be noted only when they failed to report.

The concluding stage of the Battle of the Mediterranean was fought by the Americans in a unique way. Because it was an electronic war, the key to victory for NATO lay in the wizardry of *Yorktown*'s AEGIS system. But *Yorktown* was dead in the water, immobilized so that her remaining electrical power was marshaled to run AEGIS. While she floated in the Mediterranean, moved only by the vagaries of the sea current, rolling with the gentle swells like a sailboat, she still controlled the entire battle for those ships that surged ahead of her to meet the Russian surface force.

Though *Yorktown*'s sonar was inoperative, she received input from other ships, her computers recording the locations of those subs that still survived, assigning ships to prosecute those that threatened the group. Though she could not fire a missile in her own defense, she searched out and evaluated every threat still in the air, controlling the weapons of the ships that fired upon those threats; and though she could not place herself in the forefront of the battle, she protected her ships out front, bringing down the attacking missiles by controlling their weapons.

And of even greater note was the fact that the Admiral who controlled the battle defied tradition by remaining to the rear, choosing to stay with the undefended ship that was so critical to the success or failure of his mission. While generations of admirals had led their fleets into battle, accepting the inherent risks in the front of the battle line, Admiral Pratt took an even greater risk by remaining with that ship which would become the primary target.

Admiral Konstantin realized even before the first missiles were launched that he must get *Yorktown* at all costs. It was now his one remaining opportunity. He was unaware that the cruiser lay thirty miles astern of the attacking force, and he initially searched for his target amidst the oncoming ships. Perhaps that was what gave the Americans the edge—in a war of milliseconds, they gained minutes, minutes that allowed *Yorktown* to protect the battle group from the Soviet missile salvo.

Dave Pratt sat next to Carleton, studying the consoles before them. "For every missile we launch, they seem to have two or three," he commented.

On the boards before them, they watched as the colored objects representing the opposing forces closed each other. Smaller symbols, representing missiles, appeared more brightly on the boards, moving rapidly, some merging with the large opposite-color symbols.

So involved were they that a few moments later Tom Carleton was certain he was responding immediately to Pratt's last comment. The warning buzzer, indicating that a missile was locked on *Yorktown*, had just gone off. "And they seem to have finally located us. I think you'd better be prepared to shift to another ship."

Yorktown could not defend herself from the approaching missiles. Though she could control the defense of a battle group, she was now as helpless as a baby. The ship could only track the approaching missiles, waiting impotently for the impact. The first missile buried itself in *Yorktown*'s bow, rekindling fires that had finally been controlled. A second landed amidships, plunging into the engineering spaces before it burst.

Once again lights flickered in CIC. The unnoticed hum of cooling motors in the electronic gear suddenly took on a new meaning as the men became aware of man-made equipment struggling, then faltering as the power dropped.

Carleton punched the button for the chief engineer. Again and again, he called. There was no answer. He contacted the executive officer on the bridge and was told that they too were out of touch with both engineering and damage control. He turned to Pratt. "That's it, I think." The burst of another missile interrupted him. The lights flickered, then went out. There was dead silence in CIC. Battle lanterns pierced the heavy air. No longer would *Yorktown* coordinate the battle group.

Seconds later there was a tremendous explosion directly above them. Shelves and equipment broke away. Though there were no flames, there was the smell of dust and smoke in the air. A voice came over the IC in front of Carleton. "The bridge is gone. They—" Then it too broke off.

"Come on, Dave," Carleton said, jumping to his feet. "Let's get you the hell out while there's still a chance."

A sailor yanked open one of the hatches leading to the bridge. Flames licked hungrily in at them. The door was wedged shut.

"Back here," Carleton said, taking Pratt's arm. "We'll cut out the back way."

When the hatch was pushed open, they were greeted with thick black smoke. The crackling of flames mixed with the cries of the wounded and the shouted orders of the damage-control parties. All combined to create a raucous sound that was both confusing and terrifying. It was heightened by the gruesome sights that greeted them as they raced down the ladders to the main deck.

Behind and above them, the bridge area was a mass of twisted metal. Searing flames rose above the masts. Occasional drafts of wind revealed only torn, twisted metal where *Yorktown*'s bow had once parted the waves. They were forced aft by wind-driven flames, only to be stopped by a fresh conflagration from a jagged hole in the main deck. Parties of sailors patiently extracted those life rafts that were still usable, heaving them over the side to swimmers.

Pratt raised an arm to his eyes to shield them from the heat and smoke. Staring off into the distance, he gestured silently. Carleton followed his gaze. There, close enough to leave no doubt as to its identity, was *Kennedy*. The giant carrier was burning its entire length. Through the clouds of smoke, smaller ships circled the carrier, searching for survivors. Every few seconds they could make out new flames leaping into the air, followed by clouds of new black smoke. Then those same explosions would echo faintly across the water to mingle with the chaos aboard *Yorktown*.

"I think you're going to have to jump, Dave." Carleton

had his hand on the Admiral's arm, gently leading him to the side.

"How long will you stay?"

"Not forever, I hope. But it's my ship, Dave. There're still a lot of people aboard, a lot that need help." He grinned through the soot that was beginning to cover him. "You know what tradition says, Dave, about the captain being the last..."

A final missile burst on the opposite side of the ship, hurling both of them into the water. When Carleton surfaced, he saw that *Yorktown* had broken in half with the blast. Her stern section was drifting away, totally consumed by flame. The forward part rose slowly, almost majestically, displaying the ragged metal where her bow had once been; then it slid backward into the water.

Carleton searched for Pratt among the heads bobbing in the water as men swam away from the remnants of their ship, searching for lifeboats, but none of them was Pratt. Carleton's life jacket held him well above the surface, allowing him to turn from side to side in the water. As he stroked toward one of the rafts, he saw gray hair bobbing twenty feet away.

He kicked his way through the floating rubble on the surface to Pratt's side. The man seemed uninjured. There were no marks about his face. Carleton placed his hand under Pratt's nose and found shallow, halting breathing. Grabbing the back of the life jacket, Carleton kicked toward a life raft just filling with survivors. Hands reached over the side to lift the Admiral aboard. He was stretched gently on the bottom of the raft, with a life jacket as a pillow. Only now was Carleton able to see the lump forming on the side of Pratt's head. It had been a heavy blow, and Pratt's color darkened as the swelling grew.

Tom Carleton looked briefly over his shoulder as the stern section of *Yorktown*, a flaming pyre, slipped beneath the surface with a rush of bubbling water. Then he turned back and cradled Dave Pratt in his arms until they were picked up two hours later by the frigate *Samuel Eliot Morison*, which had somehow survived the day unscathed.

THE KREMLIN

The Soviet Premier leaned forward, one hand resting in his lap, the elbow of the other on the long conference table, his chin cradled in his hand. He glowered myopically through thick glasses at an invisible spot above General Colonel Melekhin's head. The Premier said nothing.

To one side, high enough to provide an unobstructed view for each member of the State Committee for Defense, was a television set with an enormous screen. A hazy picture flickered as if it might disappear at any moment. But there was no doubt about the black-and-white image that it carried. General Keradin was dressed in the working khaki uniform of an American naval officer. A cordon of American faces ringed the prisoner on the tiny, pitching flight deck of the American frigate. Arms folded, Keradin responded to the unheard instructions for the satellite camera that whirred away a hundred miles above.

General Keradin was very much alive, his face changing expression as various people conversed with him. The KGB had acknowledged the voice signature was indeed that of the General. There was no doubt among any of the Soviet leaders that watched. The Americans intended to show that the head of the Strategic Rocket Forces was very much under their control.

Melekhin looked down the table, his eyes blinking as though he intended to speak. He could not gain the attention of the Premier, whose stare remained locked on the spot above Melekhin's head.

Admiral Chernavin, the Commander in Chief of the Soviet Navy, broke the silence, letting his breath out with a hiss. "You are sure about Konstantin?"

"I am sure of nothing at this stage," Admiral Khovrin responded. There was no effort to mask the irritation in his voice. "Since I entered—" his hand swept the length of the room, "no one has interrupted us. The last message, more than an hour ago, was that Konstantin was abandoning the flagship. There were no reports that he had been rescued by any other vessel. There have been no messages since I arrived here. That is obvious, and the obvious seems to me that he may be lost." Khovrin's fists were clenched in frustration.

"Well, then . . ." Chernavin began but chose silence, his eyes returning momentarily to the screen where Keradin appeared to be in conversation with an American.

The Premier lifted the receiver from a phone to one side of him and spoke briefly into the mouthpiece. His expression gave no indication of the response, but his eyes snapped from face to face around the table as he replaced the instrument. "Nothing," he said calmly. "Absolutely no response from Washington." He slid his glasses up slightly so that he could massage his eyes. It did nothing to relieve the headache that had been building for the last hour. "But it seems that the Americans have been able to beam that picture," he inclined his head toward the television screen, "all over the world." Wetting his lips, he repeated the last four words individually. "And, gentlemen, that has attracted a tremendous response."

Melekhin shot to his feet, his chair falling backward. "And in twenty-nine minutes, sir, I think you can expect a response from Washington, and from every other capital. They will be groveling. . . ."

"Sit down," the Premier responded calmly and succinctly. All eyes turned from the screen to Keradin's second in command.

Melekhin gazed back at the Premier, a trace of hesitation disappearing as he nodded his head once in acknowledgment. Silently, he righted his chair and sat down.

The Premier turned next to a man seated beside him who had yet to say a word. "Will you explain to those here what you outlined for me before we came in here?" Then he looked down the table. "You are each aware of what he is about to say. You have heard it before, but I want it for the record how I came to my decision." His last words became a whisper.

The man rose. Not once did he look at the Premier or any other man in the room. "The Americans catalogue the locations of most of our missiles. They also are aware of most of their targets. We launch by a preselected system, known only to a few people, which is based on the size and purpose of the strike we intend. It is quite possible that by certain means they could gain information concerning this system from General Keradin. With such prior knowledge—" He shrugged. "Well, they could defend against— intercept—" He shrugged again. "If they choose to retaliate, we do not have the benefit of such prior knowledge." He looked finally to the Premier for assistance. Finding no response, he sat back down, the fingers of one hand drumming a silent tattoo on the wrist of the other.

The Premier looked to the Commander of the Black Sea Fleet. "There is little likelihood that the Fifth Escadra can secure control?"

Admiral Khovrin shook his head.

"Nor can we hope to halt the American convoys?" His eyes fell on the Commander of the Northern Fleet.

Admiral Milchaylovsky whispered, "No."

"Then I will contact the President and inform him that we will stand down and accept the new borders as they currently exist." Historically, Soviet armies never returned to their old borders. The Premier intended to hold a line that began at Bremen in the north of West Germany and followed a circuitous route through Münster, Düsseldorf, Frankfurt, Munich and across northern Italy to Venice— once again farther than ever from the heart of Mother Russia.

But Melekhin was on his feet once again, protesting, "We cannot..."

The Premier looked firmly to Chernavin. "Admiral, would you be kind enough to escort General Melekhin outside so that he might give orders to halt his countdown?"

When Chernavin returned moments later, he was accompanied by Melekhin's subordinate—just as the Premier had planned beforehand.

D-DAY PLUS FIVE WEEKS

A SMALL INN IN THE MARYLAND HILLS

The summer season was over and the help back in college. The owner of the little country inn had to double as a waiter, and for some reason he was uncomfortable with these guests. He'd never expected to have a wedding party at this time of year. It wasn't a large one, only eight people, but it was more than the owner and his wife really wanted after a busy summer.

The lovely lady who stopped by to make the reservations one afternoon the week before, a Mrs. Pratt, hadn't really misled him, but a few moments before, he'd told his wife out in the kitchen that he never would have allowed it if he'd realized the type of people who were attending. It wasn't so much the black man, even though the inn tended to discourage mixed groups; it was something special about these men, something subtly frightening. He couldn't quite put his finger on just why. They were military—that was obvious. But there was also something in their eyes, the way they looked at you, especially the one that was about to make the toast.

"May I please have your attention—or I'll break up the place." Bernie Ryng was getting drunk. Though he laughed at his little joke, his eyes were, as usual, expressionless.

He had been the first one to come through the door that evening, and just the sight of him had scared the innkeeper. "It is the solemn duty of the best man to toast the bride and groom. Admiral—" he sloshed his glass in Pratt's direction, "—I am not one to go against tradition, but Henry and I want everyone to drink to you first, Dave—to a speedy recovery."

Dave Pratt smiled back crookedly from his wheelchair. Alice, his wife, was beside him. "Amen," she whispered silently to herself and reached forward to clink glasses with the others. Thank God he was alive. Tom Carleton, who had hovered at Dave's bedside until assured Pratt would live, said later that the doctors had not expected him to survive. That had been the first miracle. A few weeks later, Alice decided a second one had occurred when the doctors, to their own astonishment, told her the chances of a full recovery had increased tremendously. This evening she had cut his food for him, but he had fed himself. Earlier that day, as the best man, he allowed Verra to wheel him down the aisle of the little church, since he couldn't walk with her on his arm. She had refused to listen when he said that one of the others, who could walk, should do the job.

Now, with protracted pauses between phrases as he searched for words, Dave Pratt responded. "If they could have waited another month or so instead of being so randy—" he smiled somewhat lopsidedly at the newly married couple, "—Verra would have had an arm to lean on . . . instead of having to drive me down that aisle. When you—Bernie or Nellie—are ready . . . I'll be walking." The strain of speaking was mirrored in his features. He grinned at his wife and pointed at the glass on the table before him. "Alice . . . please . . ." She put the drink in his right hand, gently holding on to it until she was sure the grip was tight.

"Just a minute, Dave. Gotta make sure everyone's full up for this one." Tom Carleton deftly popped another champagne cork as he spoke. As usual, Carleton was anything but spit-and-polish. His shirt had quickly taken on a two-day-old look and his suit pants once again were slung low, emphasizing his ample belly. "I know you're supposed to be on the wagon," he said as he got to Pratt, "but a tad of bubbly won't hurt just this one time." Making sure the grip was still firm, he filled the glass for Pratt. "There—now everything's done up proper."

The Admiral smiled his thanks. "If I continue . . . to get this service, it will be tough to . . . to get back on my feet." He gestured slightly in Verra's direction. "And when I do . . . Henry's going to have to be on his toes . . . to keep me away from you."

As he took a deep breath to search for his next words, Verra came from the other end of the table and kissed him gently on the cheek, then whispered, "Thank you, thank you so very much."

"Normally . . . I would do this on my feet," Pratt continued. "Seeing it's family . . . I don't think there will be any objections." He turned to his wife. "Alice, would you stand for me?" She rose to her feet, extending her glass toward Cobb and Verra. "Here's to one old member . . . and one new member of the family . . . whom we welcome with all our heart." Pratt paused to take a couple of deep breaths. "And here's to two people . . . who tamed the lion Keradin in his own den . . . Russia . . . and made it possible for us . . . to be here today—Hank, Verra . . . to forever." His head sank toward his chest wearily, then lifted to hold both of them in his gaze. There were tears in the corners of his eyes. Slowly, with an effort, he brought the glass to his lips and sipped his champagne.

The owner of the inn caught snippets of the conversation from the kitchen, relaying each new tidbit to his wife—the newly married couple had done something very dangerous in Russia! The black man had survived two ships blown out from under him in one day! The strange one whose eyes looked right through you was the only survivor of a mission that was still secret! And the fat one had apparently saved Pratt's life. Then realization suddenly came to the inn-keeper. Pratt—so that's who the gray-haired man was. The Commander of the Battle of the Mediterranean, that man in the wheelchair, was actually in his inn!

As the evening progressed, the owner found himself down

to his last bottle of champagne. These people must have hollow legs! He was going to have to explain this to one of them, but for some reason he was hesitant, afraid. Finally, he decided on the fat man's wife. He was now a bit in awe of Mrs. Pratt, and this other woman seemed by far the quietest. When he was able to explain his problem to her— that there was only one bottle left, but that he knew where he could get more—Lucille Carleton laughed. "Oh, Tommy never remembers to carry money. I'll send someone out to the kitchen in a moment with some cash so you can run out and get some more. We plan to stay here for a while." Her eyes twinkled merrily.

The innkeeper's face fell when the black man came through the kitchen doors, a wide grin on his face. The owner's wife remarked later what a handsome devil that Mr. Nelson was! "So we're drinking you out of house and home," Nellie's voice boomed. "Here." He extracted a wad of bills from his pocket. "Buy a case. What we don't drink here, we'll take with us. You see," and his grin punctuated his high cheekbones and deep brown eyes, "this will never happen to us again—a wedding, I mean. No lady would be able to live with Bernie—and for me I think once is enough. So keep it flowing, my friend." Nelson had noticed the innkeeper's attitude toward him at the beginning of the evening and now his arm encircled the man's shoulders. "The rest of us made a deal with each other. We're not going to let the happy couple run off to bed. We're going to stay here all night." He gave the man a bear hug and departed the kitchen with a deep laugh.

Each of the party understood how Verra had felt. There were no secrets among them. When Cobb had acknowledged weeks earlier that no matter how hard he tried to convince himself to the contrary, he was once again in love, Verra had insisted that they stay apart until they were married. After all she had been through at Keradin's dacha, she needed a delay before this fresh start. She loved this strange man, Cobb, who had saved her life, but it also meant a great deal to her if she waited until they were married.

Perhaps that would put it all behind her; perhaps it would erase the pain of the past.

Cobb saw the sense to it, and so did the others—after all, they were all family. And now that Cobb and Verra were legally husband and wife, the others like slightly malicious siblings were\conspiring to keep them up all night. It was no different than in years gone by, like the days in Vietnam when they drank the hours away and played juvenile tricks on each other.

They were older now. They would never be the same. But they were going to try to bring back those bygone days once more . . . when they played those old tricks. Cobb would understand, and explain it all to Verra. It was only one night and they were all alive. It would be a celebration of one more beginning.